THE PALACE BLUES

by

Brandy T. Wilson

Spinsters Ink

2014

Spinsters Ink
P.O. Box 242
Midway, FL 32343

This is a work of fiction. Names, characters, businesses, places, events and incidents are either the products of the author's imagination or used in a fictitious manner. Any resemblance to actual persons, living or dead, or actual events is purely coincidental.

Printed in the United States of America on acid-free paper

First Spinsters Ink Edition 2014

Editor: Katherine V. Forrest
Cover Designer: Judith Fellows

ISBN: 978-1-935226-74-1

About the Author

Brandy T. Wilson earned her PhD at Florida State University. Her work has appeared in Robert Olen Butler's *From Where You Dream*, *Ninth Letter*, *G.R.I.T.S. Girls Raised in the South*, and *Pank Magazine* among other publications. She was a Lambda Literary Retreat Emerging LGBT Voices Fellow in fiction, an Astraea Emerging Lesbian Writers Fund Finalist, and was a recipient of three Bread Loaf Writer's Conference scholarships. She teaches writing, literature, and Gender & Women's Studies at the University of Memphis.

In loving memory of
Granny and Nanny
who always believed in everything I ever did.

Dorothy Imogene Shannon Worthey 1924-2004
and
Imogene Tidwell Wilson 1923-2013

Acknowledgments

Many thanks to those who made this book possible, including but not limited to the following:

Spinsters Ink for their continued dedication to women's and lesbian literature, finding our voices and our readers. It is an honor to be published by such a wonderful press and one of the oldest surviving lesbian presses in the world. A huge thank you to my editor, Katherine V. Forrest, who helped make this novel shine.

This book took a great deal of research and would not have been possible without the help of the librarians and collections at Strozier Library at Florida State University along with several of my students, friends, and colleagues who often gave me clippings, reference materials, and notes to help me in my research.

Those who inspired and worked with me on this book at various stages of its development including my mentors and teachers Robert Olen Butler, Elizabeth Stuckey-French, Dr. Sheila Ortiz-Taylor, JoAnn Gardner and Dr. Donna Marie Nudd and to the many workshops at Florida State University who gave me feedback throughout the process. The Bread Loaf Writers' Conference 2006 & 2007, especially Randall Kenan, Stacey D'Erasmo and their workshops, and to Kevin McIlvoy who also wrote about the blues and shared his soundtrack of blues to write the rest of the book to. The Lambda Literary Foundation's Writers Retreat for Emerging LGBT Voices and Nicola Griffith and her wonderful workshop there. These two conferences sustained, inspired and encouraged me to keep writing this book.

All of my writing teachers—Janet Burroway, Molly Giles, Michael Heffernan, Lynn Freed—who laid the foundation of writing skills from which I have attempted to build.

A special thank you to Dr. Jerrilyn McGregory for teaching the class that inspired this novel, particularly for introducing me to the blues women of the 1920s such as Ma Rainey and Bessie Smith. These women were autonomous, independent, and talented, making a name and career for themselves at a time when such a thing was rare if not nearly impossible for women. These women also lived and loved in ways that have been seldom discussed of the time period, which inspired my goal for the book, to give voice to women and lesbians of the past and shed light on their possible lives.

The English Department and the Creative Writing Program at Florida State University for providing me the time, space, support, and access to the materials needed to begin this project.

The awards that this book has earned me and provided support for the continuation of the project: Astraea Lesbian Writers Fund Award and the George M. Harper Award.

My early and continued readers and supporters particularly Stacy C. Brand, Sarah E. Fryett, Samantha Levy, Michael Garriga, and Kimberly Elkins who gave me the lyrics to "One Spot."

My friends, colleagues, and special people who have supported me along the way particularly Dani Blackman, Joan VanDessel, Katie Bradley, Arden Newsom, Jessica Sizemore, Devin Belzer, Stacy Tanner, Cindy Stopha, Beth Acree, Erin Sarver, Néill Gammill, Jessica Tice, Ru Freeman, Charles Rice-Gonzales, and my many students over the years.

My family, with a special thank you to my mother, Peggy Worthey Wilson, for years of love, support, and encouragement, and to my father, Jim Wilson, my brother, Jay Wilson and my nephews, John and Colton Wilson.

Jennifer Ressler for her years of support as well as for reading and editing my first full-length manuscript.

Special thanks to Rita Mae Reese who has read, talked through, brainstormed, troubleshooted, and supported this project from its inception as a fragment of a scene written in poetic form down on Harper Street where we were neighbors to its completion, the final project you see here.

And to my wife, Theresa Bullock, for whom there are too many things to list but among her many sacrifices are her readings of draft after draft after draft, her continual intelligent and insightful feedback, her encouragement and belief in me and in the novel, her kindness and support in all of the ups and downs that comes with such a project, and for everything. None of this would be happening without her. Thank you, my sunshine. You are my world.

And to all of those I have inadvertently omitted. You are appreciated.

CHAPTER ONE

I was seventeen the first time I snuck into Jimmy Small's. My hair was cut short like the city girls, and I was grubby from cleaning rent rooms. I was a backwoods, small-town Texas tomboy, born and raised, after all. Dressed in hand-me-down trousers and suspenders and smelling of dried sweat and tobacco, I naturally came off as a boy. And lucky I did, too, because it was the only way I could walk the streets alone or get into any of the joints.

I'd be eighteen in a little over a month, but to my mind, I was already grown. I'd have given my eyeteeth to actually *live* in Chicago, but I was just visiting—helping in my uncle's grocery shop and boarding house for the summer. By day, Chicago's South Side was dusty, flat, and dry, but at night it was wet with gin and Blues, secretly hanging on against the Bible-thumping temperance women like my mama. At the end of the day, if I listened hard enough the horns from the clubs could be heard out into the street, all the way up into the rent rooms above my uncle's shop. It was all my uncle could do to keep me inside. I yearned to be where the music was. So on a Saturday in the cool of the evening I latched my thumbs at my trouser pockets, lit up a cigarette from a pack I'd found in one of the rent rooms, and strolled toward Small's.

It was July 1 and the theaters and proprietors were hot and geared up for the Fourth. The Rapp and Rapp Theater's sign was glowing with red and white curved lights spelling out Chicago. People swaggered along under the lights, and trinket shops and storefronts held late hours to keep up with the neighboring joints. I could hear the buzz of electricity as I passed by on the other side of the street.

Jimmy Small's was one of those places they called "Black and Tan" clubs, a speakeasy on the corner of State and East 35th, just up the road from the shop but far away from the heady intellectuals that flooded the area, away from the successful businessmen like my uncle playing poker with his boys, away from my aunt tucked away at home up on Prairie Avenue.

The building had been a storefront a few summers back, but had closed and the windows were boarded up with plywood. Jimmy Small had come along and torn off the rotted wood and shaded the windows. The place still had its shabby tin overhang, but Small had painted a sign out front pronouncing it The Palace Café.

That night there was a crowd of people, black and white, standing around the door smoking cigarettes and pushing down on each other's shoulders to see into the building. A trombone wailed from inside, sounding like someone was sobbing yet howling with joy—all at the same time. It hit my stomach like a drum, and I knew I had to get in. I walked around to the alley to avoid the crowd and found a side door. It was clear of people, so I edged open the heavy door just enough to squeeze through.

Inside, sweet perfume and musky cologne with the faint stench of bathtub gin hung in the air as I weaved through the swarm of people. No one questioned or even acknowledged me, maybe because I was dressed as a boy, maybe because I was white—probably both. I sure wasn't the only white person there. I stood on my tiptoes, craning my neck to see over the people. Small had raised a stage that took up the whole of the front wall where a band was playing a popping tune, horns held high. I could barely see over the bobbing heads in front of me so I pushed further in to find a place to watch the show.

There were makeshift tables along the sidewalls and a smooth cherry bar that wrapped around the back, both lined with stools. The middle was open space, a dirty wood floor with a few support beams. The joint was filled up with people standing shoulder to shoulder, and most of the stools were full, especially those up close to the stage. Finally, I found my way to one open stool, dead center, but in the back next to a support beam. The heat grew so thick it crept up to my neck and beaded sweat at my brow. It was better than my uncle's poker table or being stuck at the house with my aunt, so I climbed up to stand on top of that stool and held my ground as I peered out over the crowd.

Plenty of rich folks had come down to Small's to "slum it" on South Side. Most all of them were men though. The women, the white women, the few that were there, were all fanning themselves, slinging their hats and gloves off in the heat. They swayed into their fellows, wide-eyed and giggling. They were already drunk on the bathtub gin that a black man in work clothes was scuttling up out of the basement for them. Some of them fainted, but most of them just left early, before their wax faces slid off, before the show really got good.

The band took a short break, and when they returned, they brought a singer with them. She took center stage, robust and proud as a peacock, and commanded attention with one long opening bellow, bringing the room to silence with a tough, southern drawl as she strutted into song.

She wore a floor-length gown, satiny white, and it sparkled against her dark skin. Shiny tight ringlets of hair hung all around a sparkling headband and almost touched her broad shoulders. Her dark face was lighter around the eyes, cheeks plump and smooth. Her full lips glistened in the lights, lined with a red glow. Her exaggerated lashes fluttered with the song, her honey-colored eyes alive and sparkling. From the moment the singer took the stage, she was all I could see—all I could hear was her voice, like a hot horn vibrating through my chest and into my stomach. I clung to the support beam, wishing I could reach out over that crowd, touch the gown that clung at her shoulders but exposed her healthy arms, soft collarbones and the shadow between her breasts. The men at the bar kept stumbling into my stool, but I stayed on, even when the stool shook under my feet each time she moaned a chorus. Even in that crowd and that heat, I was wide-eyed and giddy, but I couldn't have fainted even if someone had knocked me over the head.

The band was piled in a sweaty heap behind her, every last one of them dressed in matching black suits. The pianist sat apart from the rest, closer to her. He was thinner and softer looking, his hands just skin-covered bones moving across the keys. When the horns sounded behind her, folks started swaying and dancing a slow drag. The rising of the notes brought her voice to a vibrating boom:

"I'm always keeping one spot warm for you, honey," she sang.

This sent the café into a frenzy. Men hooted and hollered, and the black women wailed with her, raising their hands in acknowledgment. The song sent a warm rush from my stomach to between my thighs, and I almost buckled at the knee. This was what they called "The Blues," the real Blues, not like the men who came around my hometown joints every weekend with their guitar picking and Texas twang. They didn't have that moan, that ability to bewitch the crowd. They didn't have *her*, Jean Bailey.

I wanted to be like her—tough and beautiful, loud and in control. But more than that, I wanted, needed to be near her, touch her—make sure she was real.

At the end of the last song she bowed at the waist like a man, and this deepened her cleavage. The crowd hollered again, and I couldn't help it, I belted out a shout. My face flushed, but I steadied myself to watch her leave the stage and make her way through the crowd splitting for her like a curtain all the way to the wraparound bar behind me. She caught my stare, but turned her gaze almost immediately to the bar.

"Jimmy, you know what I want." Even her speaking voice was loud and drawn out.

"Bailey, don't give me any lip tonight," he yelled back, not at all intimidated.

As she got her drink, she turned to me again. Her eyes ran the length of me as she cocked an eyebrow and put her drink to her lip. I felt clammy and crowded with all of those sweaty bodies around me, but at the same time I got this feeling like I was the one on display, like my stool had become the stage. I slunk down, crossed my arms and tucked my hands underneath them, feeling my small breasts give me away. I could feel them forcing my suspenders to round out at the chest, bow toward my armpits. I pressed down harder and made my way to the door. As I squeezed through the crowd, I heard her talking to Jimmy Small, still loud, still smooth.

"You better shut it up, Jimmy, or I'll leave now and never come back to this shithole."

I wanted to go back then, beg her to stay whatever the trouble was with Jimmy Small, but it was too late. I was being crowded out the door and into the street.

Just outside, I thought I heard Small yelling her name, "Jean Bailey, Jean Bailey." Once out of earshot, I let it roll softly off my own lips and into the night air, knowing full well that by the time I got back to the shop I'd have to wipe the look of awe off my face, or Uncle Albert might just do it for me.

CHAPTER TWO

When I got back to the shop that night, I hadn't realized how late it was, or I would have just gone on back to the house. The front was locked up and I had to go around back. My uncle Albert would be playing poker in the little room back there, and I'd have to try to sneak by without them noticing me. I hoped they thought I'd just fallen asleep upstairs waiting to go home. I creaked through the back door and down the hall toward the stairs. It was dark, but there was a light under the door. I could hear the men hollering over each other, could smell the cigar smoke, even the booze, seeping under the crack.

Prohibition liquor was strong, and what they usually got was dangerous if not deadly. A month back they hauled one man out. He was big and it took four of them to carry him. I had to hold the door and caught a glimpse of his face, sunken, contorted, his eyes rolled back in his head. But my uncle didn't pay no mind to the law, and not much to the danger of the booze. He'd been drinking since he was fourteen. He'd boast, "Hadn't got me yet! Why should the police or a trip to the doc scare me?"

Just as I was about to pass by the door, it flew open. Jack, my uncle's old army chum, was coming out. He'd let go of the door, and it was wide open. As he scrambled to close it again, my uncle yelled, "What the hell's going on out there?"

The room went silent, save the clanking of bottles falling to the floor in an attempt to hide their contents. I started to tell them it was just me so they wouldn't jump out of their skin, but as I opened my mouth to speak, I saw my Uncle Albert, his roughly shaven cheeks, his falling jaw, a look of dismay coming into his eyes. Both of his arms fell to his sides, unleashing the woman in his lap. The woman was not my aunt, who was fast asleep at home at this hour. It was Cora, all dolled up like I'd never seen her, bright pink rouge and lipstick and stiff little ringlets of hair all about her head.

Cora, a young black woman, was my uncle's hired help, and I worked with her cleaning the rent rooms above the grocery. She spoke with an accent I could never place and wrapped her head up completely every day in a kerchief, not a lick of makeup on her face. I never saw her hair. I never asked to. Once I had asked about where she was from, and Cora sucked in her bottom lip and tightened her grip on the basket of laundry. I thought she'd slap me for sure, but she just walked away as if I hadn't asked. I didn't figure I'd get much further with the hair. Working with Cora was all right though. She let me act like cleaning the rent rooms was my job, my real job, but she was always there to tell me if I wasn't doing it to suit her. I half expected her to scold me then, but she got to her feet, smoothed her dress and turned around, acting like she was cleaning the little cabinet behind the men.

"Frankie, what the hell are you doing? Where have you been?"

Jack walked by me then and grabbed some sodas from the cooler. He was an uppity businessman who owned a slaughterhouse but never seemed to be there. Jack hardly ever left my uncle's place and was more like another uncle to me. He shook his head at me as he set the sodas in front of the other men at the table.

"I—I was shopping—for, for my mother," I stammered. This was what I usually told them when I went out walking, that I shopped at one of the new department stores and took the streetcar home. Even if I got home late on the last car, I'd tell my aunt I'd been tending the shop counter while Uncle Albert was busy. They didn't talk much, and when they did, my comings and goings were the last thing they wanted to discuss. But it was too late tonight.

"A damned lie. The stores have been closed for hours, and she's still out gallivanting," Jack muttered.

"I was just walking around, Uncle Albert. I guess I lost track of time."

He shook his head and stared back at me, as if to search my face, curious, but also with a punishing look. "You don't have any business being out on the streets at this hour, young lady. I don't know what in God's name you're up to, but you best watch your step. Get on out of here. Wait for me in the shop."

"Yes, sir." I nodded and turned to leave, pulling the door closed behind me. A strange sense of defiance mingled with guilt in my stomach.

I calmed just enough to fall asleep in the chair behind the counter. He nudged me awake and motioned me to the door. The drive home was silent. He fidgeted with his mustache as he drove, and just as we were getting out of the Model T, he shot me a glance, raising his brows.

"Frankie, I will not have you embarrassing me like that again. Do you understand? You best know your place and keep it." He didn't wait for an answer or even a nod as he headed toward the house. "We got a big load of canned goods coming in the morning. You be up and ready to go first thing." He went inside, me trailing behind.

I wanted to argue with him. Cora in his lap, surrounded by booze and cards, was worse than me being out late, but I knew well enough to keep my mouth shut. I walked on into the house with my head down.

* * *

The next morning came early, and all I wanted to do was lie in bed, smoke cigarettes and think about Jean Bailey. A plume of smoke flared into a stream of sunlight coming through the window and I watched the dust illuminate, twisting into a ribbon as I exhaled. I pictured Jean Bailey walking through it, toward me, taking my hand. A gush of blood rose in me as I imagined the texture of her hand, dark and smooth, fleshy and strong, against mine, against my flesh.

"Frankie...Frankie...Dorothy Frances! You get out of that bed right this instant!" Aunt Ida's voice crackled over the sound of her cane on the stairs, and with it, my daydream collapsed. I rolled over and grabbed the ledge of the window. The butt of my cigarette was still smoldering so I couldn't throw it out yet. I fanned at the open window until I heard the creaking of the last step near the top of the staircase. I spat on my finger, rubbed it around the end of the butt, and then tossed it out before shutting the window. The window went down with a bang, but Aunt Ida was already rapping her cane against the doorframe. I straightened up, putting my back to the window, and avoided looking her in the eye, afraid my face would give me away.

"What in God's name is that awful smell? Is that smoke, Frances?" She wrinkled up her nose and fanned at the air around her. "Frankie, why are you standing there looking dumbfounded? Get dressed. Your uncle has already left without you. You've got to get down to the shop to..." She was too out of breath to finish her sentence. In the last few years her arthritis had made getting around near impossible. She'd quit helping out at the shop, giving the job to me in the summer, and stayed at home, mainly on the first floor. Except that she insisted on climbing the stairs each and every morning to get me out of bed. I even began to wake up early to beat her to it. But she'd hear me creaking around and come up anyway, hollering over her pounding cane, afraid I'd leave without breakfast, sneak away into the day.

Aunt Ida stood in the doorway, her head following me as I hurried back and forth across the room throwing on clothes. Just as I was slipping my suspenders over my shoulders, she frowned. "What've you got those trousers on again for? You have to tend the counter today. With that big shipment coming in, your uncle can't be out front."

I turned and dug through my dresses in my trunk. I picked one out. It was a day frock, the dark blue cotton one with the white trim around the stiff collar that my mother and I had made together the previous season, and held it up for my aunt's approval. The dress was long, tight in the waist, and high in the collar just exactly like a Gibson girl and not at all the new style, a style I was fascinated with.

The day Mama and I made it, I'd been thumbing through patterns, drawing and redrawing them the way I wanted, watching Mama correct them. I had seen the new shorter hemlines and dramatic drop-waists in a catalog, the same kind of dresses on the women on State Street and hanging in the armoires in the rent rooms.

Mama had frowned down at my patterns. "Dorothy Frances, you will not, cannot, be seen out in public in such garb. I don't care about the hooligan city girls, the—what is it these women are calling themselves?" Mama had said, turning her nose up at the thought. "Ladies of the night, loose women is what they are! I don't care what they call themselves."

"It's fashion, Mama," I said.

"You're too young for fashion."

"I'm almost eighteen!"

She raised an eyebrow at me and turned back to the frock in her lap, trimming the seam with large heavy sewing scissors cutting in chops as if it were a carrot. My mother was smooth as silk when it came to clothes, to sewing. I had her knack and followed her lead though I often hated being cooped up in that little sewing room with her. It was at the top of the house, just up from my bedroom. It had slanted walls, as it wasn't meant to be a room at all but an attic. She had a little wooden table in the middle and a tiny sewing machine in one corner. There were two chairs, a comfortable, cushioned one she sat in, and an upright wooden one where I sat or stood to be measured. I hated the stagnant air of the room, the sun peering through the windows like punishment. And I hated the clothes we made.

I let out a long sigh in the now stagnant air of my aunt's guest room as I tossed the drab blue dress on the bed and unbuttoned my shirt. This was the only day dress I knew my aunt would be happy with, and it required full under-dress, corset and all, which she would have to help me put on.

Uncle Albert and Aunt Ida were childless. I was my mama's only girl, the only child at all, and I suppose that made a difference in the matter. When Aunt Ida, my mother's younger sister, married Uncle Albert, a well-to-do businessman, and moved up to Chicago, she was just a few years older than I was then. My mother and my aunt had expectations and high hopes for me that summer, most likely to get me married well like my aunt and most recently, like my younger cousin, Deloris. The coming fall, she was to marry her boyfriend, Bean. His whole name was Randal Brady Bean, but Bean was what stuck. They'd have a country wedding and live out on Bean's family land in West Texas, nothing but a dust bowl and poor folks scattered across the flatlands like so many ants in anthills. Deloris was beautiful, proper, more proper than I ever was, and always dressed appropriately. My mother approved of her and often pushed me out on double dates to chaperone Deloris and Bean, though we all knew I had no interest in dating the boys. I was interested in staying in Chicago, anywhere but going back to Texas, and had no intention of marrying anyone.

I tossed the shirt on top of my satchel and kicked off my boots. We weren't city folk since Mama had married my father, a cattleman, and stayed in Texas. And we certainly weren't rich by any stretch of the imagination, not even as well off as my aunt and uncle, but we did better than just get by. My mother and aunt had come from money, old money was what my father called it, but money lost in one way or another by their brothers, who were also mostly gone now, out west or dead. In spite of or maybe even because of this, Mama and Aunt Ida treaded a fine line between refinement and putting on airs. They expected the same from me.

I tried to be as refined as they wanted me to be, but I was usually just me. Most days I was barely ladylike according to Aunt Ida, who hated that I'd grown up in Texas a tomboy—independent and bullheaded. She couldn't stand the fact that I was most comfortable cleaning the rent rooms in pants, pants I adored. I loved the feel of them against the length of my thin legs and rounding out my buttocks. I slid them off and slipped them into my satchel along with my shirt, boots and suspenders, hiding my movements.

Aunt Ida huffed across the room toward me. "I saw that, Frankie. I don't know what has gotten into you, young lady. However grown you play like, it is your duty to represent this family."

"Don't I do my duty, Aunt Ida? I am up at the crack of dawn every day helping at the shop."

It wasn't a strong argument, and I regretted it, especially when her face fell like she had just remembered where I was going. She brushed by me, flipping wildly through the armoire to find my corset.

"Duty? A disgrace really. You playing maid for a bunch of Neeee—gros." She sounded just like my mother then. She liked that I helped my uncle when she couldn't anymore, but hated what I did, hated that the place was now mostly kept in business by black folks. It was something she was embarrassed about, and I suppose drawing out the Ne- in negro made her feel better about it, as if that extra syllable placed more space between her and them. "I have all but lost your uncle to that damnable place, and I'll be dead before I lose you to it, too." Her eyebrows were raised, daring me to say anything.

I bit my tongue and drew in my breath as she laced me in, tight, without an inch of wiggle room. When she was finished, she turned and hobbled back down the stairs without so much as a word. I pulled on the dress and left without breakfast.

When I reached my uncle's small shop, it was empty and no one was stirring above. The shop was stocked with groceries and other goods with the rooms above it. He rented these out mostly to folks just arriving and looking for work and a place to live and to those just visiting or doing the entertaining over on State. When they asked me a few years back if I would help with the shop and keep the rooms clean in the summers when I visited, I was more than willing. It meant that I'd have access to all those rooms and might find some little something left behind by a boarder: a pocketknife from a scruffy old man, a scarf from one of the women, something exciting. It also meant that I might get to talk to one of the boarders, find out where they were from, why they were there. So every summer since I was fourteen, I loved to keep the rooms cleaned and scrubbed down after people had come through. But it wasn't really my job. It was Cora's.

That morning, as I made my way to the back to put my satchel away, I met Cora coming down the stairs.

"What you up to, Frankie?" she asked and tossed a handful of rags into a cleaning bucket. "Lord, if ya ain't in your best dress." Cora was wearing her work clothes this morning, a faded blue cotton muslin dress and apron. Her face was stripped clean of any hint of makeup, and her hair was back up in her wrap.

"Aunt Ida made me wear it, said I needed to help tend the counter today."

"Well, get on out there then and quit lollygagging back here."

"Not today, child." Uncle Albert's deep growl startled me, and I jumped around to face him. I had been messing with my satchel and hadn't seen him come up behind me.

"That order hasn't come in and nobody's awake around here anyway after all that ruckus last night. You go on up with Cora today, but don't you step foot in a room unless Cora tells you to, you hear?"

I grabbed my satchel and hurried up the stairs behind Cora. "Miss Cora, what's he talking about? What ruckus?" Excited, I imagined someone coming in late in the evening after traveling all day, worn down to nothing, rags and a knapsack. I could see his dirty britches and hands dusty from the road. I could smell the sweat and oil from the car. He would have some stories to tell for sure.

"It's some ol' raunchy singer stayed here after no one else let her in. Can't believe your uncle made me let her so much as on the doorstep. Said she'd only be here a night or two and then she was going across the south, on a vaudeville bill or some such, went on and on about how it was her ticket to the big time, into pictures! Ha! A negro movie star and ugly as sin! Like I'd believe or care about all of that nonsense," Cora scoffed, rambled on about how she'd had to ring my uncle, how late it had been, and how the singer had stunk of liquor.

I knew then why my uncle had left without me, that it had been in the middle of the night, and he'd stayed here, with Cora. But I knew, too, just exactly who had come in that late. I took a breath and tried relax my face to look calm.

Cora and I were almost at the top of the stairs. "What room is it? I'll be quiet when I pass by."

"Frankie, don't even think about peeking in there. That curiosity'll get ya cursed. Now get outta that dress so we can get something done around here." Cora swished down the hall, and I darted into the room at the top of the stairs to change into my trousers.

All day, I followed Cora from room to vacated room. She stripped and remade the beds and wiped down the nightstands. I came behind to sweep and mop the floors and carry the linens to the laundry basket at the end of the hall. We'd do the laundry the next day on the wringer out back. We had cleaned just about every room. Several of the guests had gathered their few belongings by the end of the day and moved on. The rooms were all but empty except for the few long-term boarders, and I knew which rooms were theirs. There was only one other room we hadn't touched. I hadn't heard a peep from the room, not all day long, and it was nearing six in the evening. I knew it had to be the one.

After I carried out the last pile of soiled sheets and noticed that Cora had made it to the last empty room, the room right beside the singer's, I snuck down the hall to her room. I could hear Cora swishing around the bed next door, but I didn't care. I had to get close to that singer. I had been humming her songs all day long, the music behind her voice still alive in my ears, her image still lingering in my head.

I put both hands on the brass doorknob hoping it wouldn't creak like all the others when I opened it. It did, and I stopped, took a breath and pressed more slowly. As soon as my head would fit through the slit, I looked in and gasped so loud I had to bite my lip to shut myself up.

Jean Bailey was still asleep and lay naked across the mattress that barely had a sheet still attached to it. I couldn't help but step in to see more. Before I even realized what I was doing, I'd left the door just slightly ajar and was easing into the room, closer and closer to Jean Bailey. There were two other women there. One lay curled, loose fabric bunched in her curves, on the brocade camel-backed couch. The other, half dressed, was stretched out across the creaking planks of the floor where I tiptoed in toward the bed, unable to stop myself. I was dazed at the sight and couldn't think beyond my next step. Every muscle in my body tingled and my breathing was quick and full of nerves as I crept closer.

Jean Bailey was alone in the bed, one sheet crumpled between her legs, dimpled but strong. Her dark hand was fisted next to her jaw. Sunlight from the single window brightened the taut skin of her back as it fell into a darker crease at her hip. Her hair was matted and pointed to one side. Mascara, rouge, and red lipstick mingled into a smear on her cheek. There were milk bottles, reeking of gin, bunched on the nightstand, and they clanked when I stepped up to the bed. She didn't flinch.

There was a flyer on the nightstand. Even in the dim light I could see that it was for Jimmy Small's Palace Café the night before. At the top there was a picture of Jean Bailey. She wore a plain little skirt, but from the waist up she was dressed just exactly like a man. This stopped me, made me look down at my trousers as my head swam and my gut tingled. Two girls were with her in the picture, dressed pretty—fashionable, all dolled up and rosy. I picked up the flyer and shoved it into my pocket.

On the bed, Jean Bailey's ringleted wig lay in a knotted black mass above her head. I had never seen a wig off someone's head before, and it startled me. I reached out, my hand trembling, and felt the smooth foreign texture of it under my fingers. Its underside was coarse and stiff like straw, especially where it attached to the netting, but it was slick and shiny around the curls as if it were wet. I remembered her on stage the night before, her head glistening in the lights, her powerful body commanding attention as she swayed to the music and sang. I hadn't imagined her body the way I saw it now, sprawled across my uncle's rent bed. She was softer looking, her muscles relaxed under her flesh. Her body, all of it, naked as she was, was big and billowing, smooth and full of curves, dips, and crevices.

I wanted to touch her, feel her chest, the instrument that had so moved me, made me aware of my body in a way I hadn't before. I leaned in closer, gently placing one hand on the edge of the bed while reaching to place my other hand on her cheek, when her breath hit me. It was hot and full of gin. I had to turn away, just for a second. When I did, out of the corner of my eye I saw a figure standing in the doorway, one hand hanging on the doorknob. My muscles stiffened.

Uncle Albert stood with his heavy-browed frown, shaking his head, his mouth gaping at the women. He shot his finger out beside him, directing me out and down the hall. I jerked upright, my hand pushing off the bed but still trying desperately not to wake Jean Bailey. Just as I stood up, she opened her eyes and stared at me in confusion. I ducked my head and followed my uncle's finger. From the hall, I heard him yelling.

"Get up! Get out of here! I give you a place to lay your head, but I'm not running a flophouse! This isn't one of those nasty buffet flats! Get the hell out of here!"

At the bottom of the stairs, I wrung my hands. I knew that Cora must have seen me go into the room, watched me as I crept toward Jean Bailey. Her thick accent must have turned to a pompous sneer as she told my uncle.

I waited downstairs, embarrassed and scared. Uncle Albert stomped down and went behind the counter, looking anywhere but at me. He gripped the counter with both hands. There was no one else in the shop. My uncle clenched and unclenched his jaw as he studied his own hands. I shivered in front of him on the other side of the counter. He shook his head. "I knew it, girl. I was afraid you'd been messing around with the wrong type of people. Your mama was right. You got no business in the city at your age and unmarried. Just a little too curious, Frankie. Maybe we ought to send you back on home now."

Tears stung at the corners of my eyes, but I fought them down. "No! Don't send me back!" The longer he refused to look up at me, the hotter my neck got, the heat creeping onto my face. "You can't! You can't tell me what to do! You are not my father!" I shouted and wished I hadn't as soon as my uncle lifted his head.

The deep creases of his eyes fell with disappointment, almost hurt. I was breathless.

Just then Jean Bailey came barreling down the stairs. She was carrying a tapestry bag, half-closed, with red silk hanging out of the top. Her short hair was slicked back and greased down across her head in a ripple like a man's. The two other women followed her, carrying even more bags stuffed full. They stormed by us proudly, chins high, without batting an eye.

When they were safely out the door, my uncle gave a snort and started to speak, but his voice cracked. He tried again. "Frankie, what in God's name did you think you were up to in there? Stealing? Your parents didn't raise a damn thief!" His eyes darted from my boots to my cropped hair, ashamed, it seemed, of his own curiosity. It was as if this were the first time he'd bothered to look at me. "Or a *pervert*, an—invert, is what they say, a—*bulldagger*—" he sneered. "And to think I was going to let you stay on here, maybe even take over the shop someday, let me retire. Women are doing all kinds of things these days, as women—but girls like you—What was I thinking? We'll just have to let your parents get you straightened out, young lady!"

I could see the rest of my summer roll out like so many tumbleweeds. With Deloris planning her wedding, my father working, and my mother—I didn't want to think about what my mother would do with me. I ran around the counter and pleaded with him, "Please, don't, Uncle Albert. I'll be better. I'll be good. Please!"

Cora peeked around the corner at the bottom of the stairs. I stopped shivering, and my muscles went rigid. I saw her wrapped head and pursed my lips until I felt them dry out. "You can't send me back." When I said it this time, my voice was stiff. Like a stubborn child, I gave my uncle the most piercing stare I could muster and fought the sinking feeling I got in my gut under his gaze. "You can't. I will tell Aunt Ida everything."

His eyes narrowed and he backhanded me hard across the face. I had to grab the counter to keep from falling. He'd never hit me before. My own father had, but never right in the face and never so hard. I was stunned silent.

"Don't you dare threaten me, young lady! You will keep your damn mouth shut about my business or you won't have a mouth at all!" He pushed roughly around me and headed for the back door. "Get yourself dressed like a lady so I can get you home."

"I can't get dressed without—" I pleaded, pointing to my waist like he'd know I meant the corset I'd have to put on again.

"Fine. Just go get your things and wait for me in the car." He passed by Cora still standing on the stairs like a judge in robes. "Looks like you'll get the place to yourself after all," he said and then kissed her dead on the lips as if I wasn't even there—or maybe because I was there—and headed to the back.

Cora smiled, clicked her tongue and headed up the stairs. As soon as she was gone, I went to the back for my clothes. My face still smarted from the blow, and as I bent down to pick up my satchel, it pounded in pain. I touched my cheek. It was hot and swelling. I grabbed my satchel and turned to go, still holding my cheek. Cora met me at the bottom of the stairs again, holding a basket of laundry, smirking. I flew past her and slammed the door behind me.

Jean Bailey was long gone. I darted to the side of the building and leaned against the cool brick. The building across the alley was being used as a posting spot for advertisements. Papers lined almost the whole of the wall, department store ads, vacation ads, picture show ads, train ads. The new Union Station ad was the biggest with its fancy design and regal script all selling vacation fares to "anywhere," boasting "Every mile a scene worthwhile" and "Luxury Travel at its finest" beside a brand-new train looking like it would chug right out of the picture. Right then, I wanted to run, run and hop on one of those trains.

When I heard my uncle come out, I headed to the car. He must have phoned my aunt. When we got back to the house, she was on the front porch, leaning against her cane with one hand, the other hand in a fist on her hip. Any fantasy I had about her being on my side flew away once I saw her face hardened with disappointment. My uncle dropped me off without so much as a wave.

"Frances! How dare you disrespect your family like this! You should be ashamed of yourself." Aunt Ida faked a swoon with the back of her hand for effect and ushered me into the house. In the parlor, she let loose. "Perverting yourself for Niggers!"

"She's a star, Aunt Ida! She sings and, and—don't call her that! She's not. She's got money!"

"Ha! Oh yeah, she's big time all right—hell's bells." She laughed and then sneered at me again. "I don't care what she does, Frances, or how big her britches are—you are not to step foot near those people again! I should have refused to bring you up here again in the first place. Your mama said you needed more discipline, needed some refining or you were going to turn into some hussy! But I never, never in my wildest dreams thought you'd do this to us, to your mother!"

"What? What have I done?"

"I ought to put you on a train back down to Texas right now and let your mama, no, let your *daddy* deal with you—boy hidey, what would he say? Bet you wouldn't dare pull this in front of him!"

My daddy was a gruff man like my uncle but with a Texas stoicism. He never said much, especially to me, a daughter he didn't have much use for, but when he did speak, his voice was sharp and loud. I could see him standing over me in the pounding Texas sun, slinging off his heavy work gloves, stomping around in the dust, cursing at me. He'd give me a good earful and then walk away, off to the back pasture, washing his hands of the whole thing. It wouldn't be pleasant, but I didn't much fear what my father would do. He hadn't taken a switch to me since I was little. It was my mama I didn't want to face. I shuddered at the thought of what my mama would say, what she would do with me, how embarrassed she'd be after I'd begged her to come here and she let me, against her better judgment.

My aunt paced the parlor then slammed her cane against the polished wood floor. "Look at you! In those trousers and work boots! Wanting to be a man! Of all the crazy stunts! It's disgusting."

"I don't want to be a man, Aunt Ida. I just—" I didn't know what I wanted, but this seemed like the right thing to say, the only way I had to defend myself.

"Parading around this city like you know what you're doing! Imagine! Your uncle and I have bent over backward for you!"

"He hit me, Aunt Ida!"

This didn't stop her at all, didn't even make her pause. "That's just what you need, to have that rebellion beat out of you. Lord knows your mama never would. He hit the nail on the head. You know, he's probably right. The best thing for you will be for your mama and daddy to put you in one of those sanitariums to get you straightened out."

I sucked in my breath. Were they saying I was crazy, losing my mind—that I needed straightening out by some quack doctor in some secluded asylum? I'd heard about those places. I'd seen a girl back home get sent away, accused of losing her wits over some unnamed indiscretion. She came back all hollowed out around the eyes, crazy for sure. I wondered if my father—if my mother would agree with Aunt Ida. Would they really send me there if I went back home? I let out a whimper, tears welling in my eyes.

"Oh, don't pull that now. Get upstairs and clean up. Pack up your trunk and get to bed. I've got to telegram your parents after I figure out what to tell them. See what they think. First thing tomorrow, we'll either get you back home and find a man to get you right or…" She trailed off heading toward the kitchen.

"I'm not crazy! Ya'll can't lock me up!" When I didn't get an answer, I turned away. "Oh, I don't care! I don't give a damn what any of ya'll think!" I stomped up the stairs and sat down on the bed, defeated, my defiance draining, guilt and hurt taking over.

After I packed my trunk, I reached down into my pocket and pulled out the flyer I'd stolen from Jean Bailey's room. I ran my fingers over the image of Jean Bailey. It was crinkled, but she was still clear on the page, dashing in her French cuffs, her swaggering stance. Something spread through me like hot water thinking about Jean Bailey's face as she looked up at me in confusion in the rent room and then her refusal to look at me as she left the shop. My gut churned. I had to see her, apologize for what happened before they shipped me off.

When the house was quiet, my aunt in her room with the door closed and my uncle still out, I shut my door and slipped out the window, climbed a ways down the brick and jumped to the ground. My feet stung, but I didn't make a sound as I got away. It would be hours before Aunt Ida stirred, if she did, and before Uncle Albert came home. I could find Jean Bailey and, hopefully, be back before they knew I was gone.

CHAPTER THREE

Out in the street, I tucked in my shirt and spit in my hands, trying as best I could to slick back my hair like a boy's, like Jean Bailey's. When I got off the streetcar, I latched my thumbs in my pockets and angled toward Small's hoping she was there.

Small's wasn't nearly as hopping as it had been the night before. There weren't but a few people standing by the front entrance, and once I got inside, the fistfuls of people strolling about and lounging at the tables glanced my way. This time it didn't matter that I was passing for a boy. I was the only white person there. As I slid along the back bar, finding a stool, a man with a harmonica took center stage, and the faces turned away from me and back to him. There was a whole band there, but it wasn't Jean Bailey's band. The man blew out a tune followed closely by the standup bassist strumming on his right and a horn section on his left. He was making that harmonica sing for him, and the horns echoed his every note, the bass rolling out a heavy beat in an endless procession.

I scanned the room, hoping to spot Jean Bailey, but caught Jimmy Small's eye instead. I jerked my head away, staring intently at the stage, trying to sway with the tune, though I could feel him staring me down hard, inching toward me at the end of the bar.

"This ain't no place for youngsters, kid."

I jumped up off the stool and turned to him, his dark, lined face softening around the corners of his eyes. Standing there, I felt a bold calm come over me. I cleared my throat and attempted a deeper voice. "I—I'm just looking to see that singer you had here last night. She coming back?"

He shook his head. "Jean Bailey, huh? Yeah, I 'spect she'll be making another appearance, but not tonight." Jimmy Small was a well-dressed man in a tailored navy suit. As he lifted his arm to light a smoke, an elegant cufflink peeked out of the sleeve of his shiny suit jacket.

"Well, I—I was just looking to see her, but this band is good, too."

He shook his head again and strolled away, ducking under the bar in time to fill a patron's glass with soda.

The band never seemed to finish a song, just changed directions. The man on the harmonica moved over and banged out a few keystrokes on the piano and then sauntered back again to center stage just snapping his fingers. The horn section took over for a moment then rested as the bass line thrummed louder, and finally the harmonica started up again. Though the music was hypnotizing, I didn't feel like I could sit back down and enjoy it.

I caught Small's stare again as he leaned across the bar, talking to a man in work clothes who'd come back from a table at the front. I heard them mention Jean Bailey and scooted down closer to them. When I got up close—all out of place and feeling it, the man grinned a mischievous squint-eyed grin. "Bailey's over at the Old Mason Hotel tonight, performing for Ernestine Royce's crew—a *women's* party," the man said with a laugh.

Then Jimmy Small's face went stiff as he looked over at me. "Beat it, kid," he said and shooed me out like a rat.

I scrambled out the door and into the street. I'd never heard of the Mason Hotel, but a man at the tobacco store a few streets over directed me further into South Side. I walked block after block away from the neighborhood I knew.

Leaving the electricity of State Street as the sun dipped below the buildings was like stepping into the night, the real night. The sky was dark and expansive, littered with stars like the Texas sky. It wasn't quiet though. There were revelers about, even on the streets where the lanterns had been turned down or didn't exist. As I turned one corner, I saw two fashionably dressed couples strolling away, arm in arm, headed toward State down another alleyway. As I turned another corner, I saw a man slumped against the side of a brick building, and another stumbling as he kicked at an empty bottle in the street. "Drunkards, lousy drunkards!" my aunt would have said, "Prohibition hasn't done a thing but put them on the streets." Though I felt my skin glow under the lanterns and moonlight, the men never looked up, never took any notice of me at all. I was relieved. I lit a cigarette and sped up.

When I got to the block where I had been directed, I saw a couple of women dart into a building with a tattered red awning. The building seemed deserted, out of business, but as I approached I saw that "Mason Hotel" was painted in gold, formal lettering on the front glass. I ground my cigarette out under my boot, and just as I was about to follow the women, I lost my nerve. I wasn't even sure I could trust Jimmy Small. I didn't know if Jean Bailey was in there, if this wasn't just a corner joint where I could go in for the music. This was a party at a hotel. Respectable white folks didn't just blunder in, didn't do such things, and respectable young white women wouldn't be caught dead even thinking about such things, dressed up like a boy or not. It flat-out just wasn't done. Raids were common, and the police would arrest anyone they could get their hands on if liquor was in the vicinity—I imagined that these places were ones they dreamed of busting unlike the established and protected places like Small's undoubtedly was. I didn't care if I was respectable or not, but I didn't know how I was going to get in, and if something happened, how I'd get out.

I strolled around to the back of the building, leaned against the hard brick, listening. My legs were stiff and sore from walking in my work boots so I squatted all the way to the ground and onto my bottom, stretching out my legs. The night was coming on strong, the sun well below the tops of the buildings and slipping below the horizon. I lit another smoke and let it fill my lungs, calm me, give me something to concentrate on. When it was spent, I tossed the butt across the alley and leaned my head back against the brick.

Someone pushed a window open high above me. I could make out the sound of bottles breaking and a woman laughing, a deep, hoarse laugh. There was a faint sound of music and singing, maybe Jean Bailey's singing, maybe another woman, or several of them. I couldn't be sure. By now it was almost pitch-black, save the light from the window overhead. I had come all this way. I had to at least see if she was in there, try to get in. I fumbled to my feet and around the corner, smoothing down my shirt and straightening my trousers.

I pushed through the front door and found the lobby empty and dingy, a dim light from upstairs illuminating the dust that covered everything, the old counter, the floors, the few pieces of furniture. The old hotel curtains were tattered and ragged, faded to a pale green from the lush emerald velvet they must have once been. I climbed the wide winding staircase, grabbing hold of the banister, avoiding the grimy wall. The banister was dusty in places and sticky in others. I held on, slowly creeping up the stairs, all the way up to the third floor. The top of the staircase opened up to a large dimly lit room with chairs and tables lining the walls. Candles flickered on the tables. I immediately crouched down by the closest table and tried to hide in its shadow. There was a band playing at the other end of the room, just a band, no one singing anymore. The pine floor vibrated beneath me as folks in the middle danced together from one side of the room to the other, the women's silk chiffon dresses floating behind, teasing the onlookers lazing about in chairs against the walls. The dancing was what my mama would call lewd and raunchy. It was rough, and the dancers clung to each other, sliding up and down as they spun around the room. Jimmy Small was wrong. It was a women's party, but there were men there, dancing and watching the dancers and the women along the walls.

As far as I knew, no one had seen me come in, or bothered to look anyway. I stayed in my spot and watched from the darkness. There were couples moving about on each other's laps. There were women huddled in corners, whispering and giggling, but I couldn't see much more than that in the dim light.

"Lord, you ain't seen nothing till you've seen her." A woman a table down from me sat fanning herself with her own hand. She wore a great big hat that swooped over her face, a big plume sticking out of the top. She leaned in a little to talk to a plainer woman sitting next to her but was making out like she meant the whole room to hear, or at least anyone in the general area. "They gonna be off tomorrow, though. You missed her."

The other woman looked plenty interested, but not in her. She was looking across the room. "Damn," she said and shook her head.

"Yes, ma'am. They are going down South, straight to Georgia first, was what I heard. They got the biggest theaters in Georgia, all black, what they say. They'll put Jean Bailey center bill."

I slunk down against the wall trying to hide myself with the table. I scanned the room again, my eyes slowly adjusting to the dim light. I knew I'd have to find Jean Bailey tonight if I was ever going to talk to her, tell her how sorry I was I got her kicked out of the rent rooms.

Then I heard that deep belly laugh—*her* laugh. Almost directly across from me sat Jean Bailey. She met my stare but quickly went back to the woman in her lap. The woman was light-skinned, and her complexion radiated against her pink chiffon dress. Her hair was crimped and shined. She wore waxy makeup on her cheeks and pearls looped twice around her neck.

Her hands were delicate and lay folded in her lap as she sat looking demure and pristine on Jean Bailey's lap. Jean Bailey had her hand on the woman's thigh, and she nuzzled into her neck. She whispered something to the woman and turned, searching the room until she settled on me again, huddled now almost completely under the table. Jean Bailey nuzzled her neck again. The woman giggled and cooed and then turned, took Jean Bailey's face in her hands and kissed her on the lips. Jean Bailey pulled her in closer and kissed her back, running her smooth, dark hands up and down the woman's back.

I felt again what I had that morning in my bed. My chest was tight like my blood was rising in me but from my thighs up. I felt weak, like I couldn't move, and I couldn't take my eyes off them. Jean Bailey opened her legs, and the woman slid down between them to the floor and curled her legs up underneath her as she kissed at Jean Bailey's exposed knees, then her thighs. Jean Bailey slumped in her chair and let her head fall back against the wall, then reached down and pulled the woman up again in a straddle on her lap. They were kissing again and then rocking, hands moving under skirts, mouths open and gasping, and I imagined it was meant for me, that it *was* me there in her lap.

I began to make them out more clearly, imagining I could hear their breathing across the room, or maybe it was my own breathing as I watched, rocking with them, feeling her hands on *me* as they ran the length of the woman's back, onto her legs. Jean Bailey gripped the chair she was in with one hand and held the woman in the small of her back, pulling her closer and closer. I felt myself slump further down the wall, the pulsing between my legs growing stronger, my muscles tightening—when out of the corner of my eye, I caught a man walking directly toward me, cocky, strutting. I held my breath, realizing, just then, that my hand was between my legs, that I was touching myself, and that this man, anybody in front of me, could see what I was doing plain as day. Embarrassed, I quickly pulled my hand away, letting my arm fall to the floor by my side. I couldn't say a word. I couldn't catch my breath.

He sneered and then squatted over me with a jug in his hand. "Who do you think you are coming up in a place like this?"

I fumbled to straighten up against the wall. I could feel the people around me grow curious and stare. "I was—I mean, Jimmy Small sent me here, said Jean Bailey would be performing here tonight."

He just about fell out of his squat. "Well, be damn! What a lark! I'm gonna—well, did you get what you came for?" He nodded over his shoulder then looked me dead in the eye.

I turned crimson.

"You need to get the hell outta here!" He reached for my arm to pull me up.

I yanked it away, knocking him over a bit. He had to brace himself and almost dropped the jug in his hand. He reached for me again, and I struggled against him.

"Ernie, what's the problem over here?" It was Jean Bailey, standing over us both, her hands on her hips, and there was a crowd gathering around her.

I had gone over and over what I might say to her when I found her. I thought at the very least she'd take pity on me when I told her what had happened, the threat—and the smack—I'd taken from my uncle over her. But in that moment, I couldn't utter a syllable.

"Oh, hell, Bailey. Jimmy Small is telling about this place. I think the kid's just here to stir up some shit."

Jean Bailey looked down at me, recognizing me, and shook her head. "Small? Humph. This kid ain't come to bust anybody up, Ernie. Just look. Scared to death, shaking like a leaf. What? You afraid a kid's gonna steal your girl? I hear your girl likes a little cream in her coffee." The crowd laughed at that, everyone except Ernie and me. She was right. I was shaking. "Go on back to her, *Mr.* Royce, before she gets distracted."

At this Ernie stood but didn't leave.

"Come on, kid. Get up and move along. You're causing a scene." Jean Bailey reached down for my hand to help me up.

I grabbed her hand and let her pull me up, staring into her dark face, her honey eyes. Jean Bailey's voice was stern and cold, but I could smell her warmth, the strong dark musk of her and the other woman mingled together. She let go of my hand with a jerk.

"Look around, kid. You think you belong here?"

The music had slowed, and there were women dancing together and some of the women were dancing with men, but, but—I suddenly realized—they weren't men after all. I could make out the soft curves of their hips rising just under their waistcoats, the delicacy of their necks, the subtle softness in their smooth faces. They were women dressed as men and doing a much better job of it in their pinstriped suits and drawn on mustaches, right down to the wing-tipped shoes. A sharp thrill shot into my stomach. I looked over at Ernie and put it together. Ernie wasn't a man either. She was Ernestine Royce. The point of her nose gave way to pouty lips. She raised her sculpted eyebrows at me. Why hadn't I noticed before? I pulled up on my trousers, straightened my shirt, and looped my satchel across my shoulder, managing a hesitant nod.

Jean Bailey scanned the length of me, took me in. "You think a pair of trousers makes you a bulldagger, a real bulldagger?" she said.

"Maybe," I mumbled.

"Maybe, my ass." She laughed.

The crowd that had gathered around us began to disperse, but not without first shooting me some menacing glances. Ernie stood beside Jean Bailey, bowed up like a peacock. Defiance swept over me, and I was grinning before I could help myself.

"What the hell are you grinning about, whitey? You think this show is for you? Huh? I don't care if ya are a bulldagger, you can't be more than fifteen," Ernie shouted.

I was proud of the way she called me a bulldagger, like it was something to be worthy of instead of a disgrace. I reached out my hand, the same one that had been between my legs. It had a slight tremor, but I held it out strong. Ernie sneered, and I hesitated, blushing, wondering if Jean Bailey had seen me touching myself, but I didn't stop. I yanked the jug from Ernie's grip and turned it toward my mouth. It was my first taste of gin, and I took as much from the jug as I could stand to hold in my mouth and let it sting its way down my throat. I gasped and smacked my lips, then wiped my mouth with my shirtsleeves.

"I'm seventeen—eighteen in a—" I said.

Jean Bailey nodded at me, almost laughing and cut me off. "Boy hidey, you's just about grown then." When I didn't budge, didn't leave, my determination building, her face changed, opened up. "Eighteen," she mumbled. She stepped closer, eyeing me like a prize. She shooed Ernie away and leaned in to me, backing me up against the wall. Her skin was glowing in the candlelight where beads of sweat gathered around her hairline. "Woowee," she whispered close to my ear. "Listen kid, you already got us kicked out of one place, and I ain't gonna let on to these folks about that, but I can't let you mill about here after the stir you've caused."

"I didn't mean—" I whispered, trying to get out an apology, but she pressed against me harder and touched my face. And when I didn't flinch or make any effort to move away from her again, she teased my cheek with her lips.

"You just might be pretty under all this roughneck garb. And what about that sweet twang you got to your tongue? Where you from, *girl*?"

I trembled with the thrill. "East Texas—here working with my uncle, but they want to lock me up in a some nuthouse or send me back—" I cut off my ramble and cleared my throat.

She grabbed my chin. "Hmmm, what a pickle," she groaned and slid her hand down my neck and onto my chest, just above my breasts, and leaned in to my ear again. "All right, Texas. Listen. We're leaving Chicago first thing in the morning—leaving one of the girls here. Why don't you come along? I bet we can make use of you somehow." She backed up a little and looked me in the eye.

I could hear my heart beat in my ears. I was thrilled at the thought of hitting the road with Jean Bailey, leaving my snotty aunt and gruff uncle behind, but the thought of how much more trouble it'd land me in with my mama stopped me. "I—I can't—my mama—"

"Ha! Mama's girl, huh? That why you got that bruise forming on your eye? She give you that?"

I felt my face, still hot and throbbing to the touch. "My uncle." I mumbled, as if it were a defense.

"Oh, well, by all means then stay here, let them send you to some loony bin." She started to turn to go.

She was right, but I didn't know if I had it in me to go, just run away like a spoiled teenager. "I don't—I mean—"

The woman she'd been kissing before sauntered over. "Bailey-girl," she said in a grating singsong.

Jean Bailey leaned in to me one last time. "If you're coming, be here and ready to go before the sun comes up—make yourself scarce until then, little bull." She nodded to the door.

I turned to leave, stopping only to give Jean Bailey a tip of the hat gesture, but as cocky as I tried to come off, I hesitated, looking for something, anything in her eyes.

She didn't blink, but there was a softness that came over her face, something relaxed around her mouth and eyes. She smiled. Her full form was taller and bigger than me, intimidating me, but her smile was more like a grin, like a dare.

CHAPTER FOUR

The air outside was close and thick, but as I rounded the corner of the building a breeze swept up my neck, over my cheeks and brushed the sweaty strands of my cropped hair from my face. My head was swarming, but I could finally catch my breath.

I was high. The gulp of gin sloshed in my gut, and my head was loose. I cupped my hand over my mouth and blew out the hot air to check my breath. It wasn't as strong as Jean Bailey's had been, but there was a hint of liquor in it. I smiled and reached for my cigarettes crumpled in the front pocket of my shirt. I felt my face again, the swelling around my eye. As I lit my smoke, I could feel the tightness, the bruising. I shuddered at the thought of my uncle's hand across my face, the look of disgust in his eye as he turned and walked away. With each corner I turned, I heard his shrill whisper and the name he called me. I wanted to remember how the women at the party said it, how Jean Bailey said it. I wanted to hear her strong moaning voice lingering like a piano key over the syllables. But it was my uncle's voice that

rang in my ears, that deep voice that crackled "bulldagger" out
of his throat. It felt now just like the slap against my face that
stung and burned.

It was getting late, and if my aunt and uncle had discovered
I was gone they would be waiting for me, fuming at me. I was
afraid they'd nail me to the floor or ship me out that very night.
Even if they hadn't realized I'd snuck out into the night, they'd
still ship me out first thing in the morning.

I walked all the way back toward my uncle's shop, toward
State Street, where I was hoping I could still catch the street
car on up to the house. I knew the area, the streets surrounding
my uncle's shop, but they looked entirely different to me now.
Instead of the bright crisp life I used to see even in the dirtiest
of strangers, I now saw darkness, sullied and still. I couldn't see
the hope and mystery of it anymore. There were a few folks still
out and about, but everyone I saw had their head hung to their
chest, their arms crossed as if to hug and comfort themselves.
Clouds rolled overhead, seeming so low they might touch the
buildings I walked between. There was a breeze, but it was hot
and almost damp, like someone breathing on your skin. The
sidewalks looked dingy, worn, chipped and fragmented where
they had once appeared pristine and glowing.

I knew right then that I couldn't stay, that I had to get away. I
certainly wasn't going to let them send me to some crazy house
to be locked up like a criminal, and I wasn't going back to Texas
to marry some roughneck either. But I'd need money, supplies.
I couldn't go empty-handed.

I reached my uncle's shop and stood there looking at the
darkened windows. There was cash right there in the register,
on the other side of the door. It was already closed up, but I
knew the back door was loose, easy to get in. I went around
back and jimmied the lock, shaking it until the door flew open. I
fumbled through the dark of the shop and found my way behind
the counter. I snapped the register drawer open and cleaned it
out, shoving the coins and bills into my satchel. I figured it was
owed to me, my pay for helping at the shop. I'd show them just
how grown I was, that I wouldn't take their bullying me. Even in

my anger though, a pang of guilt hit me. I dug out Jean Bailey's flyer and flipped it over to scribble out an "I owe you" to my aunt and uncle. I left it in the drawer. Somehow in my panic and rush, I thought to grab some food, a couple of cans and some bread, a soda, even a pack of smokes and fit it all in my satchel with my good dress. It was enough to weigh me down considerably as I headed back to the hotel, so I took my time winding through the streets.

It was just before dawn by the time I climbed the wide winding staircase again. It was dead silent, and I imagined I'd see a few stragglers, half-dressed women strung out across the dance floor. I reached the third floor and found that the place was deserted. Broken glass covered the floor, and there were scraps of clothing and toppled over chairs scattered about the room. The lace curtains were torn, flapping in the breeze through the open windows. I stepped forward and glass crunched under my boot, stuck there. I lifted it to shake it loose, and it wouldn't budge. As I reached down to pull it out before it cut all the way through to my foot, I slid a bit. I was standing directly in a saucer-sized spot of blood, tacky and dark. There had been a fight and someone lost big. Just as I got the glass loose it slipped through my fingers, slicing my thumb and forefinger. I let out a small yelp, embarrassed as soon as it left my mouth, though no one was around to hear it. I scanned the room again—empty. I'd missed her. She'd probably headed out just after the party got rough, not thinking I'd be back after all.

What felt like a stone sank in my gut. Blood swelled in the cuts as I stumbled to put my foot back down without stepping in the blood again or on another piece of glass. I crept back down the stairs holding my fingers with my other hand to stop the throbbing. I knew I needed to wrap them up. At the bottom of the stairs I tore off some fabric from my shirttail and wrapped my fingers as best I could. I sat down on the bottom step and held my fingers.

I could hear a faint drone of sirens growing louder. I knew I couldn't afford to stick around. I hurriedly dug through my bag again, pulling out the wad of bills and digging out the coins that had slipped to the bottom of the bag. I had about twenty dollars give or take and figured I was damn near rich. It was getting light out, just about the time my uncle got to the shop. If they hadn't figured out I was gone before, they would have by now. Having taken the money and left the note, I couldn't go back. I figured I had no choice but to head out of town myself or face worse than some sanitarium or Texas. With the money I'd stolen, I could get a streetcar to the train station downtown and from there a train ticket—to anywhere, like the ads said. I could go luxury, straight to Georgia and find Jean Bailey.

I shoved the change in my pocket and packed the bills in my satchel again. Just as I was leaving the building, a black car rounded the corner three blocks down. I knew it was the police. I ran the other way as fast as I could and ducked into an alley. When I peeked around the corner, they'd slowed to a crawl in front of the hotel, then sped toward me. I tightened the strap on my satchel and ran. I ducked through small alleys, winding my way out of the deep end of South Side. I'd finally caught my breath again when I found a streetcar that could take me to the train station. The driver frowned down at me, dirty from the day, blood on my hands and shoes, but he let me on, as there wasn't another soul on the car, and dropped me at the station without a word.

Union Station was bustling with holiday tourists and businessmen in suits. People bumped into each other while staring up at the great domed ceiling. I weaved in and out of the crowds. As it turned out, you couldn't get a ticket straight to anywhere, well, not anywhere anyone would want to go. Most of the trains were set up to cater to tourists coming into Chicago and back home to their little dumpy towns.

I picked up a pamphlet giving me the schedule and found a route that would at least get me down South. It was almost the same route in reverse—at least as far as Missouri—that had taken me to Chicago from Texas, with my uncle as my escort, just over a month earlier. From there I would have to reroute further east and then get another ticket into Georgia. It was a different rail line, but I figured it couldn't be all that different.

"I'd like a one-way to Birmingham, Alabama on the Illinois Central," I said in the gruffest voice I could manage.

The ticket man raised an eyebrow. "That is a mighty long trip, son, " he said. "You'll want a sleeper car, but those are pretty pricey."

"I've got the money. What's the price?" I was still as dirty as an urchin, my finger bleeding through the makeshift bandage on one hand, my eye swollen and dark, so I wasn't surprised at his hesitation.

He looked skeptical and scanned a sheet in front of him. "Well, you'll take this line on down to St. Louis. Then you'll have to change trains and take the Southern line. It goes all the way, but there are a few stops."

I nodded. "I know. I've figured out my route. But you can sell me the full ticket, right?"

He shook his head. "I can sell you the whole ticket to Birmingham, but I'm afraid each time you change trains you'll need to get out and change the ticket. You'll have to make sure you get stamped at each leg or they won't change it out."

I dug my wad of cash out of my satchel and slapped it on the counter. "All right, I'll take it."

He studied my grubby hands and cleared his throat. When you put out the money, no one bats an eye. "Will that be first class, sir?"

"No, just give me a regular sleeper." I didn't want to draw any more attention than I needed to. A sleeper was luxury enough.

He took the cash and gave me my change and a ticket. I put the loose change in my pocket with the ticket and shoved the bills back in my satchel.

It was still another thirty minutes before my train so I found a washroom, almost forgetting I was pretty well passing for a boy and going into the ladies'. Thankfully the men's was empty. I fanned myself with my hands and looked into the large speckled mirror. My eyes were red-rimmed, bloodshot, the bruise under my left eye darkening now, the swelling causing me to squint. I widened my eyes and leaned in to the mirror. I was always fascinated by the way my eyes changed color when I cried, and even now, when I was tired and hurt. When I was little, I would sit for hours at the mirror and cry to make them change from a light gray green to dark emerald with an even darker ring around them. They were haunting, I realized. I wondered if Jean Bailey had noticed this, was fascinated by them the way I was with her honey-colored eyes. My hands trembled a little again at the thought of her close to me, a quick vision of the night before.

I wiped down my face with the cloths provided and cleaned my hands as best I could. My fingers had finally stopped bleeding, though they were sore to the touch and hurt to clean. I heard someone coming in, so I quickly slicked my hair back and ducked my head to pass him on my way out to the platform.

It was mid-morning by the time I boarded the Illinois Central Rail line out of Chicago headed for St. Louis. The train was crowded and loud, but I had the porter show me to the sleeper early, before anyone else, to get out of the noise. There were four little cot-like beds along each side stacked in bunks with one aisle down the middle. I picked the one on the far side by the last window. Coach required I have my own linens, and since I didn't have any, I just curled up on top of the tiny bed without a blanket or pillow and fell fast asleep.

* * *

"Young man, young man?" The porter shook me awake. He was in a stiff uniform. The smell of pine filled the car.

The whole of the sleeping car was full of bodies, snoring bodies, with me the only soul without a blanket over me.

"Sir, your ticket?" he said in a stage whisper. "I have been back here three times trying to get you awake."

A few people stirred, an old man coughed as I scrambled for my ticket.

The porter shook his head at the sight of me there curled up on the naked little mattress, but punched a little hole in my ticket all the same and let me be.

* * *

In the evening, the train seemed to hum along with little noise, lulling me into a daze or back to sleep. At times though, in the early daylight hours and when I'd make my way to the dining car, the clamor became deafening. The sound of the engine rumbled as if it were something guttural. The rambling around of people and the clanging of dishes in the dining car was a constant uproar. The only diversion I had was the thought of Jean Bailey. I could see her face before me, could hear her voice, and I felt the heat shoot straight through me when I thought of her. It was a comfort, a security I couldn't quite put my finger on. She gave me something, something more than the life my family had laid out before me like a jail sentence. Once I was out of spitting distance from Chicago, I was able to focus on Jean Bailey and how I'd find her.

On the morning of July 4, Independence Day, I sat in the dining car at a little booth alone, though the whole train seemed to be packed with revelers in a state of celebration and holiday. The heat and the steam from the engine floated through the window and around my head, over my face and soaked my skin. The ground below was rushing by so fast it made me dizzy. Tiny houses, spread far away from one another on small tracts of land, spun by slowly as if they were asking me to look hard at them. There were few trees, and I could see for miles beyond the houses where the crops were planted. The summer was in full swing now, most everything tall and dry. I couldn't make out anyone in the fields or beside the houses, and I couldn't see into the windows.

It seemed that the whole world was empty, deserted save for the revelers and me on this barreling, noisy train going south. It gave me the same feeling as when I sat at my window back home in Texas, staring out into the open plains, the expanse of pasture, a speck of cows here and there, the trees all lined up along creek banks as if even they knew their place. I would sit there for hours on end, trying to imagine a different world.

Chicago, anywhere but where I was, alone and lonely, exposed and awkward. The day before I left for Chicago back in May, my mama dragged me from the window and sat me down at the kitchen table with my father.

"Frances, you're almost eighteen now. I expect you'll act like a young lady in Chicago this summer."

"Don't I always, Mama? I wasn't raised by wolves!" She cocked an eyebrow at me. My father didn't say a word.

"I mean it, Dorothy Frances. You can't go around like some wild idiot. You are there to help your aunt and uncle. You just mind your manners, you understand?"

I was so excited about Chicago, I agreed without hesitation. "Then can I stay and live there?" I knew it was pretty big request, a dream really.

They both laughed at that. "Sure, just find you a nice rich man to marry," my mother said like it was a joke. But I knew it was what she wanted for me. This was her answer to everything. Anything I ever wanted or asked for or hoped for when I grew up, she'd say, "Well, I hope you marry a rich man," or "You better marry well," as if anything I wanted was an impossibility in and of itself, as if marrying and marrying well was the only possible way I could make it in this world.

"Oh, Mama," I said, as I almost always did, half in embarrassed resignation and half in dismissal. She'd always laugh at that as she did then.

Afterward I followed my father out on to the porch, and he slipped me a dollar. He stepped off the porch and packed his chew into his bottom lip. "Mind your mama, girl," he mumbled, spat in the dirt, and walked out to the barn.

Now, as I leaned my head against the window, the velvety curtains of the dining car my only comfort, the memory of the conversation gave me a sinking feeling of guilt and it also infuriated me. But there was something about the train, something about the thick wooden cars rattling down the track, something about the metal links clinking with the curves, and something about the deep golden curtains on the windows, the revelers all around me. It all gave me a thrill. More than that was the knowledge that I was on my own, really on my own, out in the world beyond Texas, beyond my mother's sewing room, my aunt's parlor and my uncle's poker table with all his lewd men, and without the escort of a rich man, a husband. I ran my hands up and down the golden curtains and thumbed the fringe at the end, sighing in relief.

CHAPTER FIVE

By the next day, the holiday travelers were long gone. There wasn't even anyone in the sleeper where I stayed most of the time and only a few short-trip travelers in the dining car. At St. Louis, I got off to stretch my legs and change the ticket. The wooden planks of the platform rattled and leaked a stream of dust that quickly became a cloud all around me. I dodged through the people.

"Watch out, mister," a grubby kid with a hat in his hands big enough for a full-grown man mumbled up at me. There were coins in his hat. I dug in my pockets and tossed him a penny.

"It's all I've got," I lied. I knew my money wouldn't last me long. I'd spent a great deal already on the ticket, and I would spend more to buy the ticket to Georgia.

The kid didn't thank me, just swept around me like I wasn't even there. There were droves of people going in every direction. I got a sudden flip in my stomach, a sick jolt. I searched the platform for a ticket counter and finally found the entrance to the depot. The woman eyed me as I walked up to the counter. There was no line, and I wondered if I was even in the right place. She was just a little older than me, blonde hair cropped at the neck and crimped in a wave about her forehead. She wore thick makeup and her large blue eyes seemed to pour into me as I scrambled to pull my ticket out. Instead, I slapped my cigarettes on the counter as if for payment for something I hadn't yet asked for. My hands shook as I snatched them away again.

"Where ya goin', sir?" she asked as if disappointed and then grinned up at me. She lingered on my face and then sheepishly looked down again, lowering her chin as she smiled. She had an interesting smile, one that suggested a motive, a smile too pretty, too perfect, teeth all lined up straight and gleaming under dark lipstick, but interesting all the same.

I finally dug my punched ticket out of my pocket and handed it over, attempting a wink at her, a wink that surprised even me especially since my face was still a little swollen and awkward. I was relieved when she didn't catch it. "I need to change this over for the next leg of my trip."

"Where's your final destination, sir?" She was all business now as she scanned my ticket.

I stammered a bit, but finally got it out. "Birmingham, Alabama, but I think I'll have to stop again."

She wore a smart little suit, gray with red piping along the lapel. Her blonde curls bounced as she turned around in her swivel chair to face about a dozen boxes like the mail slots my uncle kept behind the counter in the shop for boarders. I'd fumbled with those slots many times, running my fingers over the raised print on the envelopes, the fancy wax seals on some of them. I imagined they were letters from lost loves or invitations to extravagant events. Sometimes I would put them up to my nose to determine which because I was sure that a lost love would have doused the letter in perfume. All I ever ended up smelling was the stale paper.

"This will get you to Birmingham with a change in Memphis. You've got two hours until the train leaves." The ticket girl slid the ticket across to me. She hesitated, resting her slender fingers on the ticket. When I reached for them she pulled them back, just slightly, just enough for me to stop and look her in the eye.

She was smiling. "I've got a break in ten," she said. Her bright eyes blinked in slow anticipation as she slid her cigarette case off the counter and to her chest where I was sure to see it.

"I see you got your smokes," I said as I got the ticket from her. I patted my smokes in my top pocket.

She grinned. "In ten?"

"It isn't polite for a girl to smoke in public, out in the streets, you know." I could feel my toothy smile now, and I gave an embarrassed giggle. I was flirting back, as if I knew exactly what I was doing, as if I really had a thing for her.

"Well then, don't smoke in public," she said eyeing me from head to toe.

My stomach sank.

She nodded to the door to her right. "Meet me around back. I have a spot to go to."

Trying to recover, I noticed her name tag on the front of her tailored gray jacket. "Yes, ma'am," I said and faltered, stuttering as if it were a question, "Hazel?—of St. Louis?" I regained composure, raised an eyebrow, and added, "Are you witch or saint?"

She laughed and leaned her head back, came forward again shaking her head, "Oh, I am no saint, *sir*. Now you've formed a line." There was a hint of something not so flirty in her voice, and with it came the flooding noise of the train station.

The hairs on my neck stood on end as I glanced over my shoulder. There was a family of five lingering behind me, and a man and woman behind them dressed in their finest. The woman swiveled her hip holding herself up with one leg and then the other. I skirted out of the way and around to the back of the booth where I thought her door was and waited. The booth was sort of in the middle of the platform, behind it another line of tracks slid by. There were fewer people on this side, and I figured it was a freight train track rather than a passenger track. Soon enough a train came barreling through and did not stop. It was boxcar after boxcar all closed up. The dust flew up into my eyes. I was rubbing them and trying to cough the dust from my lungs when Hazel finally came out.

"Why don't you leave that heavy bag in here?" she asked with an easy smile as she placed her hand on the strap draping my shoulder.

I slid my satchel over my head and watched her set it inside. She locked the door up behind her and slipped a slew of keys on a large ring over her wrist. She flew through the crowds crossing to the other side of the platform, and I had trouble catching up. When I did, I found she'd jumped down behind a shed-like building on the far side away from the crowds, the depot in the middle, where the tracks split for the platform. She waved me down, and I jumped, following her underneath. It was cool and damp, strangely not as dusty as up on the platform. She lit up her smoke without waiting for me. She looked me over, up and down as if surveying. There was no longer a hint of flirtation in her eyes at all. They narrowed at me.

"Down South, huh? What're you running from?" she asked.

"I've got a job down there," I stammered out as fast as I could, "with the vaudeville circuit."

She didn't even perk her ears at this. She just kept right on. "Nobody goes down South. It's usually the other way around—unless you're running from the law. You running from the law?" She didn't wait for an answer, just shook her head. "It's a dangerous place, I hear. All those Southerners smiling to your face, then stealing your last dollar behind your back." At this, she stopped and stared me dead in the eyes. "Why did you flirt with me back there? All a part of the whole—" and she flung her hand up and down motioning to me, my trousers, my boots. "Is this your talent for the stage?"

I shivered, afraid to speak.

"Don't worry. I'm not gonna say anything. I'm just mad I can't pull it off is all. Just you be careful. You ain't doing so great either. Those trousers look like you dug them out of the bottom of your father's closet, and your shirt looks like something you'd sleep in. Conductor figures you out, you'll be shipped back to your parents quick as you get there—pegged a runaway. You know you can get locked up for that now?" She talked about it like it was an everyday thing, even with her warning. I was no surprise to her. I wasn't even interesting. *I had you figured out the minute you stepped up to my counter*, she seemed to say. She took another drag of her cigarette, staring out at the train barely visible down the tracks. Then she looked at me again, narrowing her saucer eyes. Her lashes were long, black, and lush. There were deep lines about her eyes, and I realized she was much older than I'd thought. "What's your name, kid?"

"Frances. But most everyone I know calls me Frankie—except for my mother—it's Frances, or Dorothy Frances to her if it's anything." I rambled on, "I was named for my great-aunt Dorothy on my mama's side and my uncle, Frank—my father's brother that was killed by a fever when he was just a baby. The second name was against my mama's better judgment, as she'd say." When I finished my nervous chatter, I waited for her to respond with a nod, anything, but she sat there, wide-eyed in surprise.

"You ain't some hoodlum are you, Frank, a thief?"

I shook my head and dropped my cigarette, crushing it out under my boot. "I go by Frankie," I corrected, slumping my shoulders. Suddenly I felt heavy, as if I could slink off and just sleep somewhere.

"Frankie, humph." She took another long look at me, studying me. "You might want to think about getting a new suit, one that fits. You are entirely too pretty—beautiful even—too beautiful to pass yourself off as a boy, especially in those rags even with that black eye. You got money for a suit? I know a good place."

My stomach dropped, and I could feel my face redden. "I've got enough, but I need to save it for the trip."

She shook her head. "Too bad. Those long lashes, those eyes, those strange, green eyes could hurt some poor man, but he isn't going to look twice at you like that." She opened up her cigarette case. It was empty. "Mind if I get one from you? For the road?"

I handed it over and lit it for her when she stuck it to her lips. "I ain't looking for any man to hurt."

"Help me back up to the platform?" She reached out her hand and using my hand and shoulder, jumped up and sat on the ledge pulling me behind.

We sat swinging our feet. We were still hidden by the shed at the edge of the platform. I lit up too, and we smoked in silence for a while. I could feel her stare again, almost as if she'd touched me with it. "I read somewhere that a nose like that was a sign of money. Makes sense really. They say some people can smell money a long ways off." She laughed and took a quick drag through her grin, gripping the cigarette finally with her teeth.

"My nose?" I stuttered.

"Long, strong, and with a slight notch of power. Always looking, nosing out something, no matter the cost. What are you looking for, Frankie?"

She was reading me like a placard. I didn't know it then, as you never do, but this would stick with me. You never know if what someone says will happen actually does happen because they suggested it and you followed the suggestion, or because they really know it. If it doesn't happen, you wonder if it was because you rebelled, or if they were just pulling your chain.

She grabbed my chin and turned my face to hers first looking me in the eyes then tilting my head this way and that, looking at my face from different angles. "The Chinese. That's where it comes from. They can tell a person's whole life story and their future by the shape of their face. I learned it from my cousin's neighbor. Phiso—nog—amy." She slowed to pronounce it for me, like I was a child learning to spell. "The reading of a face."

"What does my face say?"

"Oh, that will cost you." I expected another flirtatious grin to pass over her face, instead her eyebrows crinkled, as serious as she could muster, I imagined.

"How much?"

She studied my face again. "You've got a triangle-shaped face. It's connected to the element of fire. You're headstrong and determined, but we already know that based on your nose. Your forehead," she turned my face with her hand on my chin and stared at my profile. "Short and compact, nestled with your dark hair, suggests you make quick decisions and bask in their wake, whatever comes your way. Things will go your way—for a while. Those eyes though, those are the trouble here." She let go of my face.

I stayed in position for a minute, waiting for her to say more. I finally turned to her. "What trouble? Why, because of my black eye?"

"Oh and your ears. I almost forgot. Pert and open, but small and sneaky. Quite a driven young thing, aren't you?"

"You didn't tell me the trouble." I thought of Jean Bailey then and what Hazel had said about being locked up a runaway. I wanted to know which one would be my trouble.

"Just keep looking, Frankie."

When Hazel looked at me again, I lost the feeling I'd had about my eyes, about their abilities. I'd known my eyes were special, but I was hoping they'd get me more than out of trouble or do more than show me my trouble. She was speaking in riddles I didn't follow and acting like she knew more than I did about myself. It made me cringe. I wanted to know all that she seemed to know, but as she spoke, I couldn't keep from focusing on her lips, her thick bottom lip, lined and darkened with lip color. I wondered what it was they said about her, and I leaned in closer, studying them. I could feel my eyes water from staring, and my hands were shaky holding the cigarette. I was so close to her face I could kiss her. I'd never kissed a girl, not like that, though I'd thought about it especially since I'd met Jean Bailey. I'd had a few kisses—stiff, innocent kisses from the boys I'd dated as Deloris's chaperone. I'd studied silver screen smooches in the gush and gooey love-struck movies down at the Rite, where only women could go, and so I thought I knew what to do. And I'd seen Jean Bailey and that woman across the room. I didn't particularly think I wanted to kiss Hazel before that moment, but I wanted a kiss like that, and I wanted it from a girl. I knew that much, and I was ready.

My body felt charged. I could feel my heartbeat all the way up into my ears. I thought I might faint, so I reached up and fumbled my hand behind her neck and pulled her to my tilting head, my puckered lips. I pressed myself hard against her face. I could feel her breath, hot and smoky with the tobacco. Her lips were soft, though a bit chapped, and she opened them slightly taking mine in for a moment then closing them. Then she put her hand on my chest and pushed me away, a smile spreading across her face as I opened my eyes, my head still tilted like a fool. I thought she'd slap me like they did in the movies. But she laughed, which was worse.

I took another drag from my smoke and flicked it out onto the empty tracks. I couldn't speak. I couldn't look at her.

"You just give me that pack of cigarettes, and we'll call it even."

I slid one behind my ear and handed the rest over without looking into her face again. She let out a big breath, got up, and made her way back through the crowd without checking to see if I followed.

At the door, opening the booth, she was stiff like she was when I first approached her for the ticket.

"Where do they sing the Blues around here?" I still had a long wait for the train to leave. I thought I'd go hear the music, but I was stalling. I didn't want her to leave me there feeling foolish.

She pulled on her gloves as if I was a little twit trying again to seduce her, and she was done with me. "They don't. Good luck, Frankie," she said and closed the door behind her.

I stood there longer than was necessary staring at the closed door. Finally, I turned to head toward the Frisco Hotel and Café: Open Day and Night I'd spotted just across the tracks. From all the smoking I wasn't hungry, but I had to go somewhere.

The doors to the café had frosted and etched glass at the top. I could see shapes through it but couldn't make them out. I pushed through, and there were tables scattered in no particular pattern, a soda fountain straight ahead. There was a phonograph playing behind the man at the counter. It was jazz—erratic, loose, horn-blasting jazz.

I weaved through the tables and made my way to the bar. It wasn't until I ordered a soda, paying with the change still in my pocket from the ticket, that I realized I'd left my satchel in Hazel's booth.

The coins I handed over were greasy from my dirty clothes. I needed a good long bath. I finished my soda and ordered another. I lit up my last cigarette, finally looking around me rather than just staring at the soda in front of me, the ashtray at my elbow, wondering if Hazel kissed me back—however small she'd kissed me and however quickly she pushed me away, she did kiss me back—because I looked like a boy or because I didn't.

I turned my head to the side and looked at my profile out of the corner of my eye. That's when it struck me. It was my hair. It was too, too long. I'd cut it off myself, of course, back at the beginning of the summer. I'd been snipping at it for about a year, and when the hot weather came on, I just took the plunge. I was going to Chicago to be a workingwoman after all. My mama was disheartened, but even she admitted that it suited me, that it was becoming on me. My father never grumbled a word. My aunt and uncle didn't seem to notice, even when I tried to get it as short as the girls I'd seen with their Eton Crops in Chicago—at least not until the day I left. By now though, my crop had grown out and I had just let it be without crimping it in a wave or a curl above the ear. It was too long for a boy and, left untamed, too short for a girl, a girl with any sort of propriety anyway, but still looked like a girl's haircut. I was stuck somewhere in the middle, a dangerous place to be out on my own unescorted.

"Excuse me, is there somewhere to get a haircut around here?" I asked the waiter. I still had about thirty minutes until my train.

"Go out, down through there."

He pointed to a side door. I paid and pushed myself up from the counter, a sick sinking feeling in my stomach. Out the other side of the café, the doors opened onto the street. I walked a good three blocks full of dust before I found a barber.

There wasn't a single woman inside the place. I pulled my shirt down over my hips and stepped into the first open chair I saw. The man, balding with large round spectacles, draped a cloth over and around my neck, sized up my hair and began cutting without so much as a word. I watched as tufts of hair fell to the floor. I could hear the scissors slice and slice next to my ear and shave at the back of my neck. The dark hair on my neck was the thing I couldn't get to myself. It felt cool and clean as he scraped away the hair. I could barely feel his hands moving my head around, getting the right angle for his scissors.

He took the back up, short, shorter than a bob, short like a man's, but left the front long. He reached in front of me to the counter by the mirror and scooped some hair grease onto his fingers. It had an awful smell, a smell that tried too hard to be good, musk that smelled musty, a sweet that smelled saturated. Underneath it I could smell the grease, the oil. He fixed a slight wave to the top of my head where he'd slicked the hair back and smoothed me down. With a brush he dusted me and then slung the cloth off to the side, tiny hairs flying about as I stood and reached in my pocket for the ten cents, seven plus tip, the last of my pocket change. I walked back to the station, proud as a peach, right back up to Hazel's booth. My train gushed, gearing up to go, and I rushed to the counter, squeezing in front of the line.

"Hey, watch it, kid!" the first man in line said as I pushed up to the counter.

"I'll just be a minute."

"Hazel, Hazel," I said over him.

She looked startled. "Frankie, you're going to get me fired. What do you want?"

"I need my satchel. My train is leaving."

"Oh! Oh yes. I forgot. You'll have to come around to get it." She motioned me around back as she turned to grab it.

She was holding it out the door when I got around the back. "Thank you, for everything," I said and looped the satchel over my shoulder.

She waved and gave me a strange smile, looking up at my hair as I left.

As I walked to the train, I dug through my satchel for my ticket, but couldn't find it. I stopped just a few feet before the train and, right there on the platform, I pulled everything out of my satchel, my leftover food that I should have already thrown out, my extra pack of smokes, my dress, my corset, dress shoes and all before I realized the ticket was in my pocket, but my money—I hadn't pulled it out, hadn't felt it in there. I stopped, startled. I felt through the empty satchel and fumbled through the pile of things I'd pulled out. It was gone. Not a cent was left.

I shoved my things back into my satchel and went over in my head the last time I'd seen my money in there. I'd counted before I bought my ticket. After the ticket, I'd put the change in my pocket and the wad of bills back in the satchel. I even remembered shoving it far down into the bag so it wouldn't work its way out, and I'd felt it in there just before I changed my ticket with Hazel. I'd still had enough left over for the train to Georgia, I was sure. And then I remembered that the satchel had been in Hazel's booth, and it was locked up. No one could get in but her.

My head throbbed as the train whistle blew. Over the line of people at her booth, I could see Hazel. She locked eyes with me and grinned, and a shot of blood flushed to my face. I squinted at her and turned to head back to her booth, rearing to row with her, get my money back, show her I wasn't just some kid to mess with. The train began to move behind me. If I didn't get on now, I'd miss it, and I might never find Jean Bailey—she was well ahead of me, I was sure—money or no money, and I'd already missed her once.

I turned back and grabbed the handle, pulling myself onto the train just as it was pulling away. I felt heavier than I had even when I realized Hazel had seen through my disguise. I'd been such a fool, just another dumb tourist. I wondered how many others she'd done this to, or if I was the only sucker. I'd spent my last dime on my hair, and I had no way to get all the way to

Georgia. A slow-moving panic rose in me. The money wasn't really mine in the first place, and I realized I'd taken it just to show my aunt and uncle, my mama and daddy, show them I was grown. Hazel waved, her grin plastered on her face. As St. Louis rolled away, I let go of the handle and climbed into the car.

CHAPTER SIX

Time on a train is a curious thing. It's like being suspended, yet in motion. Barreling toward nowhere but barreling all the same, and there was nothing I could do to stop it. I couldn't reach up above my head and pull the lever for the driver to let me off at the next stop like the streetcars in Chicago. And I couldn't make the time speed up, almost didn't want to because I didn't know what I would do when my ticket finally ran out.

For a good five minutes I watched a single tree as we passed by, wishing I were in it, swaying to a Blues tune in its arms. To look out on the landscape made it seem like we were barely moving, like I could slide open the window, crawl out and jump to the ground running. But when I looked down at the tracks, the ground just outside the window, it was a blur of speed, as if we were moving slow and fast at the same time. And I knew I had a long trip ahead of me, a long trip with nothing but uncertainty at the end of it.

I moved to the dining car where a phonograph was skipping over "Yes, We Have No Bananas," chart-topping popular that summer. There were well-dressed ladies scooting around in their seats, itching to dance I supposed, but they stayed seated and whispered over their tea. I sat alone, irritated at the grating of the recording, and thought of Hazel, the deep creases in her eyes that now seemed wicked and menacing instead of wise and pretty. I remembered the harsh, quick kiss I stole from her. It wasn't the kiss I'd wanted to be my first, especially after what she'd done to me, but at the same time that I wanted to kiss Jean Bailey and no one else, I had also wanted to have kissed, really kissed a girl before, wanted to know what I was doing the first time I kissed Jean Bailey. I wasn't sure Hazel had given me anything more than a deeper sinking in my gut.

I devoured the complimentary stale rolls with a tab of butter and then had the porter fill my coffee. I took a long sip, feeling the hot liquid roll through my lips, over my tongue and down my throat. It was like chocolate to me with my smoke. After my second cigarette, smoked deliberately, directly after the first, I rose to go back to the sleeper car. I imagined that after I left the ladies cut loose, got up and swung each other from one end of the dining car to the other, but I knew that it was only in my imagination. When I looked back over my shoulder from the next car, they were still sitting stilted in their seats.

We stopped several times throughout the day and night, but I didn't get off the train except to breathe a little fresh air, afraid I'd lose more than my money. I started taking and reading discarded papers I could get for free, searching for signs of Jean Bailey. I even took the sensational papers, the ones that more than reported the news, the crimes, and the forecast, that reported the births of two-headed babies, whores with syphilis, angel sightings on the prairies. These were the ones that advertised the more devilish vaudeville showings, and I looked for Jean Bailey in each of them. I imagined I'd run across that picture of her dressed as a man like the flyer I left behind with my note.

Finally, a family joined me in the sleeper. I was relieved to have a little company. The man was younger than my father but weatherworn, rough about the cheeks and neck, deep wrinkles at his eyes from squinting too long in the sun. He was wiry and stooped in his shoulders but looked strong, his hands large and able, calloused with a bit of dirt under the nails. He wore his Sunday suit, I could tell, all buttoned up, trim and stiff like he'd taken it out of the Sears and Roebuck's package that very morning. It was gray, without the pattern or style of the ones from the tailors in Chicago. He wore a plain, dark tie, close at the neck like he'd choke if he bent over. The woman had her hair up and back in a dishwater-blonde bun at the top of her head, pulling at her face, which was scrubbed and clean, almost raw. Her frock was frumpy and out of date, full of drapery and dull right down to the stitching, though the stitching was impeccable unlike her man's suit. She was constantly whispering reprimands at the pretty near identical twins beside her, a boy and a girl, dressed simply and over-clean, who poked and prodded each other, mumbling under their little breaths.

I gave a timid smile and introduced myself, reaching out a hand to the man.

"Howdy do? I'm John Thornton," he said and gave me a warm handshake. They had staked the beds in the next row and were spreading out their linens, settling in for the night. They were farmers going to visit family down South and then going back again when they were well fed and clothed, perhaps the following spring, Mr. Thornton said. They were having a bad crop, and there would be very little the coming winter. Their older son, Jonathan, he told me, had just headed out West. He was going to make a fortune, they were sure, and send them money to get by.

"Where are you headed, young man?" he asked with an almost stern curiosity, as if dismissively interested yet goading in the same breath, very much like my father's stoic way of approaching me.

"I'm headed to Georgia." He'd surprised me, and what Hazel had said about runaways getting arrested kept me from saying more, made me regret saying that. "Family," I added. "I've got family down there." I knew I wasn't convincing. I could hear my own wavering voice tiptoe over the words. I crossed my arms over my chest. I knew I looked rumpled and dirty, all except for my freshly cut hair, and I was beginning to smell like a street urchin.

He cocked his eyebrow. "Nice shiner, boy. Listen here," he said and moved closer to my side of the car.

My heart jumped, and I could feel it beating in my throat.

"You go on out in that world. You about the right age, huh? Eighteen yet?"

I nodded, proud that I looked as if I were already of age.

"But just you mind your folks. They'll be counting on you, young man, to do what's right and good by them."

I thought of my family and what my uncle must have done when he found the note and saw that I'd taken all the money in the drawer. I could see him slam his fist on the counter, grab his jacket and head home to my aunt sitting in the parlor wringing her hands, waiting on news about me. I could see her lips purse and go white, her feeble hands rest in defeat in her lap. I'd been lost to her like my uncle, though not to the shop as she'd predicted. I imagined my parents' reactions when they found out, Mama's frustrated shouting, my father's stern stare of disappointment. No, they wouldn't be counting on me to do any good by them at all. The thought left my stomach feeling empty and loose.

I nodded, staring at the man's suit, anything but at his face, his eyes. I mumbled a "Yes, yes sir."

He laughed. "You'll do fine, young man, just fine," he said, giving me a pat on the back.

I let out an audible breath and sat down on my cot.

He smiled again. "I'm tuckered out too." He walked back to his family, slipped off his jacket, revealing a sleek vest underneath and a large hunting knife in a sheath clasped to his belt. He flung the jacket over the end of the bed and settled onto a cot.

I fidgeted on my own cot and slunk closer to the window, watching the pastures float by, until it was dark in the car and even darker outside. The twins snuggled up close to one another on a top bunk as if they were one cocoon. The woman and the man each had their own beds on the bottom and were fast asleep, the man's mouth open and snoring. I got up and paced about the car, stopping only to run my hand over the fabric of his suit jacket. It was made of a slick material I couldn't make out, but I knew for certain the stitching was shabby as I felt the treading. I could stitch it better, I thought. And then he snorted, sat up and his rough hand was on my wrist, squeezing hard, pulling me down, before I could flinch. I struggled against him, and he stood, leaning down to my ear. "Listen, kid, I know you are some damn runaway or something, and I'll get you thrown off this train quicker than you can say scat."

"I—I'm sorry. I was just looking. I wasn't goin' to take it," I managed, still struggling to pull my arm away.

He turned me around, trapping my arm behind my back, and pushed me to the other end of the car up against the door, slapping his hand over my mouth. "Shh! You wake my wife and children, and I'll beat you senseless," he spat.

As he pressed against my back, I felt him stiffen against my buttocks, his breathing heavier in my ear. He slid his hand off my mouth and down my neck, onto my shoulders. I let out a whimper, and he slung his hand back over my mouth. "What'd I tell you?" He pulled his hand away turning my head and pressing my cheek against the cold metal door.

I was quiet after that as his hands roamed the length of me. I was relieved when he skipped my breasts. But as his hand found his way to the top of my trousers, I squirmed and, remembering the knife, I tried to reach it. He pulled my arm up harder. I slumped in pain, and he pressed me in place with his body until he wrangled his hands back down to my pants. I squeezed my eyes shut and tried to concentrate on the cool of the metal door, my mind racing. As he fumbled with my trouser button, I felt his grasp loosen and I managed to pull my arm free, yanking the knife right out of its sheath. I pushed away from the door and him away from me enough to turn around. He lunged at me but I whipped up the knife between us, and he stopped, putting his hands up, stepping away.

I stepped closer, backing him up, though my hands were shaking. "You like little boys, huh?" I asked in a harsh whisper. I was suddenly frightened for his children, still curled up together on the top bunk, as well as myself, and stepped closer.

The whites of his eyes seemed to glow like a ghost, the only light in the car from the moon outside. His face was slack, falling to jowls.

I said, growing bolder now, and a little louder, "I ought to wake your wife, no, I ought to go tell the conductor what he's got on board his train." I crossed my free arm over my chest, rubbing the stiffness of the arm he'd held behind my back. He let his hands down, and I shoved the knife up to his face like I meant it. "And I will too, you don't get right back on that cot."

He backed up again, waving his hands as if to stop me, "Listen, kid, I was just trying to scare you."

I stepped into him again, looking up into his face. "I'm no kid you need to mess with, mister," I said but could feel my voice crack.

He stepped back again, and with a dry mouth, a flat tone like my father's, he said, "What are you gonna do, kill me? You think the conductor'd believe some kid, a runaway, over me? You think they'd let you go on your merry way?"

"Shut up and get in the cot," I said, still holding the knife up between us.

Shaking his head, he turned and walked back to his cot, his eerie shadow lurching through the car.

I knew he was right, that I couldn't say a thing without risking my own safety. When he was back in his cot, I grabbed my satchel and made my way to their side of the car to leave, backing out to make sure he didn't try to grab me as I passed by. Just as I reached the door, I eyed the woman's bed. She was wide awake but lying as still as a corpse, her blanket pulled up to her chest. Her eyes followed me, and she frowned. I didn't know if it was because I was leaving her there or if it was disapproval of me or perhaps fright. She gave me a tightening in my gut, and I could feel my jaw clench as I stepped out of the sleeper. I wrapped the knife in my corset and shoved it down in my satchel.

* * *

Since the dining car was closed, I lumbered through the dark train to the smoking car and stayed there until morning. My body was sore all over now, and I was shaken, jumping at every little noise. My eyes were dried out from the strain of trying to see in the darkness of the train. I wondered if I'd made a huge mistake, if I really could make it, if Jean Bailey really wanted me to come along at all, or if I was just a dumb kid full of romance and fantasy. I was growing terrified of what would happen to me if I were caught, if the man or someone else turned me in. Images of the man, the sensation of the cold door, the rough hand on my body flashed in my mind. I struggled to push the thoughts away.

At twilight I took out one of my papers, searching again for Jean Bailey without success. I flipped the paper over looking for a blank spot and dug through the little desk beside my chair for something to write with. I found a knife-sharpened pencil, all eaten up on one end like someone had used it as a gnaw bone. I began to sketch out a suit, one with a jacket like Jean Bailey's, but with pants. I couldn't decide on a leg, so I drew one side full cut, pleated and cuffed and the other with a slim and straight leg like the man in my car. This thankfully gave me more of a feeling of power than shoving the knife in his face had, and I leaned my head back against the seat finally able to relax.

The porter woke me when people flooded in heading to the observation deck. I'd fallen asleep imagining myself in my suit, all done up with a scarf and flower on my lapel. I tore out the sketch and put it in my pocket and stumbled, sleepy-eyed, to the observation deck. I knew I couldn't go back to the sleeping car, at least not yet, not until it was empty again, but remembered that they told me they'd be getting off that day.

A man and woman were on the deck, obviously newly in love. The woman leaned into the man as he guided her toward the open window. She was so caught up in him, she left her handbag on the seat. It was a modest bag, small, the seam almost ripping on one end, and though it was poor, the man and woman poor, in not much better clothes than I, I knew there'd be money in that bag. I stared at it for a long time, until a shadow passed over my face, and then the sun through the hills, and I remembered Hazel again and slunk away toward the window by myself.

For what seemed like days, the plains had rushed by until we finally reached the hill country. Hills. Texas and Chicago are both flat, so I'd only ever seen the hills on my trips to and from Texas. That morning, the sun hit the sides of the land and shadowed the rest in such an odd pattern that the sight mesmerized me, and I clung to the rails as we rode through. I'd always loved this part of the trip. I couldn't see the sun peeking over the horizon, but I could see where it landed as if in waves on the land. For miles the land rolled and rolled, deep valleys through them, as if someone had come along and dug straight through, just so we wouldn't have to climb. Perhaps they had. Finally, around mid-morning, we stopped somewhere in the middle of the hills.

I wanted breakfast, a real breakfast instead of the complimentary stale toast of the dining car. I was broke, but I thought I'd step out a while and see what I could see anyway. I spotted the family by the train as they stepped down. The man stopped and talked to the porter. The porter shook his head but took out a pencil and pad and wrote down what they said, waved the family on, and got back on the train, I realized, to search for me. I stood in the crowd while the family collected their bags and greeted a much better dressed clan waiting in the middle of the platform with open arms and smiling faces. I ducked my head and headed in the other direction, walking quickly across the platform.

There were birds chirping, over and over, the same song as I walked. My clanking boots on the boards and the birds rang in my ears. I was dazed from so much travel and the lack of sleep and could feel the man's hands roaming me, his eyes peering into me as if he could swallow me whole. I walked faster, but I didn't know how much longer I could go. I tried to imagine Jean

Bailey's face, wanting just to hear her sing again, wanting to feel some kind of safety in her presence. I strained to remember the horns raised high, wailing, pulling me into their song.

CHAPTER SEVEN

There wasn't a single automobile in sight and only a few horses about. Several shops lined the street and a great big market was just down the way from the depot. Farmers of all types were selling flowers, fruits, vegetables, salt pork, baked and even canned goods. The smell of fresh bread and food swarmed over me, making my stomach feel like a hollow drum.

One of the stands had a pile of fresh-baked biscuits. The smell hit my nose, and my stomach opened like a pit. I couldn't help myself. As soon as the crowd of people shopping the stands swarmed around me, I managed to loot one when no one was watching. I walked on and snatched an apple too at the corner and stuffed both into my pocket. Just as I turned the corner an older woman holding a young kid's hand caught my eye and frowned at me then turned and walked the other way. My face flushed, and a jolt of shame shot through me, but I just stuck my hands in my pockets and walked on.

In the middle of the market, a row of booths on either side, was a pole stuck to death with flyers. There was a circus coming to town that boasted a live camel and the smallest woman alive that rode their lion. It had just been put up and was crisp and new but flapped in the wind at the bottom. I took out my apple, bold as you please—figuring if I acted like I'd paid for it no one would bother me—and ate as I read, drawn to the picture of the woman on the lion. Her hands waved in the air, beckoning the crowd that couldn't be seen. Pasted above her was a picture of the camel and a clown, just their heads, drawn rough. As I got closer, underneath the poster I saw a smaller flyer, the word vaudeville in big letters catching my eye. As I peeled up the circus flyer, I nearly dropped my half-eaten apple in the dirt at my feet.

There she was, Jean Bailey. In this little bitty town. The flyer advertised a tent show, and she was billed as the "Hot Mama of Blues." The date was hard to read under the circus poster, but I saw it. A few days from now. I knew that couldn't be right, because she'd be down in Georgia by then. Or had I lost that much time on this damn train? Confused, I pulled and tugged at the flyer and ran with it to the nearest stand.

"Excuse me, sir, I am—I was wondering if you knew when this show—"

He grabbed the flyer out of my hand and tossed it on the ground. He wore a pressed cotton shirt and work pants pulled up over his great big belly. "We don't 'low that kinda devil music round here. Right, Sandy?" With that, he latched his thumbs at his pants pockets and gave a great big laugh, almost a grunt.

Sandy was sitting at the next booth and perked up when he heard his name but didn't get out of his chair. "Yes, sir, little man, and we 'specially don't 'low them highfalutin niggers come through here tempting ours out they work. Just lost a whole slew of 'em. Say they goin' up to Kansas City, make more money." He shook his head and spat in the sand, barely missing my foot. "They be back, begging for they jobs."

"Thank you, sir," I said and started to reach down for the flyer when the big guy put his foot on it.

"You ain't some nigger lover are ya, son?"

I stood up slowly, trying to figure out what to say next, trying not to let my face show any change at all. My body went numb and cold. Which was worse, a nigger lover or a bulldagger? Didn't they hang folks for less? When I caught their eye again, they were grinning, the both of them, with a wad of chew all stuck in specks on their teeth, and it made my stomach turn.

Without a second thought, I stood up taller and in my gruffest voice said, "What do you care if I am?" and waved my hand all haughty and pompous, an air of superior thinking about me.

The big guy unlatched his thumbs and stepped forward a bit, clenching his fists, and then he grinned as wide as pie. "Well, well, Sandy, we got one likes to dip his pecker in the pile. I tell you what, I done it a time or two myself. Ain't a thing like it. Right, son?"

I felt relieved and at the same time disgusted that I felt relieved. Relieved he didn't jump across the stand full of corn and knock me across the head and disgusted that it meant I now had some kind of camaraderie with these men. Was I somehow like them?

"You don't want that flyer, son," Sandy chimed in as if to calm us all down. "We ain't seen nothing like that in more than a year."

"Here. Here," the big guy said, grabbing up an ear of corn. "Don't you want some of this here corn?" Then, with a cocked eyebrow, he mumbled, "It'd go quite nice with that five-finger discounted biscuit you got stashed in your pocket." He lurched at me, pushing the corn at me.

I grinned and gave a tip of the hat gesture. "No, thank you, though. Gotta catch a train," I said and turned—but not quick enough. He grabbed my arm and tried to yank the biscuit from my pocket. I struggled free and ran. I ran all the way back to the depot imagining they'd pried themselves away and came after me, but when I got to the depot I slowed to a walk, a strut almost, proud of myself. I took the biscuit out of my pocket and ate it as I boarded the train.

My heart was racing, partly at the thought of them after me and partly at the thrill of bucking up to them. I sat in the sleeper on my little cot taking in deep breaths until we were all loaded up and about to leave again.

As we began to roll, I shoved the rest of the biscuit in my mouth, staring out the window at the crowd of people as I chewed.

I was relieved to find that no one boarded to share my cabin. In fact, there were hardly any folks on the train except up in the front in the day traveler seats. It was deathly quiet back in the sleepers. I settled in and tried to read the paper the porter had graciously left at the foot of my cot the day before. There weren't any more bawdy papers, so I settled for news.

A little while after we started off, I could hear the porter making his way to my car. I scrambled for my things and ducked out to the next one, hiding behind a clothing compartment. He peeked in and then turned and left. I had no idea what the man had said to him, but I knew well enough that I'd be in trouble if the porter found me. I decided I would lay low and wouldn't get off the train again until Memphis, a full day away. We took a slight turn to the east and left the hills behind.

CHAPTER EIGHT

As we rolled into Memphis, the sun set behind us and there was a shadowy glimmer over the Mississippi River, reflecting off the bridge, a great big contraption of wood and steel that seemed mightier even than the train I was on. I stared out and down the river imagining I could see where it emptied itself into the ocean. I'd come damn near all the way across the world, my whole world anyway, and it just seemed to drop off beyond the next bend.

We came to a stop in Memphis in the early evening. I washed up, what washing I could do in the little basin on the train, so I could get off and change my ticket for the last leg. I would need to get my ticket punched by the porter before I could change it though so I headed to the front of the train, hoping I could just slide by with a punch. When I got to the observation deck, the porter was stopping everyone. "Have you seen a boy, dirty, baggy trousers and a ripped shirt?" He told them I was a runaway, wanted for robbery, that I had a black eye and there was blood on my shirt, that it could be more serious.

As people shook their heads and got off the train, I turned to go the other way, dodging people as I went. Just as I stepped off a few cars down, someone spotted me and pointed, and the porter turned to come after me.

I threw my satchel over my shoulder and walked as fast as I could without breaking into a run through the crowds of people at the station. I looked over my shoulder but when I saw the porter trailing me, I knew I had to run. By the time I reached the inside part of the station, I'd gained some ground on him, so I slowed to a brisk walk again. I located a women's toilet, vacant, and ducked in, locking the door behind me. I was out of breath and sweating. Heaving with every breath I took in made me want to vomit. The toilet was dark and stank of pee and something rotten. The floor was wet, flooded, and I splashed as I made my way to the sink. I leaned over it and ran cold water over my hands and splashed my face, releasing my panic, relieved by the running water.

I realized I needed to change my stained clothes, that I needed a disguise. I pulled out my dress. It was all I had. The corset tumbled out with the dress, the knife from the man who had attacked me on the train falling with a clank into the sink. I jumped from the noise, but quickly went back to my disguise. Since I wouldn't be able to put it on by myself, I shoved the corset back down in the satchel. I would have to settle for a droopy, tied dress, slopped over my body like a long, dark blue sack. At least it was clean. I carefully draped the dress across the sink to keep it up off the floor. I tore off my shirt and struggled to get my pants off over my boots without getting them soaking wet on the floor and pulled the dress over my head. I tied the sash as tightly as I could behind my back, looping it twice for a better effect.

Once I was dressed, I ripped the bottom edge of my shirt that I'd used as the bandage for my fingers. I wrapped the cloth around the knife and tried to carefully tuck the knife into the side of my boot—I'd be more prepared from now on. It slipped and nicked my ankle just above the bone, just enough to bleed on my trouser socks. I took out the knife and rewrapped it, making a tie on one side of the makeshift sheath, then tied it to the outside of my boot, reinforcing it with my laces, keeping it from my skin and making it more accessible. It was hidden under my dress. I practiced pulling the knife out a few times and checked the security of the tie. Satisfied, I stood, smoothing my dress down over my legs. I shoved my trousers and what was left of my shirt back in my satchel and lifted my dress over the wet floor as I made my way to the door again. By the time I peeked my head out, scanning the crowded station, the porter was nowhere in sight. I didn't figure he'd bust his butt too long for such a petty criminal, but I knew I couldn't get back on that train, couldn't change my ticket, and that I might be stuck there in Memphis.

I went back to the sink and doused my hair with water to smooth it, looping it around on my forehead, attempting to make it more feminine. It was greasy and limp, too short from the haircut to do much of anything. Finally, I gave up. My body felt heavy with my drooping clothes and the wet heat, yet I felt like I was falling, drifting with no place to land. I leaned in and placed my now throbbing temple against the cool of the mirror. When I was growing up, my mother would always place two cool fingers across my temple when I had a headache. She would immediately calm the pain if not make it vanish completely, leaving me relaxed, refreshed. I yearned for her then, her sure hands, her stern strength, so confident in her world. Buttoned up from head to toe, perfectly held in her pristinely stitched dress that secured a dancer's posture, she was more than proper. She was exquisite. Suddenly, I wanted to see her. For the first time since I'd stepped on the train going north, I wanted to go home.

* * *

I waited in the toilet until my train left the station again and then made my way through the station toward a public pay telephone. The phone was located close to the main entrance, by the long line of glass doors.

"Yes, hello, Central? Can you connect me to 2L133?" I still knew the exchange by heart.

There was a long silence.

"Hello?" I fidgeted, running my hand up and down the cord stringing the receiver from my ear to the mounted phone.

"Ma'am, I'm sorry but I don't have a connection to that exchange. Oh wait, yes, yes I do. Texas, ma'am?"

"Yes."

I heard a few clicks on the line.

"Please deposit a dollar and nine cents."

A faint "hello" came over the line.

"Mama?" I said quietly, my nerves making my voice quiver.

"Ma'am." The operator's voice interrupted. "Please deposit a dollar nine."

"Can't you reverse the charges?" I'd heard my mother do this with my aunt once.

"Frances? Is that you?" My mother's voice was still coming through in the background. "Are you okay? What's wrong?"

I whimpered but didn't answer.

Her voice changed then. "Young lady! Where are you? Frances! Answer me!"

My mother's voice sounded distant, and I realized that I had nothing I could say in my own defense, nothing that would make her understand. I knew then that she would not wrap me up and comfort me. If my mama knew I had run away, knew about Jean Bailey, she would be disappointed in my behavior to the point of disowning me. Right then I knew I couldn't go home and didn't know if I would ever go home again. It was home or it was Jean Bailey, never both. The thought sank in me, like a burning bit of coal in my gut. My head pounded harder as the operator interrupted again.

"I'm sorry but it's a party line. We can't reverse charges on a party line, ma'am." The operator's voice was like syrup, sending a strange sense of relief through me.

I hung up, lingered only for a moment, and then walked out the wide glass doors into the Memphis heat. Outside, I took a deep breath, tightened my sash and forced a smile as I walked. I had to bounce my way back into the world, my new world, and somehow get on a train.

* * *

When I made it back out onto the platform, the city lamps were lit all around, and already I felt better than I had back in the small hill town, even better than I had in the toilet. The sounds were familiar and the city was busy, even in the early evening. There were all kinds of people about, but that wasn't anything special since it was a train station and folks had to get to where they were going. But I could hear music, the first time since I'd left Chicago. There was live music full of Blues. I could hear it all around, horns mingling with the rhythm of the bustle of feet on the platform. There was no dust as it had been raining there for two days, I heard someone say, so the streets were muddy, the air heavy with the smell of wet dirt and damp clothes.

On the street side of the station there were automobiles and horses, buggies and wagons passing back and forth. Off to my far right, a car lurched in the mud with a gang of men behind it trying to get it out and crank it at the same time. At the end of the platform there was an older black man playing saxophone, his case at his feet collecting change. He was dressed in a dirty old suit and a top hat, and, after a bar or two, he'd stop, spit out a scat and get back to blowing. As I moved closer, I could hear him thank folks for listening, and he'd sing something else I couldn't make out entirely, some sort of song about a street. I tried to hum along as I crossed the platform toward the ticket booth.

The train schedule was posted in the middle. I weaved through the crowds of people watching the men on the tracks switch a train in the falling darkness. A high screeching of gears, the levers grinding metal against metal, and my clunking boots on the board floor punctuated my steps. The horns were all but drowned out. Voices of tourists shouted "Look!" and people pointed in all directions, making me flinch with paranoia until I realized they were not pointing at me. Women in gloves and big hats and men with cameras swarmed around me. Children were running around, even at that hour, up late for a summer holiday I supposed.

When I reached the posting board, I scanned the schedule. I found the next train to Birmingham. It wouldn't leave until the next day, so I had that long to figure out a way to get on it. I straightened my dress a bit, stood up taller, and headed over to the ticket counter to stand in line until it was my turn to present my ticket for a transfer. I decided the only option I had was to talk my way back onto a train.

When I reached the window, I didn't mention that it didn't have a punch, didn't mention anything except that I needed to get to Birmingham as quickly as possible. The woman in the ticket booth was plainer looking than Hazel, but with kinder eyes, deep brown with soft brown lashes. Her dishwater hair was pulled back in a tight bun, slicked on all sides. The woman looked at my ticket and shook her head. "Miss, the ticket needs a stamp to change it over—and your escort will need to verify your destination." She pointed to where the passage needed to be punched and looked around me.

"I—I—the porter must have made a mistake. I just got off the train from—from—" I couldn't remember the last stop. I knew we'd been in St. Louis, but I was sure that that was not the stop that I needed to report. It would be the little town in the hills. Even if I had remembered the name, I couldn't say it. What if word was out now about me? What if I was recognized?

"I'm sorry, miss, whatever trouble you're in," she hesitated looking me in the eyes, "without these signatures, and without your escort, I am afraid I can't transfer your ticket."

I stood there, clutching my ticket, afraid to walk away, afraid to give up my spot at the window, in the front of the line. I shifted my weight from leg to leg as if to jog my thoughts for another excuse, a plea, but drew a blank. I strained to smile, but the woman didn't flinch. Dressed as a woman, I couldn't even flirt my way to a ticket. Panic rose in me like a sharp pinch at my sides. I was tired, hungry, and stranded.

I walked away slowly and made my way back across the platform to an empty bench. I took out a cigarrette and lit it. I knew smoking on the street, in public, as a woman might get me in more trouble, but I didn't care. It was the only thing I had to keep off the hunger and panic. The crowd of tourists was finally thinning anyway, and the train station was about to close for the evening.

Across the way, close to where the saxophonist still played for a small circle of tourists, a tall man stood passing out flyers. He was young in the face, around my age I assumed. He came a bit closer and smiled down at me through the small crowd. His eyes were light blue in a contrast to his somewhat tanned skin, especially his hands. I wondered if he worked in a field, or with cattle like my father, though his nicely tailored suit certainly didn't imply that he did.

As the last of the tourists meandered through, the man leaned against a pole behind the sax player and counted his remaining flyers. Behind him, railroad men were in the yard again changing over a freight train. Aside from these men, the station was all but deserted. I shifted on the bench, sitting up straighter. The clanking of boots approached as a station police officer came out onto the platform. I quickly stamped out my smoke and rose to meet the man with the flyers and took one from him.

There were several ads on the same flyer, some for the same theater over and over, the Abraham, some for what looked like competing venues, Bops and The Palace. Just like in Chicago, I thought. I'd heard a name or two before, one I thought I knew from the rent rooms. At the bottom, there was a picture of a woman. "Hear the famous 'Woeful Baby' sung by Tulla Bell: Sweetest Sound in the South" the ad proclaimed. I ran my hand over the picture of her, imagining it was Jean Bailey, trying to look engrossed, occupied—escorted. I could hear the clanking of the policeman's boots on the platform grow closer.

"You into the Blues, there, miss?" the tall man asked shyly but with a wide smile, nodding to the flyer.

"Um, yes, I—um—I am," I stuttered, backing away from him slightly.

"Julian Delacroix," he said and held out his hand. His voice had a strange accent to it, southern, but also something else, something altogether foreign but pretty sounding, musical. He was dressed in a three-piece suit, dark with a tiny stripe in the material, tailored to his every inch. It looked expensive and impeccably made. He'd accented it with a muted purple silk scarf around his neck and a handkerchief in his top right pocket. I was immediately jealous. I took his hand and shook it quickly and let go without giving my name. He waited but then shrugged it off.

"Are you headed to one of these shows?" I asked, suddenly growing bold.

He smiled. "There's a show just down the way there. Wanna come?"

The policeman had stopped to watch the men change the train, but he was closer, almost in earshot. "I need—I mean," I said and heard my stomach growl. Without thinking I put my hand over it as if to stop it, afraid he'd heard it even over the noise at the station. I hadn't eaten since the biscuit on the train.

"Are you all right, miss? That blow getting the best of you?" He reached up to touch my face, and I remembered my black eye. I jerked away and shook my head, hiding my embarrassment with my hand.

"You aren't here alone, are you?" He looked around, then back down at me. He reached for my hand, the left one with the cuts. "Oh no! You're really hurt. Who did this?" He looked me up and down.

My dress felt bigger, even more ill-proportioned, my hair even shorter, my hand bare naked without gloves or any of the other proper attire to go with the dress. "My luggage was—lost—I'm sorry. I—I just missed my train," I said, remembering somehow that I should act like a grown woman, a grown woman in distress, though it did not come at all naturally, or easily, more like a stacked lie. "My—my money. I'm afraid I'm destitute and more than a bit hungry," I said with a whine. "I should try to find a place to stay, a train ticket." I turned to head back to my bench, away from the policeman.

But Julian called after me. "Well, then, you're here for the night! Come on with me. It will be fun." He followed me and held out his arm. "I'll be your escort. You'll need one in this town," he said under his breath.

My hands became a little sweaty, and the thick air seemed to amplify the emptiness in my stomach. I knew I wasn't at all proper, not at all acceptable, and though it made me feel somehow more defeated to have lured this boy for his help, I had to—I *wanted* to go along. I was afraid and faint, but proud of my own cunning, proud how easy it actually had turned out to be to get out of danger, but worried about what I would do next, how I would get on to Birmingham, to Georgia, to Jean Bailey. I worried about where I'd sleep, about having no money.

Remembering Hazel, her cruel grin as the train left the station, I was leery of a new friend. But Julian's smile and excitement were infectious, and he trusted me, seemed to believe everything I said, and that made me want to trust him somehow. I looped my arm in his as he held it out, and we started off, away from the policeman, passing directly behind the sax player, his tune still drowning under the sound of the trains.

As we moved out into the muddy streets, the night seemed darker, the air wetter. There were fewer and fewer people about as we headed toward the river. Once we got close, I could smell it, dirt and rotting fish and oil. As much as the smells should have added up to be sour, they were raw, tart-like. A strange slew of people were about at night in Memphis, wandering out of the restaurants and shops and into the dark streets not nearly as well lit as Chicago. The stranger the people we passed, the more reaction we received. A man and woman approached us walking the opposite direction. They were overdressed, it seemed, for this part of town, and in fashion that was outdated but that appeared well preserved until they grew closer. There was tatter and wear at the bottom of the woman's dress and an almost imperceptible rip at the shoulder seam of the man's jacket. They scoffed at us as they passed, lifting their chins as if we smelled. I flinched, tightening my grip on Julian's arm.

"Don't worry. We can say you are my sister, visiting for a few days." His accent seemed to thicken with the darkness. He pointed out the different joints as we passed them by, telling me who was playing where and what kind of show was what.

"Where are you from?" I asked.

"I'm from New Orleans, girl. Créole, if that's what you're asking. I'm all kinds of people mixed up together. I've got a little of this, a little of that." He giggled and held his head higher. "But I'm mostly white, that's why I wear the face." He gestured toward his face, circling it with a finger as if he were wearing a mask.

I squinted up at him, at his makeup that I could now see plain as day, powdery and white, caking over his skin, making him paler. I realized that his tan hands were what his skin looked like everywhere. I looked away, trying not to stare. "I've just never heard anyone talk like you."

More and more black folks were on the streets, stepping off the sidewalks as the few whites passed, Julian and me included. I could see now that they stared strangely at Julian, not me. He wasn't white, but wasn't black either, though I suspected he'd been treated as such most of his life.

"Well, I never heard anyone talk like you either," he said, clearing his throat, and pulled me on.

"Frankie, call me Frankie," I stuttered.

Julian smiled without looking down at me. A low tune of horns and voices flooded out in the street as we approached a building lit up with a side sign spelling out B-o-p-s downward.

"Looky there. Ida Giles, 'Queen Texas Wailer' herself was here just last week."

I stopped to listen as the door to the place opened and closed, speckling the street with brief glimpses of light.

"Texas?" I asked, remembering only the honky-tonks back home. "You mean that picking stuff they do on the guitar?"

"Ooh honey, not just the guitar. No, she's really got a great sound in her," he said and slung his hand and head back. "Why you so surprised? Texans sho know how to string a tune. I tell ya."

There was no woman's voice in the tune that faded in and out of Bops. "Who's there now?"

"It's the house band tonight."

We crossed to the other side of the street and just out of earshot of Bops, we came up on The Palace. Closed for the night, it was dark, deserted and sad, starkly different from The Palace Café. I thought of Jimmy Small's that first night I'd seen Jean Bailey. I thought of all the people crowding outside the door. I could see Jean Bailey on the stage belting out a note under the lights. I sped up my steps without thinking, and Julian and I almost began to skip.

"Have you heard of Jean Bailey?"

"Heck yes! You like Jean Bailey? Oh, just you wait. Tulla Bell is a Texas Blues gal too. She's no Ida Giles, and certainly no Bailey, but she's something. You'll see."

Starry-eyed, he went on about how he'd seen her first down in Louisiana in some tent or something.

"I—I'm from Texas, but I ain't never heard any Blues there. I didn't hear the Blues until I was in Chicago."

"My Lord, you was in Chicago? That's where it's at. Why you coming back down this way? Should be the other way around."

"Jean Bailey. I'm gonna work with her in vaudeville," I stammered out, but Julian just raised his eyebrows and with a smile pointed directly ahead of us. It was a shorter walk than I'd expected. We were already at the theater. We stopped in front of a tall wooden structure pieced out like an overgrown saloon you'd see in a Western but with a modern sign across the front all lit up with Tulla Bell's name spelled out in bold black letters. Julian told me the Abraham Theater was by far the biggest in that part of Memphis since it was open to blacks and whites. There was a long line wrapping around the back, two long lines, one for whites and one for blacks. As Julian approached the whites only line, I stiffened as I saw people at the front hand over cash to get in.

"Julian, I don't—I—"

"Most people call me Jewels, but I like how you say Julian." He cut me off to greet an older white man with a too-generous smile. "Frances. This is Mr. Hammond, sole owner and operator of absolutely nothing, but who *manages* to keep me in rags." At this, both men laughed a stilted laugh.

I realized that the two men, Julian and Mr. Hammond, were dressed exactly alike, but with different colors. Mr. Hammond's scarf was yellow, his handkerchief folded like a neat flower on his lapel. Mr. Hammond stepped back allowing me into the line, bowing a bit at my entrance.

There was a small commotion from the other line directly across the way from us. Julian's smile fell as a man in the blacks line threw his hands up, telling some kind of story to a shorter black man, both just as lean but not nearly as well dressed as Julian was.

Finally, I turned and shook hands with Mr. Hammond at the same time staring down into his coat pocket, spying a bulging wallet.

"I am a talent manager, Frankie. But Jewels is right. I didn't work for my money. I was born in it." He stepped back and looked me over. "How do you know Jewels?"

Julian was still watching the other line, and I wondered what his talent was, or how or if Mr. Hammond was his employer.

"We just—I mean—from the station. We know each other from the station."

"Do you like the theater shows?"

I nodded.

"There's so many Blues singers around here," Mr. Hammond said. "Who can keep up? Jewels can tell you all about the Blues, for sure." He nudged Julian's arm, and I recognized something in his face, attraction, a level of attention, something.

Julian straightened his back and lifted his chin. "Yes, sir, I sho can tell ya." His words seemed dismissive and forced as if they came through gritted teeth.

"Jewels. That accent is so charming, just delightful. I am reminded why I love you each time you open your mouth."

Something in the way Mr. Hammond said this unnerved me. The lilt in his voice was a little too sweet, too syrupy, and I thought of the man on the train, the way he warned me with compliments.

"Julian, maybe I shouldn't stay, really. I haven't got a dime to my name."

"Oh sweetheart, I've got you. Don't worry. Any friend of Jewels is welcome with me." Mr. Hammond's southern drawl was coming out now slow and deliberate. His mustache gave a bit of a twitch. I followed him inside, still unnerved. He had a slight limp and seemed to lean on Julian as we made our way to a table.

The band gathered, and the lights in the place dimmed. At our table down front, Julian reached over and struck a match to light the candle, his face going in and out of view with the flame. I caught his eye for a second, and he flashed me a grin, like he knew more than I did, and perhaps he did. But it was a warming grin, and we both laughed.

CHAPTER NINE

When the show was over, Mr. Hammond gently tugged at my elbow and the three of us rose to leave, weaving through the loitering crowd until we reached the door and were forced into a line like cattle. Mr. Hammond held me with a dainty hand at my elbow as he sauntered behind me, but Julian was lost in the crowd.

Tulla Bell's songs rang in my ears, songs about hopping trains for free—what I figured I'd be doing first thing in the morning. Hoboing it was what she'd called it. "Katy's at the station, Santa Fe is in the yard. Gonna leave this town, if I have to ride the rods," she sang, the twang in her voice reminding me of home, of my mama's faraway voice on the line before we were disconnected. I shook it off, trying to picture Jean Bailey's face, hear her voice instead.

Julian was right. Tulla Bell was no Jean Bailey. I was relieved and disappointed in that, but the show left me with even more determination to find Jean Bailey, to catch up with her. However I got there, free or not, I'd need money when I did.

Walking out of the theater, Mr. Hammond caught up beside me, and I leaned in a little too closely, almost stumbling into him. I spied his bulging wallet there in his pocket again. I remembered my father warning me about pickpockets in Chicago before I left. "You stay away from crowds, now girl. They'll rob ya blind," he'd told me, "have they hands down in your satchel before you know what's what." He hadn't warned me of pretty ticket booth girls, and he sure didn't tell me how I might do it myself, but there was a wallet, plain as day, and seemingly easy to just reach in and grab. I couldn't bring myself to grab Mr. Hammond's though.

I feigned a stumble as the line moved closer to the door and reached down into the pocket of the man in front of me—nothing. I tried another to the other side of me, practically stumbling all over the place and must have looked drunk. There was a wallet, but when I thumbed it, sliding my fingers through the folds as I shoved it in my satchel, I found that there was no money in it, not a dime. By the time we got out, I was sweating, and too afraid to try again.

Mr. Hammond tightened his grip on me and tried to steady me. "We should get you on out of here, off your feet, before you hurt yourself." He smiled at me and ushered me on.

I wanted to walk toward the river, get a breeze up off of it, but I stayed with Mr. Hammond, relieved when I saw Julian behind us again.

"I really appreciate the show, Mr. Hammond, Julian, but I should get on to the train station now," I said.

"Darlin', the train station has been closed for a good long time," Mr. Hammond said sweetly. "You won't be able to catch anything until morning. Besides, you don't want to get arrested. Do ya?" He didn't even blink, just said it like it was commonplace and nodded to the door. Julian didn't react. He was distracted as the black folks streamed out of the other entrance.

I started to protest, "I should really just go back and wait at the station."

"You'll get picked up there for sure, unescorted and all. I don't know how you've gotten along this far, all the way from

Chicago, I hear." I suddenly realized that Julian had been telling Mr. Hammond all he knew of me during the show. "It just isn't safe. Come on along with us. Jewels wants to get you fed and set up for the night, and then get you on a train first thing tomorrow, or whenever. Who knows, you might want to stay."

I looked at Julian who perked up with a big grin, excited for the company I guessed. "I'll drive!" Julian said, as if delighted by the idea, and Mr. Hammond agreed.

I was dumbfounded. I had nowhere else to go. Mr. Hammond was right, my idea to go back to the station and wait for the morning was not a good one, especially since there might still be folks looking for me there. Julian and I followed Mr. Hammond and his brisk, tight walk, now without a limp, to his car, just around the corner of the building. Julian cranked it and got in to drive. Mr. Hammond opened the door for me to get in the back and he climbed in beside Julian. The car was fancy, brand-new, and smelled of leather.

"Don't worry, darlin', we'll get you fixed up right," Mr. Hammond said and turned around in his seat. "I've got a great old big house. You'll practically have your own wing. Safe and sound with your own maid and everything. You'll love it."

Mr. Hammond relaxed in his seat, confident and comfortable, a bit giddy, and something about him made me believe him. He was dark-haired, had light brown eyes and a sweet smile, a good-looking man, well groomed, polite with little worry in his face at all. Although he had a sharp, angled jawline, his mouth was relaxed and seemed soft, as kind as his eyes but sophisticated, grown up, confident.

I remembered the boys I'd dated back in Texas. I remembered their rough, groping hands, hard and torn from working with cattle and on farms, remembered their freckled faces, the impatience in their eyes. When they kissed me, I felt as if they would swallow me whole. It was always wet, always fast, like we were running out of time, and always clumsy. I imagined that kissing Mr. Hammond would be a foreign experience compared to the boys back home, maybe a nicer experience, and for a second, I thought about my mama's advice to me, telling me to marry a rich man. Mr. Hammond could have been my father had he been just a little older, but I realized why she said that. Money seemed to make everything so much easier. But not easy enough to make me want to kiss him.

We drove for a good long while through the city. Memphis's buildings seemed squat compared to Chicago. We came up on a dingy street with houses that looked like they were stacked on top of one another, piled high. There were women in the windows fanning themselves, and I could have sworn they were half dressed. Of course, I couldn't tell. It was dark, and they were up above me as we drove on through.

Once through the neighborhood and to the outskirts of the town, we came to a long drive paved with stones. At the end, we parked in front of the largest house, a mansion really. It was white, and I could see the expansive wooden staircase through the glass front door, winding up to nowhere, nowhere I could see above the doorframe anyway. Julian got out and walked up to the house. Mr. Hammond opened my door and motioned for me to follow. Before we reached the massive porch a woman stepped out.

"I'm home, Mama!" Julian yelled up with a wave.

The woman was dark-skinned and dressed in a tea-length blue uniform overlaid with a white apron and a little white collar. It was similar to Cora's but much nicer with sturdier fabric and tailored to fit. She was thin as a rail, but came across not in the least bit slight. Even from the yard I could see that she commanded attention. I didn't think she looked old enough to be Julian's mother though.

"Julian!" The southern charm rolled out of her mouth like smoke from a cigarette. "Why M.!" she said over us both, looking out to the car. "I didn't think I'd see you tonight. I figured you and Julian would be out all night. And who is this?" When she looked down at me, I couldn't tell if she was surprised, startled, or worried. I shrank behind Julian.

"Bonnie, you don't mind taking this kitten in for a night do ya?" Mr. Hammond yelled as he came up behind me.

"Kitten! I ain't taking in any more strays, M.! I don't care if she's your niece from Yazoo!"

"Aw, Bon, you'd do it for me wouldn't you?" Julian pleaded with her on the steps, kissing her on the cheek.

I stopped, but Mr. Hammond kept walking and then turned and motioned for me to follow.

When he stepped onto the porch, he bowed. "I'd like you to meet Frankie. Frankie, Madam Bonnie Rhodes. She takes care of us here at the *Adler Lake Estate*." Mr. Hammond named his home with sarcasm, as if it were a joke. I wondered where the lake was.

Madam Rhodes huffed and took my hand to shake it, but then held onto it, turned it over, revealing the dirt, the cuts, and the blood. She looked into my face and let out a holler. "Whoa Lord, M.! Where did you drag this one up from?"

"Down at the theater."

"Talent?" she asked.

Mr. Hammond looked to me then, and I looked to Julian.

"She's looking for Jean Bailey," Julian finally chimed in.

"Oh, that hussy! Of course, of course. Jean Bailey." Her voice was nasty then, and a snarl came over her face as she turned and showed us all into the house. The whole house was brightly lit with lanterns and candles. There was a chandelier over our heads with a hundred twinkling crystals.

"Now, Bonnie, don't be like that. What's that one done to you?"

"Oh don't 'now, Bonnie' me. You don't know heads nor tails about it."

Julian and Mr. Hammond grinned, shaking their heads at Madam Rhodes. "Bonnie, take her to the guest quarters will ya?"

"Yes, sir."

She motioned for me to follow her off to the right, down a long, dimly lit hall, as Julian and Mr. Hammond went up the stairs.

"It's not properly made up, but it will have to do tonight. Did ol' Marcel—Mr. Hammond think he was getting himself a nice young talent with you?"

I shrugged, confused. "Julian just asked me to come along and then Mr. Hammond offered me a place to stay. I—I missed my train this afternoon and lost all my luggage and—"

"You don't have to explain none to me, miss. I'm just the help."

Eventually we reached a back staircase and climbed to the top only to find another long hallway there as well.

"You know Jean Bailey, Mrs. Rhodes?" I tried to make friendly conversation.

"Madam Rhodes, please."

I nodded with a blush. I didn't know there was a difference.

"We called her Virginia back then since that was her given name, but she changed it soon after she started up singing again, after Marcel got her that gig over at the Abraham."

"Was she one of Mr. Hammond's—um—discoveries?"

She laughed at that as she opened a door to a bedroom and turned on the light. The bedroom windows were shrouded in heavy violet drapes, floor to ceiling. There was a large oriental rug that drew you in to a sitting area beside a vanity with a large gilded mirror. The bedroom was gaudy and old, musty smelling, but it was richer than I'd ever imagined. In the middle of the room were two beds, both bigger than my own back home. They billowed with pillows and ornate blankets.

Madam Rhodes pulled back the blankets and fluffed the pillows. "Miss Bailey was here a lot back some years ago, lots of those singing girls were. Most were lost, like you, but Jean Bailey was already a big name in some places. People don't know her by that name 'round here, don't know what she does, don't much get her kind of act. They's more interested in the jazz, the horns, those men, even Marcel. Much more interested in the Julians than the Jeans."

"Does Julian perform?"

She nodded, surprised it seemed that I didn't know. "Of course, that's why he's here, or that's how he got here anyway. Marcel found him down in New Orleans or some little town around there."

She instructed me to get out of my soiled clothes and into bed and told me she'd bring up a snack in a few minutes. "You look as if you could use a three-course meal, but a snack is all we have at this hour."

When Madam Rhodes left, I tugged my dress and boots off, untied my knife and tucked it under the pillow. I climbed into bed in my underclothes and pulled the blankets up to my chin. I was already asleep when Madam Rhodes came with the food. She shook me awake, startling me with her severe expression as she leaned over me, but I just drifted off again without eating a bite.

* * *

The next morning, the food was gone and Julian was waiting for me downstairs when I found my way there, dressed again in my dress that Madam Rhodes had smoothed out and draped over the end of the bed. Julian was in a silky, colorful robe I'd never seen on a man, on anyone, before and was giddy and all smiles, as if he'd found a new playmate.

"We have to get you cleaned up girl, better dressed, and fed, of course!"

We ate at the little table in the kitchen, not the one meant for company, while Madam Rhodes scurried around us doing chores. Julian acted as if he could barely wait for me to finish breakfast, seeming much younger than me in that moment. He didn't even eat his boiled egg and toast, just a few bites of the cantaloupe on the plate. I was surprised that the breakfast was so simple. Even for the rich with all the ornate décor, food was food, at least for a guest like me anyway.

"Where are we going, Julian? I don't have any money for clothes, not even for material to make clothes or anything," I said between bites. I shoveled down my food and ate most of Julian's when he pushed his plate over to me.

"Oh! We've got clothes! Loads and loads! Right upstairs, from all the singers Mr. Hammond manages."

Something about how he said this, half under his breath when Madam Rhodes was out of the room made me think he was lying.

"I—I need to find a way to a train, Julian. Is Mr. Hammond here? Can he take me to the station?"

Julian's face fell. "Frankie, he'll take care of you here, long as you want, but he won't put you on no train to go find Jean Bailey."

I didn't know exactly what he meant by that, but I wanted it to be clear that I didn't expect anything from Mr. Hammond. "I was actually thinking I'd hobo down South."

"Oh, Frankie, don't." Julian leaned in to me, put his hand on my arm. "I mean, you don't have to leave yet, do you? There's so much we can do here. So much fun we can have. Just for a little while?"

The pleading in his face reminded me of my cousin, Deloris. Every time she wanted to see Bean, she'd give me this face, hook me with a promise of fun, fun away from my parents so I'd agree. It made me feel needed somehow, and just then, it seemed that Julian needed me more than I had needed him the night before. I scooped the last bite of egg from Julian's plate and leaned back, full and satisfied, gulping the last of the juice Madam Rhodes had squeezed for me.

"Oh, all right, Julian. Just for a day or so."

He jumped up and threw his arms out, almost losing his robe. He grabbed me and dragged me out, kissing Madam Rhodes on the cheek for a thank-you as we left the kitchen.

"Do not leave a mess up there, young man!" she yelled after us.

At the top of the great staircase, Julian ran ahead of me to the end of the hall. I tried to get my bearings, figure out where my room was in relation to where we were. I was lost. Finally, at the end of the hall, he opened two double doors to a bedroom, a boudoir twice the size of where I stayed, twice as much gaudy décor. He made his way to an armoire on the other side of the bed and threw open the doors in a dramatic fashion as if he were on stage or in a film.

There was a line of dresses, exquisitely sewn dresses, each lined with a different jewel, made from a different fabric—all expensive seeming, colorful, bright and bold, but expensive. They glittered. He pulled one out, a glowing light pink one lined with what looked like diamonds. It was loose, drop-waisted, the new style. I ran to it and traced my hands over it. It was smooth, light and airy, but it was—too much.

"Julian, this is gorgeous, but I can't wear it—especially if I'm going to be hopping trains. It's—it's more like a costume, something you'd wear on stage rather than in real life." I still couldn't take my eyes off it so I had no idea what Julian's reaction was. I just knew he was flipping through the clothes wildly, pulling them out and tossing them on the bed, one on top of the other.

When I turned I saw that he'd built up quite a pile. I picked up another one, a green one, almost the same style but a little more muted, an olive green with off-white lace and appliqués instead of sparkles. "I might could do with this one, if I took some of the ornaments off. But it's way too big. I'd have to trim it quite a bit to—"

Just as I turned to face Julian who was still digging in the armoire I saw past him to the back, to a suit, a tailored, beautifully stitched men's suit. It looked like the suits on State Street, and it was small, like what the women wore at Ernie Royce's where I'd last seen Jean Bailey. I dropped the dress and went to it, touching the lapel. I could see Jean Bailey's suit jacket on the flyer I'd left behind and imagined I was running my hands over it, over her, that she was leaning into me again. I yearned to feel her warmth on me again, her touch on my cheek again, and I yearned to feel the slick feel of pants against my legs again. I slipped them out from under the jacket, unbuttoned them and held them up, about to try them on under my dress.

"Well, I'll be goddammed! Jewels! Look here, boy!" Marcel yelled from the door, half scolding and half excited.

Julian and I both jumped and turned to Mr. Hammond standing in the doorway, holding my satchel.

"Marcel!" Julian ran and kissed him right on the mouth, but there was something, something hesitant, something forced in it. Julian backed away and tried to sweep up the mess from the bed, picking up garment after garment and slinging it over his arm. Mr. Hammond didn't move, didn't react at all, and I was frozen stiff. I don't even think I took a breath. I felt just like I did when Uncle Albert had found me in Jean Bailey's room. My face throbbed again where he'd hit me though I knew that my eye looked a little better at this point, the bruising having turned to yellows and reds looking more like lack of sleep or nutrition than a black eye.

Mr. Hammond walked toward me then and stopped in the middle of the room, putting his hand on his chin. He was dressed in knickers like he was about to go play sports. "I knew there was something about you," Mr. Hammond said, as proud as a peach, pointing at me holding the suit pants. He pulled my trousers out of my satchel and his face brightened, like he'd just been given a gift. "I know just exactly what you are looking for, just exactly. Fit right in with you sissy boys, right Jewels?" Mr. Hammond's voice rose to the lilt that had banged against my ear the previous night. It was sinister.

My stomach knotted as I tried to back away. I felt naked and exposed.

Julian flushed red as a beet and cleared his throat. "Ah, I knew it! You don't look for a second like you belong in a frock! How wonderful!" He forced out a laugh and took the suit jacket from me, holding it up to me, fitting it to me. "From the moment I saw you, you seemed more like a boy trying to pass as a girl than the other way around, all skinny and with a black eye."

I crossed my arms at my chest. I didn't know why, but I was offended.

"Oh Frankie, it's okay. Jewels, show her." Mr. Hammond was gruff in his order.

Julian didn't hesitate. He grabbed something from the bed and ran behind a large screen at the far end of the room. He slung his robe over the side and emerged a few seconds later dressed—looking for all the world just like a beautiful, stylish woman—in the pink dress I had ogled earlier. He slapped on some long white gloves and did a twirl around the room.

"Julian!" I gasped. "You—you look—"

"Divine! I know!" He tossed his imaginary hair over his shoulder and swooned across the floor. He moved more like a woman than most women I knew—more like a screen siren, a movie star, or like someone on a stage, singing, though he was taller than any woman I'd ever met. "Come on! Now! You try."

He tossed the suit to me and plopped down on the bed in the middle of a pile of dresses, thumbing through them, admiring each individually and then tossing it aside as if each offended him.

I went behind the shade, wriggled out of my sloppy dress, now dirty from the mud the night before, and slipped into the trousers, the immaculately tailored shirt, and the thick jacket. I stood up tall and smoothed it all down into place and then walked out. Not only did the clothes fit well, they felt good, nice material, nicer than most of my good dresses, and excellent tailoring.

"Well, I'll be—" Mr. Hammond said and then crossed the room to me, crinkling his brow down at me. He went behind me and pulled down on my jacket. He spun me to the mirror and pulled again. "Hmmm. What shall we do about these?"

There were two little bulges in the material where my breasts were. I didn't have large breasts and had mostly trained myself to slouch enough that they didn't show, but in this suit, as nicely as it fit, my breasts seemed to stick out, larger than they actually were. I shrugged. My corset would only make them seem bigger. Julian joined Mr. Hammond. They moved me this way and that, slouched me over, bending me to try to make the least of my breasts. Finally, they gave up.

"Jewels is lucky. At least large breasts are not the razz these days and not required of the dresses. But for you—breasts are never the thing for men." He laughed at this, a hot, pompous laugh.

I stood admiring my reflection in the mirror. Even with the bumps, maybe even because I could still see the bumps, I liked what I saw. I slicked back my hair with my hands and brooded at myself.

Julian giggled. "You do look, um, sexy in that though, as a she-male. Not quite a she and not quite a male—no, no, I mean as a she and a he. Both!"

I grinned as wide and as unsexy as I could.

Mr. Hammond looped his arm in Julian's. "Well, sweetheart, you are absolutely right," he said, his voice and attention changed. I couldn't tell if he was mad or complacent. He motioned for me to turn around, show him my outfit from all sides, and when I did, he made a guttural groan that turned my stomach. I stopped mid turn. Julian wiggled away from Mr. Hammond and ducked his head to go put away the clothes.

"Quite sexy. Yes." Mr. Hammond stood behind me, put his hands on my hips and pinched at the fabric at my waist to tighten it. He lifted my arms and turned me to the mirror, still behind me, fitting me. The tighter he pulled at the sides, the more my breasts showed. I couldn't tell if he liked this or didn't. His touch felt the same as when my mother measured me up for a fitting, but after the run in with the man on the train, it made me uneasy, nervous, and I stiffened. Finally, he let go and stepped away.

"You sew?"

I nodded.

"Tell you what, you tailor this up a little bit, the way you like it, and you can have it."

Mr. Hammond walked to the door and paused. He appraised me in the reflection.

"Uh oh, Marcel, you're up to something. Aren't you?" Julian came and stood behind me, and we looked at each other in the mirror, but avoided each other's eyes.

CHAPTER TEN

That evening I bathed. It was the first bath I'd had since I left Chicago, and I thought I'd died and ascended into heaven right there in that claw-foot tub. The water was warm and scented, prepared just for me by Madam Rhodes, as if she were my personal maid. Mr. Hammond had sent up the finest soaps and hair oils and the softest bath towel I'd ever felt on my skin. Emerging all wrinkle-skinned and fresh-faced from the water, I felt just like a princess, better than I'd felt in a long, long time, ever really, as I slipped into the suit I'd tailored to fit. It still puckered a bit where my breasts were, but if I stood with just the right slouch of my shoulders, you could barely tell.

Madam Rhodes had informed Julian and me that dinner would be formal, in the main hall that night, and Julian met me outside my door to show me the way. Julian was wearing the pink gown again, gloves and all, but had added to it a number of jewels and a short little blonde wig with a headband on his head. He even had on makeup, ruby-red lipstick and rouge on his cheeks, both shining against his tanned skin but looking just as natural as I did, perhaps even more so, certainly more beautiful. He towered over me in the heels he'd added to the ensemble. He seemed to take up the entire room but also add to it, making it prettier.

"Breathtaking, Julian."

"Please, call me Jewels in this getup, darling." He curtsied for me and turned to go. "Wait," he said and turned to me again. He pulled out a pink silk handkerchief like the one he'd worn the night before in his own lapel pocket. He folded it just so and stuffed it into mine, grinning like a puffed-up rooster. I smiled wide and walked in a daze out the door behind him.

As we reached the dining hall, the room was full to the brim with guests, elegantly clad and engrossed in each other, mostly older white men in tuxedos or silken suits. The women were a bit younger but just as stuffy with stark white gloves, dark, heavy taffeta dresses, and patent leather shoes, their hair all knotted up on top of their heads, clunky jewelry hanging from their ears. They seemed so heavy it made me walk a little slower into the ornate hall.

The dining hall was like any you'd imagine in a rich man's house, a rich bachelor's house, ugly oil paintings of old white men on the wall—much like the men standing under them—gilded lighting, a long, clunky, wooden table in the middle surrounded by dark, velvet seated high back chairs. It looked like a woman had no part in the design of this area. Everything dark and heavy-handed seemed to weigh the room down.

Suited black men served drinks, cigarettes and little foods on trays, and when the first came round to us, I could feel Jewels flinch. The server was a beautiful man with soft features. I thought I recognized him but had no idea how. Jewels locked eyes with him and, without a word, retrieved a cigarette for his extender now hanging from his mouth and a drink he handed over to me. I picked up a smoke as well and once the server lit us both, we headed toward Mr. Hammond, gliding softly, arm in arm as if making a grand entrance.

Mr. Hammond lifted his eyes to us just as we approached. His eyes traveled the length of me. He looked sloppy and overexcited, as if he were drunk. I felt as heavy as the room, but fought off the feeling and tried to stroll loosely next to Jewels, who was trailing a little behind. In an instant, Mr. Hammond faced Jewels and went altogether pale, stiff. Jewels stopped, let go of my arm and stepped back, stopping there in the middle of the dining room. The room was so busy that only I noticed the change in the air, like all the warmth had been sucked out.

I wanted to slink back with Jewels but couldn't seem to lift my feet. A great many of the guests had finally noticed our entrance or perhaps Mr. Hammond's reaction and were beginning to quiet down and stare. A Victrola sat in the back and someone slid on a record. When the record started my head spun around. It was Jean Bailey's voice sounding so close she could have been right behind me. The song was muffled, like she was down a well, right behind me, but down a well. I felt a chill run up my back. I shivered and took another drag on my cigarette. I tried to focus on the lilt in Jean Bailey's voice. I tried to picture her face in my hands. But Jewels seemed larger than ever, and I felt large right along with him, like two big elephants standing dumb in the middle of a room.

As another one of the servers passed, Mr. Hammond placed a drink on his tray, looking into the Negro boy's face in disgust. I could feel Jewels shift beside me, standing up straighter but not making a move any closer to Mr. Hammond. He motioned for the Negro boy, and he brought over his tray with three full drinks on it. Jewels took another and tapped mine with his as if to toast and immediately swallowed the entire contents of the glass. I wasn't even quite sure what was in mine, as I hadn't so much as put it to my lips. When I did, I almost gasped. It was a clear liquid and smelled putrid, worse than Royce's bathtub gin. I couldn't so much as get it past my nose again to attempt another sip and was relieved that Jewels hadn't noticed.

He slammed his glass down on the nearest tray, smiling at me and then winking at Mr. Hammond. People all around me whispered and nodded in our direction. The men seemed to stare at us both in polite confusion, but the women turned up their noses and soon enough went back to their conversations. I smiled and took another drag of my cigarette, lifting my glass a little as if to toast the room and then immediately dropping it, along with my head, in embarrassment.

Jean Bailey let out a long moan in the middle of her song and then the music picked up, trotting along as she spoke rather than sang the verses. I perked up and dared another sip of that god-awful drink, but saw that no one, not a soul in the room, moved in response to the music, not even a bob or a sway. It was as if the song wasn't even playing, as if it were just background noise. This was what forced my body to finally move again. I smiled, wide and mischievous, grinning really, and smoothed down my jacket, straightened my tie and turned to Julian, taking his hand as if to dance. He curtsied to me, drew me in and twirled me around. In mid-twirl, Mr. Hammond stopped us and grabbed Julian by the white-gloved arm, dragging him almost into a stumble out of the door.

The crowd hushed around me. I put out my cigarette and followed them out only to catch Mr. Hammond pushing Julian into a room across the hall. Mr. Hammond's voice was muffled, but he was yelling loud enough that I only needed to cross the hall to make out what he was saying.

"How could you dare present yourself like this?" Mr. Hammond demanded.

"I thought—I thought that's what you wanted, that it was why you gave the suit to the little bull!" Julian's voice was flirtatious but bleeding into a screech.

"That's different!"

"Why, because she looks like a man?" Julian's voice sounded strong, manly, different than his usual lilt.

There was a pause, and I could swear I heard a slap.

"I would never have asked you to dine formally had this been my intention, Julian. You did it on purpose, didn't you? Do not try to kiss this away! I saw that boy! Another one of your sissy boys, right?"

I didn't hear Julian's reply, only what sounded like a whimper, and then Mr. Hammond flew out of the room, slamming the door behind him.

I ducked back, hiding the fact that I'd been spying. In his most sugary southern accent, he said, "Frankie, sugar will you please try to explain to Julian what's appropriate to wear to dinner?" He furrowed his brow and stared down at me, into me. "I am sure you realize, he's not quite—I mean, it's not his fault, but he's always been a little simpleminded. He's certainly not as bright as you, darling."

I cringed, embarrassed and ashamed at Mr. Hammond calling Julian simple. I wanted to defend him but was embarrassed that it hadn't occurred to me that Julian might not be all that bright. He was just sweet and kind.

Mr. Hammond took a breath, exasperated, and then took me in again, as if his eyes were drunk on me. It sent a shiver through me, and I backed away, not realizing why. "Look at you! Delicious!" When he said this, his accent harsh and gruff, immediately I saw the man on the train, the man whose knife I carried with me. I could feel his breath on me again and flinched when Mr. Hammond brushed by me and nodded for me to go in after Julian.

I felt sick and worked hard to regulate my breathing. When I was sure Mr. Hammond was safely at the dinner party and I could catch my breath, I went in to check on Julian. He was sitting on a backless upholstered bench, his manicured hands, smooth and delicate, in his lap as if he were a proper lady waiting for a date. I sat beside him. Neither of us spoke for a long time. Finally, Julian turned to me and straightened the handkerchief in the pocket of my suit.

"You're really good at sewing, like a pro. That suit is brilliant," Julian said without even looking up.

"I've been sewing most of my life with my mother. I like it. The work calms me, makes me feel useful."

"Marcel sure wants to make use of you." This seemed like a warning from Julian, but as he said it, he turned to hide his face, to hide something—like jealousy, or to keep me from prying into what had just happened.

I felt sick all over again and struggled to talk about something, anything else. "Are you—I mean—um—What's a sissy boy?" I asked though I thought I knew.

Julian laughed and took off his gloves, waving his hands to point out his dress to me. "Me. I'm a sissy boy, like you're a bulldyker."

"Bulldagger," I corrected.

Julian got up and motioned for me to follow. We went up to the boudoir again where all the dresses were hanging in wait.

In the doorway, Julian took a loud breath and headed for a trunk by the window. "Marcel and I, we've been together for years, three or four I think it is now," he said, digging through the chest.

"How old are you?" I blurted out.

"My parents didn't have much of a problem letting him take me when I was a pretty young thing, especially since I was one of about a dozen kids and especially since Marcel is rich, as if it would rub off on me and I'd bring it back to them. They'd been pawning off my talent all my life." There was contempt in his voice though he'd moved on to admiring himself in the mirror before stepping out of the dress. Julian widened his eyes and belted out a string of beebops and then a long bellowed note, almost as striking as Jean Bailey's moan but higher pitched.

I sat down on the bed. "You're amazing, Julian."

He moved to behind the screen to change clothes. "Yeah, but that's nothing compared to my playing my own music, or it used to be anyway. Marcel only wants me on the horns, if he wants me on stage at all, and never lets me sing. He won't let me near my 'cordian."

"Your what?"

He emerged dressed in day trousers and a shirt he was fixing a vest and tie around. "He says they ain't no money in what I do, says it's swamp-donkey music."

I couldn't help it, I laughed at that. "Swamp what?"

Julian smiled, smacking me on the arm like he didn't have the strength to hurt me but was trying.

"I don't know why I stick around," he said and turned his head to the dark window. "I don't suspect he'll have me for long though, now that he knows about my stepping out, or, I mean my wanting to step out." His face went all stiff, and then he darted his eyes like he'd been caught at something.

"Well, don't," I said, still reeling from the queasiness Mr. Hammond gave me.

He looked at me like I had two heads.

"I mean it. You don't have to stay here. Let's go. Let's go tonight. We can go hop on a damn train right this instant."

"The car." Julian jumped up with his idea. "We could take the car!"

I stiffened.

"Not the new car," he explained. "The old one out back, and we won't steal it, Frankie. I'll tell Marcel he can pick it up tomorrow. He'll let me go for a while. I bet he'll even give us money for the train. He's tired of me anyway." He put his hand on my arm, staring into me.

Even with my worry over the car and the nagging his stare gave me, I didn't hesitate.

"Meet me in the kitchen right after dinner."

We made our way back to dinner, Julian in a shirt and trousers and me still in my suit. The guests were all seated before their food, smothered beef elegantly plated on gold-lined china. There was a buzz in the room, laughing, talking, clicking of silver on dishes. No one even glanced up at us, and I felt like we were two scolded children being allowed to sit at the grown-ups' table. We ate silently, I more quickly than I should have and not nearly as politely as I knew how, but I was starved and the food was good, savory, melt in your mouth good, as if the expensive dinnerware had leaked into the food. When the server brought me another round and I ate it, every last crumb, Mr. Hammond seemed much pleased, but stiff as a bird. The woman beside him sipped at a drink and hardly touched her food. She was tied in so tight to her black dress that she couldn't have fit in much more than a few cocktails anyway. She never met my eye but seemed dazed and happy, smiling and sipping, nodding to her left and right, ringlets of blonde hair bouncing with her head when someone spoke. I caught myself staring and went back to my dessert. Dinner was without incident, and we both managed to excuse ourselves quickly from after dinner smokes.

In the guest room, I found my satchel with nothing disturbed inside and dug out my knife, tying it back on my boot. Down in the kitchen, I dodged Madam Rhodes and the waiters while I waited on Julian. I heard his voice in the hall before he came in. He was talking to one of the waiters, apologizing frantically, exclaiming that he had to go. When I poked my head out, I almost gasped in surprise. Julian was kissing the pretty boy waiter, more than just on the lips, more like a real kiss, a lover's kiss, more than even what Julian had given Mr. Hammond that afternoon in the boudoir. I scurried back to the kitchen, knowing what I'd known before, that Julian had lied about stepping out on Mr. Hammond.

Julian flew in and grabbed my hand, pulling me out the back door. We didn't stop to stock up on food like I'd planned. The only thing he brought with him was the pink dress he'd worn earlier, balled up into an extra shirt and tied just exactly like a hobo sack. As we were leaving the light of the house, I saw that his eyes were wet with streaming tears. I didn't have time to ask what had happened, if he was okay. When he cranked the car and skidded out of the drive, looking over his shoulder every few seconds, I knew he hadn't been given the car and most likely any money either.

* * *

At the station, Julian parked the car as far back as he could and still see the trains. We sat for a minute waiting for a train to come in. Only a passenger train was parked at the station, and we both knew we wouldn't be able to hop on it. An hour later, one freight train came through and slowed to a stop, stringing far down the tracks. This was our chance; we'd sneak onto the train just like I'd heard about in Tulla Bell's song and ride it as far south as we could.

We both got out of the car and made our way to the tracks, careful not to approach the station. The streets were just as crowded as they had been the night before, but we tried to keep our distance, staying in the shadows of the buildings, and just as we were slinking up the backside of the line of boxcars, the gears shifted and screeched. The train began to move. We walked faster, and the train gained speed. We jogged beside it, looking for an open car.

When we finally spotted one, green and rusted out, it was barely open, just enough for us to climb in and squeeze through one at a time. Julian tossed in his bundle and climbed in first, struggling only a little. When he got up, he turned to give me a hand since I could barely reach. I struggled, my feet sliding and kicking and then dangling over the gravel beside the tracks. Finally, Julian slung me into the car. Just as I was standing up, brushing myself off, a man appeared out of the darkness of the car, lurking with his brows furrowed and fists clenched up behind Julian like he'd knock him over the head. He was greasy looking with wild eyes.

"Julian!" I yelled.

Julian looked behind him and had time enough to flinch as the man raised his booted foot and literally kicked Julian out of the car, sending him tumbling onto the graveled ground by the tracks below. He tossed the bundle of clothes out behind him and I watched as they came undone and scattered onto the dirt.

Julian shook his head and then sat up, wiping his eyes like he was dizzy.

"Jump, you crazy!" he yelled back.

When I looked down the gravel seemed like it was going a hundred miles an hour, but I knew we were just crawling, having just left the station. The hobo grinned at me as if waiting for a good time to kick me off or worse. I squatted down, trying to get closer to the ground, a shorter distance to fall and just jumped. A sharp sting went up my feet and into my legs and I buckled, tumbling to the grass out of the gravel and rolled to a stop. When I'd gotten my bearings, Julian was looking me over, poking and prodding me like a protective mother bear. I pushed him off and glanced over him the way he had me.

"I'm fine," he mumbled, slicking back his hair and brushing off his clothes.

I was terrified numb. I couldn't even feel my own hand as Julian helped me up off the ground. If the train had been going any faster, we could have died from that fall.

Down the tracks, the old hobo was half hanging out of the car, laughing and carrying on with a few others in the same car. I wondered why we hadn't seen them before we tried to get on.

"We best be looking for an empty one next time," I said with my hands on my hips.

Julian threw up his hands. "We're driving." He turned and walked deliberately back, swinging his arms like he was about to take flight, leaving the clothes scattered across the side of the tracks.

I scrambled to pick up our good clothes and sped up after him. "How are we going to do that? We don't have any money. Why don't we—"

"We can't get on one of them trains, Frankie. Besides, they ain't but one more and that's another hour away. Marcel will have us by then." His accent thickened. When we reached the car, he cranked it and got in without so much as an extra breath.

I didn't argue. I wasn't jumping at the chance to try hopping on a train again. I got in and tossed the clothes into the seat beside me. When Julian backed out of the station and headed down the crowded streets of Memphis, he seemed to know exactly what he was doing, exactly where he was going, and I trusted him as he pulled two packs of smokes out of his pockets and handed me one.

We drove right out of town that night, south on what had to be the darkest, dirtiest, bumpiest road ever created. Its only saving grace was that it took us out of the hills instead of into them. For just a moment, I felt freer and more relieved than

I had since I'd left Chicago. I wasn't thinking of my aunt and uncle, my mamma and daddy. I wasn't even thinking of Jean Bailey, really. I was just staring at the open road ahead of us, miles and miles of dirt and gravel all the way to Mississippi and, Julian told me, all the way to Georgia if we could make it that far.

CHAPTER ELEVEN

The dust from the road seeped in through the windows and settled on us like soot, and the sweat spackled my hair against my forehead. We were silent for a good long time. The bugs flew through the air smacking the windshield in a strange rhythm that got Julian and I both trying to thump along. We got into rhythm, and then Julian giggled. I giggled, and then we were laughing outright, almost howling at ourselves.

"You laugh like a crazy person, Frankie—when you let yourself really let it loose, that is." Julian held his side catching his breath.

"What? What's a crazy person laugh like?"

His expression went blank like he was considering this, but then he started laughing all over again. It was true I had a strange guttural laugh, and it took over my whole body when I was really tickled. Julian's laugh was much more reserved but hardy and warm and full of something sweet.

I stuck my head out of the open window and looked up at the stars. Although I'd been out of Chicago almost a week, I hadn't even remembered to look at them again. No matter how much I hated living in Nowhere, Texas, I loved the stars and missed them. I was missing them right then even when I was seeing them. A little bit of sadness sank into my stomach like emptiness, and I yearned to fill it up again.

Julian's face was smooth as silk, his tan skin shining in the darkness of the car. He had soft features, though his nose came to a definite point and flared out a little underneath. If he set his jaw the right way, his look gave off a haughty air, but not one that would scare you off. One that would draw you in, make you want to get closer, figure him out.

"Julian, who was that boy you were kissing when we left?"

He didn't answer, but I could see his cheeks blush even in the darkness of the car. I didn't press. I just sat in silence, waiting him out.

"Tell me, girl. What is it you want with Jean Bailey? You don't seem like—I mean, you dress—you both dress like…" He stuttered over his words, but I wasn't sure how to help so I didn't interrupt. "I guess—I mean, Marcel is the manly one and I am a sissy boy. It's what he likes whether or not he'd ever admit it. You two seem like the same, both bulldyke—daggers."

I shrugged. "Jean Bailey is the most beautiful woman I have ever seen in my life. I don't care much what she is."

"Who's going to be the—don't you need a—girl?"

I laughed hard at this. "We are both girls!"

"Oh hell, Frankie, I know that, but you play like you ain't. That's all I'm saying."

I didn't really know if I played like anything, or if I just was what I was. I knew I didn't look all the way boy or girl most of the time and going around like a boy was just to keep me out of trouble. I looked down my chest, hunched over a little but smiled, "Maybe it's like you said before. Maybe it's the both that makes it—sexy."

Something like recognition came over his face just then, but I didn't know if he really followed, or even if I knew what I was saying. I didn't know if I really understood it myself and wasn't even sure I was telling the truth. It was enough that we said it out loud. It was enough to make me grin with delight that I could talk about Jean Bailey at all.

"It don't make it safe though," he said in a low voice.

I stiffened and looked up at the stars again.

Finally, after a good long silence, he confessed that he was in love with Eugene, the waiter. "He's not a sissy boy, like Marcel said, but he's black and broke, not my usual fare, with or without Marcel." Julian's voice was full of defeat even if he was trying to cover it with his flick of the wrist, flit of the hand. Before I could reply, Julian put his hand on my arm and glanced over at me with a serious face. "My people are a big drop black, dear. You should know that, I suppose. It could get you in a whole heap of trouble."

I leaned back in the seat trying to relax my stiffness, act like I wasn't rattled at all, and I wasn't—not like my folks would have been at the mere mention of a drop or would be if they knew I was there, that I was with someone like Julian, that I was following Jean Bailey.

My father once took a switch to me over a *mulatto* as he called her. She was a little girl I'd seen at the farmers' market one Saturday. I was completely entranced by her, her light eyes and only slightly tanned skin, her patchwork dress, and we ran through the stalls holding hands, giggling and making a ruckus while our mothers shopped. My mother was waiting for me at the end of one of the rows, and we almost ran right into her, out of breath and still giggling.

"Frances, simmer down and let's go." Her face was flushed and I could tell she was mad by the way she scrunched her eyebrows. I just thought she was mad that I was running around instead of standing right beside her, quiet, well behaved and prissy like a little lady. She grabbed my arm, digging her nails in and pulled me with her. "I'll pinch a plug out of you, girl," she said with clenched teeth. I knew it was more than that then and didn't even have the chance to turn around to tell the girl good-bye.

"She was running with niggers!" My mother immediately told my father when we got home. "I was so ashamed I didn't finish my shopping."

"But Mama, she wasn't black. She looked like me." I pointed at my arm, my own skin though I knew she had not been as pale as me.

My mother looked at me like I didn't have good sense.

My father stared down at me. "Frankie, don't you talk back to your mama! That girl's a mulatto, a half-breed. Her daddy is full blood. One drop of nigger is all nigger to me, and they try to play like they ain't. Charlatans! Folks intermingling. It's against God. Worse than a regular old nigger." My father grabbed my arm and pulled me out the door. Outside, I watched him break a tiny limb off one of the little trees up next to the house. He stripped it of its leaves with one hand and whacked me with it right across the back of my thighs. The sharp pain shot through me and I jumped, screaming, saying that the girl was not dark, that I didn't know. This only made him madder and he swiped me again, yelling, "I ever catch you disrespecting us again, you'll be sorry. No daughter of mine's gonna run around with trash like that." He didn't finish until I had blistering welts up and down the backs of my legs.

I shuddered in my seat, feeling again the sting on the back of my legs as Julian shot down the road. Of course, over the years my parents came to have to deal more and more with black folks just as my aunt and uncle had, and though they held their tongue for the most part, I knew the sentiment was still there. I knew that what I was doing was all but a death sentence. Finally, a good bit down the road, I switched my hand on top of Julian's and leaned in to say, "Well, I suppose I should let you know that my people are a big drop backwoods Texas hick."

He smiled big as night without a lick of fear and drove on, "Well, that's mighty big of you to admit, Frankie." At that, we both laughed again.

That night, on the dark road, Julian and I made like we'd been friends all our lives. There's something about traveling a gravel road on a midsummer night that makes ya giddy and loose tongued. By the time we crossed the state line, I could no longer imagine chasing Jean Bailey with anyone else and certainly not alone.

We made it as far as the top of Mississippi to a little tourist's rest area before we had to stop for the night. We were dead tired. Julian dug out a piece of black oilcloth and strung it up on one side of the car for a makeshift tent. It was our fort. We felt lucky and happy as clams to find the digs we did. I got out a can of food I'd taken from my uncle's shop and pried it open with my knife. We smiled over our meager meal of beans. We went to sleep full and with a feeling of victory on our skin.

* * *

In the middle of the night, thunder boomed above us and we sat up with a start. The bottom dropped out of the sky just seconds after, and we were already soaked from the pounding rain before we crawled out from under our fort. The top layer of dirt had already soaked up the rain and was so muddy I almost lost a boot as I scrambled to help Julian wad up the fort and pack it into the car. We both jumped in and rolled up the windows. I pulled out my shirt for us to dry off with though the rain was leaking in several spots and dripping on us. We tried to sleep out the night there, but mainly we just rested our eyes until daybreak and a short break in the rain. When the sky brightened, Julian cranked the car and we drove on. Luckily, the car was on harder surface and wasn't stuck, that is, not until some ways down the road.

Somewhere just outside of Holly Springs, we got bogged down where the gravel had run thin. We went slower and slower until we were finally stuck. I got in the driver's seat and Julian pushed from the back. Then we switched. By the time we got out of the rut we were in, one of the tires was punctured. Julian sank the tube in a puddle to find the hole and patched it quickly, but we didn't make it far on the gas we had after all that revving to get it out of the mud.

We walked a good long ways that day into and through Holly Springs proper, dodging stares by taking back roads until we heard a train whistle. We ran in the direction of the train and eventually found the tracks, though the train was long gone. We walked along the tracks for the rest of the day until we came upon a freight depot at sundown. It wasn't built for passengers and had only loading docks and dumping stations, great big contraptions that dumped baled cotton into the open boxcars. The rest of the cars would be filled up at the loading docks through the side.

Across the road was a general store, busy with people coming in and out, the bell on the door ringing constantly. We found a spot up next to the docks out of sight and watched through the supporting planks while we waited on the next train. The smell of cooking meat was in the air and our stomachs growled. We hadn't eaten since the night before, but we didn't have any money and only had one can of beans left. I dug it out of my satchel and we slurped it down just as fast as I opened it up. It didn't stay with us long and later that night when we could hear nothing but crickets and were sure everyone was sound asleep, we snuck across the road.

Sure enough there was a pot of meat boiling just around the back of the store. I snapped off my knife and fished out some meat, handed some to Julian and then grabbed some for myself. It was beef, cooked almost long enough to fall right off the bone, and we smacked on it hard to overcome the heat, but managed to get down enough to fill our stomachs before we heard another train whistle approaching. It didn't sound like it was slowing down so we took off across the road. When the train reached us, we ran with it, scanning for an open and empty car. The ground was rough with gravel and dust flew up into my face, stinging my eyes. We kept running, harder now to keep up with the train. I heard yelling behind us from a car.

Two or three kids just younger than me were hanging out of the car, motioning for our attention and pointing across the road. I heard a shotgun go off. We all flinched by reflex, but kept running. When it was quiet again, I swung my head around to see where the shot came from. On the front porch of the general store an old black man in coveralls stood aiming a shotgun right at us. The kids caught up and were right next to us, grabbing our arms and pulling us into the car before I knew what happened. He shot again as we climbed up. Eventually, as we met a curve in the tracks, he gave up and went inside and I sank down the inside of the boxcar out of breath.

"Woo hoo!" I shouted throwing up my fists in the darkness of the car. The lights from the town were slowly fading, but I could make out the kids who'd saved us. There were three, two boys and a girl, one about my height, one shorter and one little kid.

"Holy smokes!" One kid covered in dirt and mud just about head to toe hit Julian on the arm, excited.

"Shut up, Duck, we could have been shot deader than hell," a scowl-faced older boy said and spat out the open door of the car.

"I'm Julian." Julian stuck out his hand to the dirty kid.

"Name's Duck," the kid said, bowing up and trying to look taller.

Julian just laughed. I'd never heard of the name Duck and wondered how he'd gotten the nickname, but when Julian didn't ask, I didn't either.

"What's your name?" the older boy asked.

"Frankie. Nice to meet you."

"You don't look like no Frankie," Duck said frowning up at me.

"Well, you don't look like a Duck, either," I said and laughed.

"It's better than Frankie. Ain't that short for Frances?"

"Shut up, Duck." The oldest kid who had been working to close the door of the car sauntered over. "Duck's real name is Eugene, and he's always hated it. He came up with Duck himself when we hit the road. That's William, Willy for short, and I'm Edna Mae. I'm the oldest."

William scowled in the corner, creeping back into the shadows, but Duck came and stuck himself up in my face. "Ya'll lucky we let you on! Almost got yourself killed. Don't think you gonna stay and eat all our grub though!"

"Knock it off, Duck!"

"I guess you're right. Thank you," I answered.

"Don't mind him. He's just a little stingy."

Julian stiffened beside me. "We appreciate ya'lls help and all, but we'll just be on for a little while." He grabbed my arm and backed me into the shadows on the other side of the car.

Edna Mae shrugged and stepped back toward William and slunk down the side of the car to sit down. Duck was still in the middle of the car looking back and forth. She nodded to him and he followed.

* * *

The next morning a flash of sunlight through the slit of the car door woke me up. Everyone but Edna Mae was still asleep. She stood in the early morning light speckling the car through cracks and holes staring out the door. She was short and lean, tiny really, and her features were grubby. There was a clear line of dirt between her exposed skin and what was covered. I pushed myself off the wooden floor of the car and stumbled over to her, grabbing the side to steady myself in the moving car.

"Good morning. Any idea where we are?"

"The middle of nowhere Mississippi," she said pushing the door open wider and sat down, dangling her legs out the open door.

"How far until Birmingham?"

"Bama? Probably about a day. What's in Birmingham's got you itching to see?"

"I know there's a different train line I gotta get on there. I'm trying to get to Georgia actually, meeting up with Jean Bailey," I told her. When she didn't respond or react at all, I added, "She's my, I mean, she's a singer, vaudeville. She invited me out on the road with her."

"Well, this train don't go directly into Birmingham, but it'll take you straight up across Bama and on into Georgia. Where you going in Georgia? It's a mighty big state."

"I figured I'd find a flyer the closer I got that would tell me just exactly where."

"What? You don't know where Jean Bailey is?" Julian's voice was groggy, and he rubbed his eyes as he sat up.

"I never said I did, Julian, I'm sorry." I was picking up Edna Mae's twang.

"Damn." He shook his head and struggled to his feet. He stood over Edna Mae and leaned against the door of the car, soaking up the sun on his face, leaning out a little to let the wind blow against his cheeks. The day was brighter now, and the inside of the car was getting hot. Sweat gathered under my arms and streamed down my sides. I suddenly understood why Edna Mae had her legs dangling over the side. Her shoes were off and her trousers rolled up. I sat down beside her and untied my boots and rolled up my trousers too. When the wind hit my toes, I felt ten degrees cooler.

When we reached Alabama, we decided to stay on the train with Edna Mae and the boys. They had a stockpile of canned goods they were willing to share, and Duck was more than willing to sneak off the train when we were stopped and scour the depots for vaudeville flyers. He only ran across a couple at most of the depots as they were just freight depots, and none of them said anything about Jean Bailey. By the time we were a good ways into Georgia, just past Atlanta, we finally stopped at a depot that had passenger trains too.

It was a busy depot and Edna Mae scooted Duck out of the car with instructions to panhandle while he was looking for flyers. About an hour later, he came running back with a whole handful of flyers but only a few pennies just as the train was gearing up to leave again. As we swooped him up into the car, and I saw his gaunt face fallen with disappointment, I thought about the little boy with the big hat begging for change that I'd held out on in St. Louis and felt bad, as if it were catching up with me now.

We ate our meager supper of canned meat just before the sun was going down, and in the fading light Julian and I scanned the flyers while Willy watched Duck hand Edna Mae his pennies one at a time like they were pieces of gold. She packed each one into a sock with the rest of their loot. Finally, Julian found a flyer with Jean Bailey on it and shouted so loud we all jumped.

"Where? Where is she?" I scooted over to Julian and looked at the flyer with him.

"Says she's playing Decatur," he said and looked up at Edna Mae.

"When?" I asked.

"Says 'all weekend long' is all, no dates."

I grabbed it from him and scanned it front and back. I saw a stamp on the back dated July 10. I had no idea what day it was. Edna Mae shrugged and Julian said he had no idea either.

"It's already past," Duck finally said, looking up from his now empty can.

"Shut up, Duck. You don't know," Willy yelled across the car.

"Do so!" Duck yelled and got up to poke at Willy. Willy slapped him back, and they were wrestling before I knew what was happening. Edna Mae didn't make a move to stop them. Julian and I scooted away so as not to get hit in a tumble.

When they finally stopped, Edna Mae asked Duck if he knew what day it was. "It's the thirteenth, Friday, saw it on a sign at the depot," he said out of breath, but sure as sin.

"OOOOH!" Willy raised his eyebrows at us. "Friday the thirteenth! That's unlucky."

"Maybe it will be lucky for me," I said, trying to shake the goose bumps he'd given me.

"Oh hell, don't listen to that gypsy stuff," Edna said as she waved Willy off. "It sounds like she's playing tonight, and it's just up the road there from Atlanta. We won't stop for another two hours. You two are going to have to jump out and double back."

Julian shoved the flyer in his pocket and stood up and went to look out of the car. "That's a hell of a jump while the car is still moving." I stood up, looping my satchel over my head and across my chest and went over to the door with Julian, remembering our first attempt at hoboing a train.

"Look out over there, silly. That's really how fast we are moving. It just looks faster when you look straight down." I knew it was a lie and wouldn't convince him, or me, but before he could argue, Duck and Willy caught us from behind and pushed us out. We didn't have time to stiffen up so the fall didn't hurt nearly as bad as the first time, my satchel breaking my fall a bit, but I landed on my foot all wrong and twisted my ankle. Edna Mae yelled out an apology and then ducked back into the car without tossing out Julian's good clothes.

I hobbled up beside Julian. We walked three miles until we were back at the train depot only to find that Decatur was the other way down the tracks, that we could have stayed on the train just a little longer and landed right smack in town.

We walked the three miles back in the other direction following the track, taking big steps to stay on the railroad ties so I wouldn't twist my ankle again. Defeated and worn out, my ankle and foot throbbing, we had to find a place to hunker down before night. We headed out across a field. When we finally reached a road, Julian spotted what looked like an abandoned shed, and we made it in time to duck inside at twilight. It was pitch black, and I snubbed the toe on my lame foot something awful just stepping in the door. The shed was filled with junk. Exhausted and hurting, we curled up on whatever empty spot of ground we could find and slept in shifts. I didn't get much sleep anyway with my toe and ankle feeling sore enough to be broken.

* * *

When the light finally peeked through the cracks at the door, I felt stiff all over and a little delirious from the lack of sleep. The pain in my ankle was so bad I was almost crying.

Julian was sound asleep beside me on the dirt ground. I shook him awake. "What happened?" he asked, rubbing his eyes.

"We have to hitch or something. I don't think I can walk far on this foot." I rubbed my leg just above my ankle, trying to relieve some of the pressure. It didn't help.

A look of horror came over his sleepy face. "How we going to do that, Frankie? You're a mess, your suit ripped up one side and dirt head to toe, and well, I'm a—"

I put my face in my hands, whimpering and trying to hide my tears. I was exhausted, defeated, and wished someone would come pick me up and take me home. But I didn't even know where that was anymore. I'd given that up the minute I made the choice to follow Jean Bailey. I cried harder.

"Oh, sugar dumpling," Julian said as he sat up next to me and put his arm around me. I fell against him, crying harder still, and he held me there trying to soothe me.

"It's too hard! What was I thinking? Out here chasing after some woman who probably doesn't even remember my name!"

Julian lifted my chin and looked me dead in the eyes, the most serious I'd ever seen him. "Don't hurt to try, Frankie. And besides, who gives a hoot if she does or not? She'll take one look into those gorgeous green eyes and be unable to look anywhere else, even at the mess your clothes are in. And if she doesn't, there are others who will." He smiled, and though I tried to stubbornly fight it down, I smiled back at him. "You gotta get mad at the craziness of it all, Frankie! And that damn foot. Don't let it beat you down. Get mad and get up!"

Julian took off my boot, gently, and then dug around in my bag. He found my old dress and without even asking ripped off a strip from the bottom. He wrapped it around my ankle and up under my foot, tucking it in at the top as tight as he could manage and helped me to my feet. It still hurt, but it did feel a little better all tied up like that.

"Speak easy," he said as he held me there, helping me steady myself, "and love often. That's all there is."

Julian dusted off his pants and walked out. I wiped my face and limped out like a cripple, and we scooted down the road in the pink of sunrise. I took in a deep breath of the heavy air and hobbled on, cursing the pain through my teeth.

We were still miles from town, farmland stretching out on either side, farmland with almost no farmhouses, just miles and miles of green stalks in rows speckled white with cotton bolls beginning to pop. As the sun rose, the air thickened and seemed to crowd around us. My once crisp black suit wilted into me, and I was sweating just a few minutes down the dry dirt road. Julian huffed ahead, stopping every so often when he saw a shade tree to wait on me under, only to start again before I would quite reach him.

"Frankie, I don't know what you got me into, girl, but I sho' do want out of this damn sun." He fanned himself, squinting up at the sky, and then he stopped, looking up and down the road. I heard it too, the clomping of hoofs and roll of tires on dirt. Julian ran back to me and grabbed my arm, trying to pull me into the ditch or the field to hide.

"Wait! Let's see if we can get a ride, Julian." Julian refused to stay with me on the road and jumped into the ditch hiding as best he could in the weeds. His tan trousers and light shirt helped him blend, but I was in black. I knew I couldn't hide anyway.

When I could make out the face of the driver, I waved my arms big. It was an old man driving two horses to pull a great big wagon full of what looked like straw. When he got closer, I saw several field hands in the wagon. The driver pulled the reins and stopped right up next to me. His face was creased with deep lines under his hat, and he squinted to see me.

"What can I do ya fer, young man?"

"Just trying to get to Decatur, sir, on a lame foot." I pointed to my now scuffed up boot that I could barely stand on.

"I can get you a little down the road where I let these workers off. Hop in," he said and nodded to the back.

I yelled a quick thanks, ran around to the back, and hopped on. No one in the back uttered a word. After looking me over once or twice, they turned their blank faces and stared out into the field. When we were moving, I saw Julian's face poke up over the weeds. I glanced over my shoulder to make sure no one was looking and waved him on. He got up and ran, plopping on the back with me just as we picked up a little speed. One of the workers grinned at me when I snuck a peek over my shoulder again, but still didn't utter a peep. Julian and I were quiet too the whole of the ride, what ended up being some five or so miles down the road. We sat on the end, our feet dangling, and my toe and ankle throbbed harder and harder. I scooted over to the side and plopped my one foot up on the wagon to relieve a little pressure. When we slowed down, Julian hopped off and ducked into the ditch again. I waited until we rolled to a stop and scooted off hobbling to the front to thank the driver.

"Decatur's up over that ridge there," he said and waved his workers out into the field yelling orders I couldn't make out. He followed them out, lining them up one or two at each row in the field and they bent down to work, pulling weeds and checking the bolls. I walked up the hill and a few minutes later Julian was beside me.

"Why you so chicken of that man? What's he gonna do?"

"Put me to work, I 'spose. What else they do to niggers like me around here?"

He had a point so I just trudged on. My toe and ankle were better after the ride but still throbbing. I wanted to take my boot off, but I knew that would only make it worse, and I might not get it back on. I tried to focus on Jean Bailey, see her face in my mind again, hear her voice. I hummed a little. When I couldn't catch a tune, Julian frowned down at me and shook his head.

"We need a plan for when we get to town," he said. We were just reaching the top of the hill and could see the town begin to spread out before us. We were still a mile or so out. I stopped, breathing heavy as I leaned over and stretched my lame foot out in front of me. "I'll be your—your help," he said with a stutter and choke like he was swallowing glass.

I shrugged. "We just need to find Jean Bailey," I said and straightened up again.

We started down the hill toward town and every step sent a sharp pain through my foot and up my leg. Julian held out his arm to help me along. The sun grew higher and beat down on us, sweat pouring down my face and stinging my eyes, and I wished for home again. I wanted my mother's cool hand on my forehead, my soft bed and clean clothes. And I wanted that damn boot off.

We were a pitiful sight by the time we reached the edge of town, and reluctantly, Julian dragged me through it, stopping at the first place of business he could find. There was a colored entrance to the side of the building and Julian went in. Minutes later a short, stout white woman came out the front, drying her hands on her apron. It was a diner of sorts and she ushered me in, sitting me alone at a table. There was a group of old men at the bar by the kitchen sipping coffee and a lady with three children making a ruckus behind me at another table. Otherwise, the place was empty.

"Prop that foot up, young man," she said and stood over me as if waiting for me to order.

"I'm sorry, but I ain't got a cent to my name," I said and tried to smile.

"Don't you worry. Your man's gonna work it off. We don't 'low folks to starve around these parts," she said, though I knew my grubby, hobbled appearance didn't exactly make her feel at ease as she backed away from the table ever so slightly. "What can I get you?" I didn't see Julian anywhere, and the smell of fried eggs hit my nose, making me sick at my stomach.

"Just a cool drink is fine right now, ma'am."

She huffed off and then I spotted Julian. He was in the kitchen, shoveling breakfast into his mouth as fast as he could, cowering as the woman brushed past him as if he had something she could catch. I felt limp, my eyes welling with tears. I wiped at them and put my head on my arm on the table.

After a few minutes, she was back. "Here, you'll feel better after this." The woman shoved a plate full of eggs, grits, and biscuits against my arm and set a glass of water in front of it.

I grabbed the water and swallowed as fast as it hit my mouth. She picked it up and filled it again. When she was gone, I forced the food down, fork by fork. She was right. I did feel better. By the time I finished, the place had cleared out.

"You and your man can stay out back in quarters. Can't let you in the rooms upstairs," she said with a half snarl. "I'll meet you out there to see about that foot."

I hobbled out the door and around to the side where Julian met me and helped me into what looked like another shed. It was cool in there in the shade and on the settled, dirt floor. I sat down on a mound of tow sacks, propping my foot up on another. Julian unlaced my boot without a word.

"All right, this'll hurt," he said and yanked the boot off. I hollered and the woman flew open the door.

"Hush up, now! You gonna get the law out here." She had her hands full with bandages and a bottle of something clear.

Julian peeled my sock off and his makeshift bandage, waving at the stench. My big toe was bloody and half my toenail came off with the sock. My ankle looked like it swallowed an egg and the swelling had spread to the top of my foot, making my toes look like little nubs. I cringed just looking at it, never mind the pains shooting up my leg.

"We gotta get this thing under control before it takes off your whole leg!" The woman pushed in front of Julian and poured something onto a bandage. She dabbed it around my toe, cleaning it off. Then she held the bandage under it and poured the liquid over my toe. I yelped, biting my lip when she shot me a look. Finally, she wrapped me up and left it alone, instructing me to stay put, just like that for a day or more. When she was gone, I pulled off my jacket and leaned back.

"I guess that's that," Julian said and sat on another pile of sacks. These were to be our beds, I supposed.

"What? We can't stop here." I made like to get up but just didn't have it in me.

"Well, we're here until this foot doesn't look like you belong in the freak show!" Julian laughed at his own joke and then got up again. He said he'd work as much as he could in the diner, enough for a few days food and pocket change. "Don't worry, girl. I'll keep my ears open about Bailey."

I sank back down and fell asleep. Julian went in and out, doing whatever chores Miss Sal, our salvation, would give him. For two days, I woke only to eat and drink. Finally, on the third day, I joined him in the chores, mostly washing dishes as I didn't have to walk too much and could sit in between the lunch and dinner rush. Julian would smile at me as he came in and out of the kitchen hauling heavy bags of corn meal and flour, tubs of baking grease, and big slabs of meat from the smokehouse.

Miss Sal paid us every night, I expect to give us permission to move on as soon as we could, but I still wasn't up for a whole heap of walking and we still hadn't found anything out about Jean Bailey's whereabouts.

The fifth night, we came in from the diner and Julian was all worn out and pitiful. He wiped his hands on his apron and studied his nails, picking at them.

I sat down on my sacks and took off my boots, still smarting at the swollen ankle. "What's the matter, Julian?"

"I miss Jewel—I mean, I miss being—being pretty," he said.

I propped my foot up on the pile of sacks and leaned back. "I'm sorry you lost your dress, Jewel. Why don't we just make a new one?"

He looked at me like I was crazy.

"If we did some extra work for Miss Sal and got material and sewing supplies, I could make it."

"You could?"

I nodded.

Julian smiled and clapped his hands together like a thrilled child. "I'd dance with you if you could!" He jumped up and made like he was dancing across the room.

I laughed so hard I cried, not because he wasn't a good dancer, but at the silliness of it all, me all bum-legged lying there like a rag doll and him all grimy from work making like he was at a grand ball.

But we didn't have time to make the dress. A few days later Julian heard that Jean Bailey had been in the vaudeville show but had left it for a string of juke joints when the townspeople raised a ruckus about the bawdy show. She'd stirred up enough frenzy to warrant a revival being held by the local Baptists, both black and white, and Julian made a few rounds at the tent shows to find out where she'd gone. Turned out she was at a joint just south of town so when Miss Sal came back to our quarters to pay us I asked her for directions.

"You ain't gonna be welcome out there," she said and shook her head at me. "It's white folks what run it or own it, but white folks don't go there." But she gave me directions all the same.

She even arranged for her brother, Mr. Davis, to give me a ride. "He'd be glad to take ya as far as he can in the general direction," she said with a smile, "but he'll be on horseback."

"Well, that's fine," I said, and realized that meant that there would only be room for me. "But does he have two horses? What about Julian?"

Miss Sal just shrugged and walked out. Julian didn't look up. He sat picking through the white satin and some scraps he'd managed from a store downtown. He had even gathered a pile of sequins, mismatched, but glittering like a lap full of stars. He held each up one at a time and placed some across his arms and legs, pairing them and then rearranging them. They hung from him like tiny wings.

"You look like a displaced fairy or angel, Julian," I said with a snort.

He didn't look up, just kept picking up swatches and laying them out in rows in front of him. "Frankie, I believe I might stick around here while you go find Bailey," he said.

I was surprised, but didn't want to push him. I figured I'd dragged him through enough already and I didn't know exactly what I was getting into. Still, I was a little afraid to go alone.

"Why not, Jewel? You know I could use an escort, and we can figure out something, take turns riding or just get directions instead."

"Aw, you don't need me. Besides, place like that they might string me up, accuse me of being a white nigger or something."

I just nodded. I suspected he had gotten comfortable and wanted to rest up there for a while longer.

"You best be back here to make my dress first thing!"

I agreed, looking up from my own suit jacket in my lap as I stitched the side back up quickly. "You sure you won't come along?"

"Naw, you go on. I got some stuff to do for Miss Sal. You know, I like working. It makes me feel, well, I don't know what, but I hadn't felt it in a while." He laughed, smoothing down the swatches.

The next night, Mr. Davis picked me up after Miss Sal had paid us and gone to bed. Julian was rubbing his eyes in tiredness and reclining on his stack. Mr. Davis was a thin man, unshaven but trimmed, and had on a cowboy hat with boots and tight fitting denim, looking much like the boys I'd gone to school with back in Texas. He introduced himself and pulled me up on the horse, but after that he didn't say a word, and I was so nervous, I couldn't think of a way to start a conversation.

I climbed off the horse on a lonely dirt road in the dark, canopied with drooping oaks. As Mr. Davis turned and tipped his hat to me, I felt like I was walking to my doom, and my nerves had me shaking. This feeling, this particular moment would stay with me for a long time though. Whenever I was alone, I would put myself back on that dirt road as I turned in to the darkened night to walk under all those heavy trees, and I would remember my steps, my very breath in that instant, as if it offered some sort of comfort, some safety, as if it were the last thing I knew for sure.

CHAPTER TWELVE

This place was secret. The road to it was dark and musty. I could feel the bugs flying around me as I walked. Julian was back in town, washing dishes for our room and bit of food, still trying for pocket change. I figured he didn't really believe that Jean Bailey was out here anyway. Through the trees I could hear a rumbling noise, a clamor, and then a stop. I had to keep going. This was the closest I'd been since I left Chicago.

The dirt road was empty, though the dirt smelled like it had been moved, stirred, and there were tracks from recent travel. I walked downhill. My knees ached with each step; my toe and ankle, that I'd thought were mostly healed, throbbed again in my boot. The earth was built up on either side of me, taller and taller, and the roots of the trees showed where the road had been cut out. I felt like I was going through or into something like a tunnel. My jaw was tight, but my insides felt loose, like they were floating around, uncontrollable.

Georgia at night was just as hot as Georgia by day. It seemed to get heavier, the heat, the further into the South I went and the further down the road I walked. It fell on me, and I drooped like the trees heavy with Spanish moss. I'd been walking fast, and I could smell myself when my shirt flapped. I hadn't had a proper bath since leaving Mr. Hammond's, and until that moment, I didn't think too much about it. Even with the mending, I was still disheveled, and I felt rugged and masculine. I was musky and could feel something like pride, like the heat of a fight rumble up inside me. I straightened up and lengthened my stride. I was long and lean, and I was as much of a bulldagger as I could be at that moment, more so than the women at the flat in Chicago, I thought. I knew I'd need every inch of my confidence. I'd need every sip of my pride and false courage.

About midway down the dirt road, I stopped to catch my breath. It wasn't like I was making all that much racket as I walked, but it was the first time I could hear anything but my own footsteps or a stray critter in the woods on either side of the road. I heard a piano, horns, and then faintly over it all, I could hear a woman's voice, singing low and sweet and then loud and strong. I knew that voice, and it sent a shock up my spine just like the first time I heard it. It was clear and real, not like a record, but just behind doors, doors I would split nails to get through if I had to. I sped up and came upon a clearing off to the right where the hill fell away.

The juke joint was surrounded by shadowed cars and scattered horses. The building itself was kudzu covered, almost couldn't be seen for the green that seemed to take it over. I imagined then that it was magical, like some kind of fairyland. I stopped outside only long enough to listen again to that voice finish out a song. Though I couldn't make out the words, I knew it was bawdy, lewd in its gait and pomp, the horns tromping out the notes in long strides and then short quick thrusts. It was a striptease, revealing layer under layer of titillation. By the time I reached the door, the song had stopped and there was a ruckus and applause from the crowd. Though seeming a smaller crowd than the one in Chicago, it sounded rambunctious, vocal, not at all stunned or inhibited.

The door was wooden and rotting and had a crack where it met the building. I tried to peek through, but there were bodies crowded up against the door that I couldn't see around. The door had a long handle. I struggled with it, tugging lightly at first then in quick jerks. I inched it open a little at a time, and then it flew out and almost knocked me over. There was a slight step up onto the wooden floor, and when I stepped up, I could hear it creak beneath me. The jarring of the door had silenced the crowd, the all black crowd. They turned to stare at me, their eyes distant and distracted. They didn't look amused, and they didn't look curious. I had to catch my breath.

J Roll ran the place, or so I'd been told in town, and I spotted him immediately by the way the crowd let him through and by the way he was dressed, much fancier than the rest of the crowd. He had on a loose light yellow three-piece suit with a tied bow at the collar. His hat, wide and yellow with a black band, matched his suit perfectly. I could see the chain of his watch dangle from his coat to his pocket as he walked. His stare met my eyes after he'd made it through most of the crowd, and his face went expressionless. He seemed to bite at his lip and then stop himself. At first I thought it was nerves, but then he spat a wad of tobacco in a large spittoon at the foot of a table. Several stares followed him as he walked toward me—one from a tall woman with a large swooping hat, another from the round man that stood with her—but the rest made way for him and then went back to looking at the stage. I hadn't even seen the stage yet, hadn't even spotted Jean Bailey.

Several men dressed in suits similar but less flashy followed J Roll. He never introduced himself. I never got so much as a "Can I help you?" from him. He just stopped in from of me, staring down at me. Most everyone stood back a ways, as if I should be quarantined, even the men who'd followed him. I began to shake a bit, but I didn't drop my stubborn stance.

"I'm looking for Jean Bailey. I—I," I scrambled through my thoughts to come up with something that would get me in, "I—I work for Mr. Hammond, a talent manager in Memphis. I was told I could find her here, and from what I heard walking up, I'm in the right place."

He scoffed at me, "She's 'bout done. Go on and wait around the side door for her. I'll tell her you here. You don't want to be up in this place." His voice was gruff, but he stepped back, as if to taunt me with the stage. Jean Bailey stood there with her hand on her hip, a look of dismay, or fear, or maybe curiosity, spreading across her face. I smiled and ducked my head a little. When I looked up again and met her eyes, a hard and fast rush of heat ran right through me. She turned to her pianist, and he tapped out a song. As soon as she hit her first note, I was right back at Jimmy Small's again, feeling just like the first time I saw her, the first time I heard her and her voice made me weak-kneed. I couldn't move.

Jean Bailey swayed, looking over my head. She wasn't wearing a flashy dress like the first time I'd seen her on stage, not even her wig. She had on a man's tie and a jacket, just exactly like the flyer I'd found in her rent room. She wore a white collared shirt underneath the jacket, tight but unbuttoned enough at the top to hint at her full breasts. Her tie was tied but swinging loosely about her neck and chest. She was dressed like a man, but her hips swayed like a woman. Her hands flitted under her French cuffs with a delicacy that accented each note from her chest. I had imagined running my fingers along the lapel of her black suit jacket, cinching it at her waist, and now that it was in front of me, I could almost feel it under my fingers.

When the horns started up, she belted out a note again with them, a long moan of a note that outlasted the breath of the trumpeter and into the next. When the intro dropped down and then into rhythm, she started in on the verse:

I ain't no two-timer
I ain't no low down doer
I ain't no cutthroat boozer
But that don't stop the law
No, that don't stop 'em from comin' down on me.
Went out yesterday

Just like I did the night before
Came home this morning and found myself alone
They came and took it all
Even my old lady was gone.

Listening to her words, I could see the pool of blood at my feet at the buffet flat the morning I came looking for her. I hadn't much thought of the blood or the trouble back at Royce's since then, as I was sure it had little to do with Jean Bailey. Maybe I was wrong. I could feel the blues of the song unfetter me, as they seemed to free her, but there was a nagging, a sinking in the taking of that last verse. J Roll hovered to push me out the door. She went on with the song, and I swayed with her, both wanting her to never stop singing and waiting for her to stop, finish out the show so I could speak to her.

I still couldn't move. I didn't have any idea what I would say to her. All I wanted was right there in front of me, and it occurred to me that now that that was true, I didn't have a clue as to what I would do. Though I'd had miles and miles to think about this meeting, all I saw over and over in my mind was my face close to hers, my hand on her neck, her chest.

I got those lonesome, lonesome, blues.
Got them down and out, low down bottom blues.
I ain't got nobody, ain't got no one, no more,
But I got the blues, baby, I got the blues for sure.

I felt consumed by her voice. It filled me up and swallowed me whole. It was all around me, touching my back, my neck, my arms, my cheeks. The vibrations from the music and the rustling of the crowd in front of me were lost in her voice, too. When the song was over and the noise of the crowd took the place of her voice, I grew hot, felt faint and weak. J Roll turned to me and nodded to the door. Jean Bailey took her bow and left the stage. I turned and pushed my way back out the door into the muggy night.

Around the side of the joint there was a downed tree, and I climbed up on it to sit and fan myself with my hand. I watched the doors, the front one and the side one I'd finally spotted, for Jean Bailey, remembering her stern and swift approach to me at the flat in Chicago, and felt again the swimming of my stomach when she got close to me, daring me.

After a long time, groups of people trickled out. Some were dressed in fine clothes, others in field rags, but all seemed to know each other like they were letting out after Sunday meeting. Lighting their cigarettes and waving and hollering to each other, they jumped into cars, onto horses, and into buggies. I leaned back into the shadows. After the slew of them had driven off down the road, I dug a cigarette out of a tin that I'd wrangled from one of Miss Sal's patrons. Dust went into my lungs with the smoke. My back and foot ached, my body felt heavy with exhaustion.

I wondered if I'd drift off and then wake up there on that log at daybreak, alone and deserted. I wondered if Jean Bailey thought I'd left. The longer I waited, the more anxious I got. I slid to the ground gingerly, so as not to land on my hurt foot, and snuck around the side of the building to the other door. It was locked, but I could hear people talking inside, getting closer to the door. I slunk back into the darkness around the corner and heard the door open and close again with a bang. Someone came out and walked around the front, but I couldn't make them out in the dark. I followed, out of sight.

When I got around to the front, I saw someone in an old Model A, one that looked like it hadn't run in a while, wouldn't start for all the oil or cajoling or fixing in the world. Its seats were worn and its windows shattered. The person lit a cigarette and propped a foot up on the open door. I snuck up behind the car. When she tilted a jug up to her mouth, I saw that it was Jean Bailey, right there, just a few feet away. A rush of excitement went through me, and I stood up. I took a deep breath and walked toward her, proud as a peacock, and stood right smack in front of her, like this was all I needed to do and everything would be all right.

She was halfway in the front passenger seat. She looked up at me and started, those honey eyes dancing at me, teasing me.

Then she giggled, took another swig, and with a big wide grin spreading across her face, laughed hard.

I had made it. I'd found her. There she was, Jean Bailey, right in front of me. I wanted to sling my arms around her, let her take me, take me over. But she just grinned, and I froze. Jean Bailey's eyes didn't quite focus on me. She looked straight ahead through the windshield of the car into the darkness, to a spot where the bright moon shone down on a large live oak covered in stringy gray moss. She slung one side of a long purple scarf over her shoulder and missed, letting it fall right back in her lap. Her makeup was still perfectly placed and deliberate and heavily applied. Her red lips glistened each time she took another swig from the jug. Her head bobbled a little, and she mumbled. When she continued in a lower, scouring tone, I leaned in closer to her, sticking my hands in my pockets, afraid I would touch her by mistake. And when her voice got lower still, as if to whisper or perhaps because her voice was sore from the singing, I took my hands out of my pockets, placed one on the windowless door of the car, and squatted beside her. She handed me the jug, and I took a long, hard-to-swallow gulp. She slurred through her words, and I made out two names, Rosie and Tasha. I couldn't figure out what she was saying about them. Then she spouted a string of men's names: Joshua, Teddy, Leroy. I wondered if these were men, or if they were like the women at the flat, like me. I shook my head. I couldn't think about all of that right then. Right then, Jean Bailey was two feet away from me, swaying in and out of the seat of a car. She stopped, as if remembering where she was, and looked at me. She sat up straight, grabbed the jug from my hand, and wrinkled her brow.

"You gonna be my man, little bull?" She laughed and took another swig.

I nodded like an eager child. She caught my eye again, staring me down. "Hey! You that…you…well, I be damned. You cocky little bulldyke! You sure did!" She grinned, and there was a glint in her eye, of recognition, a hint of her dare, and for a second, I thought, respect. She lifted up the jug as if to toast me, swayed a bit, and then swayed right onto the ground, fast enough for me to miss stopping her, but slow enough for me to somehow end up underneath her. Her body all in one swoop would have been hard on me had I not felt so fine under the weight of it. I'd never had anyone on top of me, and though she wasn't facing me, she was on me, and I could feel her right in my lap but mostly against my torso and on my legs. She was bigger than me, taller and heavier. I wrapped my arms around her, and my hands held her there, grasping her solid flesh, and lucky, too, because she would have slid right down onto the ground all the way had I not been there to hold her up. I had a feeling of relief, a deeply relaxing feeling come over me, and then her body went limp. She'd passed clean out.

"Miss Bailey! Miss Bailey?" I tried to wake her, and my voice sounded small and muffled in that space under the live oaks, under her, the dense air holding us there. I was sweating.

"Hey!" I heard a voice behind me, but for the weight of her, I couldn't turn around. I heard footsteps, and then it was too late.

"Mister, what have you gone and done to the talent? Don't you know moonshine ain't the way to get 'em to work?" It sounded like some hick, but some highfalutin hick with an accent that reminded me of Jean Bailey's.

I craned my neck, still holding Jean Bailey up, her body getting heavier and heavier in my awkward sprawled out position. I couldn't budge her or me, but I got a glimpse of the man behind me, and, on a second take, a glimpse of the rifle in his hands.

"Name's Wesley, Babe Wesley. This here's my old man's property." He stopped, and I could hear him adjust the rifle. I shook, and Jean Bailey slid a little. I was too afraid to turn around and see if he was in fact pointing the gun at me.

"Folks round here call me Babe, or Baby Boy, however grown I get to be..." As he rambled on, I realized he was no more a man than I was. He was probably a good four or five years younger than me, not that that didn't mean he couldn't fire a gun.

"Well, Baby Boy, I didn't give her anything. Would you please get over here and help me get her up?" I managed.

"Why I s'pose, yes, sir. I ain't never seen a singer all sprawled out like this 'cept old Ethel down at the honkey tonk. My daddy owns that one too, but she got a hollow leg, and I ain't fooling, she really does. They say it's 'cause of the leg she can drink as much as she do without dying—and without getting caught." He laughed, tickled at his own story, and then his voice got stern. "Some folks been dying round here 'cause of that moonshine scare a few weeks back. Did ya hear about it?" He'd moved over in front where I could see him, his dark curly hair all matted and lying about his face like some kind of movie star in a hobo role. He was dirty for sure, but I was feeling dirtier by the minute in my position. I gave him half a smile, half a scowl. He held the rifle with both hands and pointed it up at the sky.

Baby Boy's gun was a hunting rifle like my father's. My father had never taken me out hunting, but I knew its sound well, the long hollow shot across a field and a thump of a deer falling. The last deer I'd seen him drag up, a full-grown doe, was still warm with life, the blood trickling out of her mouth, as he struggled to carry her across the field. He hung her up in the barn over a bucket for draining. It was a haunting sight but not as haunting as the sight of my own hands drenched in red as I helped my mother clean and dress the meat. I shivered, unable to take my eyes off the gun in Baby Boy's hands.

Finally, as he propped the rifle against the car, I struggled to reach my knife at my boot. He leaned in and grabbed Jean Bailey's arms as I pushed her up from underneath. We sat her back in the seat as best we could. Jean Bailey moved her head about as if she might wake up then let it droop to her chest again.

I stepped back, still looking at Jean Bailey, wondering how this all had happened in just a matter of minutes. "I'm Frankie, sent by Mr. Hammond—"

He took and shook my hand before I could finish. He was shorter than me, but stocky all around, not fat but strong and stout. His face was round and plump with two big dimples. He smiled.

"Why you here, Mr. Frank?"

"Frankie, call me Frankie."

"All right." He drew out his words the way I learned all Georgians did. It was different from the way we did in Texas and different still from Julian's accent.

"I'm here with Jean Bailey, managing the talent," I said, dismissively, as if we had more important things to discuss. And we did. "Now. What can we do with her?"

"I ain't never seen you before, though I seen Bailey, know her from Grady where I used to visit. She's raised down in Grady, though they hadn't let her sing down there in quite some time, just you beware. You ain't from round here, no parts, and you weren't here when she came in last night."

"No, I ain't. I came after, had to take care of some things first. But I'm responsible here—of—for her." I stuttered out my half-assed explanation and thought he bought it.

We both stood there looking down at Jean Bailey. My hand was on my hip, like a girl, and I let it slide down, hoping he wouldn't notice. He stood stiff-legged, then bent down and picked up his rifle again. He held the rifle by his side for a moment. He grinned, and then he cocked the rifle, pointing it directly at me. He was slow and steady, deliberate, not jumpy and cocky, and I got an odd sort of numbness about me, a calm as I stared past the gun and into his dimpled face, that curl flopping into his eyes, looking greasier the longer we stood there in the damp heat.

There is something about a gun. It narrows down the future. It will either be shot or it won't, and really everything in that moment comes down to it, this gun in Baby Boy's hands. Looking back, it was this moment that determined all the rest. I'd somehow felt like I had made it through what I needed to do to get to Jean Bailey. I'd passed the trials. But this moment was the beginning of it. I made it to her, but I hadn't made it with her. I loved her, I knew it, could feel it roam in me, determined like a bullet, but I knew right then, that wouldn't be enough.

My own breathing was loud in my ear. I didn't dare look down again at Jean Bailey, and he didn't look at her either. He kept the gun on me, as if he was waiting, as if he was hunting me, seeing what I would do next, seeing when to take his shot.

"I'm just doing my job," I said.

"Your job's following behind some nigger?"

I flinched, remembering the hillbillies who'd chased me off the train, calling me a nigger lover. To Baby Boy's eyes, a young white boy was with an older black woman, and it didn't matter that she was a singer, "the talent" as he'd called her. She was still a black woman. The way I see it, folks do whatever their beliefs support. I didn't know the language—how to play both sides—to the whites and get along with the blacks too. I was in no man's land, certainly no woman's land. My mouth felt dry, empty. My legs were shaking, and I tightened up my muscles to make them stop.

He let out a laugh then. Baby Boy's queer expression of curiosity and knowing hadn't changed, but he lowered the gun. "I had ya shaking in your boots!" As Jean Bailey stirred, he pointed the gun at her. "You can't ever be too careful with the niggers around here, sir. They get plumb out they mind all together with they wild ass music and God knows what all going on in there."

I couldn't move, was afraid to breathe almost, but I forced a weak smile, enough to give me some gall. "Yeah. You know how it is, though. Work's work, and I go where the money is. It's my job to keep up with her," I said and nodded over to Jean Bailey as if I was all put out. "I gotta make sure she brings in the money. But you see how hard it is to keep these highfalutin niggers in line." My words tumbled out of me, as I tried to look relaxed, tried to sound like I actually felt what I said.

"You's right there. That's why I'm here." He waved the gun on Jean Bailey, and I stopped breathing. "Just in case they start getting all crazy on me. I could shoot this one right now, just for being drunk on my property." He drew out the last two words and squinted his eye over the rifle, "Pow!" he said and made like he'd shot her. Then he backed away, laughing.

He uncocked the rifle and made like he'd put it away, but didn't. "And what's more, the white folks sees you out here, you'll get strung up right along with her."

I knew this was a direct threat. I laughed an uneasy laugh and shook my head down at Jean Bailey. Then I stupidly made like I was shooting at her too, saying "Pow, pow" to play along with him.

"Mr. Wesley, sir?"

Baby Boy cocked his gun again, and I jumped, turning around to see who was coming up. J Roll's yellow suit shone through the darkness as he came around the building. He had a wad of cash in his hand all fanned out.

"There you are! What the hell was the holdup?" Baby Boy lowered his gun, but J Roll still stopped about ten feet away, staring down at it.

Baby Boy finally leaned the rifle against the car and held out his hand for the money, and J Roll walked past me to hand it over.

Baby Boy immediately started counting it. "You know, we don't allow no mixing up in here, the coloreds and the white folks. We don't allow that, you know that." He didn't look up. I didn't know if he was talking to J Roll or me. "I suppose you met Mr. Frank here, J Roll. I don't want people to talk like we run some kind of—" He paused and put the money in his pocket and laughed. "Ah, I know, J, I guess you can't help it, couldn't tell him not to come in, now could you?"

"No, sir," J Roll said, fidgeting as he stood between Baby Boy and me.

"Help us get this singer out of here. Mr. Frank probably don't want to be having to deal with her all night. Don't she have somewhere's else to go?"

"Yes, sir. She's got people to get her there, too."

"I hope it ain't you, Mr. Frank, for your own sake."

We all stood there for a good minute or two without a word as if each were waiting out the other. I just wanted them both to leave. Finally, they turned to go, J Roll giving a halfhearted wave and thank-you to Baby Boy, and Baby Boy took my hand and shook it sharply, nodding his goodbye.

I didn't catch my breath again until I could no longer hear their tires speed down the dirt road. When I finally turned to Jean Bailey again, her head was cocked, and she was staring straight up at me, wide awake and looking as sober as I was, but stern and almost mad. I jumped, startled at her change.

Then she laughed. "I should have been a damned actress!" She laughed and slapped at her knee. "They need to find me a place in New York City! Or like I always said, I need to be on the big screen! Lordy, I got you!" She reached around and pulled herself to her feet. She stumbled a bit but caught herself. "Well, I did a little bit anyway. Maybe I needed to nod off a tad, but I tell you what, when that boy had that gun cocked at you, I could hear your knees shaking! Oh that's rich stuff! Thought you were a tough bull! Scared of a simpleminded boy! Have mercy!" Her words slurred as she made her way around me.

Embarrassed, I stammered, "He had a gun! Simple or not, it don't take much to fire one!"

"Well now, where's your gun? Knife? Don't tell me you going around like that without one."

My cheeks burned. I didn't even know how to fire a gun.

"Ah. Well. Sugar, you got guts. I'll give you that." She stopped and stared at me, her eyes lighter now, inviting. "Did you think that would just get you through? You ain't fooling me in that getup, but I guess I know what to look for," she said, eyeing my unbound breasts.

I crossed my arms over my chest.

"Now come on, kid. What the hell you want with me?" She moved closer and stared straight down at me, and her face went soft and supple as she waited. There was no amount of polite, no amount of good humor left. She was serious, as serious as the moonshine would allow.

"I—I followed you here."

"I understand that."

"I—I mean, you asked me to come."

Her face didn't change.

I had imagined this moment over and over, but there were no words in my fantasies. In my mind, I would be suave and full of strut, and she would remember that she'd invited me, dared me after her, and she would pull me to her and kiss me, dead on the lips, all romance and passion. Not at all like the kiss with Hazel in St. Louis or the kisses I'd had with boys growing up. Not like that. It would sweep both of us into what I saw as love, not so much a picture as a smile, a warmth, a thrill I felt deep in my gut, through my whole body, the way I felt when I remembered her voice.

She put one hand on her hip. "Well, honey, here I am. You the big, bad bulldagger now. AND you white. Now what?" Her accent grew thicker, and I had a hard time registering exactly what she said. "What you gonna do with me?"

"I tried to make it back in time, before you left Chicago, like you said, but you—you were gone—there was blood, and, and a big mess, and—"

She waved her hand at me and then motioned for me to follow her as she turned to go toward the building. "We gotta get on the road," she said and then stopped, turning around to me again. "But why, sugar? Why you wanna come with me anyway?"

"I had to get out of there, and I thought, I thought you could use me somehow. I just wanted—I just wanted to be with you. That's really as far as I got in my thinking." In that moment, she seemed so far away, farther than before I'd found her. I felt silly standing there in front of her saying those words. They seemed so little. She was so much more than that, so much more than me. I felt a pang, and my hands began to sweat, and I could already see myself walking back down that dirt road alone. I almost turned and left right then and there, but a panic spread through me, and my head felt like it would spin me dizzy.

"I don't know what it is exactly," I pushed on. "My family wants to lock me away or marry me off. But I don't want to be like every woman I've ever known. And you aren't. You aren't like any other woman I have ever laid eyes on. Not just because you're a singer, or even because you're a bulldagger. It's—it's—well I don't know what it is, except that I know I want to be with you. I'm in—"

Somewhere in the middle of that ramble, hot tears welled up in my eyes, and my voice became blubbery, and when I looked at her again, she was smiling. She didn't move a muscle toward me, but she was smiling. Laughing at me. I wiped at my face with my sleeve and coughed. "Yeah. Laugh at the dumb kid. But this is the last time you'll ever see me this way. I promise!" With that, my tears stopped, and I stood up straight in defiance.

"Now that's a damned lie, but I expect you'll try to prove it the rest of your life." She laughed again. "But you're pretty, and ornery, woo wee! I like that in a woman." She inched up closer to me, looking into me.

I reached my grubby hand up to the back of her powdered and glistening neck, pulled her down to me, nose to nose, and then laid a kiss on her. It was a swift, sloppy, surprised kiss. I let go and stepped back, proud, and big-eyed.

"Frankie—that's your name right?" I saw a glimpse of something like timidity and control and power all at the same time roll over her into one questioning face. "First off, you are taking this man thing a little too far. And you're white to boot. Bad mix. You ain't like that. I can see it. You gonna dress like that, fine, do a little better job next time. But you ain't a man. And don't act like your daddy or whoever the hell else you think is a man. Not for me, don't. It ain't cute. No one, man or not, is cute like that. One thing straight. This is my show. I run it. I ain't a toy, a dress up doll. And I ain't no slave. I ain't talking to you because I think you can get me some big-time deal with some white man gonna put me on a record. I got all that already. I got my gigs lined up myself with or without this circuit. I don't need that shit—" And she paused, as if thinking something over. "Listen, I ain't quite sure what you can do, but—"

I nodded. "I—I lied at the door. I'm no manager."

"Oh hell, I know you lied. Don't you know I knew who you were the minute I saw you up close?"

"You did? Well, but, I mean—" I froze, remembering she said my name and trying to remember what it sounded like. I wanted to ask questions, figure something out, but I had forgotten what, I was so stunned.

"Of course, I remember you, darlin'." She leaned in to me and I could feel her breath tickling my cheek, the tiny hairs framing my face, my ear. "I like you, Frankie. You're pretty—a smart little ballsy thing." She pulled back away from me and smiled again. Right then, I fell in love with her teeth, her misplaced white teeth, strong and wide and solid.

"Smart?" I said, feeling my face tighten into a sheepish grin, but I could feel myself turn on the charm, my eyes looking up into her.

Her eyes softened on me, and I could feel her look all the way into my stomach. "You made it all the way here without getting killed or hauled off back to your little life. I bet we can find a way to make you useful if you'd still like to come along with me, sweetheart. But it ain't gonna be as easy as all that."

There was a banging from inside the joint, like someone dropped something big, and it startled us both.

"We'll talk about this shit later. We gotta get the hell outta here right now—gotta be in Augusta by tomorrow night. Car's around back. Go get it started, and I'll be out the back in five minutes." She pointed to the back as she walked around to the front.

As she rounded the corner to the front door, I walked out of the moonlight and searched the darkness for a car. I found one. Dark. Shiny. Top-of-the-line. When I got in and smelled the newness of it, I realized just how well Jean Bailey was doing. I ran my hand along the leather seat, the polished wood trim inside the door, the chrome knobs and buttons. It was just as fancy as Mr. Hammond's and a world away from the one we stole. I had to admit to myself, it gave me a thrill, and then I remembered that Julian was waiting for me in town, waiting for me to make him a dress and take him with me. I had to go back there to do it though, and now that I'd found Jean Bailey, I didn't want to let her out of my sight. I fretted as I cranked the car and slid in behind the wheel and waited, the engine rattling in my ears.

CHAPTER THIRTEEN

Jean Bailey came out of the back door with two other women barreling out after her, bags in their hands. One of the women was crying and shaking, holding onto a tapestry bag. Her makeup was smeared, her fists clenched, her bony frame rigid and strained. Though it was dark, I could make out the tendons in her neck as she gnashed her teeth and spit her words out at Jean Bailey.

"Low-down, Bailey! You are low-down and dirty! You worse than a man! You worse." She spat on the ground and took off a string of pearls she had around her neck and hurled them at Jean Bailey. Jean Bailey picked them up, dusted them off, and stuck them in her pocket. She approached the woman to embrace her, but the other woman shoved her away.

"Don't you touch her!" This woman's voice was deeper, steady and older.

"Come on, ladies. Just get in the car. We'll get all this hashed out in the morning. I'm tired as hell. We gotta get on the road."

Jean Bailey turned to the car and to me. The two women stayed put.

"We ain't going!"

Jean Bailey didn't turn around. She opened the side door, threw the bags inside, and then stepped to the back to open the back door. She left it open and then walked around the building. The two women stood there watching her until she turned the corner. And then they looked at me in surprise, just noticing I was there, I supposed. I didn't move, didn't speak. They whispered to one another and got in the back seat.

Jean Bailey came back around the corner with a jug in her hand. She was walking fast, and she was wearing pants and a button-up shirt instead of what she'd sung in. She strutted with that jug. I glanced at her and then straight ahead at where the headlight beams lit up a speck of the dirt road we were about to follow. As Jean Bailey got in the front seat, I could feel the eyes of the two women on me, but they hadn't spoken to me and wouldn't look at me as I glanced back at them. My hands were sweating on the wheel. I could only guess that one or both of these women were more, much more than I was to Jean Bailey. I thought Tasha looked familiar, like the woman I'd seen with Jean Bailey at Ernestine Royce's in Chicago. I was immediately jealous, my insides swarming, and I gripped the wheel tighter.

"Is this what you're spending our cut on? You going to get us all locked up for good carrying that mess around, Bailey," the older woman said.

"Oh, Rosie, you know I won't let a thing happen to you and Tasha. Haven't I always protected you?"

"Phish!" Tasha's voice was a whimper, cracking as she spoke, "By cheatin' us?"

"Don't I take care of you? It takes money to do that."

"And what do you call all this, Jean? You get us hanged gallivanting around with this, this cracker," Rosie chimed in.

"This is Frankie, ladies. Frankie, Tasha and Rosie," was all the reply she gave and pointed me down the road.

I jerked the car into gear, my ankle smarting as I shifted. I hid my grimace and eased out onto the road. It was quiet for a long time as I drove back up the dirt road I'd walked down to get to the juke joint. When we were close to town, Jean Bailey leaned in to me, "You okay to drive for a while?"

"Yep," I answered before I even thought. Immediately feeling a cringe of guilt about Julian. "To—to Augusta?" I said.

"Just keep right on down the road we on, girl," she said and slid down in the seat, resting her head back and closing her eyes. "Don't worry, I'll drive when you get tired."

I bit my lip, I knew I should say something about Julian, should turn right off that road and go to Sal's, pick him up, but I was afraid it'd be too crowded, was afraid Jean Bailey would leave us both behind.

"That all right?" Jean Bailey blurted, startling me with her gruff tone.

"Yes, I'm fine to drive." It just popped out, and I sank in my guilt and tried to concentrate on the road.

"Well, then. Good," she said and gave me general directions out of town, her eyes still closed.

A ways down the road, I glanced back and saw that Tasha and Rosie were sound asleep. There seemed to be no moon about though I could still feel that it was full. I could see Jean Bailey's silhouette. Her jawline was perfectly angled into a rounded point below her lips. I felt overwhelmed at the thought of touching her. She was so grand, so lovely. I'd done it. I'd found Jean Bailey. A sharp thrill shot through me.

* * *

We made it all the way into another little town before she told me to stop. She had me pull up to a store with a wide front porch, half falling in on itself, with tiny windows at the front. I jerked the car to a stop and killed the engine. No one was around, no light on anywhere. Jean Bailey jumped out and knocked on the passenger door with her fist.

"All right, ladies. Wake up. This is your last chance to get out and get on your way—with your money. Or you can keep on going with me, like I said." She dug a wad of bills out of her pocket and fanned it out at them.

I could feel them shift behind me, startled. "Fuck it, Bailey. I'll ride. I need the sleep," Rosie said and slid back down on Tasha's shoulder.

Tasha sniffled. "Where would I go, Jean? I don't know anything else."

Jean Bailey let out a sigh. "Tasha, baby," she said as her voice softened, "you can go anywhere you want to, you and Rosie both. You both know you can pass. The world is yours!" Jean's voice was booming, and she spread her arms out wide as if she were on stage. I heard a dog barking in the distance, a few more farther away. She laughed then, a little quieter, and dropped her arms, waiting. "Just get out and go."

"But it's the middle of the night," Tasha said.

"Go on down to J's. He'll get you somewhere, set you up. You know that, sweetheart."

The pet name made me wince. I could feel another shift in the car, and in the moonlight coming out from behind the trees I saw Tasha's face close in the rearview mirror for the first time. She had small features, her small nose pointed and shiny in the light. Her hair was matted about her brow, moist and stuck there. Her eyes were swollen, red and glassy. I suddenly could imagine Jean Bailey's arms around her, pulling her close as she had done me, as she had done with the woman at the flat. I took a deep breath.

"Should I—" I turned around.

Rosie shot up and looked hard at me and then at Jean Bailey standing beside the open door. "Should you what? Who you talking to?" Her dark eyebrows came down like drapes over her lids. Her deep red lips, large and pursed, pushed out at me almost as if she were going to kiss me, but that was no kissing face—there seemed to be only hate in it. I held her gaze, focusing on her speckled, unblinking eyes, and the freckles on her cheeks. I had never seen a black woman with freckles before. She was bigger than Tasha, robust, round, but smaller and wirier than Jean Bailey. Rosie's hourglass figure and her movie star face made her spitfire gorgeous, which was why, I guessed, she was there, but that mean streak made every feature, every minute detail flare up, call attention to itself in a way that made them each seem like they belonged on someone else rather than together on one person.

"I know she a cracker, Jean," Rosie yelled from the back seat, "but who she think she is here? Shut her up, or I swear I will do it. I don't care if she is white!"

Jean Bailey opened the passenger side door and grabbed her by the collar of her dress. Pulling her halfway out of the car, she said in a low, serious voice, "You can come along or you get out now, but you gonna have to watch it. Frankie is going along with us, with me. That's how it is right now."

The violence of it all made me cringe, reminding me of my father's temper, his switch across the backs of my thighs, my uncle's slap across my face, but I could feel the corners of my mouth slide into a grin. I knew it wasn't much, but no one had ever defended me, to anyone.

"Just like that? Just like that? What happened? What did I do?" Tasha was sobbing now. "I'll fix it. You know I can."

Although I was jealous of Tasha, my heart broke at Tasha's words.

"Now look, you've upset the baby." Rosie slumped back in her seat and crossed her arms.

"My God. Would you look at the two of you? You'd think I just shot your dog. I am so tired of hearing you two bellyache. I am so tired of supporting us all. It's time I got me some support."

"As if you don't!" Rosie snapped.

I was not at all sure what she meant by support and had no idea if or how I could give it. I was broke.

"Oh hell. You still mad about Chicago? You know I didn't have jack to do with Ernie's shakedown. And look how I had to pay for that—lost two gigs over that shit. Don't I pay more to you two? More in money, clothes, jewelry, time?"

Tasha sobbed louder and Jean Bailey ran around the car and opened the door to put her arms around her. "I'm sorry, sugar.

You know this is just how I am," she said as Tasha clung to her neck. "It's time." Jean Bailey leaned in then, and in the rearview mirror I saw them kiss, a long, passionate, heated kiss and my stomach tightened, swarming up in my throat. I turned, staring out at the darkness.

Jean Bailey looked up over Tasha and shouted, "Rosie, in or out?"

"I said I'm in. I ain't leaving Tasha with you anyway, just for you to stomp her out and leave her in some shit town."

Jean Bailey slammed the door and opened mine. I sat there for a second and then moved my foot out the door. She motioned for me to get out, and I did. Suddenly, I wanted a cigarette so badly I could feel the smoke in my lungs. I fumbled for my tin, still looking at Jean Bailey sitting behind the wheel. Was it them or me? Was she going to just leave me there? In that moment, I wished I'd stayed back at the shed with Julian.

"Well, don't just stand there. Get in. I'm driving."

I ran around the car and got in the passenger side, relieved but heavy, and I missed Julian—the twang of guilt weighing on me even more now. Jean Bailey drove around to the back of the store, got out and fished out what looked like a long slender tube from the trunk. With the tube in hand she jimmied a lock on the shed. There was a beat-up old car inside. She went into the darkness of the shed and came back into the light with a can and proceeded to siphon the gas into the can. When she had enough, she poured it into our car and took the can, putting it in the back with the tube.

The smell of fresh gas filled the car as we drove away. From that moment on, it was to me the smell of a deafening and stiff silence, a paralyzing smell. It was also the smell of feeling life take you, a kind of flip in the stomach, your head forced back, eyes squinting in the wind.

We drove for hours and hours. I was wide awake, glancing at Jean Bailey any chance I got, the slight curve of her pudgy nose, her heavy, thick lashes swooping over soft, sultry eyes. Looking out into the night, I could see the cotton fields were almost ready for harvest as we sped by patches of white in the darkness.

Down the road a bit, not far, the girls in the back were snoring. I felt proud being in the front seat. I sat up straighter, smiling in the breeze through the half-opened windows.

"Reach down there and grab me that jug, Frankie."

I hesitated, surprised at the sound of her voice, so calm now, but weighted, expectant.

"Aren't you afraid—I mean, what if you get caught?" I remembered what Rosie had said about the liquor. I remembered the raid in Chicago.

She didn't answer, just took it from me, took a long swig and passed it back to me.

I gasped a gulp of gin and coughed as I corked it and slid it back into the floorboard. My head was already lighter. "What—what should I call you?" I asked.

"Call me baby. Call me sugar. Call me honey, baby doll, darlin'," And then she was singing, softly, her voice like syrup running over the words. "*But don't forget to come a callin' on me.*" She laughed, muffled so as to not wake the sleepers, but it was the first time I'd relaxed since I'd seen her in that car drunk. Hell, since I'd seen her at all, I thought. In a moment of bravery, my chest jumping, I slid my hand over hers in the seat. She smiled without teeth, raised an eyebrow over at me, and pulled her hand away, putting it back on the wheel. I could see creases at the corners of her eyes. I wondered then, just how old she really was. "Got a smoke?"

"Yeah. So I'll call you Jean?" I reached for my smokes, and I was embarrassed, but at the same time I felt suddenly cool, suddenly sexy in that moment. It was as if for that moment I wasn't focused on her, for that moment when I spoke her name, I felt myself, my own handsome appeal, and I wondered if she'd noticed. I lit up a cigarette and passed it to her, then lit my own.

"Sure, doll," she answered my question.

We smoked and then tossed the smoldering butts out the window after another swig off the jug. Somewhere on a dirt road some miles outside of Augusta, the sun was beginning to peek up over the horizon. There was a fog running over the low hills of the farmland and up over the bunches of trees between them, resting in the valleys by creeks and streams. I got the feeling we were floating away like a helium balloon but with lead weights in my gut keeping me close to the ground, hovering. I wondered if Julian was awake, if he realized I hadn't come back.

Jean Bailey cut off the headlights and shifted in her seat. Her eyes glistened in the rising sunlight, her hair, wigless, relaxed about her ears, and I could see all the little tiny hairs curling up individually out of the rest that was slicked down. Each single hair held a honey-colored hue that matched her eyes, though slicked back and together they were black, dark and solid.

I spread out a little, getting more comfortable in the seat and with a better view of Jean. She hummed, her chest rising and falling in deep breaths. Her shirt fell over her full breasts like a soft billowing sheet, and I had the urge to lay my head there and rest. I wanted to touch her. She mouthed the words to a song every now and again as she hummed, and my eyes felt heavy.

* * *

My head bounced on the seat, waking me when we hit a bump. I had no idea how long I'd been sleeping. At a fork, the curvy red clay going off and down with a dozen or so pastures planted with cotton on either side, she pulled over and got out of the car. She filled the tank with what was left of the gas and came around to the passenger side. She reached in the window and grabbed one of her bags off the floorboard and motioned for me to get out, follow her as she hopped across the ditch and into the pasture. She ducked a little as she walked.

When I caught up to her, she turned and put a finger to her lips, quieting me as if we were sneaking up on something. We walked, crouching, through the rows and rows of cotton bolls, the strips of white peeking through as if they would pop out in bursts at any moment. Finally, we reached the edge of the pasture and found a creek, smooth and cool-looking, running along down a hill. I squatted down and put my hand in the water, letting it flow through my fingers, immediately cooling me down.

Jean tossed her bag on the ground, looked around, and then unbuttoned her pants. She slid them off, gradually, over her hips as if to tease and then easily over her boots as they were loose trousers, a bit too big in the leg and waist. I stood and froze, stiff-legged, holding my breath. She stood before me with just a linen shirt on. It was a pale gray, almost white, and as she unbuttoned the shirt, her flesh sparkled in the sunlight filtering through the trees. She wasn't wearing anything on her breasts, no underclothes at all.

She stood naked, all but her boots, and when she turned I thought she'd run and jump in the stream to bathe, cool off, but she turned to me instead. She held out her hands and then ran them over her thighs, her stomach, her arms, and her breasts. I gasped and looked away, embarrassed.

"What? You can come and look at me," she was whispering, but with a forced air, "you can hover over me in bed asleep and try to touch me when I don't give you permission. You watch me up on the stage and in the car when I can't look back, but now that I show you, standing here in front of you, looking at you, you look away?"

The last startled me. It reminded me of my uncle, the way he looked at Cora. It was the same way Mr. Hammond looked at Julian. "No. I am not like that. I don't think of you that way," I managed and looked at her face.

A strange blankness ran into her eyes. "What way is that, Frankie?"

I couldn't get past it, but I was looking at her, at her face.

"Look at me, Frankie! Look at my body! I am not anything right now but a naked woman standing in a pasture in the middle of nowhere, right here in front of you."

"I—I—" I wrung my hands. The sun was bright, bouncing bright light in speckles through the trees.

Her arms dangled at her sides. Her cheeks seemed puffed and red, her honey eyes, darker, muddy and small. I noticed the shortness of her brow and the thinness of her eyebrows and how very female she was as I saw her breasts, plump and falling heavier against her body. I wanted to touch her so badly in that moment, I was suddenly aware of my face, afraid I'd somehow give the wrong expression, that my face would betray me if I looked, really looked as I wanted to at her rounded shoulders, her soft plump breasts, the dark nipples. I wanted to gaze at her hips, wide and rounded, her stomach, the raised scar from the top of her hips down to the dark mound of hair spread out like a V.

"Watch it, Frankie, you going so pale you gonna disappear," she said. Her shapely, strong legs flexed as she walked toward the stream and jumped in, splashing me all the way up on the bank.

I gasped, and she laughed as she struggled out of the water and grabbed my arm before I knew what to do, before I could get undressed too. She dragged me through the mud, and I fell in the water, my boots digging into the sinking mud as I tried to stand. She dunked me, reached down and grabbed a handful of mud and smeared it on me, and I did the same to her. Finally, I was able to wrangle my wet and clinging clothes off my body and onto the bank where they might dry on a rock, but Jean quickly pulled me back in. I stumbled naked right into her, both of us laughing, my breasts to her naked breasts, and we both froze. Her face was so close to mine and she was smiling, her eyes on me, then staring directly in my eyes for the first time that I could recall, and her face relaxed as she leaned in to me, tilting her head as if to kiss me, but just then she stopped, straightened her head and looked at me with surprise and seriousness. She looked at me with such stony eyes of what seemed like concern my body trembled from the legs on up. I wanted her to lean in to me, to kiss me there, naked in the creek so badly I almost tried to myself until I remembered the first time I'd tried it. No, no, I would let her the next time, if there were to be one.

She ran her hands over my arms as if to warm me, and I could feel the wrinkles in her fingers. We'd been in so long we'd pruned. She wiped away some mud from my face, gently with one smooth stroke and finally smiled, showing me her hands.

Rosie let out a guffaw that startled us both. We splashed away and I squatted into the water to hide myself. Rosie held up my pants, swinging them around, taunting me to come get them, and Tasha giggled. Jean smiled too and crossed her arms, waiting for me to do something. Just as I struggled to get out of the stream, I heard gravel flying in the distance, horses galloping on the road. Someone was coming. The farmers were stirring.

Rosie turned and ran back to the car—with my clothes. Jean splashed out of the stream and pulled on clean clothes from her bag. She was halfway to the car before I even moved. I struggled out of the muddy water and up on the bank, slinging off the water and wiping my boots in the grass. I covered my chest with my arms and ran across the pasture. The weeds stung my bare legs, my boots heavy with water and mud.

"Damn, Frankie. Hurry up," Jean yelled and started the car. "Grab those clothes and get in. Dress in the car. We gotta get out of here."

Out of breath, I gave up trying to cover myself and picked up my bundle the girls had tossed on the ground and hopped in the car buck naked. The car strutted out onto the road again, and, just as it did, a wagon full of workers turned off into the field right behind us and stopped. The driver's eyes, squinting into the bright sun, studied us as we drove away. I pulled the shirt over my shoulders. Rosie and Tasha had stopped laughing but were whispering in the back seat as I scrambled to pull on my pants. When the workers were well behind us, I let out a big sigh, betraying my fear. Jean Bailey looked over at me, a grin in her eyes, and then over her shoulder at the girls. They all laughed then, hands waving.

Tasha dabbed at her eyes with a gloved hand she laughed so hard. "I ain't never, never seen a white woman so scared in all my life!" she said through her laughing teeth.

As we sped up, kicking up a trail of dust, I realized I'd lost my knife, that it was no longer on my ankle, no longer in my clothes. I imagined it at the bottom of that creek. I could feel all the blood drain from my face. I buttoned up my shirt and crossed my arms. "Lighten up, bull. If you gonna be my man, you gonna have to toughen up a bit."

I blushed even harder, feeling the shift then. I remembered my words to Baby Boy, and I was still ashamed, embarrassed even though I'd only said what I said to get us out of a bind. And I may have been Jean Bailey's new man, but Tasha and Rosie, these were her people, her sisters, her blood. I was the novelty here, and she'd always make that clear. That's what I thought I knew, but couldn't say then.

But Jean said, without even looking at me, "At least you're pretty, girl." And I believed her, and the air grew lighter around us in that tight little car.

CHAPTER FOURTEEN

Augusta was hot and busy, stop-and-go traffic straight through the square. I leaned out to try to catch a bit of the breeze through the open window. The longer hair on top of my head slung into my eyes, sweat dripping from the strands. The streets were lined with wagonloads of cotton from early harvests. In the lines there were only men, men in business suits and others in work clothes, cotton-picking clothes. There was a white line and a colored line, and never once did the two meet or cross. Several men turned to watch us ease through the square.

Jean drove straight through, silent, rolling up her window to keep the dust out. We passed slowly through downtown Augusta, and everyone in our car was silent, still. Jean made a turn, and after a few minutes we were shaded again, the trees like canopies overhead letting in only small patches of sun as we drove. The car tires grew louder, passing from cobblestone to gravel. The girls shifted in the back seat. Even though I was in the front with Jean, a tiny bolt running through me with each glance at her, she was still far away, eluding me somehow.

The Ortilly Theater was a grand building with a front as large, if not larger, than the Rapp and Rapp Theater in Chicago or The Abraham where Julian took me in Memphis. A twinge shot through me again at the thought of Julian alone in that shed behind Miss Sal's, waiting to see if I returned. We pulled right up front, and Jean threw her door open as she killed the engine.

"Be just a minute," she said and got out.

I pushed down the thought of Julian, assuring myself he was fine, better without me dragging him across the country. I leaned forward to see the top of the theater building.

"Boy hidey, you act like you ain't never seen a joint before!" Rosie said and laughed, Tasha giggling faintly with her.

I slunk back into the seat.

* * *

When Jean came back out she was dressed almost as well as if she were about to go on stage, just more subdued. She wore a straight, Eton-cropped wig and a wide-brimmed ladies' hat that came down low on one side, a smart suit and skirt tailored to meet her curves, and all were camel-colored and soft looking. She wore chunky high heels that made her legs appear strong and muscular.

"Plans have changed. We're doing two shows tonight and then heading out in the morning." She didn't look peeved, and no one asked any questions.

With a lit cigarette in her hands, she opened the car door and waved for me and everyone else to get out.

"Girls, go on in and start getting ready. Mr. Ortilly's got a spread inside. Just mind you don't overeat. I want you both moving like two loose lilies tonight," she said.

"Where you going?" Tasha asked, pulling her tapestry bags out of the car.

"I've got to run some errands, be back shortly. Frankie, you drive."

"Pick up some hairpins!" Rosie yelled as she walked into the theater.

Jean Bailey got in the car and pointed me back in the direction of town. "You gonna be my manager tonight, girl, but just in name, ya hear? You best drive like you are in charge."

I was taken aback but agreed and drove on. She directed me to a general store right smack in the middle of town. Jean Bailey was dressed so fine anybody would have looked at her three times, and they did. Once inside the store, she gave me a five-dollar bill and told me to find hairpins, rouge in a light pink, powder in white or beige, and nylons in nude. "And don't get the cheap nylons either," she whispered. Jean stayed in the foyer, fidgeting with her hat and gloves. I stopped just down the first aisle and looked back at her, waiting for her to follow. She nodded her head to the right. There was a sign with "whites only beyond this point" written in scrawled black letters hanging from the ceiling. The whole damn store was divided in half. Only necessities were on the one side, groceries, hardware, and the like. The beauty products were all on the whites only side. I suddenly felt strange, on display as she watched me go down each aisle picking up the items. I handled each, searched through the choices with care, and brought them all back to her for approval.

When I came back with the last item, she sent me down the open section alone, though she was allowed there, to get gauze and a whole heap of Ace bandages. I was confused and alarmed, but did it anyway while Jean stood in the foyer, primping now. The sun lit up her face through the window. As I approached the counter, the sales clerk barely looked at me. He kept one eye on the items and the other on Jean, though, perhaps because she was dressed well, better than both of us, better than the only other two women, white women, in the store. The two women carried their flour and sugar on their hips like children, and held their shoulders back, proud, as if to make a show of being unmoved by Jean or me. When we got back to the car, I let out a sigh, glad to be out of there, relieved the task was done without trouble.

"What's wrong, girl?"

"Why didn't you just send me in or go and ask for these things? And what's the use of the bandages?" The panic rose in my voice.

Jean just threw her head back and laughed. "I usually go on out to the colored side of town for these things, but Tasha's too damn pale for most of it. Anyway, it's more fun this way. Why in the hell get all dolled up if I got to sit in the car?"

I didn't have an answer for her.

"Now go on, let's get you some clean clothes."

"But I—I mean, I'm all right. I tailored this suit myself, fits like a glove. I just need to spruce these up a bit." I ducked my head and smoothed my suit down. It was wrinkled and dirty, and I thought of when I'd first tried it on, of Julian complimenting it, smiling at me with excitement. I'd started convincing myself he'd gone on back to Mr. Hammond's, though the thought did not make me feel any better.

Jean looked me over, shaking her head. "Sugar, they are nice. You did a fine job, but you need something—you just need more. Now, let's get on down to my side of town." She had a smirk about her and was clenching and unclenching her hands into fists in her lap like she was nervous.

I smiled and drove on, but I just wanted to stop, to stop and be with her, alone without the pressure, pressure of time, or where we were, where we were going. I just wanted to stay still with her. Unclench her hands and put them in mine.

We drove back toward the theater but passed it, going further and further to the outskirts, where the town seemed to change, become rich with color and signs written in hurried, dripped paint. We parked on a street lined with stores, and though some folks glared at us, most seemed to make exception for the "entertainment" once they realized who Jean was and that didn't take long. Jean had a presence about her, an air and a sophistication, and she was tall, curved, and solid, a force coming out of that brand-new car, walking down the street click clacking in those heels. She walked right into a men's clothing store without a flinch and pulled me in after her. The men lit up when they saw her, welcoming her in and showing her suits.

"Boys, I just need a nice dark suit for this character right now," she said and nodded to me.

They didn't bat an eye. I guessed they expected she'd have someone like me around. She told them we'd tailor it ourselves if they just gave us some materials, so they measured me up quick and pulled a ready-made suit off a rack. Jean picked out another set of tweed-cuffed pants and a linen shirt and some lace-up, two-toned shoes. "You'll work it off," she assured me as she paid the bill.

That afternoon, as we made our way back to the theater, sunlight littered the dirt road in patches through the canopy of trees. It rolled over our faces, illuminating and then shading us. It was hot, but in the car against that cool dirt, in the shade of the live oaks, it was breezy and cool, and the air was fragrant with damp clay and jasmine vines lining the road. It was a short trip, and I was sad when we arrived. Jean had me pull around to the side door, and when I got out, I felt light-headed. Truth be told, I was so hungry I was having trouble standing. I hoped my face wasn't completely drained of color. It seemed that I had two modes at this time, pale as a pancake or red as fire. It was as if I walked in an extreme I hadn't known existed until then.

Jean ushered me into the door and through the back halls down to a dressing room. The girls were sitting, stripped down to their underclothes, fanning themselves in front of the mirrors that were lit with bright round bulbs. I could feel the blush rise in my cheeks as I stood still, stuck just inside the door. Bags with nylons hanging out of them, cosmetics, crimping irons, and dresses of all kinds were strewn about the room. They had a canister of lemonade in front of them, and Jean poured us both some. There was a bucket on the floor beside the girls, and Jean leaned over it.

"Oh, look here, Frankie! Good old boiled peanuts. I know you ain't had none, and if you have, you ain't had them like this." She motioned for me to come over.

I looked down in the bucket, and it looked like soggy peanut soup with the shells. I'd never even seen such a thing, much less eaten anything like it, but my stomach growled at the warm, nutty smell. I reluctantly stuck my hand in and grabbed one, but had no idea how to get the peanut out with a soggy shell around it. I hoped they didn't want me to eat the shell too. I sat down with it, eyeing it. Tasha reached in after me and grabbed a handful. She took one, squeezed it, sucked at the crack in the shell, broke the shell down the seam and then sucked out the peanut. I tried. I squeezed and juice ran all down my hand and jaw, even onto my neck as I tried to slurp it in. I couldn't get the shell to open up, but the juice was good and warm and salty with a little kick of cayenne pepper, and I wanted to get the peanut out so badly, I could feel it crunch in my teeth. I pried at it and pried at it and finally gave up, tossing it in an empty bucket Jean put at our feet for that purpose.

I grabbed another one and repeated the whole thing, and this time it split right in two and all the juice went right into my mouth followed by the peanut. I let out an audible groan of pleasure, and Jean gave a sort of half-laugh and then turned on her heel and walked back through the door.

"That woman get any nylons and powder?" Tasha asked.

I nodded that we did with my mouth full of peanut.

"Anything else?" She'd stopped eating for a second, was reaching and poking into the bucket, fishing for a better one, and pulled out a rounded one, pale and plump.

"A few things, yeah." I stuck another peanut in my mouth and was about to tell her a list of things we'd gotten when Jean came back in the door with our loot.

"All right ladies, start getting to it," she said as she pulled the supplies out, handing them each over to Rosie. She held onto the bag with the bandages and my suit.

"Oh, I will in a minute," Tasha whined, sounding childlike. I looked her hard in the face. There were no laugh lines, no wrinkles about the lips. She pulled out a long cigarette extender and puffed away. She was defiant if nothing else, and I was beginning to see she was quite young, a baby really, though well developed for her age.

"Tash! I know it will take you damn near three hours to get ready. Now shove a few more peanuts in your mouth and get on with it," Rosie yelled, backing Jean up.

Jean pulled out my suit and the materials for shaping it up and handed them over to me. "Frankie, next door there's more food. Get something in your stomach and then come on back and try on the suit."

After all those peanuts, my mouth was raw from the salt and I didn't much want anything more, but I draped the suit over the chair, put down the materials, and went next door. There was a long table in a separate dressing room lined with fruit, bread and sandwiches. I sucked down a little sandwich or two, dainty sandwiches, cut all nice with the corners rounded and everything.

When I got back to the dressing room, Tasha turned toward her mirror and pulled her slip down off her shoulder, making kissy faces at herself in the mirror and then giggling as she dabbed one cheek and then the other with rouge. Rosie snorted, pulling on a new pair of stockings. Jean tucked the bag with the bandages under her arm and thumbed through the tapestry bags they'd brought with them. "You girls are going to have to hang all these up, but put it all back in the bags before we leave tonight, you hear?"

Tasha sighed, frustrated, turning around to Jean Bailey. "What? You didn't get any new ones?" she whined.

"You've got plenty, Tasha," Rosie said, crossing the room to the line of dresses.

Tasha huffed. "You got her new clothes! You always telling us we can't afford it! How you go and buy for her?"

"I got you what you needed, sweetheart, new nylons, even more rouge," Jean said.

Tasha crossed her arms like a child and sank down in her chair. "What's left in that bag, Jean? What else did you get her?"

"It doesn't concern you, Tasha," Rosie said.

"The hell it don't! What is she doing here anyway? What can she do? Bet she can't sing or even dance a lick. Hell, don't even look like a girl most of the time—certainly ain't one of us," she said and looked over her shoulder at me with a sneer. "Damn cracker!" she said and turned back to the mirror to powder her nose.

No one said a thing, not even Jean. She just looked at me as if to see my reaction, see what I might say. My hands shook, so I stuck them in my pockets and tried to stand tall, all bowed up like I'd fight, but I couldn't get out a word, didn't have a word to get out.

Tasha threw down her powder puff and stood. She stomped across the room, deliberately running into me and shoving me aside with her shoulder muttering "cracker" in a whisper. I stepped back and let her through. She dug through the bags, slinging dresses out across the room in a fit.

"Now that's enough! Stop it! And pick this shit up! I don't want to hear any more. It's my money. You get paid, too. You want a new damn dress, go buy one!" Jean clutched the bag of bandages under her arm and slammed out the door.

I could hear talking in the hall, men's voices and Jean's.

"Out there telling lies, I bet, with a gaggle of men ain't gonna pay us worth a damn," Rosie grumbled. "She rather be out there with them anyway. Let her go on and huff off like some kind of Queen of Sheba."

Rosie was a beauty too, standing there with her hand on her hips, her slip just barely touching her at her curves as she clipped the top of her stocking to her garter belt. The girls' underclothes were the prettiest I'd ever seen, all frills, satin and lace. I was so out of place, I felt like I was glowing. I looked down at my own clothes, dirty and disheveled and pulled them off to try on the suit. The suit smelled crisp and new, a powerful smell.

Rosie slipped on a bright pink dress, satin lengthening down her torso with a drop-waisted sash about her hips, elegant and stately. Tasha moped over and pulled down a deeper pink dress, calf-length, fringe filled and tassel-laden.

"Jean will be getting dressed on down the hall, Frankie," Rosie said. "Why don't you take the suit on down there?" It was more insistent than a request.

I slipped my dirty trousers back on, gathered up the suit and materials against my chest covering my undershirt and breasts, and left the room. There hadn't been another room in the direction of the food, so I went the other way. Finally, I heard a low tinkling of music coming a few doors down. The door was closed so I knocked.

"What?" I recognized Jean's voice.

"It's Frankie. Can I come in?"

She met me at the door, her wig off and stripped down to her underclothes as well, wearing just a slip and nylons. I felt my mouth go dry and my stomach drop. There was a phonograph playing softly in the corner, some man and a horn and it thumped in my ears.

"Well, come on, let's see what this suit looks like," she said and ushered me in.

She went to the mirror, lit up brightly with bulbs lining the top, and tied a handkerchief up around her hairline. She smeared some makeup on her face and neck. I rushed over to a chair beside her and changed into the suit. It was a little tight in the chest, a little baggy in the crotch, but way too long in the leg. She turned to me, wiping her hands on a rag. Then she ran a hand along the seam of the coat and along the inseam of the pants. My breathing grew shallow and my legs weak.

"These trousers need to be taken up here and in the length," she said, standing up again.

"I can do it," I blurted.

"Oh, I know you can, but I'm not sure you have time. How long would that take you?"

I glanced over at the chair realizing that with only the basic sewing materials, cutting the suit to fit could take me a day or more. "Um—well normally a good bit, but I could just take it up a little bit and do it better when we can get to a machine."

"Oh sweet girl! You can use a machine? You should have said." She shook her head. "Well, we can do that soon, but just get these pants tacked up. You can pull it off with that I think," she said.

She was right. The suit didn't look all that bad for ready-made, and it fit me pretty well except for the length. It was slimmer, slicker than the one I'd tailored, and I vowed to learn how to do it better the next time. I stripped down to my underwear and undershirt and sat down and started on the hem.

"You're pretty damn handy. Don't let the girls know or they'll be making you mend everything they own," she laughed taking out an eyebrow pencil and turning again to the mirror.

"I don't think I'd mind, but I'd rather just make it all myself, by my own pattern."

She raised her eyebrows as if impressed but didn't stop filling in the dark lines of her eyebrows, shaping them into perfect arches. Her hands were long, slender. I was entranced by how delicate and feminine they looked, almost as if they were different hands altogether than the ones that had gripped the steering wheel all the way in to Augusta.

I was distracted, but I managed to unhinge the seams, measure them up, and put in a new, rough hem within just a few hours. Jean finished her makeup and came in and out as I worked. The last time she came in struggling to hold three hatboxes and a long, flowing black bejeweled gown on a hanger with a glittering feather boa draped about its neck. I leaped up to help her, grabbing the three boxes while she hung the dress.

From one hatbox she pulled a tight-fitting cap with intricate designs all the way around. From another she pulled a whole mess of feathers, arranged on a clip. I tried not to stare, entranced by the pretty things and her slipping into the dress and a pair of black heels. By the time I had my trousers and shoes on, she'd completely transformed into the performer I'd seen that first time in Chicago, this time in black, the dress hanging loosely from tiny shoulder straps and dropping to just above her breasts. She fastened the feathers to the hat and pulled it down snug to her head. I sat in my trousers and undershirt tying my shoes as slowly as I could, eyeing the seaming of the dress, the cut, and how layers of material draped in streams unevenly around her ankles, giving it bounce.

She dabbed at her lipstick in the mirror and then stopped to watch me in the reflection. "You gonna have to get your breasts flat before you put on your shirt and jacket," she said, taking off the hat again and placing it carefully on the dressing table in front of the mirror.

I crossed my arms over my undershirt and pressed down on my breasts, slouching as much as I could.

"No, no. Not like that. Come here," she said and turned, motioning with her hands and leaning against the dressing table.

I got up and went over to the mirror beside her. Even in that heat, my hands were suddenly cold and clammy as she grabbed them and lifted my arms. She pulled the shirt off over my head, and I shivered, but I didn't shy away, didn't make a move to cover myself. She smiled and ran her hands down my arms as I let them fall. She was so close I could feel her breath on my face, soft and warm. Then she turned and pulled out the gauze and Ace bandages.

"Turn around and hold your arms out like this," she said and spun me to the mirror, lifting my arms out again. She unraveled the Ace bandage and reached around me, draping it over my chest, the one end just under my right arm. Her hands grazed my skin and goose bumps spread down my arms. "Why didn't you stick up for yourself back there, girl?"

"I—I just thought—I don't know. I didn't really know what to say, figured it was between ya'll."

"Gonna have to get over that figuring and speak up to survive this bunch. Standing there like a cocky little boy ain't gonna cut it around here. Hold this here," she said as she pressed the bandage over my breasts. I put my hand on top of hers. "Keep your elbows up." She slid her hand out along the edges of the bandage and pulled it back and flat, then wrapped it all the way around my chest twice, tucking the end in at the back. She grabbed two fasteners and clasped them over the tuck.

I let my arms drop. The illusion was strange, like I was covering some kind of wound across my chest. I felt constricted, bound, afraid to move, afraid one big breath would pop the fasteners. I seemed to naturally slouch. My breasts were gone though. I was flat, flatter than most of the boyish looking girls in flapper outfits I'd seen in Chicago.

"Breathe, Frankie, or you'll pass out. The bandage is stretchy."

I took a deep breath, and it felt loose. "What if it comes unraveled?"

"That's what this is for, reinforcement," she said and held up the gauze. "It'll also make it smoother and won't show under your shirt."

She wrapped me all the way around again, carefully placing the gauze in thin strips barely layering one another. When she was done and she'd tucked it in tightly in the back, the whole contraption was smooth and white instead of the fake flesh color of the Ace bandage. I turned sideways in front of the mirror, trying to stand normally, or normal for a young man. I put my hands in my pockets, posing.

"Go on now, get dressed," she said with a grin.

I quickly pulled on the undershirt, the dress shirt, and tied my tie. Once the jacket was on, I really did look sharp, and I passed, however feminine my face and my hair falling into my eyes looked.

"You just need one more thing," she said and opened up the last hatbox. She pulled out a dark blue, wide-brimmed Homburg hat with slightly curled edges that matched my suit exactly.

I put it on my head and pulled it down, tucking my hair up in it.

Jean laughed, proud of herself. She stood behind me again and lifted the hat and placed it back on my head loosely and cocked to the side, slightly over one eye. I gave myself a snarling look in the mirror. I looked masculine for sure, but now I was dangerous too, just what she needed me to be, I thought.

CHAPTER FIFTEEN

Backstage at the Ortilly Theater was as hot as a steamer engine at full speed. As it grew closer to showtime, entertainment folks filled the place, crowding into the little dressing rooms on both sides of us and running up and down the halls yelling for costumes and props. I'd slicked my hair back and my tie was as tight as I could muster in the heat. Jean had placed a little pink carnation in my lapel and sat me on a wooden chair just outside her dressing room like a guard. I fanned myself with my hat and wiped at my brow with the back of my hand. The owner of the joint was to come back any minute, and I was given strict instructions to talk to him, tell him I was with Jean Bailey, promoting her, see what I could get out of it. I could hear the crowd gathering and men talking, women laughing all the way backstage. I knew I'd soon have to go out there and put on my own little show.

"You must be Mr. Frank." A large white man squeezed through the performers backstage, approached me, and stuck out his hand.

I stood, attempting a smile and a nod.

"Mr. Ortilly, and I own this joint."

Jean stepped out of the dressing room and curtsied to Mr. Ortilly.

"Miss Jean, I found your man," he said and nudged me in the arm, squinting his already too small eyes that seemed eaten up by his red, puffed out cheeks.

She nodded with a shy smile. She didn't say a word, but she clenched and unclenched her fists at her sides. A chill ran up my body. I had my instructions, but I couldn't utter a word, couldn't move to be more cordial to him, couldn't move to comfort her.

"Well now, come on out here, Mr. Frank. We've got the best seats in the house."

I followed him out into the seating area. The whole theater was packed with people, all white and all in evening attire, some sitting fanning themselves with their programs and some still standing in the aisles. A large woman stood at the front side-aisle grasping at her side as she let out a roar of a laugh. Her peach-colored gown, covered in rhinestones at the neck and waistband, was snug at her chest but flowed lavishly down to the floor. She wore a large peach-colored feather that sprang from her small hat, swishing the air as she spoke. She fanned at herself with a delicate paper fan, more to feign southern feminine charm it seemed than to dispel the heat. There were three men gathered around her in tuxedoes. All were focused on her, her every loud word and overblown gesture.

A demure woman sat alone in the row next, scanning her program and the stage. Rows behind her were filled with men and women chatting, filling the theater with an anxious air. The theater was large with row upon row of seating, three tiers of balcony seating and boxed seating along the sidewalls. The carpet was swirled with deep reds, greens, and blues. The seats were lined in a deep crushed red velvet ornately outlined in gold trim. Every piece of wood in the place seemed to glimmer a golden hue. The ceiling itself was draped in crushed red velvet matching the stage curtain and held together in a knot at the highest point with a gold wooden button. A glittering chandelier hung just below it.

It was a palace or palace-like, certainly more so than The Palace Café back in Chicago. It was grand and immaculate like a church. Just as Mr. Ortilly was about to grab at my elbow to introduce me to some of the patrons, I excused myself. I needed to go backstage one last time. I needed to see Jean again, see if all this would be okay, if she was okay and what I was supposed to do.

When I rounded the corner and went through the heavy black backstage door, I saw a man dart into Jean's dressing room. He had an almond complexion and was dressed in a tailored suit, similar in cut and color to mine. He was a broad-shouldered man, much taller than me. I wondered if he was one of the men whose names she'd mumbled the night before when I found her. Tasha and Rosie were rehearsing, singing a scale in the hallway. They didn't take notice of me or the other five or six people that had just come out of their dressing rooms, costumed and painted for various acts. This was the rest of the circuit performers, the ones Jean Bailey had left for a while to play the juke joints. I realized then that this was vaudeville, that this would be more than Jean Bailey on stage at Small's. I wondered where they'd been all this time, what shows they'd played without Jean and how they all traveled to get here. I imagined a long caravan on the roads or all of them piled into a single train car.

As I eased down the hall to the seat outside of Jean's dressing room, a flood of people passed me, streaming out of the rooms and into the hall. A black man and woman came through dressed like cotton farmers with hair up in cornrows and pigtails, red paint around their lips and black paint on their faces. Then a beautiful girl in a skintight leotard swished by me. She was small and childlike but a full-grown woman with almond-shaped eyes and deep black hair, so black it was almost blue. A white man in a tux with tails followed her, tattoos peeking out over his collar and up over his entire face, deep black marks, dotted and lined. Tasha and Rosie rushed up behind me.

"Frankie, we're about to start!" Tasha squealed in my ear. She was grinning, her makeup glistening, even in the dim light of backstage.

She squeezed my arm, and I was so startled by the touch I stepped back and almost stumbled over the chair. I heard a rustling behind Jean's door, as if I'd disturbed them. Feeling my face flush, I maneuvered through the crowd of performers and back out into the audience. Mr. Ortilly was waiting for me and ushered me to a seat—a seat right next to the loud woman. He leaned into her ear, whispered something, kissed her on the cheek and then disappeared backstage, leaving an empty seat next to her.

"Mr. Frank, my husband tells me. How do you do?" she said in a stage whisper as the houselights blinked.

"Pleased. And your name, ma'am?" I asked and sat with my hat in my lap.

"Oh, my foot. I ain't old enough for you to call me ma'am. Call me Laura—Mrs. Laura Demetrius Ortilly."

"Good to meet you, Ms. Laura." As I slid my hand in hers, I could see she was mustering up the appropriate blush, and then the orchestra began, the houselights dimmed. The audience shuffled, mumbled and hushed as the music reached an opening crescendo.

"Ladies and gentlemen," a voice boomed from behind the curtain splitting slowly open as Mr. Ortilly himself walked out to center stage, his arms extended. "Welcome to the Ortilly Theater!"

Throughout the first half filled with comedy skits, daring feats, and music, Ms. Laura grasped my arm, tapped me with her fan, and whispered her reaction to every performer, black and white alike. She especially enjoyed the contortionist and, of course, Jean Bailey who sang a couple of upbeat songs. As the curtain closed and the houselights rose, so did Ms. Laura. "Well, Mr. Frank, won't you escort a lady to the lobby for a treat?"

I rose to meet her arm, and she tucked it in mine, though she almost had to lean down to do so. I felt like a child standing next to her. I could feel my hair starting to fall in the heat and wanted to put my hat back on. Instead I forced my shoulders back, held my chin high, and walked through the crowd with her. When we arrived in the lobby, I was introduced to three more theater owners: a little man, short and stout, by the name of Douglas, and two average-looking but distinguished gentlemen, Mr. Williams and Mr. Van Holden. It was all Georgia high society, I realized, higher society than what I'd come from. I could feel my palms moisten and reached to wipe them with a handkerchief before I shook hands and added that I was Jean Bailey's "manager…promoter."

"With Miss Bailey, sir, no offense, but I'm afraid you're just a showpiece, ain't ya?"

I could feel my neck heat up. I laughed. "Yes, sir, she's managed pretty well herself. I tell you, I'm really interested in her long-term career, recording and pictures. I think she can go all the way to New York City then Hollywood, the way she's headed." They'd beaten me to the punch, but I recovered, proud that I'd put in the bit about the pictures even though Jean had never asked me to. I breathed deep and let my shoulders relax.

"Why, Mr. Frank, you don't need to be talking to these two-bit theater boys." Ms. Laura gave a flirtatious laugh and a swat with the fan at Mr. Douglas. They all guffawed and stared straight down into Ms. Laura's ample chest. Her rhinestone-lined collar swooped right down the middle of her, and given the style of the flat chest, she was the only woman around with such a show, a show she was more than willing to display it seemed.

"She's right, Frank. You see that man over there with the woman in red?" Mr. Van Holden pointed over my shoulder, and I turned to follow his arm. "That there is the couple you need to be doing business with."

"That's Mr. and Mrs. Pickard. She's the cousin to the family that owns a big-time film studio." Ms. Laura dragged me by the arm, leaning in and whispering to me at the same time.

I barely had time to nod a "nice to meet you" to the theater owners. Mr. Pickard was entirely preoccupied with a man Ms. Laura told me later "ran the whole town," but Mrs. Pickard, who I supposed mattered more in the first place, was delightful. She was, in fact, the delicate little woman who was sitting almost directly behind us, the woman who'd been fidgeting alone in her seat before the show.

"Mrs. Pickard, Mr. Frank manages some of our talent here tonight." Ms. Laura was all of a sudden polite, careful in her words, and even soft-spoken, as if she were afraid she'd break Mrs. Pickard. The woman was a waif and looked a bit too pale in that red dress.

"Oh?" She took my hand in hers, and I realized, almost too late, that I was to kiss it.

After my fumble, I gave the next part of my script, delivered with a bit of a stutter, but delivered.

"He's so modest, Mrs. Pickard. He'd like you to help him get Jean Bailey into the big time, into pictures."

This caught Mr. Pickard's attention, and he stopped mid-sentence and turned to us. "Now, Mrs. Ortilly, that's just plain silly talk. What would she do in the pictures? Isn't she a singer?"

"Well, of course she is, but she's a performer, Mr. Pickard. She can do more than sing," I broke in, my pride for Jean getting bigger with my words, though I had no idea what all Jean could do.

"I think I won't hold my breath for a nigger woman to become a movie star."

"Imagine," Mrs. Pickard chimed in.

I thought she seemed as if she were agreeing wholeheartedly with her husband, but there was a waver, an excitement in her voice that said she really was trying to imagine it.

"Oh besides, Harry," Ms. Laura spoke up, "she could do the music for the pictures anyway. And why not a musical?"

"Have you seen these new 'talkies'? That's what they're called, right? They are hideous, really, so over-the-top and gaudy!" Mr. Pickard paused only to take Mrs. Pickard's empty glass with his as if he were about to get refills but continued, gesturing with his two full hands. "It is so unnecessary, completely takes away from plot and characterization, and the action itself, a picture's unique, high-end quality."

Mrs. Pickard took out a long cigarette extender loaded with a cigarette. "Harry, for the love of God, that is what people said about film in the first place and now listen at you, so pretentious, I swear!" Mrs. Pickard dismissed him and grabbed back her own glass.

"It's lazy, if you ask me, is all," he said and lit her smoke.

She just smiled, excused herself, and walked away to get her own refill.

I stopped her. "Mrs. Pickard, should you think of a way, please keep us in mind." I knew it was pushing a bit too far and rude to her husband, but I couldn't help myself. Mrs. Pickard curtsied, and Ms. Laura and I went back to our seats.

The second half of the show was much the same format as the first, but the comedy was shorter and the buildup for Jean Bailey greater. Without introduction, Jean Bailey took the stage. The audience was quiet, hushed to stillness. When the light rose on her, the glistening on her black dress, the feathers dancing about her neck sent a shiver up me, and it was as if I could feel the entire audience take her in in a deep breath. She had her own band, and the orchestra sat silently below. Her band on the theater stage seemed much bigger than when they were squeezed into Small's. I wondered where they'd been and why she didn't travel with them either. There were a few extra players it seemed, a cornet player stood out as he played to and with her voice. He echoed her and she him. They scatted over the melody and back again. By the end of the first few songs, it was hard to always tell the two sounds from one another. About halfway through the second song, I recognized the cornet player. He was the man I'd seen backstage going into Jean's dressing room, and I felt relieved and silly.

Jean Bailey started the next song softly, humming along with the horn. Then more softly still, she sang a lullaby, followed by a swooning love song. She cut in with an upbeat blues tunes, building each one upon the next, until I thought for sure the audience would pop from wanting to jump up and move, yell out a response. But there was nothing. Only the traditional applause after each song, with an even bigger one after a favorite song, a song they'd heard before, the "Mid River Blues." It was a song that had been on the radio in Atlanta, Ms. Laura whispered to me, and she was giddy with excitement for knowing all the words. She mouthed them along with Jean Bailey, and every now and again I could hear her voice, as if by accident, as if she didn't even notice that it had slipped through. She swayed with the music, bumping my arm and then Mr. Ortilly's who'd joined us for the finale, sitting oblivious to everything else around him, that silly grin on his face.

In the second half of the set, Tasha and Rosie pranced out to the stage. They got in rhythm with the tune, with Jean Bailey and with each other, swaying and snapping their fingers, arms going back and forth to their chest and down again. As the song began, I realized they were to serve as the response to Jean Bailey's call. Jean knew her audience, knew she wouldn't get the response she'd gotten in Chicago, so the girls did it for her, showing this audience a real performance by Jean Bailey.

"Once I was crazy 'bout a man. He mistreated me all the time," she sang and the girls repeated it.

"The next man I get he's got to promise me to be mine, all mine," she sang, but the girls answered with, "Yeah! All mine!"

"Trouble, trouble, I've had it all my days," she sang and the girls repeated it.

"It seems that trouble's goin' to follow me to my grave," she said and the girls answered, "Got a love struck woman chasin' trouble to her grave. UhHmmmm."

At the end of the second set, the girls merely sang backup and danced behind Jean Bailey, and for the last song they left the stage completely, almost everyone did. The cornet player was the only one who stayed—for a duet of sorts. As the song began, Jean Bailey turned to him, her arms at her side, and I noticed she clenched and unclenched her fists again, a sort of nervous movement that no one may have noticed as odd but me. She seemed so confident and sure in every other way. Her slow southern drawl came rolling out of her mouth with the first note and never left her. It was a song about traveling alone, a song about power and money and people wanting, needing, asking. It was her song, I understood, and as she reached the last verse, she asked just once for someone to hold her tight, for someone she could call home, someone she could call "her man." As she hit that last gut-tearing note, she dropped her chin a little and glanced out into the audience. Ms. Laura was no longer nudging me, and I didn't even hear the slightest shift of feet on the floor. The broad-shouldered cornet player seemed to leave only the sound of his horn on the stage and fade into the darkness that surrounded the spotlights. There was only her, Jean Bailey, and her voice. It felt like every note touched my skin, as if each chord was her hand on my flesh, her lips against mine. I didn't hear the crowd roar around me until she'd bowed and backed into the darkness of the stage.

I'd finally seen a full set of Jean Bailey's, and I felt that I'd been fed. My insides felt full, but light at the same time, a sort of freedom—the freedom I'd yearned for since I first saw her, since I'd boarded that train in Chicago. It was an incredible relief. I felt too weak to stand, but too light to sit. I pushed off the seat and rose with the crowd. I was dazed as I said my polite good-byes to the Ortillys. Once backstage, sitting in the chair outside Jean's dressing room, I felt I could breathe normally again.

Jean approached the door and found me. Her gown was damp from the heat of the stage, but her skin was freshly powdered, her body freshly misted with perfume, a deep musky flowering scent. The scent of her filled the air and made my head swim. She grabbed my hand, pulled me into the dressing room, and shut the door behind her.

"I talked to the cousin of a film studio." I realized as it slid from my mouth that it didn't make much sense, and I tried to recover, stuttering, but she took my face in her hand and then ran her hands down my sides as she pulled me to her, resting her hands at my hips, and planted her lips on mine. I was stunned silent wanting to stay in that moment, her lips on mine, her hands on me. It was a moment I'd longed for, but it lasted only a second before there were knocks at the door, and I was ushered into a side chair to wait, dazed and grinning. She opened the door with a smile, fanning herself with the largest, longest black feather I'd ever seen, just exactly like a movie star. I knew that the movies were where she belonged.

A string of admirers flowed in and out of the dressing room until Jean Bailey posted me at the door again to turn them away. Once the crowds had all gone, and I was back inside the dressing room, Tasha and Rosie came in and rushed around, piling Jean's things into their bags. All three of them crowded around one mirror and dabbed at their faces, all three of them still dazzling in their gowns. When we left the dressing room, there were performers in the halls carrying props and costumes and heading out the back door.

Tasha handed me a bag without so much as a dirty look. I felt like she'd come to some sort of acceptance about me, but I had no idea why. She still made me tense, and now I was suspicious, too. When we left the theater it was late, and there was a bright moon, full and looming, that lit up the sky and the tops of the trees and made Jean Bailey's car glow. There was a ring around the moon, and Rosie said that meant bad weather was on the way.

"We should get out of here right after the show, Jean," Rosie said as she loaded the bags in the back.

"We ain't gotta be in Mobile for a while, Rosie, Besides, I think there's a party tonight." Tasha winked at Jean and batted her eyes over her shoulder.

"What kind of party?" I asked, but both girls ignored me, and I wasn't even sure Jean heard me over the car cranking.

"Frankie, hand me that suit coat," she said and held out her hand. "Don't want to get it all wrinkled on the drive out." She took it off me and put it in the trunk. "Now, get on in and drive," she directed me and we all piled, bags in hand, in the car.

As we were leaving, Jean leaned forward and craned her neck toward the sky through the windshield. "By God, that's a pretty moon, sisters!"

Tasha and I, mirroring each other, leaned out our open windows and peered up into the sky. I propped my arm over the door and pulled out onto the street. In the blue of the moonlight, I could have sworn I saw her blush, even smile. Her smooth almond skin rounding over her high cheekbones and delicate jaw made her face seem even more like a child's. Rosie huffed in the back seat as Jean directed me down the street and through downtown, my ankle now a dull ache as I pressed the gas and shifted the gears. We almost backtracked the way we'd come into Augusta, but just as we were about to leave the edge of town, Jean asked me to turn onto a clay-packed dirt road. The moonlight spotted the road through the trees and our dim headlights made the sharp curves dangerous. I slowed as Jean grasped the handle on the dashboard.

"What are we gonna do about your boy, I mean *man*, Bailey?" Rosie's voice cracked.

"What are we gonna do about your voice, Rosie?" Jean didn't bother to turn around to talk to her. "When you gonna learn to lay off the gin and cigarettes before a show?"

"Why's it okay for you then?"

"I don't sound like a gigged frog, now do I?"

I had been looking for a turnoff Jean told me would come up some ways down the road. The road grew darker, more and more wooded, and the moon was hidden.

"Where are we going?" I finally asked.

Tasha leaned up to the front seat. "This is The Premier. Don't you know? It was the first theater for black folks in the South! We do a midnight show here every time we come through. But it ain't like that show you just seen. It's—It's—"

"Black," Rosie interrupted, sullen and stunted, obviously meant to shut Tasha up.

"It's more than just black, Rosie. It's exciting. It ain't as stuffy—it's—"

"Loose," Jean added.

"Yeah, loose."

"The white houses won't let us do our thang the way we do it on our own. We just barely got into doing those shows over at the white theaters anyway," Jean explained.

Tasha pulled herself forward on the seat to get closer. "Yeah, and did you see that tattooed white man huffing and puffing past me and Rosie?"

"And he acting like he was the king of Augusta, careful not to even brush up against our gowns in the hallway, like we're lepers, like *we're* the freaks!"

"That ain't nothing new, Rosie," Jean said. "That's just the way it is. At least we got in and got paid in full this time." Mr. Ortilly had come to me as I was blocking Jean Bailey's door and handed me an envelope. He gave me a big smile, tipped his hat and walked away.

Jean pointed to an all-but hidden turnoff, and I took it. It was overgrown a bit, and I could hear the weeds hitting the underside of the car as I navigated the tire and buggy tracks. Just after the turn was a clearing and beyond the trees was a great big building, almost as big as the Ortilly Theater, but painted white with blue trim, almost resembling an old plantation house in the front with its large porch and rounded out columns. There were rocking chairs spread across the porch and people sat fanning themselves, all dressed well in evening attire just as the audience had been at Ortilly's, but there was not a white person anywhere in sight. My hands gripped the wheel, and I missed Jewel, my stomach tightening with my guilt. I had a sudden, strange urge to duck my head.

"Now, Frankie, don't get all squirrely, just be careful out here. We are going to sneak you into the back and up into the balcony with the rest of the white folks what like to come see our shows, but don't get into anything with them or with any of the black folks around here."

I nodded as we passed a painted sign propped in the front that read: The Premier. In small letters below the name across the bottom, I picked up the name Ortilly.

"Mr. Ortilly runs this one, too?" I asked.

"Might as well. He put up a lot of money for it back when it got scorched."

"There was a great big fire, should have seen it!" Tasha was animated now, lively and full of something I almost thought was booze though I hadn't seen anyone swig from any jug, didn't even know where the jug had gone.

As we circled around the building and toward the back, there seemed to be a hush over the crowd on the porch, and I noticed the sheriff standing at the edge of the porch watching the crowd watch us and then looking suspiciously at us himself. I felt my shoulders hunch as I circled up to the stage door, just a rickety wooden door painted white to blend with the rest of the building on the side at the back. I stopped the car, and Jean wouldn't let me kill the engine. She nodded for the girls to get out, then directed me to keep on going, back further into the dark shadow of the building and even further toward the trees where the clearing ended.

"Here. Park it right here." She smiled and touched my arm. "Now turn around, look right there. See that fire escape? That leads up to the balcony. You go on up there and knock four times like this." She sounded it out on the dash, and I nodded. "Get in there and find a seat or stand, what you can. Keep to yourself. I ain't got any idea what kinds of white folks come to our shows." Her accent seemed to take on new depths then, and it was as if, while she was finally home, comfortable, I was the itchiest in my skin I'd been since I ran away. She shook her head. "This is it, what you got in it for. Don't say I didn't warn you."

I wanted to protest. All I'd wanted was her, to be near her. I hadn't thought much beyond that.

The hairs on my arms and neck rose as she got out of the car and grabbed her bags before making her way across the lot to the stage door. I sat there a good five minutes before I moved. Finally, I got out and went to the trunk for my jacket. There under my jacket was the jug of gin, corked and hidden. I slid on the jacket, looking around. There wasn't a soul in sight, so I dug the jug out, uncorked it, and put it to my lips, letting it sting and then settle in my mouth before I swallowed. I took three gulps and put it back, hiding it as best I could. As it warmed my gut, I tucked my shirt in tighter, adjusted my tie, and buttoned my coat.

"I can take care of myself," I said, determined, but immediately checked around me to see if anyone had come out and could hear me. No one had. I smiled and strutted toward the fire escape, skipped steps and arrived on the platform a little out of breath. I had to do the knock twice before anyone answered. They opened the door and gave me a glare, pointed me to a seat to the far right by myself. There were seats all around me, but they were empty. I tried to keep my eyes on the closed curtain, keep to myself, but I couldn't. I peered over the ledge. The theater filled up. I'd never seen that many black folks all in one spot, not even at Small's, not even at the party where I talked to Jean Bailey the first time. I looked around the balcony, and there was only the man who let me in and two other men huddled up together on the other side.

The theater was nice, white with powder blue and gold trim, painted ornately on the ceiling and down the walls with designs and scrolls of writing I couldn't read from my distance. The curtain was blue velvet and the stage a deep mahogany. There was a small orchestra pit just like at the Ortilly, and the band, all black, was setting up, tuning their instruments.

Just as the theater lights went down and the stage lights rose, the balcony door opened, and a silver glow lit up the balcony. I turned just as a delicate black-gloved hand, jeweled and sparkling in the incoming moonlight reached in. The man who had glared at me reached for the hand, gave it a kiss, and helped the woman over the threshold. She was a white woman, very thin, and dressed in a loosely hanging calf-length gown, silken and white with its black-lined and jeweled waistline at her hips. Her chest and neck, almost to her face, were shielded in a white boa with several random black feathers mixed into it. She wore a white hat, tilted to the side with a black veil over her eyes. White, delicate and billowing feathers sprang from the hat, and she held similar feathers, but larger ones, as a fan in the other hand. They were very much like the feather that Jean had held in her dressing room, and I got a sudden gut punch that made me squirm in my seat.

The woman was followed by two small men dressed in dark suits, each with pastel shirts and flowers on their lapels, one in pink and one in yellow. They sat across the aisle from me, and the woman placed the feather in the seat beside her and removed her gloves and hat. She was beautiful with delicate features to match her hands. She had a long thin nose, high cheekbones, smooth and glistening in the reflection of the faraway stage lights. I recognized that face. It was the woman I'd met at intermission, the woman with the film connection, Mrs. Pickard. But neither man was her husband. I scanned the balcony to see if I'd missed him when I came in. She was there without him, with these two men.

The show had begun, but I was more interested in Mrs. Pickard than what was on stage. She whispered to one of the men, giggling and waving her feather at him. She never caught my stare. It was as if she hadn't even noticed I sat directly across the aisle from them. The two men also seemed oblivious to me, though they sat to her right, closer to me.

When an act ended, Mrs. Pickard applauded and her two men followed suit. The one closest to me gave a whistle and she giggled again. The doorman shushed them, and they hunkered down in their seats, all three of them giggling like children.

The orchestra began with a boom, taking my attention away from Mrs. Pickard and her men. It seemed all the instruments were playing at once. The houselights went completely dark with the stage lights, and then one single spotlight came up, and through the curtain, Jean Bailey appeared. She was dressed in an all-white tuxedo, a formal one with tails and a black bow tie, cane and top hat. She took off her hat and bowed to the crowd. The orchestra died down, and the curtains spread, revealing a black baby grand piano. She sat, flipping her tails up over the seat, and she began to play. The tune was quick and hopping, and the crowd stood and danced about as if they were at a show not to watch, but to dance.

Jean Bailey rippled her fingers down the keyboard and ended with a thump, only to start playing again, more softly now, hunkering down to the keys as if to hear them. Then banged out a chord and another, hard and loud and then she began singing, full voiced and full of twang. The crowd cheered, shouting and clapping. It was a song they knew—a raunchy song I'd never heard. She danced at the piano as she sang and played.

Jelly roll, jelly roll
Sitting on a fence.
If you don't get it
You ain't got no sense.

Now I'm wild about my jelly
'Bout my sweet jelly roll.
When you taste my jelly
You wanna take me right home.

Mrs. Pickard let out a loud laugh, a grunt almost, at the chorus and then put her hand over her mouth. She sat on the edge of her seat holding up opera glasses. Just as she let them drop, she turned her head and noticed me. I smiled. She did not. The smile on her lips faded, and she turned, put the glasses back to her face, dropped them and looked over at me again, and then leaned back in her seat, whispering to the man beside her.

When the song was over, Jean Bailey left the stage again for a different act. I stood, mustering up all the courage I could and made my way across the aisle to the row of seats behind them, sat down and interrupted.

"Yes?" Mrs. Pickard said, covering half her face with her feather.

"Mrs. Pickard," I whispered, "Mr. Frank, we met earlier."

"Yes. I know who you are." She turned around. The two men didn't even acknowledge my presence.

"Mrs. Pickard, I just wanted to see if I could talk with you about Jean Bailey again, now that you've seen her perform a bit more."

She turned around and peered at me. Her eyes were green, greener than mine, but a light green, and seemed to almost glow in the darkness with a translucent iridescence. And empty. She seemed so empty and far away. "Sure, why don't you come around here and join us." She gave a grin and turned around again.

I stood, catching a glimpse of the stage. It was a comedy act very similar to one we'd just seen at Ortilly's. I walked around to the other side of the aisle and took the empty seat next to Mrs. Pickard. She smelled like lilacs and powder with a hint of booze and cigarettes, but she was lovely. Her delicate hands sat in her lap, one clasping the feather. "So, what can I do for you?"

Just as I was about to speak, she stopped me and stopped the two men beside her in mid-conversation about the comedy act. "I am so rude. Please excuse me. These are my acquaintances, Mr. Joseph Williams and Mr. Randolph Jackson. Boys, Mr. Frank." I shook their hands, conscious that mine were sweaty and a bit soiled next to their pristinely manicured hands. We exchanged nods, and they went back to their conversation. "Now, where were we?" She smiled again and looked into my face.

I rambled nervously about Jean Bailey, her talent, star quality, her beauty, what she could bring to film, bumbling as I tried to sound like I knew what I was talking about. "I feel quite confident she could be a star in films."

Mrs. Pickard scrunched up her face. "That's all well and nice, but you're forgetting one big problem."

I stared back in confusion.

"As my husband pointed out earlier, your talent is a Negro. There are no Negro film stars. There is no need for Negroes, not Negro actresses in pictures. People don't want to see such things."

"What people? There aren't any yet, but there could be. We could be revolutionary. We—you—could be the first to make that happen." As the words left my mouth, I believed them and felt that I was, in my own way, revolutionary. It sent a jolt through my body, as if I'd been lit with a cold fire.

She fanned herself and tuned back to the show. Jean Bailey took the stage again. Jean's presence seemed to change Mrs. Pickard's demeanor, as if she woke up a little, was paying attention. Without taking her eyes off the stage, off Jean Bailey, she said, "And what would she do on the screen. Can she act?"

"You see her now. She's performing, acting in a way. Really, Mrs. Pickard, she's already a star, that's clear."

Mrs. Pickard took up another cigarette, and I fumbled to light it. I lit my own, and we both watched Jean Bailey tap out another tune on the piano. But then I could feel Mrs. Pickard's eyes on me.

"I don't know what that singer can do without sound," she said, finally, turning back to the stage.

"Aren't there films with sound now? Isn't that the new thing?" I was earnest.

She laughed and scrunched up her face again. Then she turned to me and furrowed her brow, pursed her lips. It was as if there was someone else now behind her face making the muscles move into place and freeze. Her eyes were clearer still, almost colorless. And a look of recognition swept across her face.

"Mr. Frank, if that really is your name, I will talk of no such nonsense with you. I know who, or at least I know *what* you are." She pulled her head back as if to get a better inspection of me, my clothes, my body. "You best be watching your step around here. We don't take to your kind or *hers*." She nodded toward the stage. "Now, if you don't mind, I'm going to get back to letting the niggers entertain me."

I was stunned. I sat back in my seat and finished my smoke, putting it out in the little ashtray on the armrest. The two men leaned forward and nodded for me to return to my seat. I didn't move. Mrs. Pickard got up and crossed in front of me. The two men shifted seats, each sitting on either side of me. I started to get up, but Mr. Williams, I think it was, put his hand on my arm, stopping me and leaned over to Mr. Jackson.

"You 'member that old crazy loon that lived out on Carson's Bluff?"

Mr. Jackson grinned, his forehead seeming too meaty for his face and protruding. "Ah, you mean that sissy boy? What a sight. Whatever happened to that old boy?"

"You 'member, dontcha? They found him down at the bottoms, weren't much left really, just a sack of meat—in a dress!"

They both laughed at that.

"In a dress!" Mr. Jackson roared, and then leaned in. "You know I heard they'd cut off his pecker! Found it down the road a ways." Then he looked at me. "I'm sorry, *ma'am*. Ain't right we talk like this in front of a lady, is it?"

My gut churned, and I immediately imagined Jewel, his pink gown all torn about him and lying in a crumpled, defeated mess. I wanted to run out of there, but they had me pinned in my seat, if not by force, by suggestion.

Mr. Williams leaned in, looking over his shoulder and then back at the stage and nodded, "You know that there is illegal. Can't a body *impersonate* the opposite sex or the law will step on in nowadays."

"Just as well. Guess that sissy boy might have kept his member had it been a law."

At this they both leaned back in their seats and crossed their arms. I was hesitant to reach for the armrest to push out of my seat, but when they didn't stop me, I got up.

I walked to the door and out into the lot again, my hands shaking. The moon had moved almost directly over the theater, and it was bright, so bright I could see all the cars, horses, and buggies. There was no arrangement to them, no pattern of parking the way there was in Chicago or in downtown Augusta. They were just there, all stopped where they stopped, and we'd parked along the edge, almost in the trees.

As soon as I reached the car, I fumbled around for my smokes and realized they'd probably fallen out of my pocket onto the seat in the theater. The moonlight spotted the hood of the car and me. I watched the spots dance in the slight, hot breeze. My jaw ached from clenching my teeth, my stomach knotted and sore from nerves.

I had crawled into the back seat, trying to pass out when I heard a woman laughing behind me outside the car. I checked the rearview mirror and hunched back down in the seat. "Shit," I whispered, and then regretted it. I could see myself now all mangled at the bottom of a cliff, those two goons standing over me, laughing. It made me want to be sick.

Mrs. Pickard was laughing wildly and stumbling down the steps, the two men at her side. They hadn't heard nor seen me. My windows were a bit fogged up by now from my breathing. They disappeared around the other side of the theater, and I heard a car start, then headlights drove away into the distance. I was relieved. I curled back up on the seat awhile. After what seemed like hours, I could have sworn I heard Jean Bailey singing all the way out in the car. I pulled myself up and out and back up the staircase. And, though the doorman shook his head, he let me in. I sat myself in the very same seat that Mrs. Pickard had taken, took up my pack of smokes and lit a cigarette, holding it in my still quivering lips. I leaned back in the seat and let it fill my lungs.

Jean Bailey was on stage again, still in her tuxedo, but the tie was untied, the shirt unbuttoned down to her cleavage. She shook her chest for the crowd and they hollered. The curtains opened up behind her, and she introduced a man from New Orleans, the man that had played the cornet for her at the last show. He played the trombone now, letting out a wail like a woman's wail. It was a sad wail, but as soon as he'd let it out, he took a breath and hopped it up. Then all the horns joined in. This music was different, jazzy and wild, but Jean Bailey could sing with anything. She let it rip, one raunchy song after another. The crowd echoed every bold lyric she put out for them, every singsong chorus, and they knew every response. And, finally, for her last song she sang about us, about me, how we were bulldaggers. Although it made my cheeks hot, made me afraid and shaky, I was proud, proud to be there, be who she was talking about in the song. She announced the song as the "Mannish Woman Blues."

The girls joined her on stage and swayed with each other behind her, making eyes at her, her making eyes at them. They flirted, making kissy faces and wiggling their rears.

We gona get on top,
And you gonna bring your daddy to town.
Daddy, call me daddy?
"Daddy!" The crowd and the girls sang back.

I smoked my cigarette, mumbling "Daddy," swaying to the music. In my gut, I was pissed and scared, but my pride, my desire won out. I knew she'd be mad at me for not listening to her, but hoped she'd let it go, make me feel better. I could feel Jean Bailey's voice from my mouth on down to between my thighs. I felt a blush rise in my neck as I let myself picture her hands on me, kissing me. I closed my eyes and let the song wash over me.

CHAPTER SIXTEEN

When the curtain was finally drawn and the theater cleared out and empty but for the ushers, I dragged myself from the seat and let myself out. The doorman and the other men in the corner who'd I'd all but forgotten were long gone. It was much darker, the moon having gone below the trees. There were only a few cars still left in the clearing around the theater.

But there were a slew of people at the stage door, waiting for someone to open it up. I walked on to the car, trying not to be noticed, and got into the driver's seat again. I was almost asleep when the girls piled in. Jean Bailey was the last to arrive and slid into the seat beside me, her eyes worn down and watery, her makeup smeared just a tad from sweating under the lights. She was still in her tux, but had her feathers all about her.

"We're going to a party, ladies!" she said.

"Woo-hoo!" Tasha squealed. Rosie was quiet, and I didn't turn around to look, but I imagined she was shaking her head and staring out the window.

Jean motioned for me to get out so she could drive. As we passed each other around the back of the car, she stopped me. "What happened to you? You look like you been scared half to death."

"Nothing." I shrugged her off and went around and got in. My stomach ached from my nerves.

"What happened, Frankie?" Tasha squealed, and I put my head in my hands.

"Woo, Mr. Frank got herself into something, didn't she?" Rosie jeered.

Jean Bailey had started the car and slid into the seat. "She don't want to talk about it. Now let her alone." She jerked the car in reverse and pulled out. We drove all the way back to town, through downtown again and then to a side street and to a building that looked like a department store with ornate apartments all lit up above it. We took the side fire escape entrance, and, just as we reached the landing, I stopped to catch my breath. Jean stood waiting beside me.

"I figured we'd have to get on the road, Jean," I gasped.

"Naw. We got a whole week before the next show, but we gonna head out tomorrow or the next day. Oh, you poor thing," Jean said and took my shaking hands in hers. "What'd I tell ya though, Frankie? You lucky you ain't dead." She raised an eyebrow at me.

"I know. But I was just trying—"

"Never mind. Just know I know these parts better than you, white or not, and you are two things they don't care for around here, bulldagger and nigger lover."

I gasped again, fighting back the picture in my mind the men had left with me.

"What? Am I wrong?" she asked.

I shook my head. I was fighting tears, more embarrassment than anything else. She smiled, touching my face boldly. It was the sweetest touch she'd ever given me, her eyes looking into mine. "I promise, you'll like this party. Now buck up. I'm taking you to a real buffet flat, girl."

She took my hand and pulled me on. Her hand was soft, and I felt the folds against mine. I followed her in, sticking close to her side.

A single swinging bulb lit the hallway. It was damp and humid inside, and I thought that if I touched the walls, white but smudged and dirty, I would feel the condensation. There were three wooden doors. We went to the end, the last door, and knocked. The girls had been ahead of us and had already gone inside, I supposed. A woman asked for the word.

"Ain't no word. This is Bailey." And the door opened to a tall, slender black woman dressed in an off-white sequined gown cut just above the knee and so low in the front I could just about see her belly button.

"Bailey! I've missed you! Come on in here!"

Jean slipped her a wad of cash.

"Lordy, Jean, I'm gonna raise rent and buy a new dress!" She took the money and threw her arms around Jean's neck and kissed her on the mouth. Over Jean's shoulder, she squinted her eyes at me, drew back and whispered, "Who's this?"

Jean introduced me to Miss Josephine *Champagne* Sherman. She held out her dainty but ungloved hand, which I took and kissed softly, looking into her eyes, before I let it go. "Oh she's a charmer, Bailey. Mmmmhmmm."

Jean smiled back at me.

"Ladies, welcome to Miss Champagne's buffet flat! It ain't all big city like up in Chicago, but come on in and make yourself at home. Refreshments are in the kitchen, some sundries up here, and well, the party, that's in the back. And, Bailey, your room's all ready. Thought you'd be here last night, but—no, no excuses. We have you now. Enjoy." She spread her arms and welcomed us in.

Jean pulled me behind her. I was still stiff with nerves but felt my muscles loosen up a bit as we moved through the crowd, white, black—every single one of them women. The apartment was small but warm with gauzy curtains on the long windows in the front room and matching material draped over the lamps, creating a hazy light to mix with the smoke from three women lounging on the divan smoking from long cigarette holders ornately decorated in silver or sequins. A fair-skinned black woman dressed in red, wearing glistening red lipstick, black gloves, and a hat with a slim red feather to match sat on the end of the couch closest to the opening to the kitchen where we were headed. When we passed, she blew smoke up in my direction, raising her chin at me, and then after she inspected me, an inspection that landed on my behind, she gave me a sly smile. A white woman sat close by in a wide, velvet-trimmed chair by the window sipping on a drink. She was dressed only in a silk robe, red and black with a floral design. Her bright blue eyes were lined in black, stretching almost to her temples in a point, and her lashes were long, too long, whipping out to the sides of her eyes. She flitted them when she sipped and then stared out the window.

The music from the phonograph was loud and boisterous, jazzy and without a singer. Two women in the kitchen danced like flappers, kicking up their feet in the back and swinging their arms about in rhythm with the music. They yelled over the music and motioned for us to join. One of the women was dressed in a fringe-covered dress, all blue, and a headband with a little jewel at her brow. The other woman was wearing a suit, a man's suit, but tailored to fit her curves. Her hair wasn't slicked back but cropped and worn in finger waves. Jean guided me through them, dancing, both of us moving with them and through them in the black and teal tiled kitchen. The kitchen held a matching teal icebox on the floor to the back. It had a padlock on it, but it was open. Inside was ice, and among the ice, big rounded bottles like I'd never seen.

"Champagne?" Jean asked.

I'd never even seen champagne, but I knew what it was. I'd heard my uncle's friends talk about it, the bubbles, saying it was closer to a pop than liquor.

I nodded. Jean poured me a glass. It was a slender flute and crystal I was sure. I'd seen an entire case of crystal in the front room, all lined up and lighted by a tiny lamp behind them. Jean poured me a glassful. I eyed the glass, watched the bubbles rise to the top, smiling at my own reflection, wide-eyed and amazed. "How does Miss Champagne get all of this?"

Jean shook her head. "No one knows. All we know is she's always got a fresh supply, and always rolling in the dough. But that's why we call her Champagne, and that's why we all come back. Well, that and a few other reasons."

We toasted and drank a big gulp. The bubbles tickled my nose but the drink was almost sweet like it was flavored with perfume or flowers. We filled our glasses again and left the kitchen. Through the front room was another long hall. It was then I realized that Miss Champagne's apartment took that whole side of the floor and possibly the other side as well. Those other doors outside led to other rooms whose doors were down this very hall. There was a bright light at the end of the hall, and Jean squeezed my hand and I held on tight.

"You ready?"

I didn't know what I was or wasn't ready for, so I shrugged. She smiled and led me to the back. It was a wide, long room like a dance hall, but no one was dancing. White curtains divided the room, and the section we walked into was bright white, draped in more white curtains. There was a red velvet divan directly in front of us. A very scantily clad woman was lying back on the divan. She smoked through an extra-long holder, blowing smoke up in the air into little rings. There was a circle of women surrounding her, watching her blow the rings.

I spotted Tasha and Rosie directly across from us in the circle. Jean nodded at them, and they waved, just as another woman came up from behind them and put her thin arms around their waists. It was her, Mrs. Pickard. And she gave me a glare, and a sly little smile to Jean. I turned up my glass of champagne ignoring the foaming bubbles in my mouth and choked it down.

"Slow down there, pretty. That shit'll sneak up on you."

I held my glass out for her to refill it.

Jean took my glass but raised an eyebrow at me. "What's the problem, Frankie?"

I knew my face had gone pale again. "That woman. That woman with Tasha and Rosie."

"What are you talking about? What in the world could that little woman do to you?"

"No, some guys with her—earlier—at the show." I wasn't explaining well. I couldn't explain it all right then and there.

"Well, that's what you get for getting all mixed up with those good old boys and their women. I told you to keep to yourself, Frankie."

She smiled but pulled her hand away.

"I wasn't trying to—Mrs. Ortilly introduced us. She's the cousin of some big movie house owner. I was trying to help you out!" I tried to keep my voice down, but I was sounding like Ms. Laura's stage whispering attempts. The women around us stopped muttering about the party and started muttering, I was sure, about us.

Jean was suddenly interested and scanning the crowd. The three women were gone from the circle. "What did you say?"

"I just told her how great I thought you'd be. Then she had her boys threaten me—well, in so many words." I couldn't bring myself to repeat the story they'd told me.

"Ladies."

We both looked up and there she was behind us, arm in arm with Tasha and Rosie.

"Ma'am." Jean stuck out her hand. "I'm Jean Bailey."

"I know who you are, and I am sure your little trollop has told you who I am."

"Excuse me, ma'am?"

"Oh dear, I'm sorry. And please, Mr. Frank, forgive my manners earlier. Those boys. They just don't know how to talk to a lady, especially a lady like you." She was rich, a snot, and she suddenly made my skin crawl—however beautiful she was, however pleasant she sounded, and however much she could do for Jean. I wanted to reach right into her sockets and pluck out those scary eyes.

Jean cleared her throat and put her arm around my waist. "I'm sorry. I'm not sure I got your name."

"Ashley Pickard. Call me Ashley." They shook hands with a delicate grasp.

"I see you've met my girls," Jean said and nodded to Tasha and Rosie but pulled me in tighter.

"Yes, yes I have. They have wonderful things to say about you." She squeezed them into her, and they both grinned.

"I'm sure they do." Jean grabbed my hand and turned around to watch the now empty red couch and scan the circle.

"Well, it was very nice to meet you. We're going on to the next room. I hope you'll join us soon, Jean." The three disappeared through the crowd again.

I was relieved, but Mrs. Pickard's leaving left me the only white girl in the room, and as the women around us huddled together in little circles of conversation, I felt suddenly out of place, alone, though Jean was by my side. A woman bumped me getting closer to the couch as if to see something, but no one was on the couch. I stumbled away from Jean. She reached to grab my hand, but missed, and I almost fell. The women glared, hateful—at me. I regained my footing but didn't squeeze back through the crowd to Jean, just stood there outside the circle. When Jean didn't make her way to me, I inched to the wall and leaned against it, but kept my cool, my cocky stance. A song started up. It sounded closer, closer than the phonograph in the front room that was now being drowned out. The song was slow, seductive, and a path cleared in the crowd. A woman came through. She had dyed red hair, light skin, and was wearing a long satin and velvet trimmed dress with tiny straps. She sauntered out to the couch and the crowd closed in around her. I couldn't see what she was doing and didn't try. Finally, Jean weaved her way out of the crowd and back to me.

"I wondered where you'd gone off to," she said and grabbed my hand, pulling me off the wall.

"Did you not see that woman almost knock me down?"

"Yes, I tried to grab you but missed."

"Why'd you leave me out here so long?"

Jean turned to me, surprised. "Frankie, what is wrong with you? You have traveled halfway around the country, by yourself.

Why the hell would you need me to come over here and rescue you?"

I shrugged. I didn't know why, but I wanted her to.

"Come on, girl. You gonna have to grow some thicker skin to hang around with me." She squeezed my hand. "Maybe this will help." She leaned in to kiss me, right then and right on the mouth, her soft lips against mine, right there in that bright room with all those women. I could feel the stares but I didn't care. I was finally with Jean Bailey. I was hers. I wrapped my arm around her waist and then brought one hand up to her neck and pulled her in, kissed her back. My stomach jumped, and I felt again like I did when she sang, her voice plummeting through me like fire down into my stomach, making my legs go all weak and trembling. Her lips went to my neck, then back to my mouth again, and then she pulled away and smiled. "Damn," she said.

Ashley Pickard had come back, alone this time, and eased over to us and up to Jean's back, dancing into her. Jean turned around, saw who it was and then turned to me and rolled her eyes. She leaned in to kiss me again.

"Let's get out of this crowd," she whispered and pulled me toward the door.

As we turned to leave the room, Ashley raised an eyebrow at Jean, as if in warning. Jean just shook her head.

I grinned so big I could feel it all over my face. And we walked away, down the hall and into a room, a bedroom with an iron bedstead with deep burgundy drapery. There were no windows and only a simple vanity and chair in the room. The bed looked rumpled and slept in, and the sheets were crumpled up to one side, the pillows wadded up at the top. Not at all how we would have left my uncle's rent rooms.

I could hear the phonograph in the front room again. It was blaring out a rambunctious blues song, and I could almost see the hips swaying in the front room to the same beat as the stomping feet. Jean lit a candle on the vanity and then led me in by the hand and shut the door behind us. She put her hand on my face and kissed me softly, unbuttoning my shirt with her other hand, and then running the hand over my stomach and around my back, pulling me to her. She reached up to my breasts softly gliding her hand over my bind, grabbing at the gauze that pressed my breasts down. I stopped her.

"You want me to pretend you're not a girl, Frankie?" she asked.

"No. I just—I just. I'm—"

"Spit it out, woman." She laughed.

"I'm a—" I stopped, because I wanted to say virgin, but I wasn't sure it was the same thing with a woman. "I mean I've—I've never done this before."

Her face softened. "Oh honey, it's okay. Do you want to?"

"Yes," I answered without hesitation. "But, can I ask you something?"

She nodded.

"What, I mean, who are Tasha and Rosie, really? Who are they to you?"

She let her hands fall. "They're like my sisters, Frankie. Nothing more, really."

"I've never seen anybody act to their sisters like you have to them." I crossed my arms over my chest and backed away.

She moved toward me, rubbing her hands up and down my arms. "Okay, okay. Tasha and I are lovers—Rosie and I have been too at some point. But I want you right now."

"Tasha's not gonna—"

"Yeah, I know. Tasha's jealous. But she knows me, knows how I am, just hasn't seen me with anyone else in a long time. They're my best friends, my family, Frankie."

"So I'll just be—"

"I'm with you, Frankie, right now, right here. Take it for what it is or—" She smiled and pulled me to her, kissed me, and then turned me around to face the vanity mirror. I didn't want to hear the rest any more than she wanted to say it. My head was spinning but she was touching me.

She slid my shirt off and unhooked the gauze. As she unwound it, she kissed my neck. When it was loose enough to fall on its own, she let it go, turned me to face her again and pushed me down on the bed. She was over me before I got my bearings, kissing me, my neck, my mouth. Her one hand held her up while her other worked at the buttons on my pants. She slid her mouth to my ear. Her breath was warm, and I felt it all the way down my shoulder. It was as if she touched me, my skin with her very breath. Her shirt was open, and her flesh was glistening through it. I could smell her through her clothes, a deep musk mixed with something sweet like lilacs. I'd never smelled the lilacs on her, and I got a flash of Ashley, her face as she watched us in the other room. Disgust and lust all mixed together and rolled over her tiny features, blushing her cheeks, deepening her color against her white gown as she fanned herself with the feather.

Jean stopped. "Frankie?"

Her honey eyes seemed more innocent, younger then than they ever had, her laugh lines softer, her face smoother.

I shook my head. "I'm okay," I mumbled and rolled on top of her.

A wide smile spread across her lips. "Gonna top me, huh?"

"What?"

"You gonna take control, be on top, top me?"

I grinned and leaned in to kiss her again. Her lips were swollen and hot, and I let my tongue dance over them and into her mouth, warm, soft and wet. Her shirt was open and her chest bare. I ran my hand between her breasts and then cupped one in my hand, running my fingers slowly over her nipple. She closed her eyes, let out a small breath. I wanted to touch every inch of her, her warm dark skin almost glowing under my pale hand. I ran my hand down over her stomach. It was muscular with a layer of soft flesh curving it out at the belly button. I kissed her belly button, letting my tongue pulse there. I sat up straddling her and she sat up to kiss me again down my neck and then pressed her mouth over my nipple before falling back to the bed again.

My trousers were loose about my hips and she found her way into them with what seemed like no effort. As she slid her one hand to me, touching me, with her other hand she took my hand and pushed it between my legs and then hers. I fumbled with the clasp on her trousers and then slid my hand in them, finding her folds, wet and slick. We rocked there and she moaned a deep, almost startling moan and pulled me to her, grabbing my hair, pulling my head back and arching my back, pushing me further and further into her. Her body pulsed, grasping my hand and releasing it.

She let out her breath and flipped me over again. She kissed at my stomach, ran her tongue over my nipples, my stomach, and pulled me out of my trousers. She put her whole mouth on me, smooth, silken, warm, like a bath, like being inside of her. I couldn't stop moving, rocking my hips to her mouth, until I shook and writhed without a sound but breathing hard now. She held me there, and when I stopped trembling, she sat up again to kiss at my neck, my cheeks, and my mouth. She fell into me and tangled her arms and legs into mine, resting her head against my neck.

* * *

Hours later, I woke up to a single slit of light that slid under the doorway. I squinted my eyes at it and rolled over. The bed was empty but for me and the pillows. I heard laughing, a soft slow song, and clinking of glasses. I rolled off the bed and stumbled to my feet, the room dark and shifty. I felt around on the bed, between the cotton sheets, and found my shirt. I threw it on and pulled on my trousers.

As I eased the door open, the light was blinding. The back, where all the people had been, was dark. There was a yellow light still humming from the front room. The air was hot and still, and I only half-buttoned up my shirt as I left the room and moved toward the sound, tiptoeing, barefoot. Down the long hall, the voices became clearer—Jean's, Tasha's, Champagne's, and laughs I didn't recognize.

"Fold!"

"Damn, woman!"

Most everyone at the party had left, and the only ones still there were a small group of women, Jean and Tasha included, some fully clothed, some half-clothed, and some naked, each with a handful of cards, sitting around a table that had been moved to the middle of the room. It was a large green felt-covered table, poker chips scattered across it. Two women sat on the couch, lounging back and sipping drinks. Tasha stood, wearing only an undershirt and panties, right behind Jean, whose back was to me. Jean tossed her hand onto the table. I felt invisible.

"I guess I gotta take this off now."

"Yes, ma'am, you do! About damn time!" Champagne said over her cards.

As Tasha stepped back, Jean scooted her chair back and went to unbutton her shirt. She turned her head and caught my eye. "Hi, darlin'."

I tried to smile, to wipe the timidity from my face.

"Come on over here." She held out her hand and motioned me over.

Tasha backed away and sat down on the couch next to one of the women, almost right in her lap, and the woman put her arm around her.

I went over to Jean and sat in Tasha's chair. Jean leaned in and kissed me on the cheek.

"All right, all right, lovebirds. You got your man now. Now get that shirt off, Jean!" Miss Champagne said. She was already half undressed herself.

"Oh, hell, okay, okay. Baby, won't you help a girl out?"

I stood and pulled the shirt from her shoulders and draped it over the back of the chair. It was the first time she'd called me baby, and I could feel the warm smile spreading on my face as I sat again.

Another hand was dealt, and another, and another. They passed a jug of gin, and we all swigged. The record stopped, and Jean asked me to select another. "They are right there, lined up beside the player. Find something…soothing," she said, her words slurred, slower, and the lines around her eyes deeper.

I rose and found a record. Just as I was placing a new one on and lifting the needle, I heard loud stomps, men's voices, and a pounding at the door down the hall. They stopped, then moved closer. I dropped the needle, and it made a screech. I grabbed it again and placed it to the side. Jean was shaking her head and grasping for her shirt, but no one else moved, frozen, their smiles sliding from their faces. Jean motioned for me toward the kitchen. "Hide," she said.

I ran into the kitchen. Within seconds, the men were inside, and I could hear the women scrambling for their clothes, squealing, covering themselves, running about the room, tripping over chairs. It was the police, I realized, and my stomach lurched. I was underage—a runaway—at a buffet flat with black women and liquor. I could only imagine what they'd do with me. I slowly opened up the cabinet door, moved a few bowls and rags and made just enough room for me to curl up and squeeze in. I ducked, pulling my knees up to my chest and made myself into a ball, pulling the door closed behind me.

"Line up, ladies. Face the wall, hands behind your back."

"What are you arresting us for? This is a private residence!" I didn't know who said it, but I heard a slap, and then there wasn't any more talking, just the men yelling orders at the women.

I heard footsteps come into the kitchen, and I squeezed myself tighter until they turned and went back into the front room. There were footsteps pacing down the long hall, doors opening, slamming shut.

"All right, let's go," I heard a man say and then walk out the door, closing it loudly behind him.

Minutes later, the whole place was silent, deafeningly silent. I stayed wadded up in that ball for a long time. My foot was asleep, and my neck was burning from the strain. I had to pee. Wide-eyed, I pushed the door open and stiffly unfolded myself, falling into a loose heap on the stark tile. The teal green of the kitchen made me feel sick as I rubbed at my eyes in the light.

When I opened my eyes again, Champagne was standing over me, dressed in a housedress, cotton and worn, her makeup smeared, her hands on her hips.

"Pussy. Damn white pussy!" she said.

I scrambled to my knees and then to my feet. I had no idea why she was still there. I thought everyone had been arrested.

"How the hell? Oh, never mind." She waved her hand as if to dismiss me.

I looked around and the place was empty. "Did they take Jean?"

"Of course they did," she said and sat down at the poker table and lit a cigarette.

"How come you didn't get arrested?"

"Oh hell, girl, I bought them boys off a long time ago."

"Well, we have to get them out!"

She looked startled for a moment and then left the room. I followed. Her strides were long and deliberate, down the hallway. She swept into an open door at the end. "Get in here and put this on. We can't have them figuring out what you are, and they would." As I rounded the doorframe, she threw a frock at me. It was simple but dressier than her housedress. It was thick and coarse, a wide collar and a belt at the waist. "Go on. Put it on."

I turned to go to the bedroom where I'd slept, but stopped, stood still. "I need to pee."

"Fine. Down the hall."

I left the room and went down the hall. I peed and changed my clothes. I wasn't wearing any underclothes, and I hadn't bothered to wrap my breasts up again. Even though I was dressed when I walked back in the room, I felt more naked than I'd ever been. I pulled my arms about me.

"Stop that." She walked toward me. "Take your hands away."

She came over to me, ran her finger down the front of me, eyeing me up and down. She walked around me, looking.

My throat burned.

"Are you about to cry? Oh, hell, child. I ain't that bad. I just wanted to look." She stepped closer. I flinched and tears slipped down my face.

"I just wanted you to know what it feels like."

"What? Why?" I was almost shouting through my crying.

She laughed. "That's Jean Bailey's life, girl, and if you ain't helping her, you're just one of those men, or women, that eat her up." She looked sternly at me then, my cropped hair, my white skin.

I crossed my arms over my chest again and moved away from her.

"I let you white women in mostly because you bring the money, but you remember this: you don't *belong*. This is a black woman thing. Ya hear? Bailey, she is a black woman, and you, you just ain't, and this thing won't last. You don't understand her; you can't. She'll get what she needs from you and move on, move on back to the women she really loves, or the men."

I wondered if she was talking about herself. I wondered who the women, or who the men Jean really loved were. "I don't care. I love her, and I want to help get her out. So what can we do?"

"You know it ain't likely they'll let her out with you. Might even lock you up too, or worse."

"Don't care if they do. I came this far, ain't no reason to skip out now." I wasn't sure of where my gumption had come from, but I knew I had to get her out, get her back to me.

She shook her head. "Get your hair presentable, as much as you can, and then you're gonna take me to Bailey's car so I can get the cash she has stashed in the trunk."

She left the room. I didn't think there was any money in the car, figured she'd had her money on her, but sure enough, when we checked, there it was, divided evenly into two separate stashes in a box in the trunk.

Champagne was dressed in a woman's suit now, hat and gloves to match. I closed the trunk, and we left, walking the five blocks to the police station, right off the other side of the square by the market. The sun was just about to come up, and the sky was pink and orange above us in the clouds. The streets were empty, completely deserted.

"I can't believe she still keeps her money stashed like that in her trunk. That low-down cheat of a husband of hers gonna keep her scared and running forever, I guess."

"Husband?" I stopped.

She grabbed her stomach and laughed hard, covering her mouth to muzzle the noise. "You didn't know? Oh, my! Yes, Jean's married. Been married half her life to a sissy boy from where she grew up. It was more like she adopted him than married him though. And, by God, he sure has given her a run for her money."

Champagne explained that they'd grown up together, like cousins almost. That Leroy, that was his name, had had a rough go about it, brought up bad or something and got into the drink, running liquor, but the real problem was that he was a drunk, an irresponsible one—a mean one.

"I guess he can't help it, but he used to beat the tar out of her. She got her kid and hid in New Orleans. She still loves the man, bless her soul, but she ain't about to let him get at her money or her kid."

I didn't ask about the kid, too, I was so stunned. But I didn't have to. Champagne realized I didn't know about that either and had a good laugh again. "She's got one little sissy boy she found in an orphanage somewhere, beat to hell."

"How old is he?"

"Oh, he's almost grown, pretty good on his own now, but she's had him since he was a tiny little thing."

We came up on the police station, a small building with bars on all the windows. There was a crowd of women standing around outside. It was the whole poker game crew from Champagne's, but I didn't see Jean.

One of the women saw us approach. She was wrapped in a blanket, still half naked. "It's about time, woman, too late though. We've been sprung!"

"Who the hell bailed you bitches out?" Champagne hollered at them.

"Wait a minute! How the hell didn't you get brung in?" Tasha demanded of me.

Champagne laughed. "I found this one curled up in my cupboard like a little mouse! Clever little cracker, ain't she?"

They all laughed as I scanned about looking for Jean.

"Where the hell is Bailey, anyway?" Champagne asked, and Tasha nodded over our shoulder to a car parked in front of the station. It was a brand-new car, nicer than Jean's even, and there were two women inside. The windows were a little fogged, and I could see they were in a heated discussion. It was Ashley Pickard and Jean. Ashley saw me over her shoulder and nodded in my direction. Jean turned around, and in a minute was out of the car and in front of me, reaching for my hands as the car pulled away.

I had been holding my breath, and I let it out, let my heart sink into my stomach and back up again. I handed over an envelope with the bundle of cash and Jean pulled me to her. "Thank you," she said in my ear. She hugged me and then put her arm around me as we walked back to Champagne's.

CHAPTER SEVENTEEN

When we reached Champagne's again, I was exhausted and took a seat on the couch in the front room. All I wanted to do was go to the bed we'd had the night before and curl up with Jean for a long sleep, but she had business with Champagne and went with her to the back. Just as I was about to doze off on the couch, Jean came back in, ready to roll.

"I'll need to change," I said as I stood up and rubbed my eyes.

But Champagne talked me into keeping the dress, so I bundled up and carried my other clothes.

Out at the car, Tasha and Rosie told Jean they were skipping out on her, said they'd meet us in Mobile. They'd wooed a couple of Champagne's girls, two of her customers, well-to-do black women from Atlanta who'd come over for the show. Tasha and Rosie had managed to talk the women into rolling them all down to the next show and footing the bill. Jean tossed them a look and turned without a sound to start up the car. Her mouth was set when she got in to drive, stiff and determined. I was glad we were alone.

We didn't speak until we were well outside of town. She turned down a winding dirt road, and came to a bridge I thought for sure would collapse, or she'd jerk the wheel just enough to take us plunging over the side into the dry, narrow creek below. I gripped the seat.

Jean laughed, a wide smile on her face.

"Where are we going?" I was sure this was not the way to Mobile, down on the coast.

"I'm going to stop out to see some of my people. We'll only be a little while."

"Did you live around here?" Though I already knew the answer to this, it was all I could think to say. My giddiness had turned to nervousness alone with her in her car.

"Down south a ways. My folks is peanut farmers. Got a whole farm to ourselves. But it don't pay the bills really, and I don't want to live with a dirt floor to match my yard all my life."

"Peanut farmers? I don't think I knew where peanuts came from."

She laughed. "What? You ain't seen a peanut plant before or a field of peanut plants?"

"No. I don't think—I wouldn't have known it if I had, I guess."

"Well, by God, you will. No wonder you hadn't had boiled peanuts before. You have eaten them regular though, right?"

"Of course." I knew my voice was cold and distant, and that she was trying to draw me out, but I didn't want to talk. I just wanted to hear her talk to me.

"Where did you think they came from?"

I shrugged. "I never thought about it much."

She shook her head. "If I could take you to my folks' farm right now, I would."

"Let's go." I tried to be chipper, show that I was interested.

After a while, she cleared her throat. "I'm afraid that even if I didn't have a show, or perhaps in spite of it, I can't ever go back there. My mama made that clear. Boy, damn, I miss it though. This time of year would be getting close to about harvest time, all the peanuts you could stand coming off those bushes. There was an old oak tree that had one big branch off to the side, a big old branch, and I'd get up there, swing my feet, and watch them bring them in. I'd sing church songs, and the songs my mama sang when she worked. I'd sing any old song I knew the words to and pretend there were people down below watching me. It's always been in me, the singing. I just couldn't help myself. But I tell ya, as much as I miss the home place, all I ever wanted was to get on out of there."

"I understand." And I did. I could see a younger Jean, her sweet, soft, dark face, her frilly cotton dress, swinging her bare feet, her bare legs from a tree. I could hear her sweet child's voice stretching and trying for the sounds she made now, those deep moans, those low notes, that bluesy, smoky sound. But I had a hard time fixing the place, the farm in my mind.

All I could see was my own home place, the pasture sprawled out from horizon to horizon, the trees lined up in their places along the creek banks. My little yellow room at the top of the house, hot and stuffy. My father out there in the pasture running the cows, my mother in the kitchen banging dishes, their faces falling in disappointment, their angry disapproval of me. A sinking feeling set in, my back ached, and my shoulders felt tired and heavy. As I got further and further away from home, I realized how much harder it would be to ever go back. I'd been so worried I'd get caught, that I'd be found and forced home or put away somewhere worse than that, worse than marrying me off. I missed them, but I was too afraid of them to suffer my sentimentality.

Even with the weight of it all, I felt calm as Jean drove over the bumpy road, up over a hill with a little house below. The house was surrounded by trees, live oaks and pines, and, just like back home, a slew of large pecan trees. There was an old black man in the front yard stooping and putting pecans in a wicker basket.

Even after all that had happened with Jean, I felt somehow connected to her, a connection she couldn't have with Tasha even. We were connected in our exile.

"I can't go home either," I confessed, and my stomach tightened. I didn't know if I was more afraid of not seeming grown enough, that she'd eventually insist I go home to my mama, that I was a danger to her, or if I was just afraid she didn't care, wasn't interested in where I'd come from and why I'd left. I wanted her to ask me, but as we pulled up to the front of the house, she turned her head to me.

"I know," she said and opened the car door.

The man in the yard stood up and a woman came out onto the porch with a broom in her hand.

"Jean Bailey!" The man held the basket up close to his body with one hand, waved with the other and then came running at us. "Ma! Jean Bailey's come!"

The woman shook her head and went to sweeping the porch.

Jean got up out of the car and hugged the man.

"Ma! Come on," the man said.

"Auntie Foy?" Jean yelled.

She continued to sweep at the dirt, ignoring them both. Jean motioned for me to get out of the car.

"This is Frankie—" When she hesitated, I realized that she had no idea what my last name was.

"Frances Corbin, sir." I stuck out my hand, surprised at myself for my forward friendliness.

He took my hand and introduced himself as William Jimmies.

"We call him Uncle Bill, and that over there is Aunt Foy," Jean clarified and walked across the yard.

"Auntie Foy? What's wrong? What'd I do?" Jean pleaded as she walked up onto the porch. Aunt Foy was still sweeping. About five feet away, Jean stopped and put her hands on her hips. "You do remember me, right? You ain't gone all senile on me have ya?" Jean moved in closer and bent a little toward her face. "Look here, it's me, Jean Bailey."

Ms. Foy swept a few more times and then she stopped. She shook her head and said, "Tsk, tsk, tsk. Jean Bailey, my foot." She finally cracked a smile. Jean smiled with her, and they embraced, mumbling about love and being gone so long. "Why ain't you wrote and tell a body you was coming, and what the hell are you wearing anyway?"

"Why, Auntie Foy, you won't come see me sing no way. Why warn ya?"

I stood close to Uncle Bill, who I could feel looking me over.

"When you gonna do yo mama proud and use your real name?"

"Aunt Foy, don't talk nonsense. Listen, listen here, meet Frankie." She motioned for me to come up on the porch.

She nodded politely at me and then looked out into the yard. "That your car, girl?"

"No, ma'am, that Jean's car," I said.

"Woo wee!"

"Brand new, still smells like leather," Jean Bailey said. "Don't worry Aunt Foy, there's still some to spread around."

"Oh, just you keep that grub to yourself. I can't take your money, and you know it. Your mama would have my hide and yours too she ever caught up with you."

"You know my mama ain't gonna say two bits to me ever again after that show I put on down there. Devil's work, she's convinced. And may be, what all I know, but I know I love it, and I know it can help folks like us out of the bushes. So you gonna take what I'm giving, but I ain't giving handouts. I want to know if you could put us up a few days here, Aunt Foy, Uncle Bill? What do ya say?"

Aunt Foy crinkled up her brow and leaned around Jean to look at me. "It ain't proper, chile, white girl up in here with all these black folks. Why don't you get her a nice place in town then come on out? I don't want no trouble."

I started to protest, say—I didn't know what I'd say, but Jean just nodded.

"Yes, ma'am, I understand."

"You girls can stay for dinner though. Now go on in the house and get you something cold to drink. Miss Elsie's in there by the stove as sure as anything."

"We're just gonna get some things out of the car, and we'll be in, Aunt Foy."

We both turned away and walked toward the car. I looked up into the trees, the hot sun pouring through them in spots across the yard, one giant spot directly over the car making it light up and look newer than it had in the moonlight the night before. The night before and the lack of sleep were starting to settle in my bones. All I wanted to do was grab a fan and sit under one of those great big live oaks with Jean Bailey, just stop, just listen, and just sleep next to her, her breathing on me, her arm draped across me, the warmth of her skin touching mine.

Jean took me around to the back of the car and opened the trunk. There were two packages shoved up in the back. She put one in my hand, grabbed the other, and we went inside.

"Mind that door, Miss Priss," Aunt Foy shouted as the screen door slammed behind us.

"Yes, ma'am," Jean said.

The house was dark, and I had to squint to see from being outside in the sun. In the parlor were lace curtains, camelback couches and chairs, and an old beat-up piano in the corner. There were stacks and stacks of newspapers and magazines beside every chair and in front of the woodstove. It seemed they saved them all year round for the stove. It was hot inside and a little damp, but once we moved to the back of the house, there seemed to be a lightness about the place. I could catch the sun coming in on the side, and the whole back of the house was a screen-covered window that had a long wooden awning propped up on the inside. Jean directed me to put down the package beside hers on one of the end tables in the hall. I followed her to the kitchen. The smell of beans with pork rose in the air. There was corn bread in the oven. My stomach growled audibly. It wasn't dinnertime quite yet, but there were two plates set out on the table.

"Miss Elsie!" Jean shouted. The woman turned, startled, and then ran up and hugged Jean. "This is Frankie," Jean said and nodded at me.

She greeted me politely and turned back to the stove and stirred. She was a stout old woman, dressed in a cotton shift and house shoes. "You girls get washed up now."

Jean led me to the back to the lavatory, what looked like a newly built-on room with just a sink and a toilet. We both washed our hands, and just as I was finishing up, Jean stood behind me, looking at me in the mirror, worry in her eyes. My own eyes were worry-free, but red-rimmed with dark circles underneath, like a child's after a long cry. I took a deep breath, and tried to wake up.

"I'm fine, just hungry," I said with a smile, anticipating her question. I needed sleep, but I needed food more. Even more than that, I needed to show Jean that I wasn't another silly girl, a runaway to boot, that she needed to worry about.

Our food was waiting for us. Aunt Foy, Miss Elsie, and Uncle Bill all pulled up chairs beside us as we ate. Mostly they wanted to know all about Jean's travels and shows. I was relieved. I didn't want to answer questions about myself. I ate more quickly and sloppily than I ever had before, and when I finished before anyone, the warm soupy beans settling inside my belly, I was embarrassed but did not turn down a second helping.

When we were all done, I felt as if I could drift off to sleep sitting up in that hard wicker chair.

"Why don't you girls lay down a bit before you go," Aunt Foy said, and we both jumped at the chance.

She put us in the parlor, each a couch to ourselves. I was asleep before my head hit the armrest. When we woke up, it was early evening, and we had to go. Miss Elsie loaded us up with corn bread and fruit, a jar of water and a jar of lemonade for the road.

Jean drove. When we finally made it out to the highway again, the setting sun made a big ball over the horizon and was reflecting blindingly off the road ahead, and I was relieved when it finally set. With the sun gone, it was cooler and we were more relaxed with each other and with the drive.

Jean leaned back a little and reached over to me, putting her hand on my leg. She'd glance at me and then back at the road and smile.

"What? What is it?" I asked.

"You are a pretty thing, ain't ya? Woo wee."

I blushed hard, relieved that it was dark enough now that she couldn't see. I lifted my chin. "Thank you," I said and tried a sheepish smile without looking over at her.

She laughed. "It's all right. I know you know you pretty. I like a girl that knows what she brings."

"I'm not that vain!" I protested halfheartedly, a flirtatious lilt to my voice, and smoothed down my hair. We both laughed. She slid her hand over mine and squeezed. My stomach was so giddy I could hardly sit still.

"Now, tell me about how you got down here." She took her hand back and put it on the wheel and leaned her other arm on the door, making as if to get comfortable for the story while she drove.

"What do you want to know?"

"Everything."

I told her all about the fight with my uncle, about sneaking out of the house and stealing the money from the shop, being determined to find her, and she told me about Georgia, about growing up poor with only her songs to get her out, her determination to get out.

We talked and drove all night and into the next day, and the next, barely stopping to eat or sleep on the side of the road. It seemed we made it across the South from one shady diner to another, eating separately, like we didn't know one another, me going in first and her coming around the back to the colored entrance, sitting sometimes in separate restaurants altogether. The napkins grew damper and damper as we made our way deeper and deeper into the South, closer to the coast.

Right outside of Georgia, we pulled over to pee and took turns squatting in the heat of the day, hiding in the tall weeds along the roadside.

As she got back in the car, Jean let out a sigh and started driving again. Without looking over at me she said, "I really like you, Frankie, my little bull in a dress." She laughed. "Your crazy white ass followed me halfway across the country and hunted me down—AND, as Miss Champagne told me, you was willing to put yourself on the line to come bail me out of jail when you'd gotten away scot-free. Damn. Ain't nobody ever done anything like that for me before, especially some little cracker bull."

The memory of seeing her in the car with Mrs. Pickard shot through me then, but I pushed it away. She put her hand on my thigh and leaned back in the seat. I could feel myself smile, could feel her draw me in. "I like you too, Jean." It was probably the dumbest thing I could say, but it was what came out. We both laughed and she put her hand over mine.

"It wasn't my money though," I said. "Hell, I didn't even know you had it."

"And I'm damn sure glad you didn't have to use it either. That's got to last a good long while, at least until New Orleans, and better if it lasts long after. That's why I'm picking up an extra show at the coast."

"What's in New Orleans?"

She laughed. "That's where I live. Don't act like you don't know. Champagne told me she gave you the whole sordid history, no-good husband—and my son and all. Don't worry. My son, he's a grown boy, and taken care of, for the most part takes care of himself—got himself a gig, the talented little thing. But the house is paid for, the help is paid, but only until I get home."

"You think I could get work there?" I suddenly didn't feel as curious as I felt guilty that I had no money to contribute.

"Oh honey, we'll keep you fed."

I sat up straight. I wasn't about to let her think I intended for her to take care of me, keep me like Mr. Hammond kept Jewel. "I want to contribute, Jean. Take care of myself."

"We'll figure out something. Don't worry," she said and took a deep breath. "Boy hidey, girl, smell that? The salt is coming up in the air. Means we getting close."

The weeds beside the road swept by in a blur, and dizziness swam into my head. I tried to think of the ocean, the gulf where we were headed. I tried to picture us there together, but I couldn't get an image in my head. Not of us. "I've never seen the ocean," I told Jean.

"Never?" she asked.

I shook my head. "The only beach I've seen is in Chicago."

"Oh, that ain't no beach!" Jean laughed. "That's a lake with a little sand around it."

"My Aunt Ida and Uncle Albert took me there once or twice every summer I visited, like it was the best thing going. The water was always cold, too cold for me, even though they'd only let me get my feet wet." Jean laughed at that, and I continued. "They'd put me in my Sunday best, and we'd stroll up and down the long sandy shore, dodging people playing in and out of the water. Aunt Ida would fuss to keep a parasol over me so I wouldn't get any sun on my face. She'd say, 'Look here, Frances,' as we strolled along passing in front of the long line of lounging boys on blankets, 'one of these young men could take real good care of you, and move you up to Chicago in style,' and she'd push me out in front of them, as if to parade me."

I paused, scoffing at the memory.

"What'd you do then, girl?" she asked after a minute as if I'd left her in suspense.

"Oh, I'd walk ahead but usually stared out over the water, trying to ignore her and the boys."

"Ha! I bet. What she wouldn't say to look at you now, huh?" She was smiling.

"What do you mean?" I asked.

"All tough and independent," she said and smiled at me, her eyes softening at the corners, reminding me of that first time she looked at me at the buffet flat and dared me to chase after her. "And damn beautiful," she said and ran her finger along my jawline before grabbing the wheel again. I looked straight ahead as if embarrassed at her compliment, but I wasn't embarrassed at all. She made me feel like I was bigger than my little life, and I wanted to ride that feeling as far as it could take me.

CHAPTER EIGHTEEN

When we turned directly south down a tree-lined road, sandy and rough, all I could see at the end of it was blue sky. The car windows were down and a fishy smell came through them with the breeze. Just over a small dip, the ocean rose, and I could see nothing but water between the trees along the small, thin beach. The water stretched ahead for miles and miles, pale blue water, paler than I'd imagined, the sun glistening off it to the west, reds and golds, dancing on the small waves. The ocean in the gulf was calmer than I'd imagined an ocean could be, low tide, as Jean told me later. When we pulled up, the tide was going away rather than crashing in the way it would be the next morning.

We stood on the porch of Mr. Otis Buckner's little juke joint by the water where we would be staying in a tiny room upstairs. Jean would sing at the end of the week, a solo show she'd do before the vaudeville crew arrived. They weren't set to do another show until the weekend, at a theater in downtown

Mobile. That morning, I met Mr. Otis, a sun-worn black man with a spattering of white hair. He happily fed us homemade cheese grits and biscuits. I finally felt full, had finally eaten enough that my stomach didn't rumble an hour later. I'd lost a considerable amount of weight and my clothes, even the ones I'd just tailored, were starting to hang about my hips and swim over my bony frame.

The beach was empty in the morning light, and I could see that there weren't any houses around. We'd pulled up in the twilight when we arrived, and the place had looked deserted, the knotty trees hanging their branches eerily over the drive in front of the faded and unpainted wood frame building. A single lit sign was over an almost invisible door that read "Swamp Song." A swamp was nearby, Jean told me. "Not prime real estate," she'd said. She grabbed me on the porch and pulled me to her. I breathed in the sweet musk scent of her that mingled with the damp sea salt air, and pulled her closer to me, kissed her hard with a half-open mouth, sliding my tongue next to hers. She grinned through the kiss and kissed me back, then slid her mouth to my neck, kissing softly just enough to make the hairs on my neck and arms stand on end. She reached both hands up to my face and held me there, making me face her, making me look her in the eyes.

Her eyes were open wide and clear. "You're my man, Frankie."

I could feel her all about me, and it was as if she were inside me in that moment, inside my body, my blood. She was *with me*. I felt a sense of relief spread over me, and I grinned as I laid my head against her chest.

She held me there, and the breeze from the gulf licked at the back of my neck, whipping my hair wildly. She smoothed my hair down and then lifted my face up by my chin. "Those eyes are haunting," she said and kissed me and then grabbed my hand and led me down the steps, down the little path through the sea oats to the beach. We dipped our feet into the gulf, letting the water tickle at our toes, the two of us standing there side by side, barefoot and holding hands, my pale foot almost blending with the sand and her dark foot standing out like an oyster shell. Her hair, a little longer now, was loose and curled in little knots about her head, shaggy and wild. Her honey eyes were brighter, lighter in the sun on the beach.

"What's your husband like?"

She didn't seem surprised at my question. Staring out over the water, she answered, "Leroy Bailey. That was a million years ago. I haven't seen my husband in five years, Frankie. He's a crazy fool, as sweet and pretty as you please, a sissy boy, but crazy, a crazy drunk. Probably locked up or dead by now the way he drinks and carries on."

"Why didn't you divorce him so you could—remarry or—"

"Ha! What's the point? Ain't like I could marry *you*."

The realization of that hit me, and I wanted to change the subject.

She laughed. "We tried to get a divorce, but it was a whole heap of paperwork and money that hardly seemed worth the trouble since neither one of us wanted to be married to anyone. Marriage don't agree with me in any way, shape or form. I ain't gonna go to the trouble to get unmarried if it's not like I'm really married anyway."

"What about your son? What's he like?" I asked, my voice scratchy. The soft salt air blew into my face, and as I breathed it in, it tickled the back of my throat.

"Ah, Jeremiah, he's a charmer, but he ain't mine. I mean, I didn't have him, but he's my son all the same. He's my little sissy boy, though he's all grown up. I've got a soft spot for the girly ones."

We sat down at the edge of the beach, our toes getting wetter and wetter with the rising tide.

"I sure do miss him. I miss him every second of every day," she said and paused, her eyes watering. "It hurts so bad sometimes, like a piece of my guts is ripped out, but he's got his own life now. I gotta let him live it, and I gotta live mine. And thank God, he ain't nothing like my husband, except for the sissy boy part, so I don't have to worry."

I thought of Julian, how he'd explained that he was a sissy boy, how he'd left home. I wondered if his family missed him like that. I wondered if he went back to Mr. Hammond. "I met a sissy boy back in Memphis. He helped me get to Georgia."

"Ah, I see," she chided as if there had been more to the story.

My cheeks flushed. "I didn't *marry* him!" I laughed and poked at her, and she flinched, putting her arm around me.

"Yeah, I've been around a block or two."

I suddenly felt I never had to say anything. She'd been there before, seen what I'd seen before me. "Where haven't you been, Jean?"

"I've never been to California." She lay back in the sand and shaded her eyes. "This is why I'm so black. I'm a sun worshipper. My mama always told me I'd be blacker than tar, and she was right."

"I love your skin, your color," I said, laying back beside her and propping myself up on an elbow to look at her profile, her skin glistening in the sun.

"Why? 'Cause you ain't got none of your own?" She laughed.

I shrugged. "Maybe. I don't know."

"Frankie, you are lovely, pale and lovely. Beautiful in your own way." She was bashful in her compliment. She pulled me over her and swept my hair out of my face, tucking it behind my ear. "Green—and brown, those eyes, don't think I've ever seen such a color." As she kissed me, I could taste the salt on her lips. We were gritty, sandy, as we rolled about, slinging it over and over us again. She brushed some of the sand away form my face and pulled me by my chin.

"I want you to meet my family, Frankie, my son and my friends. They all in Nawlens," and she said it just like that, slipping into an accent I hadn't heard from her. It was wet and loose, uncontained. "God, I miss them. I miss home. Nawlens is more my home than Georgia ever was. The Paris of the South, they say. Like no place you ever been, Frankie. I got a house right close to the Quarter you'll love, or I think you will." She let me go and lay back again, shielding her eyes. "Hey, how you get to know all this shit about me, and I don't know jack about you?"

"You haven't asked the right questions," I said and stood, dipping my feet in the water again to wash off the sand, only to stick them in the sand once more and get them covered.

"Aw now," she said, teasing. "Tell me some things!"

"Well, I'm an only child. I grew up in Texas out in the middle of nowhere. My daddy is a cattleman. They ship me off to Chicago every summer hoping I'll find a nice rich man—"

"Texas, yes, you told me that. You miss your mama? Bet she misses you."

I hadn't thought about my mama in a while and not the idea of her missing me and felt an ache in my ribs as if I'd been kicked. I wrapped my arm around them, breathing short breaths, and sat down again. "Maybe. It does get lonely out there. They seemed pretty eager to get me out of the house, married off, though."

"Tell me something else. What was it like growing up? What did you dream about?"

"Getting out. I dreamed about getting out of that dumpy little town, out of my parents' grasp. I dreamed about traveling like all those people that stayed at my uncle's rent rooms. I dreamed about falling in love, like most girls, I guess." I leaned back on my elbows again on the sand. "But mostly I just wanted out on my own, do my own thing, make my own way. Sitting by a window smoking a cigarette without having to smash it out and wave the smoke away so my mama or my aunt didn't catch me. Wearing whatever the hell I wanted to, dress clear up to my knee and clear down to my navel, if I wanted. Trousers and a button-up even."

"Speaking of smokes, you got any?"

I didn't. I hadn't had any since we'd left Champagne's. We had been smoking Jean's, what few she had left. Suddenly a cigarette sounded better than anything in the whole world. I was just then aware that my hands were shaking, nervous from talking about myself, my family, but I was excited that Jean wanted to know.

"Oh, hell, Mr. Otis will have some. He sells everything up in that joint. Though don't nobody buy anything unless they here for a show and need it real bad, so it won't be cheap."

We stood and headed back to the porch where we found Mr. Otis mopping the floors, the deep wrinkles darkening on his hand as he gripped the mop. He gave us a whole can of tobacco and a whole stack of rolling papers. Jean pulled out a silver case and handed it to me as I finished up about ten of them. I stuffed them in, and we sat back on the porch in the rocking chairs and smoked a few of the ones I'd rolled.

* * *

We spent all day and the next on that porch, and then sometime in the middle of the week when Mr. Otis went out fishing, we spent the day in our room. It was a third-floor room, an attic really, with sloping, unpainted wood-planked walls and a big feather mattress in the middle on the floor. There was a tiny window overlooking the beach and the water, and I woke to Jean standing there at the open window, smoking one of my rolled cigarettes. She was wearing a long cotton nightgown worn so thin I could see the silhouette of her body. Her nipples were perked in the breeze, and I stood and walked up behind her, putting my arms around her waist and then on her hips, kissing at her neck and moving my hands up her stomach, barely touching her breasts. She blew out a drag and put the cigarette out on the windowsill. She turned to face me, put her hands on my face and smiled.

"Good morning."

I grabbed her hand and pulled her back toward the bed, lifting her nightgown up and over her head. I was wearing just a man's shirt, one she'd had stashed in a bag in the car. She unbuttoned me and slid me out of it. The bright morning sun cast shadows on the sloped ceiling.

"Should we worry about Mr.—"

"He's gone. He won't hear, wouldn't anyway."

I closed my eyes and pulled her onto the bed, on top of me, kissing her. She ran one hand down my stomach, pulsing the tips of her fingers against my skin. Her weight on me now, she slid one arm under me, and I pushed my hips against hers, my hands following her hand. I fumbled at first, timidly searching her body, waiting for a response. When I opened my eyes again and saw that hers were closed, her face intense the way it got when she sang, a flood of warmth ran over me. I let out my breath—breathed with her breath in my ear—and gave in to her with each pulse.

* * *

That afternoon we made our way downstairs, rumpled and spent, searching for food. Mr. Otis had not returned, but he'd left us cakes and cold meat. We devoured it all, pouring the food and water down our throats like we were starved. I watched her eat and could feel her lips on my skin again. I kissed her once in mid-bite and sat down grinning beside her. Every day after that we spent in a similar routine as the day before, sometimes going out to the beach and rolling around in the sand, but mostly keeping to ourselves in our room or on the porch. Mr. Otis didn't seem too much bothered by us and not too much interested, either.

* * *

The night of Jean's solo show, Swamp Song was packed to the gizzard, as Mr. Otis said. I hadn't seen Jean Bailey since she'd left me on the beach that afternoon. I'd fallen asleep on the sand, waking to the waves tickling at my feet, my calf muscles, the backs of my knees, the water creeping up my leg slowly with each wave. When I finally got up and came back in, my trousers rolled up above my knees, wet and sandy, there was already a room full of people. I didn't bother to go upstairs, didn't bother to change my soiled clothes. I was wearing the extra trousers and shirt Jean had bought me, and I liked the feel of them, loosely hanging on my skin, my sweat and my own musk mingling in them.

The large, open room was wall-to-wall with people, and I was the only bulldagger there, the only white person, too. Mr. Otis had stools scattered about, though most folks stood. I stood leaning against the wall closest to the door going out to the porch. The breeze from the gulf began to cool my sunburned skin as a piano man started to play. My skin prickled, and my damp clothes began to feel scratchy against my flesh. I felt stiff and tight, and my lips burned. I smoothed my hair, dirty with sweat and seawater, and it mostly stayed in place.

Jean Bailey wasn't on stage yet, and a small band, different men this time, gathered around the piano testing their horns, scattering thumps on drums. There was a hum, a low murmur that rose above the crowd and the sound of it, and the stops and starts of the horns pushed me further and further from the center of the room. A man dressed in a dark navy suit, crisp and neat, hat straight up on top of his head, leaned in to whisper in a woman's ear. He nodded in my direction, and as the woman peered over her shoulder, her eyes narrowed to slits. They both quickly turned around and headed for the bar through the other side of the crowd.

I stepped out onto the porch, my hands in my pockets, and I shivered in the wind. I strained to hear the waves over the horns growing louder with the piano joining in, and just as they seemed to drown out with a gust of wind over my face, I heard Jean Bailey's soft hum begin over the music, over the crowd and the waves. Her hum led into a low moan, and then the horns followed with a toot, then a low hum to match, going back and forth until the drum beat joined, slow and methodical, and finally a clinking of the high keys on the piano. As she moaned again, I felt her voice shoot through me and vibrate out over the waves. I eased back closer to the door and made out her words.

One spot, baby, I got this one spot.

It was the first song I'd ever heard her sing, the night I felt she'd sung it to me, the night I locked eyes with her as I slid down off the stool holding my breasts, feeling them give me away. It had only been a little while since then, and already I felt so different. A feeling of sadness and longing like an ache came over me along with the reminder of the excitement I'd felt that night, the thrill and the fear all mingled together.

I went back inside and crept from the door toward the center of the room, braver now. The heat inside swept over me, and my clothes felt softer now but clingy. In the middle of the crowd, I caught only glimpses of Jean Bailey in a blue, sequined dress, shorter than her others, tiny straps at her bare shoulders. She wore a matching headband with a slick little feather springing out of the side. Three long strings of pearls swooped and swung about her neck, down through her breasts and ending at her navel. The man with the hat stood directly in front of me, swaying with the music, his arm wrapped around the woman, dressed in yellow chiffon, like the women who danced across the floor at Ernestine Royce's. How different the material had looked to me then, slumped down in a dirty corner, my hand on myself, hiding, and full of fear.

I felt bolder now and the colors themselves seemed not to fade, but to brighten with me. I began to sway with the couple in front of me and the others crowding around me, a deep musk gathering in the heat under stiff suits and newly made dresses, sparkling in the dim lights. There was no wax on their faces, and I didn't look over their bobbing heads at Bailey. I swayed and closed my eyes, felt again that punch in my gut I'd felt as that first drop of gin hit my stomach, that drop I'd felt when I'd grabbed the jug from Ernie's hand and acted like I wasn't scared, like I was grown and proud.

I smiled. Swaying there in the middle of the great room at Mr. Otis's Swamp Song, I felt like myself again, or perhaps for the first time. Jean Bailey's voice came through over the voices around me and through the horns, hitting that note that sank her voice deeper into me, into my thighs and buckling my knees.

I'm still keeping it warm.
Yeah, I'm still saving this one spot—
This one spot for you, baby.

As she slowed to draw out the last note, the crowd around me grew still, and I opened my eyes to a clear view of her face, already glistening with perspiration, her lips lined in red and glossed over from the song, seeming to quiver as she closed her eyes, the lashes coming together delicately, fluttering there like wings. I turned and headed to the side for the bar. I grabbed the can of tobacco and the papers and nodded at Mr. Otis. Sitting at the bar, I rolled five cigarettes, smoked two in a single sitting and then found my way back to the center of the room.

There was a rumble about me as she sang a bawdy trumpeted tune. The words were new to me, but they spelled out plain as day that she liked women, liked women like me, and didn't mess around with men. The woman next to me gasped as her man let out a laugh. She slapped him on the arm and then caught me staring, jerked his arm and turned back toward the stage.

As Jean sang, she swung her hips to the tune, popping them from side to side with the drumbeat. She didn't flirt with anyone on stage but made eyes at several of the women in the audience.

"There's one right there, a real live *invert*, and a cracker!" I heard a voice from behind me. It was a woman's voice, but a man's followed it.

"Woo! We got ourselves a bulldagger right here in the swamp! Would you look at that?"

The rumble moved away and back again, and the heat around me let up. There was more space now and a shuffling of feet. At the end of the song, someone bumped me from behind, and I jerked around, unlit cigarette in my mouth.

"Tough one ain't she!" he said and smiled down at me with a soft, sweet face. It was Julian, and he looked at me as if he was not at all surprised. His eyes danced about, dark and sparkling.

"Julian!"

"Frankie?" He seemed suddenly confused, looking me up and down as if he hadn't recognized me. "I thought yous dead or locked up somewhere."

"What? Why?"

"New digs and everything! All highfalutin!" he said and turned, waving his hand at me as if to dismiss me, but then he stopped and dramatically turned back to me.

"Julian! I—I—" My stomach sank. Julian looked tired, dressed in worn and ragged clothes.

"So you didn't get mixed up with Baby Boy?"

"What? No, why?"

His face was suddenly serious, and he looked away from me, back at the stage. "I thought you's dead way the white folks were talking," he said.

"I'm fine. I handled that boy just fine," I said and tried to laugh remembering what I'd had to say to play along with him, how I'd had to pretend to keep Jean in line. I cringed at that thought and at the thought of leaving Julian behind. "I'm sorry, Julian, I—"

"Girl, it's okay, a boy like me knows how to take care of him's own self! I knew you's gone the minute you found miss pretty up there." He nodded toward Jean Bailey on the stage. "But you treading on slippery water, or whatever it is they say. These folks will not be kind—to your kind. White *and* dressed like that." He laughed, putting his hand on his hip.

Jean Bailey moved on without a stumble to the next song, even bawdier. Julian grabbed my hand and swung me around, twirling me, not at all in rhythm to the song. My gut swam with guilt, but I was happy to see him again.

"Don't belong, nope, but we dance like we feel, right?"

I nodded. I didn't know what he was saying, what he was talking about. He didn't seem to be making much sense, and this worried me. He seemed happy, though, so I just danced with him.

The crowd was full up to the neck in gin. Milk bottles clanked as we danced. Julian pulled me into him, into a slow drag, pressing his body to mine and swaying back and forth as the music tromped out slower, all in one spot, his hand at the small of my back, the other clasping my hand now. At the end of the song, he twirled me around and dipped me. A swirl of bright colors—yellow, blue, green, gold, brown, red, white, purple—all flashed and sparkled under the lights as he dipped me down and then swung me back up again. In one motion, he put me upright and turned me to the stage, just in time to see Jean Bailey take her bow and wink at the crowd, a crooked little smile growing on one side of her mouth as if just for me.

Julian leaned in to my ear as I watched her leave the stage, "You still owe me a dress, little bull."

I turned around, and he just smiled at me. I felt a warm rush of comfort. It was the first time I'd seen another familiar face in a long while.

Julian stayed with us that night and the next. Jean Bailey was glad to see him, an old friend, she said, and they caught up on Memphis gossip. A couple of days later, Julian pulled out the material he still had and more he'd gathered for his gown, and I set to sewing down on the porch. At the end of the week, Jean would be performing at the Razz Theater in Mobile, and he wanted to wear it then.

Julian came down and sat beside me in the next rocker over. He seemed excited about the dress, but distracted, watching the waves as if in a trance. He didn't speak for a long time.

"Frankie, I sure was lonely without you, and no dress to boot."

I stopped stitching and put the dress in my lap. "Oh Jewel! I missed you! I did."

He didn't look at me, just kept staring out at the waves.

"I'm so glad you found me here at Swamp Song," I said and took up the stitching again.

"Yeah, I had to get a wiggle on." He crinkled up his brow. "Pert near walked here after that old boy came in spouting off about how he'd cornered a rat, that's what he called you." He turned to the dress, ran his hands over it in my lap. "I thought you's dead for sure."

"How did you—how did you even know this place—"

"Miss Sal done all she could, she said, and moved me right along." He shook a little, like a shiver, and smiled, sat up straighter. "I had adventures getting here! Just like you, I did. I shimmied down here like a cat, ate right out of a can like we did on the train, and then even managed to cook up a squirrel in the woods one night, like we used to do back home. Didn't even trip up one bit."

I must have made a face at that and Julian started laughing like he'd never stop, holding his stomach and leaning back like he'd fall over.

"I knew well enough to stay off the beaten path but they's a man I knew up in Hattiesburg, used to get me gigs, and he brung me down here."

Jean came outside, kissed me on the cheek. "Jewel used to perform down here, sugar," she said and sat down in front of us on the steps.

I wondered how long she'd been standing behind us, listening to us talk.

"You gonna do a gig then, Julian?" I asked.

Julian shrugged. "That was way back before Marcel—"

Jean turned to him and waved her hand. "Julian, forget Marcel. Come on the road with me."

His face lit up for a minute, then he sank back down in his chair as if remembering something.

Jean got up and went back inside, and I thought I heard her go out the front door. Julian stared out at the waves again. I tried to concentrate on the stitching. About a half hour later, Jean came back down with a big black case and handed it to Julian. He stood up with a jerk and seemed afraid to take it.

"Now listen, this was left out in the storage from one of Mr. Otis's regular bands. You can't keep it, but I bet you could use it for a good bit, earn yourself a little dough. And it's only one key."

Julian smiled and clapped his hands, almost jumping up and down. He took the case, sat down and opened it up. He pulled out a box-like instrument, black with swirls of ivory inlay, big white buttons on one side and smaller cream-colored buttons on the other. He pulled it apart and air gathered in the crinkled folds. He pulled up a knob on top, and as he stuck his hand through the strap on one side, he fingered the keys with the other, then with both. A high note came out and sang into the air.

"Hold on just a minute," Jean said and ran back inside. When she came out she was carrying a washboard and had fashioned picks onto her fingers. She ran her fingers up and down it one time, and then Julian started in with her.

The music was rough but fast and made me want to dance or just move. I tapped my foot and clapped along with them, finally getting up and dancing around them. Jean and Julian kept on for a good long while, even after I was too hot and out of breath to dance any longer and had sat back down in my chair. Around midday it was time for food and for Jean to get ready, so they stopped for a spell. After Jean had gone back inside, Julian gingerly put the accordion back in its case and I packed up my sewing. He reached over and put his hand on mine, patting me. "Thank you, girl," he said. I stood up with him and gave him the biggest hug I could muster around his tall frame.

* * *

I wasn't able to finish the dress, with all the appliqués and pretty stitching Julian wanted, but Jean fitted him in one of her suits, too big, but suitable. I dressed in the nice suit she'd bought me back in Augusta. We drove off to the theater, smelling pretty and feeling proud.

The whole crew was at the Razz piling props into the back door, and Tasha and Rosie pulled up right after we did. Backstage was crowded with people, and Tasha's and Rosie's women along with me and Julian went through the backstage door to claim our seats. It was a dinner theater, and we'd eat while the show was going on. Just as we were making our way out to the main floor, Julian stopped.

"I'll be back. Save me a seat, Frankie," he said and disappeared backstage, leaving me with the two women from Atlanta, all dolled up and snotty. They spoke to each other, and I smoked half the cigarettes I'd rolled before we left. I crossed my legs and bobbed one on top of the other and was about ready to go back and get Julian when he appeared again—in sequins.

"Julian?" I almost didn't recognize him.

"It's Miss Jewel Delacroix tonight, ladies!" he said in a high-pitched voice. He spread his arms out wide and sauntered toward me, swishing his hips and turning all the way around so that I might get a full view of the gown. It was floor-length, a bold black-and-white silk, sequins lining every inch of it, with a drop waist. He wore a wig of ringlets, and I recognized the wig. It was Jean Bailey's, the one she'd worn the first night I'd seen her. He was small enough that unless you looked at him, really looked at him, you wouldn't be able to tell he was a man, and as was the style, he didn't need to stuff the bosom. But he must have been wearing some sort of corset because the dress curved around his hips the way it would a woman's.

His ringlets bobbed as he attempted to sit like a lady, crossing his legs in exasperation and whipping out a fan. His face was painted, his lipstick pink and perfect. He pulled a cigarette daintily out of my case, Jean's case she'd loaned me for the night, and I lit it for him as he squealed and fanned away the smoke.

"Us *ladies* aren't supposed to be smoking and carrying on like this in public," he whispered to me and nodded over at the Atlanta women. They had stopped talking and were staring at Julian in horror.

As the theater grew crowded, the ladies excused themselves and did not return. Julian and I sat and smoked until we got our food. I was thrilled to watch him eat. He picked up the fork with two fingers, his pinky extended, but still managed to shovel in the beans and rice he'd ordered. I laughed with each new course. As the show began, we sat in the corner in near darkness searching for the food on our plates, giggling and whispering.

Close to intermission, the waiter returned. The waiter touched Julian on the shoulder. "Ma'am, I am so sorry to have to do this but—" and he stopped to take in a breath, organizing his words. He was a large black man dressed in waiter's whites, a napkin draped properly over one arm. "I've had some complaints."

Immediately I thought of the Atlanta women. "What sort of complaints?" I fumed.

Turning to me he said, "Sir, this here's now a white theater. Ain't allowed to have the Negroes sitting amongst the white folks. No matter how elegant they may be." He smiled back at Julian, and I almost detected a wink.

"Oh sir," Julian spoke up in his girly voice, "we understand."

"No, no we don't." I stood and threw my napkin down on the table. I didn't understand. Julian had been able to pass in Memphis. "Juli-Jewel is Creole, and we are here with Jean Bailey."

"I'm sorry, sir, but that don't much matter. You can stay, but—"

"Yes, yes. I'll go, Frankie, you stay," Julian said and patted my arm. "I'll just be backstage. I can watch from there." He stood, dabbed the napkin at his lips and smoothed down his dress.

"But I—"

"It's just how it is," he said and sauntered down the aisle toward the stage door, swishing as he went, proud and alluring.

I sat back down, but I couldn't finish my meal. As soon as intermission let out, I went through the stage door to look for Julian. We'd go somewhere we could both sit, I thought. I figured there had to be somewhere. The halls were crowded with the crew. I looked up to the side of the stage to see if Julian was setting up to watch from behind the curtain. There was only a man dressed in black, moving a prop. I made my way down the hall.

Out in the street, it was dark and damp, like it would rain, but I couldn't tell if there were clouds for all the buildings and the streetlights. The back alley was empty, so I walked through toward the front of the theater. As I rounded the corner, I heard people talking, mingling about for intermission. There were lights from a police car pulled up to the front of the theater, and a crowd had gathered there. As I made my way toward it, I heard a scream.

"Let go! Let go! I am going, just let me go!"

"No. We're arresting you."

It was Julian in his black and white sequins, struggling with an officer. His wig was falling off to the side as he struggled. "But officer, why? What did I do?"

"Perversion, deviant sexual behavior and impersonating a female." The officer pulled Julian's hands behind his back and when he struggled, the officer hit him over the head with what looked like a long stick.

I pushed through the crowd screaming, "Wait! Let him go! Don't!" But all it got me were a whole lot of stares. The police officer shoved Julian in the car and drove away. I ran to the back of the theater, through the back stage door and pounded on doors. Eventually, I found Jean and told her what happened.

"Aw, sugar. Ain't nothing we can do but bail him out after the show when I get paid."

I was terrified and shaking all over. Jean hugged me, kissed me on the forehead, and left. I sat in Jean's dressing room for the rest of the show, dreaming up ways to get Julian out. I felt responsible. It was my fault he was even here, much less in jail.

When the show was over, I begged Jean Bailey to take me to the station in her stage gown. I couldn't wait for the girls to get all undone. Reluctantly she followed me out to the car and drove us to the station. I let Jean go in alone since she had the money and since I was still underage.

A few minutes later she came out again. "I'm sorry, honey, but they won't let me get him out."

"What? Why not?" I was frantic, tears streaming down my face.

"They say he's mentally unstable, tried to hurt several of the officers. They've contacted his parents and are shipping him off to some crazy house in the morning."

My stomach lurched. I remembered the threat my uncle had given me. "No!" I said and opened my door.

Jean stopped me, grabbing my arm just as I was about to get out. "Look here, you can't. These big-time Mobile police ain't gonna mess with a little white girl dressed as a boy come to bail out a black pervert. Hell, they'd just arrest you too, and Lord knows what they'd do to ya."

I looked down at my clothes. I knew I couldn't go in there, knew I couldn't really pass as a man, not if they were really looking at me. I knew she was right. I'd be in the same boat as Julian if I did.

"Jean! Will they hurt him? What will they do?"

"He'll be fine. Worse they'll do is rough him up a little."

"Should we call Mr. Hammond? Could he get him out?"

"No, sweetie. There's nothing he can do either. Best we can hope is they let him out soon."

"Where is the place where they're sending him?"

"They wouldn't tell me, Frankie." Her face was serious, and she put her hand on my hands, both wadded in my lap.

"We have to find out, Jean! We can't just leave him here! I've already left him once. I can't—"

"Frankie, I know, but I did all I could do right now. You ain't gonna get anywhere with those damn hicks right now either. I am not going to risk my neck or let you do it either for some simpleminded sissy boy. He'll get us all killed! Now that's that."

I sucked in my breath, feeling scolded.

"I'm sorry, Frankie. It's just the way it is," she said, softer now, and started up the car. "When we get to New Orleans, you can call up the station and see if you can get some more information out of them, see if you can get a hold of his parents or something." She patted my knee and drove away.

The clouds had gathered when we left the station and were now spitting out rain. Just as we got out of downtown, the rain began to pour down on us. When we got close to Swamp Song the roads were near flooded, washed out to the sides. We knew if we tried to go any further we'd get stranded, that the bridge might be out anyway, so we headed out of town, toward New Orleans.

CHAPTER NINETEEN

New Orleans was hot and wet, the air heavy, but the whole city seemed drenched in color. My stomach knotted up every time I thought of Julian, but I tried to just think that he would be well fed, taken care of, and that I'd be able to get a hold of his parents soon and maybe talk them into letting him come with me instead of sending him away. At least I'd thought to pack up the gown I'd almost finished for him with Jean's stage clothes. I planned to complete it as soon as I could, have it ready for him when I saw him again.

I peered out the window, staring up at a large church steeple, ornate and intricately patterned with gargoyles on the eaves. There were people performing in the streets—jugglers, horn players, a guitarist—and vendors with their wares, but we drove by so fast, I couldn't see what they were selling. As we rounded the corner off the square, the shutters on the homes and shops were ragged, painted but worn and half-hanging on the windows. We turned into Treme, Jean's neighborhood, and the houses seemed more alive. They were still worn down and so close together that they seemed almost stacked on top of each other, but they were bright, covered in flowers and vines.

We pulled up to Jean's place, a mustard-yellow house squeezed up next to a dark pink one next door. Her house had great big windows like doors, teal shutters open wide and white lace curtains hanging lank behind them. Though we could have just stepped through the windows, Jean unlocked the heavy front door, the handle and knocker pure brass, and let me inside. The walls were worn and painted over, peeling in places from the heat, I suspected, but the floor was polished, painted to look like tile. There were three divans in the front parlor alone, and a great big painting over the fireplace. It was of a black man with a horn, but the shapes were sharp and edged, the colors bold and almost nightmarish.

"Mrs. Bailey!" A small but stout old woman with a thick Cajun accent appeared on the stairs, scurrying down. "You weren't supposed to be here until tomorrow." She wore a crisp, white apron over her dark and frumpy uniform. She had rags in her hands that flitted about, nervous and jittery, as she ran up and put her arms around Jean's neck.

"I'm sure everything is fine," Jean said as she gave the woman a warm hug and kiss on the cheek. "Where's Jeremiah?"

"He's due to be back any time now," she said.

Jean introduced her to me as Mrs. Benoit, and she gave me a stiff nod.

"Why don't we show Frankie the house?"

Mrs. Benoit nodded again, and we followed her through the house, around the stairs, and to the back where open French doors led out into a courtyard with an almost overgrown garden.

"It's beautiful!" I said, and Jean took my hand.

"This ain't nothing," she said and led me back to the house, back through the parlor, the front room, onto the sun porch, and up the half-winding stairs to the bedrooms, Mrs. Benoit presenting each room as if it were a grand palace. We finally reached the master bedroom, large and heavily draped with an overstuffed feather bed atop an oak bedstead. We stepped out onto the balcony, and the damp heat hit my face, still a bit sunburned from our time at Swamp Song. The house was warm, but the stone floors downstairs made it cooler. The wood floors upstairs had almost the same effect.

"I let you get settled," Mrs. Benoit said and left us there.

Jean took my hand and pulled me to her. "I've got something for you." She pulled me out of the room and down the hall to another room, all open and unfurnished except for one couch by the long windows that led out to the balcony. In the middle of the room there was a wide structure covered in a sheet. She held out her hand as if to present it to me.

"What? What is it?"

"Uncover it!" Her eyes lit up, and she shooed me toward it.

I peeked under it slowly, lifting one edge and then another, looking up at her and teasing her, like I was afraid it would bite me. I grinned as she came and threw the sheet off. It was a brand-new sewing machine, table, and a dress form. Even my mother didn't have a dress form, though she always said how much easier it would make fitting the clothes we made. She said she could stick pins in it where she couldn't into me.

"Jean! It's too much! How did you—"

"Oh, don't be silly!"

"But what am I gonna—"

"You're gonna make money with it. You're gonna finish that gown for Julian, and then you're gonna make some for me and some to sell." She blew off a little dust that had gathered on top of the machine, despite the sheet.

I stood there, half-holding the discarded sheet, almost afraid to approach the machine.

"What? How?"

"Listen, Frankie, what else are you gonna do? I already told you, I don't need a manager, especially here in New Orleans. I want you to make clothes. You're really quite good at it. Figure it out—I don't know. How else are you gonna support yourself?"

I could feel the heat rise in the room, and the stillness made me feel stuck. I hadn't even thought about it. I'd made it this far cunning my way, but I half starved until I found her. I was no star, had no talent. What the hell did I think I would do in her world?

"Come here, look, look at this." She pulled me closer and pushed me up to the machine, pointing at the foot pedal. I fumbled over and stuck my foot on it, amazed at how fast it made the needle move up and down. I opened it up and stuck in some thread, pulling it through. I ran my hands over the dress form, imagining Julian's dress there.

"See! A natural! Frankie, vision! You've got the guts; now get the vision. Like me, Frankie. I'm going to be in the pictures, films, Frankie. Mark my words."

My eyes watered, and I tried to blink them dry.

"Mama?" A timid voice spoke from behind us, and we turned around. An older boy stood in the doorway, his thumbs latched at his trouser pockets. His trousers were pressed stiff, and he wore a blue cotton undershirt with sweat gathering in large rings under his arms. He was thin, but muscular, and he was shy with a soft voice. He reminded me of a younger Julian, and my chest felt tight.

"Jeremiah!" Jean rushed him and squeezed him hard, kissing his cheek. Jean was as natural with him and in her home as she was on the stage, as she was with me. I suddenly felt stiff, out of place.

* * *

Dinner was late, and I was exhausted when we finally went to bed that night. I'd crawled into the bed and gotten up next to her, lay my head on her shoulder. "Thank you, thank you for everything, for the machine, everything." As soon as I said it, I felt like a child, like I was just another one she'd adopted on the road.

"You're welcome," she said, and there was a distance in her voice.

"I want to find Julian," I said.

"I know you do, sugar." She pushed my hand off her leg and shrugged my head away, as she pushed off the sheet. "It's hot, Frankie, and I'm tired."

She rolled over, and I rolled away, staring out into the orange glow from the streetlamp, wishing for even the tiniest breeze to sweep through the windows. I could feel the sweat beading at my forehead, but I had a chill at my back.

* * *

The next morning, I woke up alone in Jean's bed. She wasn't even in the house. Mrs. Benoit said she was out with Jeremiah, would be gone most of the day.

"She left you this, said to have fun," Mrs. Benoit said and handed me an envelope with two dollars in it. I felt bewildered and suddenly awkward, especially there in the house without Jean. I went out and wandered the streets alone. Jean wouldn't be performing a show for another week or more. This was the last of the circuit, the big show, the finale. Jean would be staying here for some time, and I would be staying with her, but I felt lonely without Julian, and I was worried, terrified something awful happened to him. But I had no idea how to find him. I stopped and phoned the police station in Mobile.

"Yes, can you give me the name of Julian Delacroix's parents?"

"Who?" The voice on the other end of the line sounded hurried.

"Julian Delacroix, sissy boy you folks arrested."

"Why? Who's asking?" The man was gruff now, impatient.

"Oh, I'm writing up a little article on the arrest, sir," I said as sweetly as I could muster, "for the newspaper."

"Oh, oh, yeah, uh they's the Delacroixs of Carington Parrish, John and Emma, I believe."

"Thank you, kindly, sir," I said and hung up, reciting their names and their town over and over again as I walked.

I was excited and eager to contact them, but my feet were tired from walking, and I was sweating something awful. Late in the afternoon heat, I sat at a shaded open-air café on Rampart Street, blocks from Jean's house. I watched the people walk by—beggars, drunks, and prostitutes pretending not to be. It seemed that the color barrier didn't much matter in New Orleans, or at least there wasn't much of one in that area—Back O' Town was what they called it. There were all-white establishments in the city; I'd seen the signs. But this open-air café wasn't, and there were black folks and white folks, and just about every shade beyond and in between—Creoles, Cajuns, Caribbean folks and island people—all about. It was like another country in New Orleans, and I loved it.

I was close to a church with a big steeple and gargoyles, where vendors crowded the streets, and I could hear the low moan of a saxophone in the distance. The street smelled like piss, but when the wind rose I smelled fish and was reminded of Swamp Song, our little room there. I could barely understand the waiter and couldn't read the menu since it was all in French, so I nodded at his suggestion. He served me a crepe filled with cheese and the strongest, most bitter coffee I'd ever tasted. The crepe was smooth and crisp, flaking off and then oozing into my mouth, and I got used to the coffee with a little cream.

Close to sundown, I paid my tab and dragged myself down the street toward the music. I strolled up to what looked like the oldest building around, its dilapidated unpainted doors about to slide off their hinges, the rust around the bars on the windows crusting in. I peered through the open windows and saw a man behind a standup bass strumming on the stage. The man at the door was taking money to get in, so I walked on back toward the square.

On the corner a woman sat at a table laying out cards before her, big cards with strange pictures on them. She wore draping clothes and had a slight lisp when she spoke to the man in front of her. After all the cards were on the table, her hands hovered over them and she leaned in, whispering something to the man that I couldn't make out. I walked closer and stopped.

"Think of a question, any particular thing that's on your mind really and hold it there, see it in your mind's eye."

The man leaned back. "My mind's—"

"Just picture in your mind what you want to know about," she said, and she began to shuffle the cards again.

He nodded and closed his eyes.

After the cards were shuffled, the woman touched the man's arm. "Okay, cut 'em," she said and she placed the stack of cards in front of him. He cut the deck and pushed it back to her across the table.

"Keep seeing what you see there," she said as she dealt out the cards one at a time. "No, don't look here, close your eyes."

I looked away and closed my eyes too, listening to the slap of the cards, her hesitation over each one as she clucked her tongue.

"All right, I see you are coming up on something, a big change, but you are lost in it." She pointed to a card with a big wheel on it, tiny creatures surrounding it and one in the middle, and then to a card with a cup and what looked like a court jester. She flipped a final card. "Desire," she said, "of course." She looked up at the man, as if peering into his face to find an answer. "You must harness your desires before they consume you. You must take responsibility. You must own yourself."

"Okay, but—"

"You must find your home, son, in here," she said and pointed at his chest. Then she looked up at me and said, "You looking everywhere but."

The man shook his head, pulled out some money and placed it on the table, then turned to leave.

The woman snatched up the money and shoved it down the front of her dress. Then she smiled at me. "You want to know your future, child?" she said in an alluring voice.

"I—I'm sorry, but I don't have much money," I said, turning to go. Truth was, I didn't want to know my future. I was terrified at what she might say about me, about Jean and me. I was afraid I already knew.

"Is fine, gimme what you got," she said and motioned me over.

"I'm sorry. I've got to go," I said and walked on down the street. I rounded the corner and took a moment to lean against the building and shut my eyes, eyes that Hazel in St. Louis had told me would cause all my trouble. The river was behind me, and I opened my eyes and turned to it just as a boat cruised by, a great big white riverboat with lights and music and a big paddle wheel at one end, churning and churning through the water. I watched it roll down the river for a long time.

It was getting dark, and people bumped me as they reveled in the streets. I was lost. I couldn't remember exactly what street Jean lived on, hadn't thought to take note of it when I left. In the darkness, the streets all looked the same: same balconies lined in wrought iron, same brightly painted shutters on the open windows, same big brass adorned doors. When I finally wound my way to her street, the only way I knew it was the right one was when I spotted her car, the only car on the block. Jean was standing in one of the open windows smoking a cigarette, one foot propped up on the sill. She had one hand on her hip, and she stepped away from the window as I came in the door.

"Where the hell have you been, Frankie?"

"I—I was—"

"Why didn't you tell anyone where you were going?"

"I did. I told Mrs. Benoit."

"You didn't tell her where, just said you were going out."

"I didn't think I needed to. I didn't know where I was going anyway." My voice broke. I was suddenly so tired.

Jean stood there, hand on her hip, and then stabbed out the cigarette in an ashtray. "It's all right, girl. Just tell me when you plan on being out half the night. We waited almost an hour to eat, thinking you'd be back."

"I'm sorry," I mumbled. She still felt miles away, her movements stiff and cold. "I found out Julian's parents' names and where they live, though."

"How the hell'd you do that?"

"Called up the police station."

Jean smiled a forced smile. "You eaten yet?"

"I'm not hungry," I said as I reached for the cigarette case. I lit a cigarette and stared out the open window. The street was dark, and the lights in the house seemed to glare in my eyes. My guts churned with each drag.

* * *

The next day it rained. It rained all day, and the next and the next, and the streets that weren't cobblestone were turned to mud and couldn't be driven on, even in a buggy, and they were so nasty you wouldn't want to walk them either. I stayed holed up, as Jean had called it at Swamp Song, but this time I was alone in the sewing room learning how to use the new machine by trial and error, as I worked on Julian's gown. When I couldn't find a listed phone number, only an address, I'd written to Julian's parents asking where he was, making up some story about how I was concerned for his well-being, telling them I thought I could help him get better. I sent it hoping to hear back by the time I finished the gown. My sewing wasn't perfect, but the sequins and appliqués were turning out to be a great way to cover my mistakes. As I placed it on the dress form, I was proud of how it hung in its own shape.

"That's right pretty, Frankie," Jean said and walked into the room. She ran her hands over the dress and then walked up behind me as I pinned on another appliqué. She slid her hands around my waist and over my hip bones as I adjusted. The warmth of her hand and the pressure of her palms made my stomach quiver. My knees gave way just a bit, but I leaned back into her embrace, relieved at her touch. I barely moved, hoping to keep her there, keep her close to me after all the distance I'd been feeling. I had spent the days in my sewing room while she was with her kid. She was usually already asleep when I got in bed. She pulled me away from the dress form and kissed me hard, then turned and walked back out of the room, but that was the most we'd spoken in days and I was relieved, too relieved to protest or ask for more.

* * *

Soon Tasha and Rosie arrived in high style, though their sugar mamas had purchased rooms in the Quarter without them. I was relieved to see them, their familiar faces, and rattled on and on about my big adventure in the city, about the woman and the tarot, the boat I'd watched.

"You haven't taken her to Shiva's yet, Bailey?" Rosie said, smiling.

At the time, I didn't know what they were talking about, and they didn't go on about it, but the next week, the weekend of my eighteenth birthday, we all loaded up in Jean's car and drove down to the docks to Shiva's.

"You're eighteen now, girl! We gotta do it up right," Jean said.

She had bought me material to cut a tuxedo from and a pattern to follow, and I wore it tonight. Mine was black to her white one. We both wore a lavender silk handkerchief, folded to stick out of our top pocket like a blooming flower. Tasha and Rosie were dressed in shimmering low-cut dresses, slinky and silvery in the reflection of the streetlamps. We drove way down a road that paralleled the river and parked in a deserted lot behind a warehouse. We walked toward the dock a block or so away. At the end of one of the piers, set off among a few dilapidated structures, dark wooden storage houses and buildings, there was a riverboat, docked. It was smaller than the one I'd seen on the river that first day. And it was older and less kept up, but it was painted a clean white and trimmed in ornate eaves lacing lavender around each layer of the structure.

As we approached the boat, I could hear the sharp tuning of a clarinet, and then a trombone, a cornet, and finally the beat of the rhythm section joined in. There was a long, roped plank that led onto the boat, and a man dressed in a black suit stood at the door. Jean took Tasha's arm and looped it in hers, nodding for me to do the same as Rosie came up beside me. Jean and Tasha went in first, exchanging nods with the man at the door, whispering something to him.

Inside, there were several men in tuxedos and women dressed in evening gowns. But there were also men in gowns, wearing elbow-length gloves with elaborately painted faces and large feathered arrangements stuck in their wigs. They were tall, even taller in their heels. One was on stage singing with the band, and I thought of Julian, Miss Jewel, again, and the knot in my stomach almost made me want to cry. The man's voice was stronger than Julian's but still easily passing as a woman's. I could tell he was young, maybe even younger than Julian or me. He nodded at Jean as we came through to the dance hall, the largest open space on the boat, but smaller than most of the places in the Quarter where I'd been out by myself that first day.

We found a table close to the stage. The singer was dressed in a tight lavender gown, white gloves up to his elbows, his face painted like Julian's had been the night they took him away. The singer was singing a slow, sad song about waiting, the long lonely hours of an empty house, and a man who'd left. I scanned the room and noticed that there were women passing as men as well, just like at Ernie Royce's in Chicago. This time I felt like I didn't need to hide, like I was exactly where I was supposed to be.

Jean took my hand, and I stood tall and proud, running my other hand down my side to smooth my tux. She led me to the dance floor, swinging me around and dipping me as the song ended. "Happy birthday, Frankie," she said as she stood me back up. I smiled. The next song began, and I guided her, step-by-step, through a ballroom dance, a waltz I'd learned back home. As we dipped into the last of the song, the last of the steps, Jean gliding with me across the floor, her fingertips barely touching the palm of my hand, I thought of my mother.

Mama had showed me how to stand for this dance, showed me how to barely touch my partner's hand and glide with him, how to turn and hold my head. I could see her small frame, strong and knowing as she showed me the steps. We were in our front parlor, and I'd pushed back the furniture to make space in the middle of the room. I didn't have a partner to practice with since cousin Deloris and Bean hadn't arrived. My mama smiled as I stumbled over my own feet, but I could see the pride rise in her face when I perfectly mimicked her posture, her movements. "Such a long, pretty back," she said and clasped her hands together.

Jean's hand slid out of mine and down to the small of my back as we ended the dance and went back to the table. Jean danced with each of us and then with several other women in the hall.

I excused myself and went outside to the balcony. We were now far away from the docks, though I hadn't even felt us move. I walked around to the back of the boat to watch the big wheels turning and churning. The water spitting up into my face felt cool and fresh. A woman joined me there. She wore a tight-fitting gown, but her hair was slicked back under a man's hat. She had a painted-on mustache as well as dark lipstick.

"*Ma chère catin,*" she leaned in and whispered to me. Her voice tickled at my ear, but I didn't understand her. "*Ma chère catin, avez-vous une lumière?*" She held a cigarette to her lips and pointed at mine.

I lit it for her. "I'm sorry. I don't speak—"

Dramatically she clasped my hands in hers. "French? My dear doll." And she bowed her head. "What is your name?" Her accent was still thick.

"Frankie. My name is Frankie," I said.

"Lisset." She smiled and took a drag of her cigarette. "The other woman with you—is she your girl?"

"Jean Bailey? Um, yes," I said.

She nodded. "*Catin,*" she said. "Is she not, how you say? Are you a—are you for pay?"

I ran the words over in my head, confused. "No, no, I am not for pay."

She laughed and took my hand, "Oh."

Jean found us like that, my brows furrowed and Lisset tugging at my hands.

"*Ma chère, Lisset!*" Bailey threw her arms around her and smiled, giving me a wink over her shoulder.

"I am afraid I have made an offense to your girl, Bailey."

"No, no," I said, waving her away. "A misunderstanding, I'm sure. I should learn French." My embarrassment rose in my throat, making my voice high and uneven.

Jean laughed at this and led us back inside. "We'll have to go soon."

"Why?" I asked as we sat back down.

"See that man over there?" Jean nodded toward a large white man, a string bow tie at his neck. "He's a sissy boy all right, but he don't like to mingle with the Negroes or any women, especially if we ain't entertaining him. Thinks we're trouble. He's about to raise a stink with the owner. I can see it in his eyes." And just as she said this, the man angled toward the doorman, leaning in to talk in his ear. When he moved away and went into another room, Jean rose, and we all followed.

Lisset stayed behind. "Oh, no. I plan to dance. Besides, I do work for Monsieur, the owner. He would never ask me to leave." She crossed the room to a woman with long blonde hair. I longed to stay there, too, but followed Jean out the door.

* * *

The vaudeville circuit's finale show took up most of Jean's time over the following week as she prepared and rehearsed new numbers. I had finished Julian's gown and was working through a pile of mending for the girls. One afternoon, after working almost all day, my shoulders ached and my fingers were sore from pinpricks. I stood up and stretched and wandered out the door for a walk. I made it all the way down to the river. I saw that Shiva's was docked there before the evening show. Lisset was there, but I almost didn't recognize her. She was in thick trousers and a muddy-colored shirt. Her hair, wavy now, fell loosely about her shoulders. She carried a crate inside and then came back out again, and I called out to her. She met me on the plank.

"Hello…Frankie?" she asked, making sure she remembered my name.

"What kind of work do you do here?" I asked and Lisset explained that she did odd jobs, setting up for the shows, running in supplies.

"It's good money, but tough sometimes," she said.

"Are there any more jobs?" I asked, sheepishly. I loved sewing, could do it all day every day, but I wasn't really making any money at it. The thought of earning my keep a bit, having some pocket change, and getting out of the house was pretty tempting.

"Sure. You need to work?" she asked.

I nodded, and that's all it took. She introduced me to the riverboat people, and I was hired on the spot. I followed Lisset down the plank onto the docks to a line of crates. The crates were wooden, splintering on the edges and scraped against my skin, and they were heavy. I heaved one up the dock, up the plank, and then down below decks.

"Here, wear these," Lisset said after our first trip and handed me a pair of work gloves. "Your hands, they will be torn to pieces."

I put them on, and we spent the next hour moving crates. We didn't unload the crates, just stacked them there, and when we were done Lisset sat down and wiped her brow.

"Now for a wee nip," she said. Back behind the crate she had a stash. "I get one bottle per load, boss's discretion, of course," she said and grinned, uncorking and tipping the bottle up. It was clear, but I could smell that it was liquor. She passed me the bottle, and I tipped it up, letting the now familiar gin sting my throat.

Then we headed upstairs. We cleaned the entire ballroom, dusted, swept, mopped, and then put pristine white tablecloths on all the tables. Just before we were to open, we placed and lit candles on all the tables. The whole place sparkled, and I felt like I'd accomplished something big, though I'd only done what was asked, only done my job. At the end of the shift, the boss paid me in cash and told me to come back the next afternoon.

* * *

When I came home and told Jean about it, she pissed and moaned about the job and me working, said it'd land me in prison before my parents ever put me there. She said I was running liquor and didn't even know it.

"I know what's in the crates," I protested, though I didn't know for sure. "You know they can't do squat to us out on the river." I knew this only because it was what Lisset told me when she stashed the bottle back behind the crates.

"Yeah, but they can if they catch you putting it on the boat."

I didn't care. I was making my own money, a lot of money. Over the next couple of weeks, I bought things for the house, groceries and supplies, but I also bought all kinds of material and patterns and was coming up with new ones. I thought eventually I'd design a gown for Jean.

The night of the final show, I helped Jean get ready, called the theater, and booked the cab. She begged me to quit Shiva's, begged me to come with her, be there to help as her manager. She'd wanted me to see the show, and I'd wanted to see it, but the boss had me on the boat that night, me and Lisset both, so she couldn't cover me. There was a big party. He needed me and I'd make a lot of money, I told her.

"Shit, Frankie, we don't need the damn money! That ain't what—oh hell, girl, do what you want." She turned around to the mirror and smoothed her hair with a hot comb. She was dressed in her tuxedo again, her breasts bursting out the top. She let out a deep sigh and pulled the comb carefully down the back of her head and then jerked it away. "Dammit!"

"You okay? Want me to get something?" I rushed to look at the burn on the back of her neck, but she shooed me away.

"No." She held the burn with two fingers, dabbed something on it, and then went back to combing. Just as I was about to leave the room, she turned to me. "You got a letter today. From the Delacroixs."

"What? Where is it?" Finally, Julian's parents had written back.

She pointed to the nightstand, and I ran to rip it open. Inside was a simple note. "I believe you've got the wrong Delacroixs. We do not have a son. We wish you both well."

"Damn." I sat on the bed. "It's not them." I was determined to still look for him, but I'd just have to find another way.

Jean looked over at me with worry on her face, and then went back to her mirror.

"Frankie, I got an offer for another show, get me back on the road for a bit. You want to stay here or come along?"

"I—I guess—" I didn't want her to go without me, but I'd just settled in. I liked my job. I felt like it gave me something, something of my own.

"It's in Texas," she said and turned back to the mirror.

"Oh," was all I could get out. My hands began to sweat. "Are you trying to—what do you want, to take me back to my parents?" I was fuming, scared, and frantic.

She put the hot comb down and stood up. "No! God no! Frankie, I just thought you might want to see your folks, tell them you're okay, is all. I don't expect they'll make you stay now. You're eighteen."

I took a deep breath. "I'll think about it."

She smiled. "You know you're still my man, right?"

I nodded. "I love you." I'd felt it before, but never said it. It just fell out of me then and seemed to sit there in the air with my breath, tepid and still. I turned away from it, away from her and left the room, not waiting for her to say it back, not expecting her to.

* * *

Shiva's was crowded, and I was dressed up that night, dressed for the showy people, though I knew I'd ditch my jacket and tie, roll up my sleeves and move crates from the backs of cars, from the hull of the ship, from everywhere, until the boat was stocked and we were on the move. Until then, I stood with my boss and Lisset, who was dressed almost identical to me, and greeted the people as they came on board. At eight o'clock, just as I imagined Jean's show began, we were sent to unlatch the boat from the dock, which was just a way of telling us to roll up our sleeves and get to the real work. A dark car pulled up to the end of the dock. Lisset and I paid the driver, unloaded the contents, the bottles clanking in the crates, and pushed them into the hull, then unlatched the boat. In the hull, we moved the crates toward the opening to the kitchen and left the crates open for when we'd need to come down for more supplies.

As we rose from the hull, the hum of voices grew louder. The hall was filled with patrons dressed in evening attire but not as flamboyant as the night I'd first been there. It was hot down in the hull, and I was relieved to be in the open air on the deck again.

"Lisset, you and Frankie mingle tonight. There's a group of high rollers here. Show them a good time."

"I'm no trollop, Mr. Millet, just so you know." I'd understood why Lisset had asked me that the first night, understood that Mr. Millet sometimes supplied that kind of entertainment to his patrons.

He laughed. "Of course, girls."

I followed Lisset into the dance hall. We both had the bartender mix us a highball. I let the liquor swill in my mouth, tasting it before it slid down my throat.

A group of men came barreling in, wearing summer furs about their jackets. They took seats close to the stage where the performers soon would appear. I scanned the crowded room. A large party filled a table close to the windows that opened to the deck. There was only one woman in the party. I recognized her right away, and I almost let my drink slip from my hand. It was Ashley Pickard. My stomach lurched, and I could feel the liquor rising in my throat. I excused myself and went into the kitchen, down into the hull. I fumbled in my pockets for a cigarette. I smoked it down quickly, filling the hull with a lingering haze in the stale air. I stomped it out and went back up. Lisset was in the kitchen mixing three drinks.

"Bar duty?" I asked, trying to hide the quiver in my voice.

"No. *Ma chère catin*, your dance card has been filled." She raised an eyebrow and handed me two drinks.

Out in the dance hall, Ashley waved for me to come over. I could feel the blood drain from my cheeks.

"At least you aren't blushing, *ma chère*. You're always blushing." Lisset stood beside me sipping her drink. "*Jolie catin*, Frankie, go."

As I walked across the room, I realized that this time Lisset was *calling* me a trollop, a whore. She was calling me a pretty whore, but still a whore.

Ashley's eyes brightened when I set the drink in front of her. She had a white fox fur on her shoulders. She sat up straight as a board, her chin at the perfect level to show her jewels, one hand extended to me. I took her hand and bowed. When I bent to kiss her hand, I looked up to her grinning face, flipped her hand over and kissed her palm. Her fingers wrapped around my chin and pulled me to her. Her eyes were like glass, like nothing, like an empty bowl.

She introduced the men around the table, one of whom was, in fact, her husband, and another, her brother, the one in the movie business, she reported. She stood then, forcing me to lead her to the dance floor. "But, Mrs. Pickard, there is no music."

"There will be." She lifted her hand to mine and led me in a waltz.

I could feel my boss's eyes on me, his delighted grin. The whole room had their faces turned toward us as she spun us around. Finally, after a few turns, the music started, a slow waltz to match our dance.

"I'm a married woman, girl. You don't need to be threatened by me," she said into my ear, as she dipped me slightly.

"Why does that matter?"

"It does."

"Jean's married, too. It doesn't matter."

"Don't confuse me with her kind, or yours." She spun me around before I could answer. "But I forgive the misunderstanding."

I scoffed.

"I'd like to do what you asked of me, dear, for Jean Bailey. Where is she now?"

I didn't answer her. I didn't want her near Jean.

"Frankie, that's it, isn't it?"

Without looking at her face, I nodded, my head perfectly turned away in the dance.

"Frankie, you can trust me," she said and stopped, grabbed my chin and made me face her. "I am in love with my husband." Her eyes were sincere as she moved again, turning me in the waltz.

Her husband was watching us dance, his bushy eyebrows raised at the spectacle, but not in surprise, or shock, or jealousy, and I believed her.

"My brother is here to see Jean Bailey, to see if he can put her in a film. He's heard a song of hers he wants her to do."

"She's performing the last of her vaudeville shows tonight at the Carlton Theater, uptown." I blurted it out and let go of her hands, stepped out of the dance and returned to retrieve my drink at the table. I nodded at the men and turned to walk away.

"Take us there. She won't see us. Won't even return my calls." She was in my face, insisting.

"I have to work."

"I've arranged for you to take us there." She turned and headed out the door, motioning for me to follow behind, her fur tapping on her shoulder as she walked.

* * *

Lisset was standing with our boss when I left the boat, docked for a moment just to let us off. I'd wanted Lisset to come along, but the boss needed her there, needed us both, but wanted the wad of cash the Pickards had given him.

Uptown, the lights twinkled. The show was packed, inside and out. I squeezed the lot of us through the backstage door and positioned them at the side of the stage to see Jean. It was toward the end of the show, and she seemed more alive than ever under the spotlight. Her face had a glow about it, a soft hue, as she belted out the last line and took a bow, but she didn't get the response she usually did, there was no roar of applause, no standing and clapping, no hollering at all. It was just a quiet clap, long enough to be polite, but then everyone stood and gathered their things and turned to leave.

When she exited the stage, her face was worn down, like she'd just lost a fight, and when she saw me she looked confused. She grabbed me, kissed me, and then held my face in her hands, questioning me with her stare.

"The Pickards are here to see you. They want to put you in pictures." When I saw her eyes flicker in excitement, I knew I'd done the right thing.

She turned to them, greeting them warmly, and I left the theater and walked to catch a streetcar, finding my way back to Bailey's, half on foot. I was too defeated to go back to the boat. I just wanted to curl up in bed.

The house was dark but for a single lamp in the front parlor. Mrs. Benoit sat under it, a book in her hands.

"Mr. Frank?"

"Mrs. Benoit." I nodded before lurching for the stairs.

When Jean finally arrived home, I was half asleep in her bed. She curled up behind me in bed and put her arms around me. She didn't mention the Pickards, didn't mention their offer or what had happened, and I didn't ask.

CHAPTER TWENTY

Texas in the middle of August feels like stepping into an oven. The sun beats down on you with no shade trees for relief. In Texas, even the trees know their place. They line up along the creek beds and speckle small patches across miles and miles of pasture to suck up any source of water they can.

I'd asked my boss at Shiva's if I could take some time off for the trip, and after the hefty tip I'd earned him for going with the Pickards, he let me off with little to say about it. We left New Orleans and had been driving for what seemed like days. We finally arrived covered in dust and muck from the road, pulled up to a gate, and drove down a winding dirt road to a canvas tent set out on the hard, cracking black land common in that area. Jean Bailey was set to play a tent show all weekend long, something I didn't even know we'd had when I was in Texas, though Jean told me they'd been playing there for years.

I stepped out of the car just miles from my hometown on a bright Friday morning, and my face felt tighter in the dry air. There was no wind, no shade, nothing but sun and heat swarming me, making my clothes stick to every inch of my body.

It had been almost six months since I'd been home, just over three since I'd left Chicago and my aunt and uncle. I had considered making my way home the next morning after the first show and staying for the weekend until I headed back to New Orleans with Jean Bailey.

For all I knew, my family assumed I was dead. I imagined my mother would be mad, but would throw her arms around me just the same, happy to see I was still alive, proud to see I'd come home. I admit, the prospect of seeing my family after all this time, and the prospect of my own bed, good food from my mama's kitchen, and maybe even some of my own clothes sounded mighty inviting, and I was excited. But I was also scared to death. I was afraid of what kind of repercussions I'd meet, afraid my aunt and uncle had turned me in for the money I'd taken, afraid my parents would try to make me stay, though I was of age now. I knew they couldn't force me to stay if I didn't want to, but they might take up my uncle's idea and still be able to lock me up in some institution if they had me certified insane like Julian. I quickly brushed that thought away as Jean grabbed my hand and pulled me into the back of the tent where she'd be getting ready for the show. She kissed me, then pushed me away again with a sigh.

"You going on back to your folks, ain't ya?" she said, almost pouting.

I didn't know what she meant or if she was joking. "I haven't decided when or whether or not I'll visit, but either way I'm going back to New Orleans with you."

"We'll see," she said and turned to rummage through her clothes.

"What? What do you mean?" I walked over to her and reached for her hand to pull her closer to me, and she jerked away. "Jean, why don't you go with me?"

She let out a quick, biting laugh, and turned to me. "Yeah, that'll go over right nice, won't it?" Her eyes deepened to amber.

I sat down on one of her trunks, sinking my chin to my chest. I wanted her to come, I did, but I knew she was right. I knew that my mama would have a wild-eyed fit, and my father would do God knows what all at the mere sight of us. "I'm sorry, Jean. I—I know. I shouldn't have even mentioned it. But I wish I could take you home. I wish you could meet my family, see where I come from."

"I know enough about where you come from, girl." It was as if she were spitting her words at me.

I jerked my head up. "I'm eighteen now. Remember? I'm not a runaway anymore, and they can't make me stay, can't do nothing to me!"

"Oh hell. You don't have to pitch a fit on my account. You go on back, sleep in your nice, safe house with your pretty, white kin."

"What are you talking about? What does my family have that you don't, Jean? The house I grew up in ain't even as nice as yours in New Orleans."

She looked at me then and frowned, breathing heavy, as if she didn't know what to say. "I worked my ass off for every inch of what I got, girl, and you know it," she said calmly. "The stuff—that's not what I mean—oh hell, girl, you'll never understand this shit, 'cause you white!"

"This was your idea, all of it!" When she didn't respond to me I got up and took a deep breath. "Jean, I don't care about all that anyway. You know that. I left it all, and don't give a damn if I ever go back. I want—all I want is to be with you, to be free with you." Even as I said this, I knew I still had to go back, or would have to eventually. I couldn't run forever.

She turned to me and her face seemed stunned. "Oh, don't you play that damned martyr shit with me! You think you so grand? Huh? Am I supposed to be impressed that you walked away from what you had given to you on a tin platter, just because, just because you could? It don't matter, little bull. You can walk away, turn your back on it all you want. It's still right there for the taking anytime you want, just have to reach out your hand, anywhere, anytime."

"What makes you think they will just open their arms to me, welcome me back? When I walked away—don't you understand what that meant? You have no idea what my family is like. They're just as likely to spit in my face and kick my ass out the door again themselves just from looking at me." I pressed my hands on my chest and smoothed down the front of my shirt and trousers.

"Oh, poor pitiful," she said and glared at me. "Don't you understand, Frankie? You got that pretty face, however much you try to hide it with that haircut and clothes. I ain't got that option. But it don't come down to being a bulldagger, Frankie. You're white. Always gonna be white. Can't take that away. And you always gonna have it to fall back into, just like you did when you went to prance around for easy money on that damn riverboat instead of sew. You could really be something, Frankie, but you'd have to work for it. Instead you just lean right back on your hind quarters and rest on your whiteness—just like you did that night in Georgia with that stupid Baby Boy!"

Her words stung and I grimaced remembering my words, calling her a "highfalutin nigger" and acting like I had to keep her in line, and especially at pretending I'd shoot her.

"Just like second nature, ain't it, Frankie? And I'm black—a nigger, just a dumb, lazy nigger you got to keep in line, right? Ain't that what you said? Always gonna be." She threw up her hands and walked out of the tent to the car.

I was stunned. I'd had no idea that she'd heard it all. That seemed so long ago, and I wanted to protest, defend myself, explain that I'd done it just to get us out of a jam, remind her he'd had a gun, but it seemed useless. It was as if she had drawn a line in the sand and put me on one side, her on the other and was building bricks up in the middle. There it was, right there smacking me in the face.

Cars were lining the lot beside the tent by this time and people, all black people, were milling about, and I could suddenly feel their stares, their force against me, pushing me out. They weren't the patrons. They were the talent and the help. I'd felt like I'd had a place, at least in that, but I didn't. I didn't belong there, never would, no matter how hard I tried. There would always be this between us.

* * *

At the show that night, I stayed in the back mending several of Jean's gowns and costumes right up until the very last. I didn't watch the show, but from what I could hear, she sounded tired, worn down, and I blamed myself. The crowd was warm though, much warmer than her last gig, but something was off.

As she was closing out the show, I wandered out into the crowd, now mostly white folks all lined up in neat little rows of seats barely reacting at all to the music. At the end of the show, the crowd gave a regular round of applause and got up to leave. In the back of the tent, I spotted a familiar face and my stomach tightened. It was my cousin, Deloris and with her, Bean. I weaved through the people, standing on my tiptoes every so often to catch a glimpse of which way she was going. When I got a little ways from her, I yelled her name. She turned to look back at me. I could swear she saw me, but she just ducked her head and turned to walk out.

* * *

That night in the back of the tent on the makeshift cots they'd left out for us, I couldn't sleep. I could hardly keep my lids closed. I was so hot sweat soaked my hair and poured down my temples. I couldn't keep even the lightest blanket on me. Jean Bailey had downed a good third of a jug of some local booze Tasha and Rosie had brought up and was snoring on a cot not five feet away, seeming peaceful and serene. At daybreak, I heard a car start up. I got dressed and peeked out the tent flap.

Just as my head was out into the bright light, a large, big-bellied man in uniform reached in and grabbed my arm. He pulled me out. The air felt stagnant in the heat. There were cars lined up in front of the tent, blocking the road, police cars. I couldn't focus on what the man was saying to me. Finally, Will Ingram came up and took me away from the large man. Will was a boy I'd double-dated a few times with Deloris. He'd made a policeman now, he was telling me. I still could not quite figure out what was going on until they dragged Jean Bailey out, kicking and screaming, and put her in cuffs and in a police car. She caught my eye as she sat and waited, fuming at me, as if it were my fault.

"Frankie, you're in a whole heap of trouble here. We found enough booze to book everyone here. What are you doing messing around with these folks?"

This woke me up. I struggled to get my arm free from Will, and then he turned on me, pulled my arms behind my back, and cuffed me.

"And I'll be damned if you ain't dressed like a boy!"

He put me in a separate car from all the rest since I was the only white person there and took me away first.

The whole booking process was a blur. I remember Will calling my mother, trying to explain, and hearing my mother's screaming voice even though my own ear wasn't up to the receiver. "And you'll need to bring her something decent to wear, ma'am," I remember him saying as he looked me over. I remember Will putting me in a cell, a whites only cell, and being the only one in there. I could hear Jean Bailey pitching a fit somewhere in the jail, but I couldn't see her. I sat on a worn-out bench, my bare feet on the cold concrete floor. Will looked down on me through the bars with a satisfied grin, like a cat's.

Within the hour, my father was there to get me out. He didn't say a word, barely even greeted me as Will opened the cell and gave me my boots and a dress my father had brought me from home. He turned away so I could dress in private. I took my suit jacket off, but the dress was loose without a corset so I just slung it on over my shirt and trousers and pulled on the boots. When I was dressed, I followed him out of the cell carrying my jacket. Down the hallway, I saw Jean Bailey leaning up against the bars, and when I looked up again, Ashley Pickard was there in the station holding her pretty little gloves as she signed papers and handed over a wad of cash. She was alone, without her husband or her brother. I can't say I was surprised, though I had no idea she was even in town with us, and I was a bit relieved knowing Jean Bailey had someone to bail her out when I knew I couldn't, not right then anyway. As my father turned the corner to go out the door, I told him I forgot something. "I'll be out in just a minute," I said and he nodded without a word and walked out the door.

I ran back to Jean's cell and put my hands around hers on the bars. "I'm so sorry I can't, but Ashley is here. She's getting you out. I'll meet up with you back at the tent."

"Go on, girl. Don't worry about me. Go on back with your family a while, and I'll see you back in New Orleans," she said. Her honey eyes dimmed, and I could see she was hurt or disappointed, but she was playing tough.

"But, but I want—" Big tears came up in my eyes, but I didn't let go of her hands to wipe them away.

"Frankie, don't worry." She leaned in close to the bars, pulled her hand out from under mine and wrapped it softly around the back of my neck, pulling me to her. She kissed me on the cheek and whispered, "I love you. You're my man," and let go. She turned then and sat back down on the cot in the cell.

I felt her words stir through me—comforting me, exciting me—just like the first time she'd dared me to follow her. I turned to go. As I walked through the station again, I nodded at Ashley and then went out to my father's beat-up old Model T. He'd already started it and put it in gear before my butt hit the seat. We were both silent the whole way home.

* * *

My house looked as it always had, like nothing in the world had changed at all, and yet it was startling. Its copper roof shone in the sun, the white paint peeling only in a few spots at the bottom from weather, but otherwise pristine—simple, but pristine.

My boots crunched through the rotting pecans in the yard and clunked on the steps and onto the front porch, loud to my ears on the silent prairie, the most quiet I'd heard in months. I turned the knob and walked in, sticking my hands behind the folds in my skirt to hide the tremor.

My mama stepped out of the kitchen and into the front hall, wiping her hands on a dishtowel. "What in God's name! Dorothy Frances Corbin!" She tossed the towel over her shoulder and came to me with her arms outstretched and hugged me so hard I cried. And she cried. And it was what Jean Bailey knew she'd do and what I'd imagined, really known deep down she'd do. She put her hands on my shoulders and pushed me back, looked me over, shaking her head. Nothing much had changed, except that it had, and there was something there in the middle of the room waiting, waiting for someone to say something about it, but no one did.

"Go on upstairs and clean up. I bet you're hungry." She looked around me as if to see what I'd brought home. "Where's your trunk, Frankie?" Her voice was stern finally, for the first time like I was in the trouble I should be, but because of clothes of all things.

"I—I don't have it, Mama."

"Well, what did you do with it? Did you sell it or some such nonsense?" She raised her eyebrow, and my father walked out the back door as if to avoid the whole scene.

"No, Mama. I left it at Aunt Ida and Uncle Albert's. Didn't they tell you?" I assumed my aunt and uncle had told my mother everything, that I'd taken off, taken the money from the register and left everything to chase Jean Bailey, that I should be locked away or married off.

"We are no longer on speaking terms," Mama said and walked back into the kitchen.

I followed her. "What? Why not?"

"You know damn good and well why," she said, eyeing my trousers and boots sticking out underneath my dress. "Now get on up there and change out of those nasty clothes and put on something for a proper young lady."

"I'm sorry, Mama." I turned to leave, but she kept talking as she brought down a fry pan and got out some eggs to scramble.

"I can't say as I blame you for leaving up there, Frankie, though I am none too happy that you didn't tell me, and that you didn't come straight home. But I'm more annoyed at your aunt. I didn't even know you were gone until after you called, and I called up there."

I stood there puzzled as she continued. "I'd like to pretend this whole jail business never happened, ya' hear me?"

I started to speak, defend myself, but she cut me off.

"I don't wanna hear it, Frankie. What happened, happened. That boy at the police station told me all I need to know. As far as they are concerned, it was just a misunderstanding, wrong place, wrong time kinda deal. You understand? I've called the paper, and talked to Jessums. They have taken the arrest out and won't mention it again. Just you mind it don't happen no more."

I nodded.

She turned and got down a bowl. "That woman, your aunt, now I tell ya, she has gone and lost her mind. And your Uncle Albert, he ought to be so ashamed. I can't believe he can show his face in that town."

I gave up going upstairs and sat down at the kitchen table. "Would you believe she is talking about leaving him? Getting a, a what is it? A divorce?" she said in a loud whisper and continued, "I just about fell over in my chair. Frankie, run out to the storeroom and get a slab of salt pork."

I left following her orders, shaking my head as I bent down into the storage for the meat. My mama always had something to say about somebody that wasn't doing what she'd like them to. Nothing had changed at all. I came back and handed her the meat. "Are you talking about—because of Cora?"

"I don't know what that woman's name is! For heaven's sake!" She cut the pork into long, thick strips, just the way I liked them, and my stomach growled.

"You think she should stay with him, with Uncle Albert, after he betrayed her like that?"

"Oh, you can be so naïve, Frankie. I mean really. What do you think is going to happen? You think she'll be able to just up and walk away? How's she going to survive? It was just some stupid nigger woman anyway, the damn heathen that he is. It's not like he'd take up with her or anything."

My gasp was audible, and my mama stopped, pressing her hands against the counter as she stared over her shoulder at me.

"Oh I know it, honey, it's just awful. But this ain't news to you."

I flinched, could feel that she was about to lay into me and braced myself for the onslaught. I could only imagine what she would say about my own behavior if she thought this about my uncle.

"You knew all this when you walked out of that crazy house. I can only imagine the war you had to witness there, and you getting hit in the crossfire to boot! I don't know why you let me go on like this. I tell you, Frankie, I hope when you get married you don't have to deal with any of this, but men are men, always will be. I'm just proud your father don't have that kind of temperament." She turned and put the pork into the pan. It sizzled, and the smell went right to my stomach.

I touched my face where my uncle had slapped it. Of course, there was no visible trace at all. I realized she had no idea what had happened. My aunt had made up some kind of story to save my hide or hers, I didn't know. I was so relieved that my aunt and uncle didn't mention putting me away in an asylum I could have jumped for joy. But right then, I knew I had a clear choice, just like I'd had when Baby Boy was standing there pretending to shoot Jean Bailey with a gun. I could go along with her, stay in this comfort, this warmth for a bit and then slide out easily with one lie or another, or I could set things straight, tell her just exactly who I was, what I planned to do, and just take her judgment, take whatever she'd dish out.

"Mama, I don't know what all Aunt Ida told you, but I didn't leave because of any fight they had. I didn't even know if they had one."

"Oh?" She flipped the pork and cracked an egg into the bowl on the counter.

"I left with—I mean I've been traveling in the vaudeville circuit, doing piecework, sewing, for Jean Bailey, the singer? She's famous." I tried to make it sound as glamorous as I could.

"Well, that's right nice, Frankie." She didn't even turn around, and I didn't know if it was because she didn't understand, or if she was just waiting to give it to me good.

"I've been making the most beautiful gowns you've ever seen. And—and I even made this." I held my jacket up and ran my hands along the lapel, as proud as a peach, though I knew it was a bit rugged now, and certainly dusty and dirty after getting there.

"Yeah, I see that getup, figured you'd joined the circus after Deloris called to tell me she'd seen you in it."

"I knew it! She did see me! The little brat didn't say a word."

"Can you blame her? Who'd claim you in that? You look like a clown, Frankie."

I tugged at the dress over my clothes and pulled it off over my head. "This is how I dress now, Mama. I like it. Jean Bailey wears suits sometimes, too." When she didn't respond, I kept on, pushed a little more. "Jean Bailey is a blues singer. Have you ever heard her? She has the most beautiful voice! She's makes her own living, making records and traveling to shows. She has a gorgeous house in New Orleans."

She dropped her whisk in the sink and turned to me. "Well, it's good you got out in the world a bit before you settle down. Lord knows I never got to. It will help keep you when you find a man." She smiled as big as day and scooped the pork onto a plate and drained off the grease to ready the pan for the eggs.

"Mama, I'm not—I mean, I don't want a rich man—any man. I don't want to get married—ever."

"Well, want in one hand and—"

"Mama! Really, I mean it. I'm not staying here. I'm with Jean Bailey now, and I'm going back out with her first thing Monday morning," I said, though I didn't know if Jean would play the rest of the weekend shows as planned or if Ashley was still around or what, but my mama didn't need to know all that. "I'm going back to New Orleans. Jean's got a standing gig there, and I can make enough gowns and clothes to keep myself—"

"Blues? You mean nigger music?" She stirred the eggs without turning around, but I could hear the dismissal and the sneer in her voice, and my father came back in before I could respond.

He tossed his hat on the table and sat beside me without a word.

"It's almost done, GW."

He let out a sigh and leaned back in his chair. "Frankie, why don't you tell your father what you plan to do?" She giggled still stirring the eggs.

I pushed away from the table and ran up the stairs to get cleaned up. I needed food before I could work up the nerve to tell my father. Though I was too old for it now, I could already feel the switch on the back of my legs.

"Get one of your old day smocks out of the closet, Frances! Don't come down here in that clown outfit!" she yelled up at me.

I wiped down my face and hands at the lavatory in my parents' room and then walked the extra flight up into my own. Everything was just as I'd left it, as if I'd been gone only a day or so. Even the mess I'd left while packing was still there, extra clothes scattered about in front of the dressing table, my vanity strewn over with barrettes and ribbons from before I cut my hair. My bed was made but barely, just enough to get my mama off my back about it, and all my old toys were still shoved under the bed and in the armoire. There was a picture of Deloris and me at the fair on my nightstand. I picked it up and dusted it off. It was from the previous summer, but it seemed a lifetime ago. As I looked around the room, a strange sensation came over me, as if these weren't my things, this wasn't my room, as if I'd never lived here before, that it was a stranger's room I was sneaking around in. Standing right there in it, I missed it, I missed my room, my space, the feeling I used to get there, safe, alone, comfortable, and secure, confident.

I pulled back the lace curtains and looked out over the prairie. A jackrabbit hopped up over the weeds away from the house, but otherwise nothing moved, not a single blade of grass. The line of trees at the creek in the distance did not sway. It was still and dry and vacant for miles and miles. A panic rose in me, like my feet would stop moving if I stayed here staring for too long.

The smell of the food struck my nose, and I felt weak. I dug out my yellow frock with the little white flowers and changed clothes. The frock was soft and always made me a little happier when I wore it. It was loose, bigger than it had been before I left. Even my clothes felt like they were no longer mine. I tied it tighter around my waist and tromped back downstairs.

"Frankie, now what's this you want to tell me?" My father's voice was gruff, but monotone. He was already eating the full plate in front of him.

My mother put a plate down in front of me but did not sit to eat. She cleaned up the pans in the dishwater bucket and wiped at the counters as if she was waiting for me to begin. I ate. I tried to eat slowly, but with each bite, my hunger grew, and I shoveled it in. When my plate got close to empty, my mother put more on it.

With half a mouthful of eggs, I tried to get the words out to my father. "I'm going back on the road with Jean Bailey, gonna make clothes for her."

"Your daughter thinks she's a gypsy or something, and with a bunch of niggers!" Mama's voice was mocking.

My father didn't respond right away. He shoveled in a last bit of eggs with some toast and wiped his mouth, shaking his head. "I don't think so," was all he said.

I didn't bother waiting for more. "I am too. I am going, and you, neither of you can stop me. I'm grown, eighteen now. You can't keep me here, make me marry some roughneck."

My father looked up at me, a look of hurt in his eyes, as if I'd attacked him, and I guess I had.

"I didn't mean. I meant—I meant, I'm in love, in love with a woman. I'm in love with Jean Bailey."

My mama finally sat down across from me. "Oh Frankie, you can be so silly. You been watching too many of those Hollywood pictures." She laughed and took a big bite of toast.

My father took a deep breath and then looked up at me. "I don't care what you've been doing out there, up in Chicago, or even all over tarnation with those people, but you are home now, young lady, and you will act right and stay put." His voice was stern, but when neither my mother nor I reacted, he threw his fork down, pushed away from the table, and stood up. "You best have that shit out of your system, or I'll damn sure beat it out of you!"

"Oh GW, calm down. If she wants to be an old spinster, let her!" My mother was laughing hard now, and my father shook his head and left out the back door again.

I stood up too and went up to my room, frustrated and angry.

* * *

At supper that night, my father came in with Will, and I knew it was a setup, knew it the minute they walked through the door. My mama had practically dressed me herself before dinner in the nicest dress she could find that still fit me. She even tightened the corset in such a way as to make my breasts appear larger, with cleavage, but left just enough room for me to eat and breathe. Will was all fidgety and grinning, and my daddy was calm and collected, as if he'd solved all the problems of the world and could now get back to his real work.

Will was a good-looking boy, dark hair, broad shoulders. That night, at least, he was in civilian clothes rather than his uniform, and he was cordial, not at all imposing as we sat down to the food. My mama was so giddy, she was downright clumsy as she placed the roast on the table and cut us each a slab.

"Well, we got the last of them off the land and seen 'em out just this afternoon," Will said, cutting into his roast.

My stomach knotted. Jean was gone—without me.

"Weren't too much trouble, I hope?" My father tried to further the conversation, but Will just shook his head and filled his mouth with potatoes and meat.

After dinner, my mama practically kicked us out of the house together. "Why don't you two go on out to the swing a while?" she said and pointed to the big swing out back that my father had built out of welded-together wagon wheels and wood for the seat.

When we'd sat a while, I leaned in to Will. "You gotta get me a ride out of here, Will. I gotta get back to Jean Bailey, on down to New Orleans."

He looked startled. "What's your hurry, girl? Look here at the sunset. Ain't it the most beautiful you've ever seen? The big old Texas sunset. They ain't got that down in Sin City."

He was right. It was gorgeous, the pinks, purples and yellows blending together over the horizon, and only in Texas where you could see from horizon to horizon. Soon the big Texas sky would give way to night, and light up with twinkling stars. I supposed this was their plan, that I'd be seduced by it, by Will, and just go on and give in, stay here with them forever.

"Frances, I—I'd like you to marry me. Now, don't worry, I plan to court you first, show you just what I can do you for, but I've already cleared it with your daddy, and it's all set. I know we don't know that much about each other, and you've gone off and had yourself a wild adventure, but it's time now, and I can learn what you saw, and we can be together and have babies—a family."

When I didn't respond he took a breath and started again. "I got my own place now, brand-new house that needs a mistress, needs tending to, ya see. It's a bit small, but too big for just me, and we can grow with it, Frances. It's right downtown, close to the station, and to—to all the shopping and stores and stuff. I could get you anything you wanted."

I didn't look at him. I couldn't. He was right. I didn't know him, and he didn't know me, couldn't know me, ever. The thought of a little house right smack in the middle of this two-bit town made me feel like I was already in an asylum, tied up in a straightjacket, couldn't move, could barely breathe.

"Will, it's a nice offer, really, but I'm just not what you want. I promise you, I'm not."

"Oh Frances, but you could be." He ran his hand along my cheek, and my stomach churned. I backed away, and he inched in again, clasping my hand, but he was a gentleman and didn't press me further. I was relieved and a bit sickened at the same time.

"Will, you really think I could be a good wife to you? Have children and the whole bit?"

"Of course, Frances. We'd have beautiful kids, a whole brood of them!" He smiled and let go of my hands, turning to me, facing me and looking me in the eyes. "And I'd treat you right, I would. I'd never hurt you."

I smiled at him. He was sweet and sincere, and even though the thought of cleaning up after this man for the rest of my life, cooking for him, sleeping in his bed, made my skin draw up, I knew I couldn't just flat-out refuse him, couldn't just storm off like a spoiled child.

"Would you let me think about it, Will?"

"Certainly!" He seemed thrilled. "Take all the time you need, darlin'. Like I said, I plan to court you right."

"I will let you know as soon as I am sure, I promise," I said and put my hand in my lap.

He stood, smoothed down his shirt and pants, put on his hat and offered me his arm to walk back up to the house.

When we walked in, my parents were waiting in the front room, expecting, I was sure, to get the news of my engagement, or at least of our courtship. When I just told them all good night, their faces fell, but not in complete defeat, as they could see that Will was still smiling. He kissed me sweetly on the cheek and let my arm go as I went up the stairs.

A few minutes later up in my room, I could see my father walking back out with Will to take him back into town. He gave him a big pat on the back before they got in the car. I undressed and got into my bed, pulling the covers up to my chin as I listened to my mother hum through her chores in the kitchen. Soon enough, she was in bed too and my father had pulled up to the house again and a few moments later joined her.

There was a dead silence, nothing moved at all, no sounds at all, not even a cricket. As quietly as I could, I got out of bed and packed up a trunk full of clothing and other items, silly items really, from my childhood, but things I felt I needed with me. I felt I had something, a life in them, the way Jean Bailey kept her life in her own trunks, and now I had a trunk of my own. I lifted the trunk up onto my back and struggled quietly down the stairs, half wishing they'd wake up, beg me to stay.

At the bottom of the stairs, I slid the trunk to the floor and eased down the hall to the kitchen. I felt in the dark for the towel drawer where I knew my mother kept her mad money, money only she—and I—knew about, money she kept back in case she needed anything, or in case they got in a real bind, which they often did. I could tell by the feel of the wad that it was more than enough to get me a ticket, so I just slid a couple of the bills off the top and left the rest. I felt guilt creep up in me but I swallowed it as I shoved the money in my pocket and crept back out to get my trunk. At my father's car, I put the trunk in the back and cranked up the car right quick, hopped in, and drove off as fast as I could, crying, knowing I'd never be back. I drove to the station in town and caught the next train out to New Orleans, back to my job and back to Jean, leaving word to let my folks know where the car would be waiting for them.

CHAPTER TWENTY-ONE

By the time I reached New Orleans on that long train ride, I was dirty, tired, and stank like the train. I'd cried for a good long while and then slept the rest without even dreaming. I tried to picture Jean's face when I walked through the door, but I couldn't.

I stepped out of the cab in front of her house, and I felt a silent stillness, a vacancy. The air was a bit cool for New Orleans at the beginning of September. I unloaded my trunk, ready to settle down, ready to make a life, my life here with Jean Bailey.

Mrs. Benoit stood in the entryway to greet me. She told me Jean was upstairs. As I pulled the trunk up the last of the stairs and into the bedroom and sat down on the edge of the bed, Jean came in off the balcony. She smiled but didn't approach me.

"I'm so sorry, Jean. I wished I'd been able to bail you out, come back with you." I stood and crossed the room. "But I'm here now," I said and put my arms around her.

"I'm glad you're back."

"Me too," I said and let out a sigh.

She kissed the top of my head. "Sugar," she said and held me by my arms, looking into my face.

It just then occurred to me that she hadn't really hugged me back, just stood there letting me wrap myself around her. "What? What's wrong?"

"Listen, I'm glad you're back because I've got to get back on the road."

I groaned. "But I only took off enough time to go to Texas." I knew for sure I'd lose my job if I left again.

"No, honey, you don't need to go," she said and sat on the bed. "You stay here, look after the house, keep an eye on Jeremiah, keep your job."

I was a little relieved that she wanted me in her home, my home now, and that I could keep my job. "How long will you be gone?"

"I don't know," she said and looked at her hands. "Could be months, a long time, Frankie."

Panic struck up in me. "Well then, no! Never mind. I'll just quit the damn job. I'll go with you. It's fine. I can get another job if I need to, right?"

"No, Frankie, you just stay and get some of those pretty gowns done."

"You know good and well I can sew anywhere."

"Not as good as you can with the machine."

I shrugged. "It don't matter. I want to be with you," I said and sat down with her, putting my hands on hers.

"Frankie," she said, still looking at her hands. "You can't come with me. I don't want you to."

My head spun. I gripped her hands until she pulled them away.

"I've had a bad run of it, Frankie. You know, you've seen the audience at my shows. You heard me at the one in Texas. I'm fading fast, girl. I got to do something quick before I lose it all."

"What are you talking about lose it all? It was a couple of shows, a bad night, snooty people. It ain't you! Look how well you did back in Georgia, especially at The Premier."

She shook her head and looked like she might cry, though I'd never seen her even tear up. I put my arms around her. "It's okay, Jean. I can help. I'll go with you, be there, be your manager. Hell, I'll even get the crowd riled up if I need to."

At this she shoved me away. "I don't need—I told you. I don't want you there, Frankie," she said and looked up at me, her eyes cold, distant.

I put my hands on the bed by my sides and felt them go numb.

"I'm going with Ashley Pickard. We are driving out to California, just the two of us."

My gut ached like I'd been kicked, but really, if I didn't lie, I'd admit that I'd known the minute I saw Ashley at the station. I'd known this might happen, that she'd run off with her, that she'd leave me for Ashley Pickard. She could offer Jean a career I could never imagine, a career in films. I could feel the anger pulse through me. I wanted to strike out, make her hurt like I did. In that moment, when she was still sitting two inches from me, I felt her absence as if she'd already left, and I cried. I cried like I'd never live through it.

"Frankie, I'm sorry, sugar, I am," she said as she stroked my hair. "I just need to catch a break. I didn't mean to fall for the woman. It just—"

"Fall for her! What? You fell did you? I'll say!" I stood up and paced a bit then ran back to the bed, put her face in my hands and looked into her eyes, her honey eyes. They seemed so different now, a sickly sweet, but they were still beautiful.

I put my lips on hers and kissed her hard and she kissed me back.

"You know I love you. You're my man, Frankie," she whispered in my ear, and I pushed her away.

"How could you do this to me? Why?"

"We tried. We did. It didn't work. We can't go on playing house forever. Don't be so naïve, Frankie. We are just so—"

"Different? What exactly do you have in common with Mrs. Pickard?" I felt like my words were like nails, but they seemed to just slide away from me as soon as I said them.

"How do you think I felt watching you walk out that jailhouse with your daddy, huh? Wasn't nothing I could do—for you or me. I just had to sit there in the piss-stained cell until—"

"Until *Ashley* bailed you out."

"Did you want me to sit and rot? Wait on you to get me out?"

She was right. I hadn't gone back for her, not sure if I could have even if Ashley hadn't been there. The mad money would not have covered the bail.

I put my head in my hands. "Why, though? Why did you have to fall for *her*?"

"I fell for you didn't I?" She laughed a little. "But I ain't marrying nobody—not again. I ain't the marrying kind. It's who I am, sugar. You know this," she said and got up. She started to undress, get ready for bed. "Come on, honey. It will seem better in the morning. You are so young. I'm just one bright spot in a long line of them for you, just one, perhaps one of the firsts, but you gonna have so many more. You're gonna love so often and so hard it will make your tail spin, and make me seem like—well just the beginning. This is just the beginning, darlin', I promise." She reached for my hand, trying to lead me to the bed.

I jerked my hand away. "What? Why would I stay here? You're leaving me!" Tears streamed down my face.

"I want you to stay here, Frankie," she said and grabbed me, hugged me to her, stroking my back, trying to calm me, and led me to the bed. "Stay as long as you want."

I leaned into her until I was on top of her, and she pulled me down closer, pulling at my clothes, kissing at my neck. She rolled me over and unbuttoned my trousers, slid them down my thighs and was inside of me again. I pulled her down and kissed her, rocking into her, getting lost in her until I felt that my face was wet with tears, and I remembered she was leaving me. I pushed her off and rolled over to the other side of the bed.

* * *

When I woke up the next morning she was gone. Mrs. Benoit found me still sobbing in bed by midday the next day. She didn't report anything about Jean, not even when pressed, except to say, "She's gone. But you stay. You stay here."

Jeremiah came in and urged me to get out of bed. "She'll be back. Always comes back eventually, Frankie. But—" He stopped, sat down beside me, and put his hand on mine. "She don't ever come back alone." His big brown eyes were sympathetic, and I thanked him.

When they left me there, I fell back on the bed and looked about the room. I took in a deep breath, searching for Jean's lingering scent, her deep musk from the pillows, her clothes, anything.

* * *

I spent days lurking about the bedroom searching for clues, clues to something I could do to get her back, and looking to see if she'd left me anything—a letter, a note, anything.

At night, the orange glow of the streetlamp, or the orange moon hanging over the city, low and full to bursting, flickered in through the open window with the billowing gauze curtains. I imagined I could still feel Jean there, as if she were snuggling against me in the heat that was slowly giving way to fall. She'd been gone for weeks without a word, and I tried not to think about her sitting in that car with Ashley that August morning after Champagne's bust, tried not to imagine them kissing in some side alley outside a cabaret club. I tried not to imagine them in California, the sun on Bailey's face the way she loved. I tried not to imagine Ashley admiring her under the lights in some stark room, set for a movie, the movie she'd sing in. I hated Ashley Pickard for a long time. But really, I knew Ashley was the least of our problems. She was just an opportunity, a pretty way out.

* * *

I stayed in Jean's house for a month, moping around the bedroom, barely getting cleaned up enough to go down for food once or twice a day. Finally, I ventured outside and after a day of wandering the Quarter, I decided to find Lisset again and try to get my job back. I'd taken the time off to go to Texas but didn't know if they'd still keep me on after I didn't show up for over a month. When I found my way back to the boat, Lisset was so happy to see me she ran up and hugged me. She vouched for me right then, and Shiva's hired me back. Mrs. Benoit tried to talk me out of leaving Jean's house, but I couldn't stay there any longer. I moved in with Lisset who had an apartment in the Sixth Ward, adjacent to Jean's neighborhood. She had room for me and for my sewing machine, table and dress form, so I settled in at Lisset's and worked.

Although I was better after getting out of Jean's house, I wasn't happy. I'd let my hair grow longer and wore trousers that might as well have been the hand-me-downs I left Chicago with the way they hung on my thinning frame. I barely ate and barely spoke to anyone.

"Going to have to stop the mooning, Frankie," Lisset said to me one day as we unloaded crates onto the boat. I could feel her stare.

"I'm fine," I said and kept working.

"No you're not, but you're going to be, *ma chère*," she said, putting her hand on my shoulder. "They's a girl who asks about you, wants to get to know you."

"I ain't interested."

"Aw, it is fine. You mourn Mrs. Bailey, but then you find another. You move along."

* * *

She was right. I did. After a few months, I cut my hair. I slicked it back with cream. I cut more slacks, a few shirts, and bought more gauze for my breasts.

I met people, lots of people like Lisset and me. Over the next few months, I sewed a lot of clothes and moved a lot of crates, made an honest wage, and saved every penny I could.

I'd made up my mind I was going to start trying to find Julian again and get him out of wherever they were holding him. He may have been simpleminded, but he wasn't crazy and didn't deserve to be locked up. I could take care of him. We could take care of each other. I owed him that much.

I finally tracked down his parents when Lisset showed me how to get a hold of public records and police reports at the library. When I did, that's when I figured out they had him up in Jackson Parish at the asylum there, closer to where his folks were. After I found out where he was, I had to figure out a way to get him out, which took months. Thankfully, Shiva's hosted a variety of clientele, many of which were more than happy to offer their advice for a drink or two. Finally, at the start of the next year, I hired a lawyer, Mr. McDermott, with the money I'd saved, and bought us train tickets upstate and marched right up to the asylum to make our case.

The building looked like a run-down school or hospital, and no one was outside though the grounds were very pretty, serene and covered in trees and green, green grass. The doors were locked, but we could see a nurse sitting at a big round table right through the doors. She got up and cracked open the door.

"We're here for Julian Delacroix," I said, pretty as you please. I was dressed in my best suit, my breasts flat, and my hair perfectly primped under my hat, which I took off to greet her.

"These are not visiting hours, sir," she said, still half holding the door so we couldn't get through.

I leaned on it, opening it more. "We are not here to visit, ma'am—"

Mr. McDermott squeezed in front of me and cut me off. "I'm his lawyer. We have an appointment with the doctor."

She raised her eyebrows and ushered us in, shaking her head. She walked around the desk, looked through some paperwork, and then waved for us to follow her down a long corridor off to the right. The place seemed deserted, but I could hear strange noises all about, some talking, or mumbling, or even moaning, coming from the closed rooms.

"Doctor, these men are here to see you about Julian Delacroix," she said as she stepped into a brightly lit office about halfway down the hall.

He ushered us in and offered us a chair.

"We are here to take Julian home," I said. Mr. McDermott put his hand on my arm as if to stop me from saying more.

Mr. McDermott introduced himself as a lawyer working on Julian's behalf. "It is my understanding that because Mr. Delacroix was in a bit of a scrape, his parents voluntarily placed him here, and that he could leave as long as he could be cared for."

"Yes, this is true. Are you here on the behalf of the parents?"

"No, we are here for Julian," I said again, getting a little agitated.

"Frankie, you hired me for a reason, let me do the talking. Why don't you wait down the hall at the nurses' station?"

I fumed, but got up and left the room, stomping down the hall, and found a chair by the nurses' station to wait. About a half hour later, my lawyer finally came out with a stack of papers and motioned me over to the nurses' station. I had to sign two or three papers, taking responsibility for Julian as if he were a minor. Once these were signed and handed over to the nurse, she left to go get Julian.

"I think they were more than happy to get rid of another mouth to feed, especially one that wasn't really sick," Mr. McDermott said.

When Julian came down the hall, he had a wad of clothes in his hands and nothing else. He was wearing an all white jumpsuit like a prison suit without the stripes. His head was shaved clean and he looked pale and thin. His face lit up when he saw me, and he ran to give me a hug, yelling my name.

On the train ride back, Julian and I talked and talked like not a day had gone by, fast friends again. He said that the asylum hadn't been all that bad, but he seemed shaken, not quite the same. He took a long while to say a thing. He paused and thought longer than he used to, almost like a silent stutter. He said that the cops had beaten him up pretty good, and his parents couldn't take care of him. So when the cops offered the asylum, they jumped at it. They'd made sure he was nursed back to health and then never came back.

"I was lonely," he said and looked out the window. "The people were crazy!" He waited, looked back and me, then out the window again. "I ain't crazy like that, Frankie, and there weren't no one to talk to, dance with."

"I finished your gown, Miss Jewel," I said, more thrilled than I realized at the idea of getting to finally try it on him. I'd sewn lots of gowns, mended more, but of all the gowns I'd made from scratch, his was the one I was most proud of as I had sewn and unstitched and sewn it again and again until it was perfect, and it had never been on a body yet.

I'd told Lisset all about Julian and what happened and she agreed to let him live with us there in her apartment until we could find something bigger or get our own place. She had even arranged a coming home party for him, though it was just us, our boss, and one or two patrons from Shiva's.

Julian was thrilled, and I thought he'd cry when he saw the gown, insisting on putting it on right away. As he slid it over his thin frame, I saw only two spots where I needed to take it in a bit, but he said he didn't mind.

"Gives me wiggle room!"

Lisset had an old phonograph and we borrowed records we'd found at Shiva's. Lisset made a big dinner and we ate and danced most of the night. I was relieved that Julian was safe and had made it through without much harm, that he was with me again.

"I've been lonely, too, Julian," I said after I told him about Jean and that she was long gone now.

"It's okay, Frankie, we'll find some hot tickets over at that boat," he said, and he was right.

* * *

Eventually, I fell in love again, and got all beat up with it, found myself alone again, save for Julian when he was between romances with rich older men. I roamed the streets of New Orleans, finding friends, and as Julian had told me to do way back when we first hit the road, I loved often. But nobody would ever be Jean Bailey.

I made my own way, my own home and, with Julian's help, set up my own dress shop in the Quarter. I took pride in my work, at the boat and in the clothes I made. I designed hundreds of dresses and even a line of suits and kick-around clothes, shirts and fitted slacks, tailored just for girls like me, tomboys, as Julian called us. I wrote to my parents and told them where I was, and my mother began sending regular holiday cards, though I never saw them or my aunt and uncle again. I never went back.

I heard that Jean finally packed up and left for California for good. She made records that I bought and listened to on Lisset's old phonograph. Each record was smoother than the one before, more and more harmonious with the horns that bellowed with her voice. Her last record wasn't even a race record but was released on a big label.

The year I turned twenty-one, Jean came back to the South to do another circuit. I tried to make it to a show, but it was canceled, with no word as to why. Months later, I got the news. I was closing up shop at Shiva's, mopping the dance floor and cutting up with a few of the regulars that always stayed late while we cleaned up. Lisset came up, two drinks in hand. "Here, take this, *ma chère*," she said, her face frozen.

I leaned my mop handle against a table and took the drink. "What's this for?"

Lisset ushered up a girl to me, tears streaming down her face. She was pretty, a petite little Creole girl. I put my arm around her. "What is it?"

"They say you knew Jean Bailey," she said.

"Yeah, I know Jean. What is it? Tell me. Did something happen?"

"She's gone, Frankie," Lisset broke in, and the girl went to crying harder.

"I know that, Lisset, she's traveling, doing the circuit again, I imagine."

"No, Frankie, she passed away. She's dead."

I let my arm slip from the small of the girl's back. "No," I said and backed away.

"She died up in Georgia," the girl let out.

The world around me blurred, and I felt like the boat had begun to move, knocking me off balance. "What happened?"

"She collapsed on stage one night and they couldn't get her back," the girl said.

And then one of the regulars chimed in, "Truth is, I heard it was a car accident, drove right into a fence post."

The image of Jean's car smashed up against a post lingered with me for a long time, cutting at me, in my gut. "Ya'll knew about this and nobody told me!" I sat down and downed my drink.

"I didn't know," Lisset added. "I hadn't heard a word until just now."

Over the next month, it was all anyone talked about, and then no one talked about her at all.

Some said she was drunk. Some said she got a bad batch of liquor. Some say it was her old sissy boy husband, that he had come back and beat her up bad—left her for dead. Some said she had a bad heart, that it just gave out, all of a sudden like. There were so many stories—one even sounded so close to me, it made me shiver. She'd been in New Orleans, distraught and looking for some lost love. When she didn't find her, Jean drove all night to Georgia and fell asleep at the wheel.

All that is known or reported in anything reliable is that by the time anybody found her, it was too late. It was a white man who found her and reported it. He wouldn't touch her because she was black, wouldn't put her in his car and carry her to help, however damn famous she was. He left her there and called the police, who found her dead some hours later. She died alone on the side of the road in Georgia.

When I heard, I fought back that image, making myself see only my own image of her right outside of Augusta where we'd stopped to swim in that creek. I saw her ahead of me through the tall weeds, half-naked, her dark skin glistening in the sun.

* * *

The last time I ever laid eyes on Jean Bailey was on a little reel, a clip, from the film that hardly anybody ever saw, showing before the movie I'd paid to see. I was sitting in a dark theater, stiff cloth seats, new and not yet broke in. My date, a girl I'd only known for a short time was with me, her legs crossed delicately at the ankles, her hands in her lap when they weren't in the popcorn.

The reel was scratchy and grainy, lines rippling through, but I was startled as I made out her familiar face, the face I'd once held in my own hands, those full lips, high cheekbones, long lashes, and I remembered her bright, honey-colored eyes though the film was in black and white.

My date leaned in to me. "What is it? Have you seen that one?"

I didn't, couldn't say a word. I just watched as Jean Bailey leaned against the bar, her suit jacket on over a button-up just barely showing her cleavage, her chest rising and falling as she belted out the lyrics. The sound was canned, but her voice was clear and easy.

I'm saving this one spot, baby, this one spot for you.

Her glistening lips were pursed in that last shot, her head tilted back, just slightly showing her neck, and her shadowed eyes, half-closed.

For more Spinsters Ink titles please visit:

www.BellaBooks.com

Bella Books and Distribution
P.O. Box 10543
Tallahassee, FL 32302

Phone: 800-729-4992